from The Atomi

MW01125180

Captain Hartman glared at the helmsman. He watched for him to move. *I repeat, run for sheltered water. That is an order, mister.* He eyed each officer on deck.

What the hell was the old man doing, I wondered, as my stomach rolled over?

The helmsman knew from experience a sea this rough could break an aircraft carrier in half. He stared at the second officer in command, as if to pass, in the split second between blinks, a frightful message to a secret co-conspirator. He gulped, his eyes begging for help as the color drained from Cal Bradley's face.

Lieutenant Bradley took a deep breath and nodded affirmation to Captain Hartman. I saw muscles tighten down his neck, his jaw clamp shut and his lips freeze in place. Bradley's tense stare told the helmsman a captain's order was a captain's order, no matter how stupid it sounded. He would not buck the system.

Turn the damn ship now! Captain Hartman shouted, his short fuse ignited, his eyes searing with rage. He was an Annapolis graduate who expected his orders to be followed in an expeditious manner. He spread his feet to keep balance and crossed his arms over his chest.

Lieutenant Bradley swallowed hard and repeated the captain's order. *Turn the ship, sailor.* You could see in his eyes he knew this was wrong.

The helmsman caught the look, and began to squirm. I knew that move. I had to pee when I got scared, too. *Affirmative, sir,* he said and nodded, numbly. The man focused, and spun the wheel.

Damn state of affairs this is, I thought. Three officers on this deck are petrified and the other one's off his onion. Together we control the fate of a multi-million dollar ship and over five hundred lives.

To Tracy –
my friend.

Happy Valentine's Day

THE ATOMIC SAILOR

A story about fathers and sons,
family secrets, and generations of sailors
struggling with PTSD.

by
Laurice Lazebnik

Historical, Fiction, Narrative

ISBN 978-1495206382

Cover design and page layout by
Jennifer Hauschild | Hauschild-Design.com

*This book is dedicated to my mother
who honed my imagination.*

*A percentage of the proceeds from the sale of
The Atomic Sailor will be donated to the
Wounded Warriors Project to honor and
empower wounded warriors.*

*For more information visit
WoundedWarriorProject.org.*

THE ATOMIC SAILOR

PROLOGUE

A seaman apprentice stands waiting at the fringe of a mangrove swamp.

It's been a week since the USS *Cape Esperance* departed the port of Diego Garcia for this unmapped Indian Ocean island. It has been a week since this cockeyed sailor, soaked with beer by his betting barmates, dove down a wooden table on a bet he couldn't execute a perfect carrier landing. He was well on his way to big money when the military police appeared at the request of the barkeep. The sailor was lucky. The captain only gave him one week in the brig on piss and punk before assigning him temporary duty with the ship's Holy Joe.

It is this sailor, short on stature and intelligence, who watches his shipmates disembark from the ship's launch onto this uninhabited strip of jungle. Seasoned sailors refer to him as Stubby, a 2-6-10, which decoded means (when he's caught it will take two surgeons six hours to remove the captain's boot implanted in his ass.)

Stubby is oblivious to the approaching storm. Sweat stains his dungarees. Half a pack of burnt cigarettes litter the sand by the time his three mates leap from the launch that has transported hundreds of other stir-crazy squids for a day's R and R. Stubby watches the transport leave his shipmates on the beach and turn seaward for the next load of sailors.

"Hey, dipshit. How'd you get out of the brig?" the larger sailor asks, flicking his cigarette into the sand. He plunges through brackish water into the swamp leaving his shipmates on the beach. "What you hiding, horse fly?"

Stubby mashes his Lucky Strike on the sole of his shoe. "Nothin." He shreds the fag, smears it into the sand with the toe of his sneaker and rolls a fresh pack up his sleeve.

The big fellow shoves him aside, plucks the fartsack from the jungle and thrusts his fist inside. He slaps the back of Stubby's head, curls a sweaty arm around his neck and knuckle-rubs his forehead. "The boys gonna love you for the suds. Stubby, my boy, you ain't completely stupid."

"Who said I was?"

"Aw, some lowlifes from the ship. Hey, watch it, clumsy," he says and shoulders the knapsack.

Seasoned crewmembers from another *Cape Esperance* launch follow a long line of half-naked men snaking up the jungle path blazed flat by still earlier herds of sailors. It is January, 1952. The seamen have eight hours to get rid of pent-up piss and vinegar before the ship's bell signals the end of their Cinderella Liberty.

"Tired of bread and water in the brig? You thirsty, horse tick?" Two other shipmates slosh through the tidal pool, shadowing the larger sailor into the tangled jungle.

"Wait! Wait for me!" Stubby stomps across the saltwater swamp. "Wait!" He skulks through the ooze following their trail of chatter and broken boughs. "Slow down." The humid lushness of the afternoon air fills with echoes of tin cans ricocheting off rocks, hearty laughter, and drinking contests.

"First man to flame a fart wins a cold one. Sailor, you're out this round. We don't want your gassy ass firing an SOS back to the ship."

Stubby pulls down his briefs, sprawls on the jungle floor between the men and lets a wet one rip.

The big sailor smiles. "Nice ass, lass."

The men groan, ignore his challenge, and jaw on and on about skirts and shirts while they suck down more Budweiser Lager.

"Was that the ship's bell?" Stubby asks, sitting upright between tangled tree roots.

"Nah," the larger sailor nods he's heard it too. "You hear an Australian bellbird? Let's play another game. You in?"

Warm dusk deepens into a bleary, drunken darkness as the men bruise into one another and moan. Their wrestling now and then exposes a slash of latent flesh.

"Which way to the beach?" the low-ranking sailor says. "He struggles to stand, but sinks to his knees. "Somebody help me."

"Come on, clueless." The big guy jerks Stubby to his feet and crumbles an empty pack of smokes, tossing it into the jungle.

"Here," Stubby says, and fumbles with the bulge in his T-shirt sleeve. Cellophane rattles as he squeezes open a fresh pack of Lucky Strikes. The cigarettes hemorrhaging from the pack are bent and broken. "Take one of these."

The big sailor takes one. "Now stop pestering me, gnat."

Stubby ignores the jab, whirls around, and plucks a lighter from his shipmate's pocket. He stumbles toward the big guy to light his cigarette, but the Zippo slips from his hand. "Anybody wanna play soccer?" he says as he bends from his waist and peers into the undergrowth. "What happened to our game?"

"Your hairy ass would be wasted on soccer," the big guy says. "Gentlemen, we're alone on this island tonight. Shall we give the last beer to the silly young lass and take a poke at his pretty pink ass?"

"I dunno," the second sailor says, his hands shaking as he opens the last can with a church key. This could end up a real cluster fuck."

"I lost your Zippo," Stubby says. "We're all lost, lost in an impenetrable jungle."

Crass hands clasp Stubby"s shoulders. "Let me help you drink that last beer."

"What the … I don't want …" He gulps and chokes. "Hey! Let go of …"

The sailor's struggle ends when he's pushed to his knees and a size fourteen sneaker comes to rest on the back of his neck. Panting and sawing snorts coupled with his threats and curses blend into the general jungle clatter. All go undetected in the raucous swing of nocturnal predators.

"You bastards!" Stubby whispers when it's over, and whimpers until dawn.

CHAPTER 1

I can't remember my father ever holding me. It seems strange that memory should surface now, circling inside my thoughts like that typhoon he bragged about surviving. The bastard's been dead for twenty years.

Focus, I tell myself. This is not the time to get into that dark funk, not on my first field assignment for the bureau. Screw this up and the agency will have me sorting paper clips. Damn, it's cold in Michigan. My shoes are soaked, my feet are frozen and it's barely nine o'clock. Let's see … it's Tuesday. I'm looking for condo 123.

My only memory of affection from my old man was when I rode in his rusty blue Ford pickup with the missing door on the passenger side. He must have known that truck was dangerous. I remember pressing against his good shoulder and wrapping my arm around his neck to keep from spilling out on loose gravel when the damn fool cornered hard, or spun donuts.

What a stupid thing for a father to do with his kid in the car. He was a terrible father, yet, I remember feeling safe squeezed in there between the seat and his warm back. And spinning was fun. I remember our laughter, and the smell of his crisp, starched uniform. It held the same perfume as the stiff, ironed aprons my mother wore to work. Door 103. Keep moving.

My father was at sea for long stretches. He came home for a week, a couple times a year, except for the time he spent with us when he broke his shoulder. That's when he gave me the wooden toy he said he'd carved with his jackknife. "It's not a boat, stupid. And it's not a battleship." He talked with his good arm crossed over his white cast. "It's a seaplane tender!"

The gift came with tiny airplanes and a tall wheel, a crane spool on one end. He wound it with string, then showed me how to land jet fighters on the flat top by catching the wheels with the string. I enjoyed scooping airplanes from my bathwater and guiding them into the air until he rushed the water into a whirlwind like the typhoon that hurt his shoulder. Father's waves sunk my ship. He plucked it from the tub when I cried and put it in his pocket. Father didn't like crying.

I swallowed my tears, and while I held out my hand, he explained how the hangar deck was below the top deck, and was an airplane garage where sailors stored planes landing on deck or lifted from the sea. He dried the little ship on my towel, and while holding it between his knees printed the name, *Rendova* along one side and *Cape Esperance* on the opposite.

"Eat your cereal, Davey." My father liked giving orders at our morning table. "You want to grow tall and sail seaplane tenders like your papa, don't you?"

Mama laughed. "He won't have to eat many cornflakes to grow bigger than you, Willard." Mother liked to tease him.

This time her words fastened on him and lined his face with pain. "How many times do I have to tell you," he spat through clenched jaws. "My name is Willie and I'm tall enough for the US Navy!"

When my parents fought I ran outside to hide in the high weeds by the pond. I was a short kid, like he must have been. I wondered then whether I would grow to be taller than him, so my mother wouldn't tease me, or if I would inherit his stature and face her insulting humor.

Sounds of laughter left our house the day he hung his uniform in my closet. He told us he was home to stay. The Navy no longer needed him. I didn't know the details. I was only seven.

Usually, my mother was happy to see him, and soon after his arrival they would send me out to play while they ducked into the bedroom to make the rusty bedsprings squeak. But this time, instead of joyful sounds, I heard sobs.

"How could you let them?" She screamed so loud the swamp frogs stopped croaking. "Don't touch me, and stay away from my son." I heard a crack and an explosion of glass.

"You've got to believe me," I heard him yell.

"Was it the first time?" She was weeping now. "You're lying. You're an imposter, an embarrassment to our family. You promised." I heard a squeak that I knew came from the bedroom door. "You're not even a man." The sound was followed by the familiar bang of the screen door flung so hard it slapped against the siding. "Liar!" she called after him as I saw him take the porch steps two at a time. "No one loves a liar. Willard, you're not the man I married. You're not a man at all!"

I hated it when she cried, but I promised myself I would never love a liar, either. I backed into the cattails and pretended to be my favorite television character, FBI Agent Elliot Ness. I pretended to see an imaginary gangster run into our dark garage for cover. After a time I followed the criminal, but stopped short when I heard a creaking groan overhead. It was then that I looked up and faced my father, swinging by his neck from the rafters.

Mother rushed into the musty garage after she heard my scream. When her initial shock was over, she pulled me from where I had sunk into the dirt floor, shook my shoulders and said, "Look at me." She grabbed my chin and forced my face toward hers. "Stop crying, Davey. Dry those tears. You are not like him. You are strong." She made me blow my nose. "Davey, you are now the man in our house. A strong man would never tell anyone what he saw here today." I lowered my head and swallowed the tear knot that blocked my throat. "Can you do that, Davey?" she asked.

I agreed to do whatever she asked, but this shame marked my life. I didn't speak of his death after that. And now I can't remember his face.

It wasn't until twenty years later when I joined the FBI that I found order, predictability, and control in my life. That calm changed when I scrolled down the contents of one particular computer file. I no longer had the option to block memories of the man, who for a short time, was my father.

I read *James H. McLaughlin* on the brass plate beneath the door numbered 123 and feel strangely alone. It's quiet up and down this condominium complex. Unusually quiet.

CHAPTER 2

A sharp rap of the brass knocker spikes a twinge through my numb cheekbones. An answering chime of wind on icicles pushes pain into my eardrums. The screech of a snowplow blade scraping bare pavement sends shivers up my spine. I rub the dull ache at my temples. My roommate's words work their way through the pain.

"Are you daft?" he had said, having just heard me volunteer for the Michigan assignment, my first after graduation from the FBI Academy. "Just because you look like a bear doesn't mean you can survive cold weather. They're having a blizzard in Michigan right now. Don't you watch the news? It's been snowing up there for three days and the forecast is for another week of snow. Look, you were brilliant during tropical survival training. Take the Florida assignment."

He may have been right. I rap numb knuckles on the entrance door. The Federal Bureau of Investigation suspects this man of plotting to swindle the Veterans Administration out of compensation for injuries resulting from the atomic tests in the South Pacific. We could be wrong. He may just be a subversive older veteran with issues who enjoys stirring the pot. Or, he could be like the example from one of my textbooks, a habitual liar. It's my job to find out. James H. McLaughlin hasn't managed to overthrow the government, yet, so I should be able to wrap a mutiny led by a man his age in a couple of days, tops.

"FBI, open up," I say to a carved oak door. It's snowing sideways, denting my forehead when I look into the wind. What is taking this guy so long? Is he hibernating in there like an old bear? I lean my ear against cold wood, and hear what sounds like a television news show. "Wake up!" I pound. I'll probably have to remind the old guy he had called the bureau three years ago. I wipe the frosty buildup dripping from my eyebrows on my coat sleeve. My mind drifts as I recall seeing the suspect walk with a cane at the restaurant in Swainsville yesterday.

It's a ten-hour drive from Jackson, Michigan to New York City. If I wrap this case expeditiously I can surprise my girl. I like surprising my girl.

The television news bleats through the door. It's something about a car bomb in Baghdad. I fist-bang the door again, longer this time and take a deep breath to sound professional. "This is the FBI Open up." My colleague was right. I don't have a clue how to survive the cold. I rub the back of my head. My woman would know how to make me feel better. News from Iraq abruptly stops from behind the door.

"Hang on, I'm coming," a deep voice penetrates the door. "Forget your key again?" He sounds like a person familiar with bellowing orders, his voice loud, laced with authority.

Chilled to my core, I identify myself exactly as I have been taught, removing any threatening tones or impatience from my voice. When I rub my hands together I feel like I'm touching a corpse. At first I relish the weird feeling, like I enjoy other intimate relationships that are offbeat. But the pangs of pain poke icy tentacles up my arms and bring me back to now.

I hear what sounds like slippers shuffling on carpet ... a grunt following a scrape. A chain jingles. Then the door is ajar. A single eyeball glares down at me through a narrow slit. "You're not my daughter."

"Are you James H. McLaughlin?" I ask with a slow, thick tongue, my neck trussed inside a wool overcoat, snow-soaked by snowmelt. My arms feel swollen and as heavy as logs.

Weight is nothing new to my torso. My mother was tall and thin. She told me once my roundness came from my father's family. Gluten has a certain affinity for my bones.

I take in the landscape while I wipe my nose. I wonder about the stacked condominiums lining this frozen lake. Looks expensive … gated community … pool house. Snow-covered boulders rest between ghost-white shrubs. It could be pleasant if it were warmer. I wonder how much retirement income a retired Navy officer gets a month? I blow my nose, then poke frozen pegs into my breast pocket, a routine reach for my bifold. The Florida assignment sounds pretty good right now.

"I'm on official government business with the FBI. Are you James H. McLaughlin?" I snap open my credentials, hold them close to the door and attempt to locate another hand-kerchief with the other hand. I'm not in time for the percussive sneeze … a serious hit on his door.

"I'm McLaughlin. What do you want?" His coffee breath steams through the crack. I see him scowl, squint, and then he closes the door.

I inhale and hear a security chain scrape down what must be a channel, then exhale and watch the door swing wide revealing a face framed by a trimmed gray beard.

"Are you showing me identification, son?" He squints and nods toward my outstretched hand.

The old man looks more like a cat ready to pounce than a subversive threatening the American way of life. I nod, angle my credentials so the sun will shine on my polished silver badge.

"Get in here young fellow. My glasses are fogging." The now open doorway is crowded with his bulk. "Freeze to my deck, and I'll have to chip you off with a jackhammer." Icy wind and snowflakes bluster in as I stumble past him.

As I shake slush from my hair, I say, "Thank you. I appreciate this," and mean it. The smell of fried bacon lingers in the air.

I follow McLaughlin's gaze to my shoes, oxfords with thick soles and elevated heels, the kind short men wear to look taller. He eyes me like I'm a dim bulb, and herds me into an inside hallway.

"Where the hell are your boots? Ditch those shoes. Shed those socks, too." I attempt to pull them off, but my fingers are too stiff to hold. "Roll the socks down from the top," the old man orders, and bends down to pull the elastic over my heel and toe. "Like that. Fetch a towel from the bathroom. It's over there." He motions down a passageway with a brush of his hand. His head shakes from side to side as he issues instructions. "A man can get frostbite real fast in this climate."

I take a mental note. McLaughlin is comfortable being the one in control. He seems to like playing with his prey like a cat, pulling strings. Okay. I can be his puppet if it gets the job done. As I totter toward the bathroom I can smell my armpits. Odd, I think. I'm sweating and freezing at the same time.

"Does the FBI fill you in on weather conditions?" he calls down the hall as I reach for a towel folded neatly on a shelf by the toilet. "That agency never did take care of their people, but then," he says in a murmur that lacks amusement, "neither did the Navy. I was cold for thirty-three years, never had the right clothing for the part of the world I was in."

Since I have been invited into his bathroom, I check the medicine cabinet and see a small box of tampons and a round dispenser of birth control pills. A woman lives here. The container is cinnamon colored, like the brand Leticia, my girlfriend uses. A young woman.

"Looking for something?" McLaughlin says from the doorway. For such a large man he moves quietly. He's holding a weapon in his hand. It's a forty-caliber automatic pistol, a Smith and Wesson. My hand brushes past my empty holster as I reach for the ceiling.

"I repeat. Are you looking for something?"

I seem to be in trouble with the puppet master. My pistol lays flat in his hand. "Yes sir. Em, I am trying to find an aspirin, or something stronger for my congestion." I'm embarrassed I've been caught snooping. I'm mortified I've lost my weapon. If this guy is playing me, he's good. "I … I have a headache … could be catching cold."

He opens the medicine cabinet with the barrel of my gun. "You'll find Benadryl in there. Look on the bottom shelf. It's a small blue pill." He sticks my pistol in his pocket, turns, and shuffles down the hall.

"Sir, that gun is government property." I poke my head into the passageway to watch. "The snap on the hammer that keeps it in my holster must have come loose when I slipped off my shoes." My hands are still in the air. "You may want to check the safety, sir. That gun is loaded."

He pauses, takes the Smith and Wesson from his pocket. "When did they start using automatics?" He flips the gun in his hand. "I thought feds used a snub-nosed revolver, like a .375 or a .38."

"They were too slow and cumbersome," I say, and wonder how he knows so much about firearms issued to federal agents. "They only hold six rounds before we have to stop and reload. The automatics are faster because they take clips that hold eight to ten rounds." I'm giving out too much information. Before I know what's happening, I'm volunteering even more. "Automatics are standard issue now."

He turns my weapon over in his hand, holds it out, aims and sets his sight on what looks, from where I stand, like a sagging chocolate cake on the kitchen table.

"The Glock is popular with city cops," I say, "but my personal preference is the weapon you are holding in your hand. May I have it?"

The old man ignores my question, fake-shoots the sinkhole in the cake, then shoves the gun deep into his pocket. He steps out of sight. I hear him whistling.

This is great, I think. I feel the leather pouches along my belt. I'm relieved to find my two extra clips. What if this guy goes postal and starts shooting? What if I have to jump him and knock him down? What if I break one of his bones? What if?

I can't break up an old man. His spine would snap like a dry wishbone. The paperwork I'm required to file would take a month ... and my ass would be glued to a chair for the reminder of my career. This is the worst day of my life, and it's not even noon.

I return to the bathroom and take two pills from the Benadryl bottle, memorize what I have seen in the cabinet and step into the hallway. On my right a door stands ajar. I can hear him rattling around in the kitchen, so I nudge it open with my big toe. Inside are shelves loaded with thick, woolen blankets.

At the end of the hall is a generous room, empty but for a single cot and metal shower stool. A stack of cardboard boxes stands vertical near the door. The furniture is spare and compact, sized for a sleeping compartment aboard a submarine, not the master bedroom of an upscale condo. This room could be where he sleeps.

"Need a hot drink to thaw your insides?" he calls from the kitchen. "I was just brewing some joe." A teakettle whistle screams. Metal scrapes on metal.

Hot liquid might save my life, keep my insides from freezing together. I feel the cold, wet band on my Jockeys. My handcuffs are still jammed in my waistband, warming the small of my back. "Thank you," I call and step inside the bedroom. I can see into a closet, glance behind a door. No one is here to surprise me later.

"Find a towel?" he calls from the kitchen.

I find a stool in the front room near his electric heater, sit and rub my feet with his towel. "I'm good." My eyes spin as I inventory the room. Along one wall are bookshelves with a row of framed family photos. A canvas book bag with *Jackson District Library* printed on one side leans against a side table. "Warm feet make a difference," I shout towards the kitchen.

I stand in my bare feet and take a few steps toward a framed photo on the wall. In the center of the picture stands the same man who is now brewing coffee in the kitchen. A banner behind a string of adults in the photo reads "Happy Birthday Admiral McLaughlin."

Admiral? I wonder if my FBI file could be mistaken. The report about his rate at retirement had been vague, if not confusing. It stated he had been a master chief petty officer during his career, the highest rung on the ladder for an enlisted sailor, but the file didn't say what rank he was when he retired. This picture shows an officer with a wide stripe on his sleeve and scrambled eggs on the brim of his hat. If this guy is an admiral, he might be more dangerous than he appears. An officer's rank could give him the clout to be a threat if he turns out to be subversive.

Next to a shelf bearing a heavy vase stuffed with peacock feathers is a photograph of a woman in a nurse's hat. She has confident, full cheeks, a capable broad nose and a large, full mouth. Stuck to the picture frame is a handwritten stick-it note that reads, "Daddy, Mom wouldn't like you climbing ladders, either." It's signed, "Corny."

"Do you take your mud blonde and bitter or blonde and sweet?" the old man says from the kitchen.

"No sugar. No cream." I take a step towards a fat gray feline curled into a circle on the couch. The furry coil springs like a cobra, humps its back, and sweeps a warning paw at me.

I retreat. My life isn't unfolding as I'd hoped. I had wanted to save the world from criminals since I was a kid, not quarrel with cats. My favorite author had been Sir Arthur Conan Doyle. I loved Sherlock Holmes, watched every movie Hitchcock made, and never missed an episode of FBI Agent Elliot Ness arresting gangsters on TV. I still read crime novels for enjoyment, but I used to read them because I might learn something that could help me later on.

The study of physiognomy possessed me when I was ten. I pasted newspaper pictures of criminals in a scrapbook, and attempted to profile potential offenders by the placement and shape of their eyes, or the length of their noses.

During undergrad at George Washington I studied history and criminal justice. When I discovered a book on the ancient art of face reading that the Chinese call Mien Shiang, I knew I was on the right career track.

After graduation I worked three years on the local police force where I observed a range of depravity I thought impossible in American culture. I arrested a father for selling his children to the sex trade. I investigated a kidnapper who harvested body parts from healthy people then sold them to a transplant ring servicing a local hospital. All during that time I was able to remain detached, objective and cool, no matter what assignment they threw at me. I was able to make my mind cold and impervious to the dark, harmful thoughts of those who wished to harm me. My partners accused me of having no feelings. I just did my work by the book.

At FBI boot camp I could have taught the course on being a chameleon. When I was a kid I learned how to stay quiet, watch, listen and blend into the background. That's how I survived my indifferent family.

After graduation I was stuck behind a computer, scrolling through endless missing-person records, cross-checking names against bureau files. That's when I hatched the plan to get a copy of my father's service record using the FBI's powerful search engines.

I had a hunch that if I found his files I could exhume the secrets hidden in the black hole of my memory. If I could understand his short life, learn the facts my mother refused to share, I may be able to find order in my life.

As the retired admiral shuffles from the kitchen, I glance into a second room. A double bed and a chest of drawers hug the back wall. Reflected in a dresser mirror is an open closet door exposing a pink bathrobe. My girl has a bathrobe about that color. The cat-o-four paws and twenty claws is now coiled in the center of the bed, reclaiming a soft dip in the comforter, watching me. No one is home but the informant and this attack cat.

"Ever order the multi-grain pancakes at the Big Boy?" the old man asks from behind me.

"Sir?" I cough to stifle my surprise. Caught. He's not smiling when I turn. I straighten the signet ring on my finger.

Blue eyes set wide apart on a square face fits my profile of a person with enormous restraint. I hope I'm right. These cautious slits could protect his thoughts at all costs. He must have seen me snap the photo of him at the restaurant drinking coffee with two men. Damn.

I didn't tell anyone at the FBI Academy about my early work on criminal physiognomy. My theories about quick-tempered people with close-set eyes would have been labeled a gross generalization. My study of eyebrows of different heights indicating ingratiating, untrustworthy people would have been dismissed as a cops-and-gangster game.

The old gentleman softens his gaze, smiles, and hands me a mug. "You shadowed me. Why?"

I swallow hard, relax my jaw to keep my face unreadable, and thank him for the coffee and Benadryl. My supervisor at the Ann Arbor field office warned me this case might turn into a waste of agency time. Could this guy be testing me for the agency? I've heard that happens with new agents. I clear my throat to make it lower, professional. "Someone in the Bureau seems to think you have information that would interest the FBI," I say. "May I have my gun?"

McLaughlin scratches his beard. "Hang your coat up so it dries." He looks around the room. "We used to have a hall tree.

He nods toward a chair. "Hang it there. So, Washington thinks I have interesting information?"

I have McLaughlin's photo, but still need a physical description for my written report. The man is over six feet tall, stands straight, looks … maybe seventy, although his records show he was born in 1921, which makes him … eighty-five. He wears glasses. His clothes are spotless. His trousers ride low on his hips, held up with thick, red suspenders. The toes on his shoes are shined smooth and the heels are clean with crisp edges. His personal hygiene reflects career Navy. I take out my note pad. "Mind if I ask you a few questions?"

His gaze measures me from my bare feet up, like the expensive tailor that streamlined my topcoat to make me look taller. He tilts his head. "Yes, you remind me of Slick."

Slick?

CHAPTER 3

Who the hell is Slick? I wonder as I check the time and record 9:15 a.m. and the name *Slick* in my notebook.

I survey the room. Prescription medicines line the table-top beside his oversized leather recliner. A bottle of Pepto-Bismol stands watch, a sentinel at the end of his lifeline of pills. Envelopes wrapped with rubber bands rest on a large print copy of the *New York Times*. Neatly folded sections of the *Christian Science Monitor* stacked on the floor barricade his chair from the rest of the minimalist décor. The effect is orderly clutter. A photo of a teenage boy leans against a table lamp. I wonder …

"He's my son," he says. "Haven't seen him in a long time."

His files mentioned McLaughlin had two children, and both had been in the military.

"Your eyebrows are just like his, a hedge, like a clipped mare's mane snaking across your forehead with no break." His face stretches into a wide cheek-crunching smile. "You're one of those men, like my son, who will carry every hair on your head to your grave." He rubs his balding head. "Lucky for Slick he didn't inherit my genes. I've got a full head of skin." He laughs. "I used to have a mustache, but Faye said it looked like a dying caterpillar." He glances at the end table I've been surveying. "I take those horse pills to humor my daughter, not because the doctors order me."

I stand, sipping coffee and wonder why his son wouldn't have his genes. The old man's eyes disappear under sagging lids. His cheeks soften.

"When I was a kid my father would get after us every spring," he says, "give us a dose of sassafras tea to thin our blood from all the pork we ate that winter. We had no pills. I was the one sent out to peel bark from the tree." He nods for me to sit on his sofa. "Peach bark is an Indian cure from my mother. She was Cheyenne." He leans over the side table, takes a pill from a bottle and holds it between his teeth. "I hate those white coats who parade around as doctors." He swallows hard. "When we needed one the most, they were never around. He died young."

Could all this be true? The guy is a US Navy admiral, he's half Native American and his father died when he was a kid, like mine. I wonder if the big pharms boil peach bark and squeeze it into those pills he's taking? I'll be the patient listener if he wants to spin more stories, and then I'll check his facts. Is the man dozing? "Sir?"

"Oh, I was just thinking about what doctors didn't do for my father."

"What happened to him?" I ask, and turn to warm the back of my legs on the heater beside the sofa.

"Papa was only forty-nine when he died. His sickness came at a time in my life when I needed a father the most. He had Brights. That's a kidney disease where you drown in your own water. Today they treat it with diet … limit your salt intake." He shifts in his chair. "There was no money for doctors or medicine during the Great Depression. I think Papa knew he was going.

"Papa was a careful man. When he got a bottle of whiskey from a moonshiner, he poured a saucer full and lit it. If the flame was blue, he'd drink. Any other color flagged poison." The old man rubs his wrist across his mouth. "He'd let me set on his lap and have a taste every once in a while." His blue eyes turn the color of grape slush. "I used to drink. Do you?" He points at some empty decanters on a tray set on a side table.

"Never moonshine, sir," I say, and wonder how to confirm his story.

A 1976 fire had destroyed the bulk of military records at the St. Louis warehouse including the old man's promotion records. I was lucky to get a copy of some of his service history. I had reviewed his files and prepared a list of questions. This old veteran could give a wealth of background information the government could use later to fill in the potholes left after the fire. If I do my job right, I should be able to sort truth from fiction. But first I need to bond with the informant, get his trust. I finish the coffee and set the cup on the end table.

"I never drink while I'm working. Thanks, maybe another time." I clear my throat. "I grew up not far from Annapolis. I imagine you spent a few years there?"

"I'm no Naval Academy ring-pounder." He scowls. "I'm a mustang ... came up through the ranks." He growls. "I did attend a few schools in Annapolis." One side of his mouth draws up in a smirk. "At the Naval Academy a sign on a classroom wall reads, *All enlisted men are sly individuals who bear constant watching.* Across campus the sign in the enlisted men's quarters reads, *A commissioned officer is the natural enemy.*" His grin broadens.

"Slick had a lot of body hair, too. Your resemblance to him is remarkable." He sighs. "It's good to have some company today, even if you are FBI."

I wiggle my feet. The stinging sensation is like a tickle I need to scratch. I'm wondering what happened between him and his son when I hear a door slam from the direction of his kitchen.

A tall, silver-haired woman saunters in carrying a basket of folded laundry. A cigarette dangles from her lips. Smoke shooting from her nostrils as she exhales makes her look like she has elephant tusks. She has on low-rider jeans, and a tight knit top with a plunging neckline that reveals at least five inches of crinkled cleavage. Her smile sparkles like a flash of sunlight on an otherwise overcast day. She passes McLaughlin a wink and addresses me.

"You must be the FBI agent who dropped his gun." She balances the basket on a bony hip and bends down to extend her liver-spotted hand. "I'm Pony." The woman's pendulous bosom falls forward. The tattoo of a hummingbird stretches down one breast. The bird's beak is inked narrow to suck nectar from an elongated flower painted on the opposite breast. Stenciled over her heart is the head of a snake with its mouth open and a tongue ready to strike. If more of the reptile exists, it must be lurking under that long flap of skin.

I stand on my bare feet and take her hand. I'm embarrassed she knows about my missing pistol. She must have been listening from a room I hadn't noticed off the kitchen.

"Can I have my hand back now?" she asks in a breathy voice. "Or am I under arrest?"

Oh my god, this old lady is coming on to me. She must be three times my age. I drop her hand.

Pony turns toward the old sailor. "Governor, it looks like I'm done here." She bends at the waist, straight-legged, like a broke-open shotgun, and places the basket on the floor. "I think I lost one of your blue socks, hon, and I put a meat loaf in the icebox for lunch." She shrugs and checks the bottom of the basket.

Her tank rides up and her jeans slide down revealing a tattoo at the base of her spine just above what must have been the crack in her ass. Her skin looks firm for a woman her age. Soft. That tattoo is the prettiest little butterfly I've ever seen inked on bare, pink flesh. Her frank femininity grows on me as calmly as a vine climbing a trellis, until I feel my shorts move.

"Is there anything else I can help you with, honey?" Pony says, standing upright and turning to address McLaughlin. The butterfly flies right as she turns her hips left. Her eyes catch mine. She grins. "What do I have to do to get investigated by this little hunk of Hollywood manhood?" she asks, winking at the admiral and tipping her head toward me.

The old man sees me studying her tattoos, and sighs. "Pony Puente, this is David Dugan? Pony, you may as well tell the boy about your tattoo. I can see he's dying to ask."

Pony's hand travels around to the back of her jeans. She grasps a belt loop, wiggles her hips and tugs her tight pants higher. "I don't recall why," she says looking straight into my eyes, "but I can tell you how." When she grins her entire face becomes an inviting smile. Her eyes sparkle. Her pug nose tips up at the end.

"I was a WAVE in the Navy about fifty years ago, on leave in Las Vegas. One morning I woke up at the Hilton with six sailors and this tattoo." She pulls down the back band on her jeans revealing what was meant to be a Monarch butterfly, and winks. "Best night I ever had." Her laughter is infectious. Even the admiral guffaws.

"Excuse me, honey," Pony says, balancing the long ash of her smoke as she disappears into the bathroom. I hear the toilet flush.

My imagination soars. I wonder if room service in Las Vegas hotels includes a drop-by tattoo artist, or, if one of her seagoing amours could have done it while she slept? "The tattoo … did it … ah, did it …"

The woman aborts my question with an observation. "You are a curious little guy." She steps up next to me. "You single?" She runs her hand from my ear along to my chin, and pulls my jaw up so I have a clear shot at her eyes. "I saw you looking at me." She winks. "I've got a body made for sin, and I'm real lonely."

The old man raises a pepper gray eyebrow. "Pony, stop teasing him. He's not rich enough for you. He works for the government."

"Listen Moby Dick," she says, turning toward McLaughlin. "I've dropped my standards. I'll take any man who can drive at night and go to the bathroom on his own."

"I'm oiled out," the old man grins. "How Fuen Fuente ever got his hands on a prize like you is a mystery to me." He turns to me. "Her husband was a fine man and a good friend of mine."

A crooked grin slides across Pony's face. "Oh honey, Fuen didn't find me. I found him ... used the process of elimination. I dated every sailor, flyboy and doggy I met, plus most of the men in Jackson County before I found a good one." She gives me a sweet smile. "He didn't have a chance once I made up my mind. How old are you, good lookin'?" she asks, glancing at the bulge in my pants.

"T-twenty-seven."

"I have a grandson your age," she says, and puckers the tips of her thin lips. "Are you having sex with your girl?"

"Ah," I gasp. "My, ah, my girlfriend, she's from New York. Ah, yes. We've had, sure, we have sex all the time."

"You can't surprise me, hon." Her grin glitters from the gold caps on her teeth. "I have eight children. They could never surprise me because I've already done it all." She pinches my cheek and turns serious. "Your ears stick out like a taxi with both doors open. A good haircut could fix that." She runs her hand down the side of my face, gives me a wink, and saunters over to the admiral. "Gotta go, kiddo." Pony plants a kiss on the old man's lips, and disappears into the kitchen.

When I hear the door click closed, I realize her departure has left a vacuum, has taken the life out of the room. I am drawn to that woman's striking good looks, despite her age, regardless of her grandchildren. What is going on between my legs, I wonder? I am at full attention. This reaction is new for me. I stick my hands in my pockets to adjust my briefs, then look up to see a sly twinkle in the old man's eyes.

"So, you liked my little Pony," he says, his eyes running down my torso. "Your kind of virility usually means a man has something to conceal. You have a taste for flashy ladies, son? Or, do you have secrets?"

"Ah, this is unusual for me … to have … oh, I'm dreadfully stupid in matters of sex."

"You're entitled to be a playboy at twenty-seven." He squints at me through bifocals. "Hell, I was a playboy when I was your age. You look older than twenty-seven." He leans in. "You need to trim those black burrs from your ears if you want to make it with women. I don't know why, but they don't like their men too hairy." He finds a pair of small scissors on his side table and tosses them across the room.

I make a two-handed catch, not bad, considering I have to remove both hands from exploring my pockets and the scissors have sharp tips. Is he kidding about trimming my ears, I wonder, in the middle of an official interview, and after Pony set my manhood astir? "Maybe later," I say.

"Son, if you were in the Navy your shipmates would see those burdocks as a sign you were a dirty, foul-smelling scrounge. Any sailor with sprouts like yours would have been picked up by four or five of his shipmates, hauled down to the showers and scrubbed with sand and canvas. When he was clean, they'd take a Kiwi brush and scrub him again. Unclean habits are not the Navy way. Complain and the men would work you over again. Complain to higher authorities and you would be thrown out of the service for having head problems." He points. "Go clean up. I'd tell Slick the same thing if he were here."

That sounds strikingly close to an order. McLaughlin is not my commanding officer, after all, and I have no intention of trimming my ears. Not here. Not now. I'm an FBI agent on official business for the United States government. "Admiral McLaughlin, I think …"

"That was an order, son."

Son? I like the sound of that word coming from his mouth, but he's not my father, and I'm not about to respond to his command. Maybe not having a real father watching my every move as I grew was a blessing. My stepdad dismissed his part in my upbringing as Mother's role.

I rub my fly, unable to bring down the flag. Damn this is an uncomfortable business. I focus my lust like a stud, and imagine tracking Pony, sniffing her scent this way and that like a bloodhound. I know I can't follow her. My agency training imbedded duty as primary in my psyche. Besides, the old sailor still has my gun. I'll humor him now to get what I want later.

"Okay, I'll do it," I say, and adjust my pants on my hips. In the bathroom mirror I check my smile to see that my teeth are clean. "I can do this," I say aloud. I'd watched my barber remove the hair once, years ago.

CHAPTER 4

Spiral clippings fall into the sink bowl as the retired admiral observes me from the doorway, his silence ripe with expectation.

"I'm twenty-seven." I set the scissors down and turn to leave.

He blocks the door and circles his index finger toward the sink.

I acquiesce, return the bowl to ship-shape condition, then drop the burdocks into the waste bin. He nods toward the scissors. "Yes, of course," I say, holding them under hot water, drying them, and presenting them to his open hand. "And, no sir, I've never reacted to a woman like that before. I feel like I've been drugged."

"You've dropped some of your pretty curls," he points.

I bend to sweep the black hair from the floor into my hand. Scattered under the sink are small blue tablets and some pink and white pills. "What are these?" I hold one of each up for his inspection.

"What bottle did you take the Benadryl from?" he says, looking at me as if I have a room temperature IQ. He fumbles for a prescription canister on the medicine cabinet shelf, and holds it out so I can read the label. What's in here? Are they small blue pills?"

I read the label. "Benadryl." Then pick up the plastic canister next to it containing small pink and white pills and compare them to those from the floor. They were slightly larger and blue, but shaped almost the same.

"Son, you may have swallowed my Viagra. The bottles spilled out a few days ago. I could have mixed them." His starter-smile turns into a broad-faced grin. "No wonder you have a record-breaking boner." He hits his leg with his palm, and breaks into peals of laughter, holding the doorjamb to keep from falling.

I can't help it, his laughter ignites mine. A snort erupts from my nose and turns into a belly howl. "You use Viagra at your age?" I ask when I catch my breath.

"Sure, for blood pressure, and I use it sometimes when I need a little help," he says, shaking his head to regain composure. "It's not a sin to waste a good erection for a youngster your age, but it would be disastrous for me. Those damn blue pills cost me ten bucks apiece. Did you find them all?" He tips his head sideways to see under the sink, then points to one I missed next to the wall.

I capture the last blue pill from the floor, slip it into the canister labeled Viagra, and return the container to the medicine cabinet. I slip two Benadryl into my mouth. He's still laughing as I take a stab at focusing on my mission instead of this man's sex life. I work stubby fingers through my thick, curly hair, regain my composure, and join him in the main room. "To answer your question, sir, I'm twenty-seven years old, and, I don't need help from your blue pills." Without thinking I bite a broken fingernail, and tear it clean with my teeth. "Now, about my purpose here ..."

"I heard you the first and second time. You're twenty-seven. I'm old, not deaf." He gives me the once-over. "Your ears look better. By the way, I was short, too, until I was in my late twenties." His grin is gone. "I was always hungry as a kid. Best food I ever ate was in the Navy. Once I got three squares a day I started to get taller." He steps through the kitchen doorway. "I'll wager you still have a couple of inches lurking somewhere under that mop of hair." The teakettle screams the water is boiling. "I'm making more coffee. Who told your agency about me?"

"A retired Secret Service agent gave me your card. He was an intermediary between the intelligence services."

"Ah, a cutout, another anonymous face for network security." He disappears in the kitchen and the steam screaming stops. "That's typical Washington bureaucracy," he calls behind him. "No one gives a direct answer, and no one speaks for himself."

I wonder how he knows cutouts are used so agents from one intelligence service can't talk directly to operatives of another agency. That's insider information. He might have read about the Abel spy ring of 1971 when information compartmentalized for agents at the bottom of the pyramid was only know by a few controllers on top.

Ah, I remember it now. The fiasco was leaked by the media after 9/11. That's where he got it. Focus. I'm not here to add to his knowledge of the CIA or the NSA. I'm taking charge of this interview, and I'm doing it now. "Sir, tell me ..."

"I asked you if he was a cutout?"

The manual advised agents to stay calm and remain quiet if they land in a situation where the informant is taking over, to divulge information only if necessary, and then in small bites. My case officer advised me to withhold information completely, to see what the informant had to offer. If I follow protocol, the old man might slip and drop some unexpected detail.

"Yes, he was a cutout," I say, caving in on FBI protocol. Why do I feel like I'm in the middle of a role reversal like the scenarios we practiced at the academy? "The cutout told my case handler that a retired Navy officer, a James H. McLaughlin living near Swainsville, Michigan might be willing to talk with an FBI agent. Official paperwork indicated this man was asked to participate in some criminal behavior." That should be vague enough to hook the old man.

"You're not the first FBI agent to come knocking."

Now we're getting somewhere. I see him shuffle to the refrigerator, take out a carton of milk and pour some into his cup.

"Java?"

"I'm not used to this cold weather," I tell him to soften the mood. I follow orders and shift closer to the electric heater.

"I asked if you want some coffee."

"Yes. Sure. Thank you, sir."

"Move the newspapers from the couch to the pile by the door," he calls from the kitchen. "What do people call you, Dave or David?"

My position on his couch gives me a clear view of him in the kitchen, and, it gives him a straight shot at me from the doorway. I realize I'm tired, stressed about my gun, and my neck is stiff. The procedure manual warns agents to stay alert and careful in situations like this. My head feels like it may blow apart if the Benadryl doesn't kick in soon.

Screw the manual. If the guy shoots me, he shoots me. I won't attempt taking my weapon by force. My head really aches. I hate Michigan. It's too icy, too cold, and too far from my girl. I wonder if the absence of feeling in my feet will be permanent. I hold my bare toes close to the heater.

"My friends call me Dave, but my family calls me David. I'm afraid I scared your cat."

"That would be Murphy." A cupboard door slams. "He's my daughter's guard cat." Metal clinks on pottery. "Don't take his rejection of you as personal. He hates all government workers." A heavy door slams. "You like cats?"

"No."

"I cat-sit by day while my daughter works." He shuffles into the living room carrying a steaming mug in each hand, but stops when he sees my feet against the heater and steam effervescing from the wet cuffs on my pants. "I wouldn't do that if I were you." He places a mug on the table beside me.

"Warm your feet gradually and the pain will be less. Get near the heater, but not that close." He trudges to his chair and positions his mug on the end table. "I remember the pain of thawing, of being so cold my entire body throbbed. Fear and the brown bear kept my feet from freezing on many occasions."

I sneeze and move my feet. "Excuse me. My ears are blocked." I sneeze again and blow my nose. "I don't think I heard you right. Did you say you slept bare, or slept with a bear?"

CHAPTER 5

I could have been fired when I used the computer at work to search for my father's discharge records. I had always been curious about why he had quit the Navy, a topic forbidden from discussion by my mother. I found an answer right there in the small checked box before the word dishonorable. The short explanation typed on the standard form read "... *found unfit for duty while on the USS Cape Esperance by court-martial.* A note at the bottom read, 'Technically sound but socially impossible.'

That family secret opened the door to another forbidden topic, our family disgrace. I thought it was the fight he had with Mother that triggered his death. I found him hanging in the dark after he ran from our porch. What inspired him to hang himself in that garage? Was it connected to something I had said, something I had or had not done. Even now that I'm an adult I'm afraid to break my oath to her and ask about that day, afraid of her answer.

Pieces of my family puzzle are sliding together. It makes sense that his demise could have been connected to his court-martial. Had the bureau known instability flowed in my bloodline, I would have been barred from the agency.

Another secret door is blocking my personal investigation. Why was this blight, this dishonor stamped on his record? What could my father have done that was so bad that the United States Navy didn't want him? I noted the legal proceedings were held in San Francisco and memorized the list of witnesses typed along the bottom edge of the report.

After graduation from the FBI, I was given the opportunity to choose a case for my first assignment. The McLaughlin name jumped out at me from the file. This name was the same as a signatory on my father's court-martial document. I found six service records for James H. McLaughlin serving in the US Navy, but only one who had served on the *Cape Esperance* and the *Rendova* around the same time as my father.

"Sir, was *brown bear* a code for a brunette liaison?" I say to the James H. McLaughlin standing across the room from me.

The old man smiles. "I'll tell you all the lurid details, but first stuff your shoes with newspapers. I've already been through that pile," he points at the *Christian Science Monitor*. "Newsprint will draw the moisture and dry the leather without cracking. Don't put them too close to the heat or they'll scorch." He sits back in his chair. "Now what did you ask? You want to know about the brunette who crawled in bed with me?"

I rub my foot. It's as sore as a gumboil. "No, sir. Not the bare brunette. The brown bear. You were telling me about a bear that saved your life."

"They grew rather large on Kodiak Island, too big to take to bed at night and cuddle," he winks, and takes a sip of his coffee.

I continue to separate the pages of yesterday's paper and wad them into balls.

"They run up to fifteen hundred pounds. I worked for a contractor in Alaska when the Japanese bombed Pearl Harbor. Quit my job and enlisted on the spot. New recruits were assigned to guard the US government's fuel storage dumps near Fort Kodiak. It was a port that almost never iced over. Cold temperatures were extreme that year. When light ice surprised us by skinning the bay we had to improvise. Oarsmen were ordered out in twenty-four foot whaleboats to break up channels of open water so seaplanes could taxi to and from shore and take off. The whale boats were crude, but they were all we had at the time."

"Didn't you take basic training?" I finish stuffing the paper balls into my shoes and set them back away from the heater.

"My CO gave me a book to study. He said I'd be tested in three weeks. I could skip boot camp if I passed, so, I passed. I earned my college degree the same way, except for a few specialty schools I had to attend."

His information jibes with the service record I reviewed this morning ... *McLaughlin has proved tireless, energetic ... with laudable interest in his work, has the ability to grasp administrative problems, is considered an excellent leader, and is hereby recommended for promotion when eligible.*

The old man takes his seat in his black leather chair. "Nobody trained us. They just told us, 'Take charge of this post and all government property in view.' We made it up as we went along."

I can feel his eyes on me and hear a hum as he settles into his oversized recliner. "About the Kodiak bear, sir ... "

"Ever see one of these operate?" He pushes something on the arm and the chair begins buzzing. A slow motorized movement tips him up to a standing position and sets him down on his feet. "I ordered it from the TV. You'd be surprised what they sell on channel thirty-nine. That's what I look at when I'm not watching CNN. This old tugboat does everything but scramble eggs." The motor purrs as the chair reclines.

"We were untrained and at war on Kodiak Island," he says. "We had to improvise ... used to sing this ditty when we got frightened walking armed guard duty. 'Walk this post in a military manner and take no shit from the company commander.' He chuckles to himself. "We made fun of everything. We had to laugh. Couldn't cry." The chair clicks to the upright position and he sips the black brew he calls coffee.

"We weren't like kids today. When we enlisted we didn't have enough sense to be scared and admit it. Most of us just wanted three meals a day and a roof over our heads." He leans forward and slides his cup onto the table.

"The belly-robbers from the mess hall threw spoiled food inside garbage dumpsters near my guard post. It wasn't long before the local brown bear population stopped plucking cranberries from bogs near the fuel dump. Scavenging dumpsters was easier. I watched them move around at night while I sang songs from my guard position. I had my iron sweetheart slung over my shoulder, just in case."

"Iron sweetheart?"

"That's what we called our weapons. The bear were big, so big that when they stood on their hind legs they were taller than a man ... ten or twelve feet high."

Sunlight from the window exposes a determined expression on his square face, illuminating him like I imagine the Alaskan midnight sun must have exposed those hulking prowlers. I bend forward so I won't miss a word.

"We were given orders to let the bear have anything they wanted, not to shoot unless they attacked. The brutes lumbered close in to dig garbage, so close I could smell their musk." He wrinkles his nose. "They never came after me. I didn't know it at the time, but they preferred garbage to my sweet ass." He cackles. "Fear of an attack kept my blood pumping, kept my skin shivering, kept me pacing, kept me from freezing to death. Fear of those bear saved my life."

It didn't take much for the old man to suck me into his story. My curiosity about subjects service-related had been keen since the topic was banned from my childhood home. I had to sneak to a friend's to watch *McHale's Navy* on TV, drink Cokes and smoke cigarettes ... all forbidden pleasures. Last week when I couldn't sleep I turned the tube on at 3:00 a.m. and was pulled into *Tora! Tora! Tora!* with Jason Robards and Joseph Cotten. Kept me awake until five.

"Not everybody reacted the same way to fear during those frigid arctic nights," he says. "I still remember the sky up there. It stretched so large the stars bulged and seemed ready to pop. My buddy, Warren G. Baldwin, had a different reaction to fear. He was a bear of a guy and no one to mess with.

"One midnight when both Baldwin and I had the fuel dump watch, this cocky, chicken-lieutenant they assigned us was showing off his authority just for his own amusement, sneaking up behind us, trying to take away our weapons."

"Chicken-lieutenant? Was he a coward?"

McLaughlin shakes his head. "He didn't know enough to be a coward. He was one of those butt-stupid guys that took ROTC in college and was given a division of twenty men to command before he understood how to tie his own shoe-laces. That may have been the first time in his life he had ever held authority. He was green, inexperienced, and didn't understand the responsibility that goes along with authority. He played big shot with the wrong stooge when he screwed with Warren G. Baldwin.

"My friend told me later he felt a presence behind him, felt pressure on his weapon, felt as if it was being pilfered from his shoulder. He acted on instinct like he had been trained if attacked from behind. He pulled his knife, whipped around and slashed the intruder across his middle. The knife cut through his uniform and sliced the lieutenant's belly wide open. Baldwin said he watched the surprised look on the lieutenant's face as his guts spilled out on the white snow."

My stomach whirls.

"I came a-running when the lieutenant screamed. He was kneeling, bending over, trying to gather them, sweeping his steaming insides together across the ice with his arms, the red stain expanding around him. I hollered for the sergeant of the guard to bring a litter. We laid the guy back, gathered his guts and stuffed them inside his belly. Baldwin and I helped strap him into a wire mesh stretcher and then watched as hospital corpsmen carried him away. They flew him to a hospital in Anchorage."

"Did you see a counselor to help get through the trauma?"

"That wasn't an option at that time."

"Weren't you upset?"

"Cried six pints." The admiral flexes his back and pulls the lever that snaps his footrest into place. "I need to keep my legs elevated." He wrestles himself into a comfortable position, a labor of tugging and straining that leaves him puffing. "Feeling coming back yet?" he asks and leans forward to look at my feet. "Just keep 'em away from that heater, son."

I cough and rub my bare feet. "Did the lieutenant die?"

The old man leans toward me. "If your feet are prickling you're too close." He pushes the heater away with the cane he retrieves from the side table. "Never found out if he made it."

In my imagination I see steam from the warm intestines spilling red on the cold white ice. The smell is that of fresh red meat … sweet, a hamburger scent that I recall from my mother's hands after she mixed ground beef with bread crumbs and eggs to make her signature meat loaf. The image and smell give me goose bumps. I will never be able to enjoy meat loaf again. I come back to the sting I feel in my lower legs. "Think my feet have permanent damage, like frostbite?"

"Probably." He grins. "How long did you stand out there?" His forehead hatches a serious frown.

"Long enough for my core temperature to drop."

"Get yourself some boots, son. Waterproof ones, not the fancy leather kind. Fifty dollars will get you a good pair at Meijer's." His frown deepens.

"I've told you all I know about the incident. If you try to pin that officer's death on Warren G. Baldwin, you're forty years too late. Warren's dead." He looks at his watch. "I'm getting hungry. Want to help me eat some of Pony's meat loaf?"

CHAPTER 6

My case handler said my first objective was to determine the credibility of the stool pigeon. He said the guy could be feigning help, or stonewalling. It was his opinion, after reading my reports that McLaughlin was sharp enough to pull off a major fraud even at his advanced age.

My boss reminded me about John Walker, the retired chief warrant officer who sold Navy secrets to the Russians from 1968 to 1985. Walker's ring included family and friends selling key settings for the KL-47 cipher machine used by the Navy's command center for Atlantic submarine forces. Russia learned about advance movements of the American nuclear fleet and Navy secrets from the technical manuals Walker sold them.

I grimace. If I screw up I could compromise national security. Without thinking I slug down the grit at the bottom of my coffee mug. I'm determined to probe every corner of the informant's personal life until I find the loose brick in his security wall. "I'm not here investigating Baldwin, sir." I swallow a lump of something hard ... a coffee bean. "Why did the FBI knock on your door the first time?"

The old man's face changes into a knowing grin, like he's sure I'm fishing and there's no way I can hook him unless he takes my bait. He pauses. His lips tighten across his face.

"They were looking for my youngest brother, Paul." It's clear his years in the Navy taught him a direct question requires a direct answer. "He went AWOL from the Air Force when they didn't live up to the promises the recruiter made. They gave him six months in the brig when they found him."

The tangent his story takes intrigues me. "Six months? How long was he absent without leave?"

"He went AWOL one month before they contacted me. Two agents in shiny brown suits stopped to see me every week. Three months later the military police found him working for an electrical contractor in Salt Lake City. The Air Force gave him a bad conduct discharge. He went back to work for the same contractor after he served his time. My brother died when he was forty-five."

I suck air through my teeth and stop short when I hear the sound I'm making. "The Air Force doesn't fool around."

"Neither does the Navy. You're not interested in Paul McLaughlin. What do you want from me, David Dugan?"

Just then Murphy bounds from the bedroom, lunges over my lap and jumps to the headrest behind me. I grab his foot to prevent his tail fanning my face, but the damn cat slashes me with his free paw and leaves a thin line of new blood across the back of my hand. He leaps to my lap.

Before I can react, he plants his other foot, pushing needle-thin claws through the fabric of my pants into my flesh. "Ow!" I leap to my feet, and Murphy shoots into the bedroom. If I only had my Smith and Wesson, I think, I would …

"I thought Murphy had changed his mind about government men." McLaughlin doubles over in laughter and hits the armrest with his open hand. "I guess he doesn't like you either. He puts up with me because I'm retired."

I sink back on the sofa, rub my leg and ask. "Are you currently a member of the National Association of Atomic Veterans?"

It's his turn to be surprised. The old man jerks forward in his recliner, spilling his coffee. "So you're investigating the NAAV?" His eyes catch mine. "You could have saved a lot of time if you asked me straight out. But, you young people don't work that way." He grimaces. "Okay, Agent Dugan, I'll answer questions about the NAAV, as long as the answer info isn't classified. But first, tell me who turned me in." He crosses his arms behind his head and leans back.

I think we're getting somewhere. "You did, sir. My records show you reported to a JAG officer …," I stop to check my notes, "it was an E.F. Fuente."

"Fuente?"

"We need your help with the veterans who tried to enlist your help. We need you to walk those men through the filing of their fraudulent claim. And we'd like to talk about the class action suit filed by the NAAV against the US Government."

His hands flop to the arms of his chair. "So, old Fuen pulled through after all. He never mentioned it after I phoned him, and I didn't ask. When did he contact you?"

I find the notation in my spiral notepad. "It was five years ago September."

"Hmm. When I didn't hear from him, I thought the brain trust in Washington had dismissed my tip because of my age. That must have been just before his heart attack. Why did they wait so long?" He pauses, and holds up his hand as if he has answered his own question. "The insidious leaders in D.C. held off opening the class action suit until most of the defendants were dead. There were too many of us … over 200,000 at first. We would have broken the budget." He leans back, and stares at the ceiling. "We put too much trust in our leaders, in Congress. Those bastards left us to drown in a pond of paperwork … a sea of promises … an ocean of hope. They could have done right by disabled veterans. I'm not sure the current batches of mouthpieces do a better job." He glances over at me. "Why is the FBI investigating me now?"

I take a deep breath remembering how intimately familiar I am with deceit. I broke the oath I swore to the bureau by not divulging I had a conflict of interest with this case. I compromised an oath to my mother by exhuming family secrets. I'm in deep and I can't stop now, not until I root out the secrets missing from my father's service record.

"Are you daydreaming, son?" I hear him ask. "I blame television for your generation's short attention span. I asked you a question."

I remember my mother saying that daydreaming helps her make sense of the world, helps her make it through the day. "I know it was a while ago, but can you remember what you told Mr. Fuente?"

The admiral scowls. "I get annoyed when young bureaucrats like you discount what people from my generation say because we're over eighty. You assume we're all senile."

I won't let him bait me. I turn to a clean sheet on my spiral pad. "Don't leave anything out."

He straightens in his chair, like he might if he were testifying before a court-martial. "I was at a meeting of the NAAV with an organizer out of Sacramento. Joe Ortega was his name. He invited me to meet with a fellow veteran diagnosed with colon cancer." The old man clears his throat. "Melvin Gibbons turned out to be a tall, string bean who said he had been in the Navy and knew his cancer was service related. He asked if I could help him with the paperwork to apply for compensation. When I asked Gibbons if the atomic tests he had participated in were on land or at sea, he studied the planks on the floor and said nothing.

"Ortega talked instead. *Look, sir,* he said to me. *Gibbons was never aboard any of those ships and he didn't witness any atomic or nuclear tests. He's just a poor sailor who served his country on a ship that never left the Mediterranean. He has two families to support.*

"I looked at Ortega like he was nuts and told him I didn't get it. Then I asked him how he planned to prove his cancer was service related.

"Gibbons said, *My brother Earl was on the* Albemarle *with you in the Marshall Islands. He died ten years before leukemia was on the list of cancers that were eligible for compensation. I take care of his wife and kids. Now both his son and grandson have leukemia. They've topped out their insurance and the medical bills have eaten away their savings. My wife and I help where we can, but now I'm sick and we're broke. My brother always thought a lot of you, sir.*

"Then Ortega jumped back into the conversation and said since I knew my way around Navy paperwork, it shouldn't be hard for me to switch names on his DD 214 discharge, and place Melvin on the ship with me instead of his dead brother. Then Melvin could get the cash his family deserves. I remember Ortega's words exactly as he spoke them. *Look at it this way, sir,* he said laying his hand on my arm. *You would want to help a fellow shipmate, one of your own men, wouldn't you? God knows Gibbons deserves it.*

"*Let me see if I got it right,* I told him. *You will file a phony claim to represent Gibbons' service as something it wasn't. You need my help to create a bogus DD 214 discharge portfolio. Gibbons' colon cancer would then be classified as one of the cancers adjudged service-connected and would be recognized as a reimbursable disability. Gibbons would recoup damages long overdue his brother and would be repaid for taking care of his dead sibling's family. Do I understand your intentions?*

"I must have had it right because they both had this grin of accomplishment hanging on their chins. I told them I wasn't sure the faked DD 214 was the best way to go. *There may be a safer way to get Melvin Gibbons some money.* I removed Ortega's hand, told them I needed to sleep on it and asked for their contact information.' The two men wrote the information on the back of a bar napkin.

"When I got home I forwarded the napkin to Fuente. He thanked me, and told me this sort of sting by disgruntled vets was not uncommon. *Hell,* he said, *those poor bastards spend their last days trying to figure out how to feed their families after they are gone.* He said he'd take care of it, and advised me to keep mum on the counter sting, so I never did call Gibbons."

"Admiral McLaughlin, why would you turn a fellow veteran in, a dying veteran?" I say. The old officer leans forward and stares at me, like he has located something deep inside my eyes to hold his focus. I feel an uncomfortable heat inside my head.

"Fraud is not my way, son, and it's not the Navy way."

I feel my chest tighten, and try to disengage his stare.

"Phonies like Ortega and Gibbons who try to benefit from diseases that kill others ruin it for the rest of us, give all veterans a bad name." McLaughlin's eyebrows furrow into a deep gash at the bridge of his nose. He appears disgruntled. "Why did it take the FBI so long to get moving on the class action suit the NAAV filed against the government?"

My eyes smart and begin to water. "My agency couldn't begin the investigation of Ortega and Gibbons until an official claim was filed on the class action suit." I try to blink away a tear. "The agency had to wait for paperwork, and as you know, our system moves slowly."

"Slower than a snail on crutches."

"Right. So, when the claim was received and rejected because it was fraudulent, Ortega would follow up with a lawsuit to attempt to prove to the courts that his claim had merit." I rub my eye, which ignites my dry-eye burn all over again. "The defense of that lawsuit would be where the fraud would be proved. Are you following this?" I see him nod. "With your help, sir, we can prove fraud and they will go to jail."

The old man exhales his next breath slowly through his teeth … a weak whistle. "You'll have a hell of a time getting information now. Gibbons may already be dead. Congress has already labeled the NAAV subversive. And those veterans aren't dummies. They'll sniff you out. This isn't easy for me. I feel like I'm playing at the wrong end of the field." McLaughlin's voice has become a monotone, steadily increasing in volume. I sense he's having second thoughts.

"I checked," I tell him, "and Melvin Gibbons recently underwent a major surgery. He's still alive and lives in Sterling Heights, Michigan, near Pontiac. He may just be waiting by the phone for your call."

Murphy shuffles from the bedroom, brushes against the old man's leg and comes to a stop in front of me. He lowers his head and hovers. It's hard not to twitch. He takes a step toward my shoe. "Scat," I say and kick my foot toward him. The cat jumps and hisses. I sense McLaughlin's eyes on me. "Will you work with us, sir?"

"Not if you hurt that cat," he says. His nostrils flare, and his eyes flash like a delayed fuse.

"Nice kitty. Don't scratch me again," I say as the old man's eyes roll upward. Embarrassed, I look away and hear a sigh that sounds familiar, like disgust.

"Why the hell do you think I would have broached the condition of affairs to Fuente if I wasn't willing to help?" The cat jumps into his arms. His frown deepens. "Sometimes I think if you federal kids had brains you'd take them out and play with them." His volume gets louder. His voice remains strong and steady. He strokes Murphy.

"I need you to contact Gibbons," I say, focusing on the evidence needed to prove the claims are fraudulent. "Explain to him how to circumvent Navy bureaucracy."

"Okay. Okay," he says. "Let's say the man has managed to stay alive. Just what do you want me to lay on him?"

"After thirty-three years inside the system? Come on, sir."

McLaughlin softens. "You're right, David. It's not that hard, if you'll help. First, I need you to check St. Louis to see if Gibbons' records are among those burned in the warehouse fire of 1976."

I'm surprised he remembers that fire. This old albatross is sly. I'm beginning to see how he soared from the stripes of warrant officer four to the star of a rear admiral.

"If the records are there," the old man says, "the FBI can get them pulled for up to six months without a trace. When no records are found, Ortega, Gibbons and I are clear to fabricate. I can write a letter and say Earl Gibbons was on the *Albemarle* with me in the early '50s, during Operation Sandstone."

"That should work," I say. "Phone Gibbons. I'll run a wiretap and record the conversation. Find out if he's still interested in pursuing the fraud. Make the whole thing sound like it was his idea. Can you do that?"

"I feel like a henchman," he says.

"Call Ortega next. See if you can get the two of them to write their plan down for your review. When the document arrives we'll have another solid piece of evidence. Offer to return a revised, signed copy to them in Pontiac as a goodwill gesture. I'll drive you in. As soon as we've got their voices on tape, we can all go home." I pull a folded paper from my shirt pocket. "Here are some suggestions from my boss. Use them if you like."

I have specific instructions from the Ann Arbor office. First, determine if the informant has a personal axe to grind. Always question his motives. And remember, gaining his trust weighs heavily in this case. Report your findings to base before you go forward with the investigation.

The boss told me at our last meeting that I had to be in D.C. a week from this Wednesday to guard some foreign dignitary's hotel hallway, so the wrap had to be soon. He reminded me the agency had strict procedures about investigating fraudulent actions against the government. Procedures had to be followed by the book. Foul ups could cause the case to be thrown out of court. If the informant had legal problems, I was authorized to deal. If he wanted cash, money could be had. My favorite part of each meeting with him was when the senior agent stood and adjusted his tie. He said nothing more, just eyed the door until I took his cue and backed out.

I emerge from my thoughts to notice the admiral's hands are gripping the arms of his recliner. His fingers are white. I walk toward a window and pull back the drape to put some space between us. "Mind if I get more coffee, sir?"

"Water's in the electric pot in the galley."

I scan the sky for an end to the snow, then step into the kitchen. The sound of boiling water soon fills the room. The pitch of the steam screams progressively higher until it stops and slips back into a whistle midway up the scale. "Can I get you a cup?"

"The cow is in a cubby on the back of the refrigerator door."

I click the metal spoon in the pottery mug for an interminable length of time before I realize the sound might annoy my host. After handing him his brew and taking my seat I say, "Sir, are you aware of any trouble you might have with the law?"

"With the police?" His eyes narrow. His face reddens.

I watch him inventory my bare feet resting on his deep pile-carpeted floor, my shoes drying near his electric heater, and my bulk now testing the springs of his leather sofa.

"You are a cheeky little bastard." His voice is a whisper. "What does my criminal past have to do with a group of old sluggers attempting to defraud the country they swore to protect? You know something I don't?" His face is crimson. The level of his voice is rising.

"Bear with me, sir. Just answer the question."

"It's none of your damn business." His teeth are clenched.

"I'll take that as a no."

"I wonder," the old man grinds out the words, "if the FBI trains agents to be cocky ungrateful bastards or if you new recruits learn it on your own?"

I keep my sight trained on my coffee mug. "Why doesn't anyone in this town know you are a retired US Navy admiral? When I ask about your rank all anyone knows is that you are a veteran."

"It doesn't matter who you used to be around here." McLaughlin's tone is sharp.

My forehead feels warm. I look up and catch his glance leaving my face and moving to the front door. It occurs to me that he is big enough to throw me out. He is old but a larger man than me, and he still has my gun.

"My wife was a shrink," he says staring forward, his tone calming. "She said if people catch wind of my rank, they'll ask me to march in parades, officiate at funerals, and speak at banquets. Neither of us had much use for that. I've always hung close to the deck." His eyes find mine. "And I was doing okay until you rolled into town. Who have you questioned?"

"Under the Patriot Act the bureau can get information from anywhere, the library, academic institutions, brokerage houses, travel agencies, doctors. We can access personal information from property tax records and professional association memberships. Our supercomputers use advanced networking that can analyze billions of bits of data about people like you in order to discover patterns and useful intelligence products."

"Is the government listening to my telephone conversations?"

"We have that capability."

"You would need a subpoena for that. Who would issue one?"

"A Jackson County judge with a special clearance issued one for me. He was trained by the Terrorist Task Force."

"What probable cause or reasonable grounds did the FBI use to investigate my involvement in terrorism? High treason?"

"All I told the judge was that I needed your records for an ongoing national security investigation." I watch the old geezer's eyes glaze over. "No one knows I'm investigating you, or ever will. There will be no entry on your record. Patriot forbids recipients of a Section 215 to tell anyone they have received one."

"There go our First Amendment rights." He slams his fist down.

"The only limit to the government's power here is that the investigation may not be based solely on your First Amendment activities."

He takes a deep breath, and pushes himself forward in his chair. "Look, David. I've dealt with regulations most of my adult life, and when necessary I've found a route around them. I learned early on that when one of my men was ordered a court-martial for a minor charge, I could advise the clerk who worked on the legal forms to misspell a few words, make a few typos. The judge would throw the whole thing out for sloppy paperwork. That's how the Navy operates, spit-polished and bleached white."

"Are you a good citizen, sir? Do you need some help with your sins?"

"Thank you, David. My sins are not up for public scrutiny. I'm not in any trouble. And you are annoying me." He releases the lever and his footrest collapses. "What the hell are you fishing for?"

"Were you forced into Medicare from the military health care system?" I ask, throwing bait.

"Damn it! Be direct with me. If you want to know if I hid any gambling debts that could make me vulnerable to breaking the law, just ask me."

"Have you?"

"That's none of your damn business."

"I'll take that as a yes, sir."

"Are you offering to pay me to help with your investigation?

"If that would make it easier for you, yes. The agency has a whistle blower's fund for cases like this." McLaughlin had no doubt seen it all during his lifetime, and his normal manner told me he rarely lets anything bother him. This time he seems offended. His breathing quickens. He turns his head and shifts in his chair.

"Selling information is not my style." His face wrinkles like he is in pain. He opens the bottle of Maalox on his side table, swallows a draft, and pulls his lips flat against his teeth. It would have been a smile if his eyes had not shown such menace.

"David, let me explain. When I found the fleet I found my level, like water in a puddle. I starved through puberty and high school, grew up skinny. In the 1920s, we would have taken pot luck with buzzards if Mama had permitted it." He coughs, withdraws a cloth handkerchief from his pocket, and wipes his brow.

"The blow of '34 flattened our crops," he says. "The constant wind threatened our landscape of twisted scrub pine and tangled thorn bushes with extinction. It blew the soil away. We learned the hard way not to hide under a stand of cottonwood when a lightning storm rolled in. My family lost everything. The barn burned. The roof blew off the house. The countryside turned hard and dry and rust colored like a raw desert. And then we lost the farm." He rubs the stubble on his chin.

"I was going nowhere if I stayed in Oklahoma. My belly gurgled three times a day like a leaky radiator. I weighed a hundred forty pounds and was five-foot-eight when I enlisted at nineteen. Ten years later, I weighed two-ten and had grown six inches. The Navy fed me, gave me opportunities to achieve, to advance, and to earn respect. Regulations gave me discipline, taught me when to be aggressive, and gave me the tools for restraint. You could say the US Navy filled me with order and grace, became my religion."

I tip my head in acknowledgement, still trying to understand why this man, Navy blue clear through, would turn in one of his own. My boss may buy the old man's answer, but I'm not convinced. I wonder by what standard McLaughlin defines *right*.

My next question has nothing to do with the NAAV, and nothing to do with Ortega or Gibbons. The question has everything to do with what I'd stumbled across in my own father's service record, a connection the two men had on the *Cape Esperance*. McLaughlin's name was typed on the form in black ink.

"Were you ever involved in a compromising situation during your Navy career that could be used against you?" I grow nervous as soon as the question passes my lips. Should I have taken this risk? I could get busted for less.

His eyes pelt mine. "You mean blackmail?"

CHAPTER 7

My watch reads three. We've been at this since morning and my attention is drifting to the shadows his pill bottles make against the wall. McLaughlin's wit is still keen as a blade. He's cooperating, answering every question I pose.

"Circumstances that surround blackmail in the Navy often involve homosexual behavior," he says.

"Yes." I scribble a scroll along the edge of my notebook.

"Personal financial problems are also high on the list, but sex is king." His tone becomes grave. "Homosexuality is illegal, yet it occurs. It doesn't mix with Navy policy. I've first-hand knowledge of the Navy's unofficial policy. It's not pretty. What's the matter with you," he says. "Does it bother you to talk about homosexual behavior?"

"Go ahead," I say, surprised that when I ask about blackmail his mind jumps to gay sex instead of common theft, assault, or infidelity. "I'm listening."

"Concealed homosexual encounters could and have jeopardized national security," he continues. "A compromised sailor could be blackmailed to pass along classified information. When suspected homosexual activity is discovered immediate action is necessary. While I was at sea the policy was ingenious in its simplicity, and brutal in its execution."

The admiral's jaw hardens. The muscles in his neck tense. "I've been aboard ships when sailors caught their shipmates in a homosexual act. The crew threw a blanket party for them … flung a blanket over their heads and beat the crap out of them. Sometimes an event would be held for a sissy the men merely suspected of being homosexual. We'd uncover the truth up on the bridge when the fellow turned up in sick bay all banged up. I heard of a poor sot who was tapped on the back of his head, hauled up to the topside and dumped over the fantail. We found him missing at muster the next morning when the head count was short. It was the CO's job to write the standard 'missing at sea' letter home to his family."

"That's murder." I'm wide awake and fascinated.

The old man rubs his chin and motions for me to close my mouth. "Every sailor aboard knew what happened, yet would swear it had been an accident, and that the kid had been clumsy and fell over the side."

The retired admiral goes on to recall the unofficial policy for officers that had been at sea for too long and had crossed the line of acceptable behavior. Official policy required officers to resign at once.

"A skipper I knew implemented his own unofficial policy. He called the offending officer into his cabin, announced he had the goods on him and told him that to avoid embarrassing the Navy or his family by making his behavior public at a court-martial, he was expected to go to his quarters and bite the barrel off his pistol."

"Commit suicide?" I ask to clarify his colorful language. If this was a common practice in the Navy, I wonder if my father hung himself to prevent embarrassment to our family. The Navy had already thrown him out. My father couldn't have been a homosexual. He married my mother. They had me. I suppose he could have been bisexual.

I recall something linking the word *liar* to his last day. My memory is like a chain, connecting me with Mother's last words to him. "You promised to take care of me." My recollection clicks back yet another link. I can hear her weeping. "You don't have a job. And now this," she said. "You promised I would be the only one. You are a liar. I can't love a liar!"

The old man nods an affirmative to my question about suicide and brings me back to the present. "I remember an officer who was granted permission from his CO to bid his family farewell," he says. "Our ship was docked in San Diego. The man took a taxi into town to see his wife and kids. Then he had the taxi drop him at the Eleventh Naval District Head-quarters at the foot of Broadway and San Diego Streets. He climbed to the top and jumped. The building was right there in the harbor. I could see it from the ship."

I am intrigued, yet my mouth is so dry that swallowing the knot in my throat is painful. Disturbing information intrigues me, feeds into my insatiable appetite for stories of offbeat sex and violence. Yet the admiral still hasn't answered my question. "Sir, have you any firsthand knowledge of ..."

His face holds the emotion of a rock. "David, I am not a homosexual and have never participated in homosexual activities."

His tone tells me I have hit the wall with my last question. His stare penetrates my eyes, then moves to the door, a look familiar to me. I'd better make sure he's the McLaughlin who knew my father before he pitches me out and I lose the one lead I have to uncover our family's secret.

"Sir, I apologize," I stand to change the tension in the room. "I got off on a tangent there that we didn't need to explore." I walk in front of his chair, fold and unfold my hands. "Sir, I know you are clear on our mission here today." I'm talking too fast. "You witnessed a malignant growth when you met with those two veterans a long time ago. We need to know that you will stay the course and help your government re-move the tumor. The only treatment we have for this cancer is your testimony."

He blinks, and turns his head a notch.

I slow my speech to gain control. "You happen to be in the middle of a minefield, sir. If it's fraud, heads could roll. We need your cooperation to catch these guys. Are you commit-ted to see this through?"

The gentleman rubs his arm across his forehead and leans back in his chair. "Sit down, David," he says, takes a deep breath, and exhales. "First, I understand where you're going. No offense taken."

No, he doesn't understand. This is more than an interrogation for me, and more than searching out causes for my family's failures. Most FBI investigators are nosy by nature. I am an exception to the extreme. I take pleasure in delving into exotic personal secrets, shaking out a family's bones to expose clandestine activities outside the investigation. This interview with the admiral is like taking a journey for me, traveling incognito under someone else's skin. No one will know about my kinky side. Who would question an agent of the Federal Bureau of Investigation?

"Weren't you listening? I told you I'd cooperate," he says.

"About your conversation with Fuen Fuente," I say, attempting a dispassionate tone. "Did you tell him what you witnessed, what you heard?"

"That answer would be an affirmative."

"Tell me what you remember, who was there, what was said."

He taps his forehead with his index finger. "I have it all right here. Some first-class brains have told me I have the closest to total recall of anyone they have ever known." The battery in his motorized recliner buzzes as he elevates himself to a standing position. "I want to show you something." He fumbles for his cane, and groans with each tottering step down the corridor to the room at the end of the hall. His posture is straight, giving no hint of his advanced age. He returns a few minutes later with a yellowed folder, stops at the end of the hallway and leans against the wall. He is breathing hard. "You think I'm the kind of man," he pauses to force a breath into his lungs, "who would defraud the United States government? Read these." He shoves the packet into my palm.

"Certificate of Achievement." I follow his order and read aloud from the top sheet. "Joint Task Force Seven, faithful service, devotion to duty on the *Albemarle*." A second certificate reads, "Joint Task Force 132 for meritorious service at Eniwetok, Operation Ivy, 1952." Still another was from the USS *Rendova*. The last line of the certificate of recognition for service performed during the Cold War reads, "The people of this nation are forever grateful." It is signed by William S. Cohen, Secretary of Defense.

I will check the records tonight against the man's file. If they are accurate, he has served the Navy long and well. "Mind if I borrow these?"

The big man stiffens against the wall.

"I'll bring them back tomorrow," I say. "Are you all right?"

A deep frown creases his forehead. His face turns crimson. "You think I'd fake my records?" His eyes scorch mine. He points toward the door. "Get the hell out of my home."

I'm stuck. I cannot move. Aftershocks from his words feel like branding irons burning the word *idiot* on the walls inside my gut. I just stand there, sweating. I don't know what to do.

I have felt this heat before. A memory flashes through my mind of the time my father and I embarrassed my mother at the diner where she worked. He had accused her of being too friendly with a customer at the counter and picked a fight with him. When her boss ordered us all to leave she thought she had lost her job. The arguments had been loud that night and my stomach churned then like it is doing now. I gaze longingly at the open bottle of Maalox on his table. I shouldn't have asked about his sexual preference. It was insensitive of me to question his career achievement records. I should know where to draw the line between my personal and professional life. I can get pulled from the case and lose my job for a stupid mistake like this. I could wind up humiliating my family like my father had, and I could ..."

The admiral steps toward me, breathing heavily.

I back beyond the range of the big man's powerful fists. Will he blow, wad his fists into bludgeons, and hammer me flat?

He stands there, glaring at me, then steps back.

I get this man. His limp arms and wilted hands won't harm me. This retired Navy officer understands the link between power, influence and responsibility. He lives the rule of rank, respects the authority behind an FBI shield, and keeps his strength in check with self-control. I marvel at his sense of balance, and wonder if I will ever be able to achieve it.

The real smacker to the truth about Admiral James H. McLaughlin, I realize as the redness drains from his face and his body begins to slump, is that nothing in his aged and weakened condition indicates he could end my career with a single phone call. But I sense he could. His connections at the bureau and respect from the men with whom he has worked would make that possible.

I watch him as he staggers backwards to brace himself against the wall, watch as he fights for control of his breath, and watch as his hand moves up his chest to cover his heart. I see his skin turn gray.

It's his heart. My own heartbeat accelerates. I rub sweaty hands on my pant legs, and feel as guilty as hell. I look around for a landing strip in case the old gentleman collapses. The frosted glass door behind me creaks.

"What's going on here?" A soft voice turns hard as it cuts through the tense air. The sound of boots scraping across thick carpet pulls my attention to a woman in her forties. Her eyes are accusing. Murphy bounds from the bedroom and takes a stand between her feet.

"Who are you?" Her eyes dart at the admiral and then back at me. "Daddy, do you need a pill? Do you need the hospital?"

"Can't talk." He pushes himself away from the wall.

"What are you doing here?" She takes her father by the arm and leads him to his recliner. "Did he hurt you, Dad?" As the old man settles, her glance travels to me standing there in my tailored dark suit, white shirt and tie, and bare feet. She steps between us, into my space. "You've upset my father! He's not a well man. What's the matter with you?" Murphy moves in beside her, leans forward and hisses. "You bully. Get out or I'll call the police."

This isn't supposed to happen to an agent of the federal government. I've never been thrown out of anywhere before in my life.

"Honey," the old man interrupts, his head stretches low, "he … he is the police."

"I don't care if you're an FBI ace. Get the hell out!" The woman snatches my coat and shoes, pushes the door open with her hip, and throws my belongings into the snow. Then she grabs her father's cane and pokes the tip toward my face.

"Okay, okay. I'm going," I say. The cat hates me. The woman hates me. And my informant has ordered me to leave. I elevate my arms in surrender, and back from one storm into another. The wind does the rest, and whips me into total submission. As I huddle barefoot in a snow bank looking for my shoes I hear a familiar sound.

"Dugan!"

I look up and see Admiral James H. McLaughlin leaning against the open door frame.

"You might need this, son," he says, dangling my weapon from his hand.

CHAPTER 8

I log in at the Ann Arbor field office at five that afternoon. My socks are wet. My feet are cold. I dictate the report. My memorandum notes the informant has verified agency records admitting two men had asked him to falsify military service records. I drop the tape in the stenographic bin and rap on the door of the head operative. It's time for me to request the agents I will need to involve in the investigation.

"McLaughlin is not in trouble," I tell my boss and take the seat he indicates. "He doesn't want money, and will cooperate."

The senior agent stands and scratches the back of his head.

"The informant seems to be motivated by civic duty," I tell him. I'm not proud of my people skills earlier today, but I am expecting an attaboy from the boss for being so thorough.

"Sounds like a rare fish, Dugan. That's the worst kind to work with."

My heart hiccups.

The senior operative paces the worn wool carpet with his hands pushed deep inside his pockets. "We can't predict what he will do. He could extricate himself from the investigation if you cross him." He came to a stop in front of me. "You need to play on his ego. Thank him for his help. Be his friend, but find out what he knows. Are you up for it, Dugan?" He walks around his desk to his chair.

"McLaughlin has a lot of war stories."

He spins on his heels and sticks his finger out at me. "Listen to every one of them. Ask questions. Be interested. Get him indebted to you. Offer to pay his car expenses."

"He drives around in a golf cart, when it's not snowing. I could offer to give him a ride, buy him breakfast. He likes to eat at this chain restaurant."

"Good. Take him out. Is our agent with the concealment device still shadowing you?"

"Only at the restaurant."

"A third party could be watching you watching him. Did you two agree on your cover?" I nod. "Make it believable. Your academy recommendation reports you were high on imagination." He laughs. "Oh, and I want a complete report from you here in this office," he taps his desk, "after every meeting. And, I mean complete. Remember e-mail and cell phones are not secure. Use them only for non-sensitive information. If you need to talk to me in an emergency, use the State Police radio frequency in your car. Keep your source confidential at all costs."

"He has an overprotective daughter. She refers to her dad as an admiral."

"Admiral?" The man rubs his clean-shaven chin. "His paperwork didn't indicate he was a big fish. This could change everything, raise the stakes. You better put a wire on him, just in case."

"I don't have cause. No judge would approve a …"

"Conceal the audio surveillance gear the first chance you get, then snuggle it straight to me."

"Snuggle it?"

"Sorry, Ace. I forgot you're green. In the field we refer to sending information safely as snuggling. Got it? We transmit on frequencies close to powerful radio stations so the information is hard to detect." He laughs. "It has nothing to do with foreplay." His smile dissolves. "Don't activate the tap unless you have cause. I'll take care of the judge if you need a sub-poena signed. I almost forgot. You're scheduled for training on the tenth at Quantico, and to be in D.C. next Wednesday." He rubs the back of his head. "What do you know about his daughter?"

"She knows I'm with the bureau, and if she's anything like her father, she won't blow my cover. The woman threw me out of the house earlier today, threw my shoes into a snow bank. I had to walk around barefoot on the ice to find them."

There is a pause. He says, "Nice personal touch, Dugan. Sounds like you're good at playing stupid. Use it." He stands and signals our meeting is over by straightening his tie. "Keep me in the loop."

Traffic is light as I drive west on I-94 to the one bedroom apartment provided by the bureau for stopover agents. Walls of piled snow line both sides of the highway like construc-tion barricades. Blowing snow has drifted and covered the slick, black ice patched along the freeway all the way from Ann Arbor to Chelsea. Conditions are slippery. Damn danger-ous.

I plant my pistol on top of the refrigerator, and sit down for my first full meal of the day. The foam take-out container is from what I had been told was the best restaurant in Chel-sea. The bouillabaisse, crowded with clams and plump pink shrimps, has a hint of cayenne which warms my insides. I locate a cold Heineken in the back of my refrigerator and begin to relax my brain box.

The admiral's commendations and service record take no time to skim. The information is glowing, until I come to a sobering court-martial. Soon after James H. McLaughlin en-listed in the Navy, he was docked a month's pay, spent five days in the brig and lost his chance for a good conduct medal. He was twenty-three. The young sailor pled guilty to being "drunk and unable to go on duty while the country was in a state of war."

I step to the window and pry the blinds apart with the long neck of my Heineken. The treadmill of his career puzzles me. How the hell did a man step from a low-grade seaman to a high-ranking officer in the Navy with a court-martial on his record?

Light streams from the street lamp through the blinds throwing a ladder pattern on the floor behind me. Why would a blemish like a court-martial be insignificant to a promotion board for one sailor, yet pop out and cause another to be booted out after seven years of service, like it did with my father?

Nothing makes sense. The man who gave me life must have screwed up royally in his seventh year to have been given a dishonorable discharge. And this drunken sailor must have done something outstanding during his thirty-three years of service that warranted his unusual climb in status. But what?

Arched street lamps spin a yellow glow pooling on the parking lot snow across the road from my complex. A neon Meijer's sign scrawls across the roofline of the strip mall. I step outside, stick my hands deep into my pockets and jog toward the glitter.

On my way back an hour later with bags billowing under an arm, I phone McLaughlin. "Sir, please don't hang up. I'm the FBI agent your daughter threw out in the snow. We need to talk. Breakfast Monday morning after your daughter leaves for work? That's tomorrow. Yes, of course you know what day of the week it is. I'll be there around eight."

I tap out my girlfriend's number with my thumb while I climb the stairs. She would have enjoyed that fish stew I had for dinner. Both of my shoulders ache. My neck is stiff again. She doesn't answer. I unpack my plunder with efficiency, align my new footwear on the closet floor, and set my suitcase beside an empty six-pack of Heineken. I swallow two aspirin from the bottle behind the bathroom mirror, swing the silvered glass closed, and lean in for an inspection.

My thumb touches redial on the compact phone as I turn my head. My nose is too long. I wonder why my woman has not mentioned these sea urchins lurking in my ear cups. Maybe excess hair doesn't matter to some women. My back muscles are on the verge of spasm. I ache for a woman. Hell, I just ache and I'm drunk. I snap the phone shut and plug it in to recharge. After a steaming shower I crawl into bed. I can't sleep. My head aches. Where the hell is that bitch?

CHAPTER 9

I wait on the steps outside McLaughlin's condo until I hear his clock chime eight.

He opens his door at first knock. "Corny just left. It's safe," he says. The cat attempts an escape, but the big man blocks him with his foot.

"I apologize if I frightened or upset you yesterday," I say.

"Agent Dugan, I've crash-landed a helicopter, been wounded twice and survived thirteen months at sea. A young buck like you can't shake me up. My daughter Corny is another story. She scares me with regularity."

"She terrifies me."

"Hold your fire, son. I forgot something." The old man steps back inside to retrieve a brown paper bag and his cane. He pats each pocket down until he locates his key, pulls the door closed behind him, and tries the lock.

A movement in the window beside the door draws my attention. Murphy is standing sentry with one paw pressed flat against the window. He mouths his message and extends his claws against the glass. I get it.

"New boots, David?" The old man's focus is on my feet as I help him down icy steps.

"Fifty bucks at Meijer's."

"Well done," he says. "You're not as thick-headed as you look." He backs into the passenger seat and lifts his feet inside one at a time. "I swear you're a clone of Slick."

I start the car, and adjust the heater. "Does your son live nearby?"

"You investigating me or my son?"

"I just wondered if he followed your example and joined the Navy?"

"Air Force. He was a pilot."

"What does he do now?"

"He flies airplanes. Anything else, or are you done with my son?"

"Do you see him often?"

He said "No" with a finality that told me the topic had run its course. "I appreciate your coming out in the cold to give me my gun yesterday. I guess I'm lucky Corny didn't use it on me."

He fakes a salute.

"Sir, can you recall for me the conversation you had with those two sailors who approached you at that NAAV meeting. I believe it was Ortega and…"

"Those sailors asked me to help them fake a dead brother's service record so the surviving brother would be eligible for a bogus government compensation settlement." His eyebrows shoot up. "Are you senile, son? I've already answered that question twice." He looks straight through me. "Do you think repetition makes a statement more or less true?"

Don't annoy this man, I remind myself as I fasten my seat belt. I train my eyes on the rear-view mirror and back the car from his parking space. "Why would they ask you to help them?" I come to a stop and turn towards him. "Why you?"

The admiral takes a deep breath. "I never understood that either. My best guess is they thought I understood the system because I worked inside for thirty-three years. Maybe they thought my rank held enough weight that a statement from me verifying their claim wouldn't be questioned. I don't know."

I take a mental note. His mind seems okay after the incident yesterday.

"That's my Mercedes." He points to a golf cart in the carport. Two slow moving vehicle signs are fastened to the back bumper. A Stars and Stripes is mounted on each of the front fenders. "It gets me where I need to go, except when the ruts in the snow get deep, like today. Thanks for the lift."

"Thank you for the hot coffee yesterday." There must be some reason he's not driving a car. Maybe it's his age. I step on the accelerator. The tires spin, catch, and whip the vehicle sideways.

"When the snow melts into puddles over street ice," he says, "it complicates driving. Try throwing the transmission into forward, then reverse, and repeat that until it catches."

I spin-rock the car until the tires uncover a sliver of bare ground, catch and lurch ahead. We skid past a lumberyard and slide sideways down Main Street. His silence for the remainder of the ride unnerves me. "Someone may be tailing us," I tell him.

"Noone could tail us the way you drive. Not even a Girl Scout selling cookies."

"I mean, we should establish a cover, a reason for my being with you if the subject surfaces."

"That occurred to me, too," he says. "Being my chauffeur is out. Let's see, how would you like to be ... how about being my nephew from New York? You could be visiting your favorite uncle because ..."

"... because I'm working on a project like the genealogy of our family."

He reaches across the front seat and offers up his hand. "Hello there, David McLaughlin. How's that old bitch, your mother holding up?"

We have a good laugh and continue spinning and skidding in the direction of the restaurant. I like the idea of being his relation. "I apologize for questioning the veracity of your certificates of achievement. I didn't mean to upset you. It's my job to verify everything. The paperwork you gave me was authentic." I skid to a stop at the second of the town's two traffic lights.

"Glad to hear it." McLaughlin pulls a handicapped parking tag from his inside coat pocket and hooks it over my mirror. "There. That should help your parking karma. Full throttle, young man. The lights green and I'm hungry."

Inside the restaurant we encounter the smell of baking bread, the background buzz of country music, and the toothy smile of a hostess. The admiral introduces me as David McLaughlin. "He's writing a book about our family. Will you give us one of those nice big booths in the back where I can spill the family secrets without whispering?"

She leads us to a booth, places paper mats on the smooth gray tabletop, and hands out folded menus.

"I've got a wolf in my belly that needs to be fed." The admiral hands his menu back. "Did I smell cinnamon rolls?"

"Cook just took them from the oven," she says. "They're full of sugar, and not for you. Sorry." She shrugs. "I'll send Rudy right over with coffee. Welcome to Swainsville, David."

I nod to be polite and straighten my tie.

The old man tells me about Rudy, how he graduated college as a biology teacher at a time when there were no school jobs. He joined the Guard. His wife left him while he was in Iraq, ran off with his best friend. He was involved in an explosion that killed all his buddies. He lives with his grandmother and works as a waiter. "He's getting some professional help. I don't know much more than that. He's not ready to talk about his bad dreams. I think he's better but it's taking time. It happens that his grandfather sailed with me off the coast of Africa."

A young man with huge ears approaches our booth with two pots of steaming coffee. Rudy sets mugs on our table with one hand and fills them with the other. "Your usual, Admiral?" He pulls a complimentary copy of the *Detroit Free Press* from under his arm, and passes it to the old man, all the while looking me over. "What will it be today?" he asks me. "The hostess says you're writing a book about the McLaughlin family."

"Good news travels fast," the old man says. "We better order. I eat almost the same thing every day. Rudy knows." He glances up at the waiter. "Give him the same, keep the sludge coming, and don't forget the ketchup."

I nod to the waiter that I will take the same, curious to know what that is. "Admiral," I say, "I have reviewed the paperwork you gave me. And ..."

Rudy picks some money off the empty table next to us, and slips it into his pocket. He hands a menu to a new customer that I recognize from the Ann Arbor field office, disappears into the kitchen, and returns with a bottle of ketchup. "Admiral," he says. "I don't recall you mentioning a David McLaughlin before. I thought I knew everyone in your family."

We both turn at the same moment to look up at him.

"You know now, Rudy," says the old man. "Are you giving me that ketchup, son, or are you keeping it for my birthday present?"

"How do you fit into the family tree?" Rudy prods, ignoring the old man's question and placing the ketchup on the table. "You're pretty dark for an Irishman," he says, "unless you come from the black Irish McLaughlin strain."

"Could I have one slice of buttered rye toast?" I ask.

McLaughlin holds his palm flat. "Did I tell you about the invasion of Ireland by the Viking fleet and the bastards they left in their wake?"

A frown creases Rudy's forehead.

"Don't let the rye bread get to you, young man. Just because he's refused one of the world's greatest biscuits doesn't make him all bad." He catches my eye and nods toward the waiter. "Rudy's writing a who-done-it and has been using our family history for his characters. He's a natural detective … got the ears for it."

"He doesn't talk like you," Rudy says, "and he certainly doesn't have your good looks. No, he's too short and chunky to be a McLaughlin."

"The biscuits will be fine if you don't have rye bread," I say, and inhale some coffee. "Am I really bad looking?"

"You're unimaginably ugly." The old man is licking ketchup from a spoon.

"Oh, come on. I know I'm not handsome, but I'm not that bad." I take another sip of coffee and set the mug down hard.

"You look like a sea lion that needs a shave," the navy veteran says.

"Rudy, do you think I'm attractive?" I ask.

"Not to me," the waiter says.

"You know what I mean … attractive to women."

"Let's see, David," the admiral says. "If I reversed my polarity I might be able to give you an opinion." He winks. "Let me look at you. I'll give it a poke." He removes his glasses, cleans them with his napkin, and settles them on the bridge of his nose. He wraps each stem around an ear, leans in and tilts his head. "Yes."

"Yes?" I ask.

"It is my considered opinion that you are … hopelessly unattractive."

"Give me some more coffee, Rudy. You two are depressing me. I am so hungry I'd eat buttered cardboard if you would bring me some."

"You look like a cop," Rudy says without smiling.

"Take it easy, son," the admiral tells him. "David's from the shallow side of the McLaughlin gene pool. Keep it light or he might start bawling."

Rudy moves across the aisle to clear a table.

"He has big ears for a waiter," I say.

The old man grins. "They are well developed. My mother used to say that large ears like his could hear voices from the spirits. Keep on Rudy's good side. You may need him for a conduit to the other world someday." His face goes blank. "He spotted you easily. I thought people in your business worked undercover."

"I do, or at least I did, sir." I watch the agent in the next booth shift in his seat. Damn, I think he's taping this conversation. "Do you ever let Murphy, your cougar, outside?" I ask and press my handkerchief to my wounded hand, annoyed it's started bleeding.

"Murphy? Sure, sometimes he jumps ship." He picks at a small foil cup of half-and-half. "By the time I get this open, my coffee will be cold."

"Let me help you." I skin back the foil. "Your bank records show twenty-five dollars deducted from your account every month for the last twenty-five years. I checked further and the same amount was wire-transferred to a bank in Lawrence, Kansas. It went to a special fund for some kind of widows and orphans society."

McLaughlin stiffens and looms even larger on his bench across from me. He leans in and whispers. "You nosy bastard. You've dug into my personal records." His voice becomes a low growl. "You better have a damn good reason or your superiors will hear about this invasion of my privacy."

I know it's common for subversive groups to launder money through charities in remote American cities. I'm on safe ground, but the old man's ire makes me uncomfortable. "It's my job to check, sir." I force a smile. "You could be asked to take the stand and testify, or you may be deposed."

I remember from class that using a smile while asking a touchy question could make it more palatable. "If an attorney digs into your past and pulls out something that makes you appear untrustworthy to a judge or jury, you could be compromised as a witness."

I nod. Nodding is supposed to send a subliminal signal that what you are saying is true. "It's my job to investigate anything that looks suspicious and make sure there is a plausible explanation."

This old guy could simply have a sweetheart stashed in Lawrence, Kansas, although, for twenty-five bucks a month she would have to have a damn good sense of humor. "Under the Patriot Act not much is sacred. Want to explain this contribution?"

"David, if the government allows you this much latitude to snoop, sooner or later you'll dig up the skeleton in my closet. I'll save you some time. My grandfather was a horse thief."

I'm in the middle of a sip when I laugh and cough at the same time. Cold coffee shoots from my mouth. I watch him shake his head as I clean my face, and then the table with another paper napkin. "Sir, you shouldn't tease the FBI."

He opens his palms to me. His laughter ignites. I glance at the agent in the next booth. His recorder must still be running.

"Come on," I say. "You mean like in the old Wild West?"

The old gentleman takes a sip from his mug. "Can you handle an answer to that question?"

I'm not sure he's teasing, but I am sure he's testing me. "What does a horse thief have to do with twenty-five years of fund transfers to Lawrence, Kansas?" I glance across the booth. The admiral's eyes say *shut up and listen*. Okay. I'm addicted to old movies, especially westerns. I've seen most of them and should be able to recognize a plot if he plagiarizes.

Something I learned in a criminal behavior class stirs my memory, something about abnormal behavior reappearing generations later in the same family. I hope that professor was right and it skips a generation in my family pedigree or I'll end up hanging from a rope like my father.

I calculate the admiral would have been in his sixties when he got his land legs back. He would have still been spry enough in retirement to follow his dishonest grandfather's lead. I focus on his story as McLaughlin's family skeletons clatter from the closet.

CHAPTER 10

"I don't know why my grandfather, John McLaughlin, rode away from his home in DeWitt, Iowa to join the Confederate Army. He was nineteen," the admiral tells me. "His brothers served on the Union side. Families near the Mason-Dixon Line sometimes split their allegiances. About five hundred miles east in Dover, Ohio, another contrary son-of-a-gun, William Clarke Quantrill, left his home and job teaching school to join the rebel gray coats. No one knows how the two men met but we do know they rode together for almost five years."

I'm already sucked inside his story. Books about the Civil War have been favorites of mine since childhood. I recently finished the diary of a Union Army foot soldier who spoke of Quantrill as one of the worst of the bad guys.

"It didn't take long for Quantrill to be commissioned a captain in the Confederate Army, and it took even less time for him to be branded an outlaw by his fellow grays. His company earned a reputation for being thugs and cutthroats.

"According to a local newspaper, early one Sunday morning in 1863, Quantrill's men walked their horses into Lawrence, Kansas. The rogues murdered a hundred fifty men and boys, then looted the town and claimed their kill in the name of the Confederate Army.

"Quantrill's raiders killed a hundred blue bellies in Baxter Springs, Kansas later that same year." McLaughlin takes a long breath and continues. "That gang of thugs moved on to Kentucky to ransack small farms for food supplies and to steal fresh horses. A platoon of Union soldiers that had eluded the bandits in Baxter Springs, surprised the thieves and shot Quantrill dead in 1865."

"Excuse me, sir, but what do Quantrill's raiders have to do with your grandfather, the horse thief, or the wire transfers from your bank? Ah, em. You've spilled ketchup on your shirt."

"I'm getting to that," the old man says, looking down and dabbing at his shirt with a crumpled paper napkin. "General Lee surrendered at Appomattox in April of 1865 not long after Quantrill was killed, but the raiders robbed and killed for another eleven years before they disbanded. One by one they melted into the red clay and tumbleweed scrub of the Oklahoma desert.

"Grandfather McLaughlin survived the rough-and-tumble years among those scoundrels and their loose women with only one battle scar ... a missing index finger. John McLaughlin was thirty when he married and tracked his family down in Concordia, Kansas. He took his Cheyenne bride, my grandmother, to meet them. Bloodlines run deep in the McLaughlin clan. McLaughlin's were decent folks. They took him in and his bride was welcomed as one of their own.

"My Great-grandmother McLaughlin was a curious woman. Her son's missing trigger finger intrigued her. She asked him about it one night at the family supper table. John shrugged and said, 'One of my pals shot it off to remind me to behave.' Then he added, 'The bastard told them all to call me Three-fingered Jack after that, since I had but three fingers left. The name stuck.'

"It didn't take the outlaw's folks long to smoke out the truth after he let it slip he had ridden with the most dangerous rogue to fight in the Civil War. They had all heard of Quantrill and his thugs, knew warrants had been issued for the arrest of the raiders for murder and rustling horses, but agreed it was to be a family secret."

The old man pulls a hand-bound book from the brown paper sack on the bench beside him and pushes it across the table.

"I brought this from home for you. There's a picture of my grandfather about forty pages in."

I flip through pages of family tree diagrams, sections written about the Irish branch of the family, immigrants living in New England, and First Nation ancestors. I draw the book closer when I see a photograph of what looks to be a ruffian accustomed to hard times. "Is this him? Your grandfather looks thin. How tall was he?"

"Six foot five."

"He looks mean."

"He was mean."

I study his slim face punctuated by a ragged beard, topped with a dusty, felt hat. Below the brim is a skull with deep depressions where his eyes and cheeks should be, features flanked by sagging flesh. The man seems to be squinting at what must have been the camera lens held by a frightened photographer.

"After the groom had folded into the family," the old man continues, "John S. Wise, a federal marshal for the Oklahoma Territory, rode out to visit the McLaughlin homestead. The lawman suspected, but couldn't prove, that John was Three-fingered Jack. He had a hard time getting close to the tight-hearted, horse-thieving murderer, but somehow convinced the groom he knew he was a wanted man with a price on his head.

"John was surprised authorities had connected him with Quantrill's raiders, and had traced him to Kansas. He and his fellow cutthroats had all used false names. John assured the marshal his rough behavior was behind him and pledged to lead a decent life with his bride, Mary America Rogers. The marshal took him at his word, but insisted they seal the deal with this promise: If John McLaughlin broke the law again, John S. Wise would turn him in and collect the reward."

Rudy appears at the booth. McLaughlin is silent while he refills our mugs.

"We seem to come from sturdy stock," I say, leaning back and looking at my watch. The old man struggles to his feet, mumbles something about a rest room and walks down the aisle.

Rudy returns. "I know you're not his nephew. Give that old man grief, and you'll answer to me." He moves to the next table and fills their coffee mugs.

I don't like threats, but I catch the message. I wonder how he knows I'm a cop, then look down and see that my holster is in plain view from where he stood above me. I slip the gun into the back of my pants, and sip coffee until the old man returns and resumes his story.

"My grandmother claimed she was black Irish, but the family knew she was Cheyenne. Many years later, the couple's fourth son, Walker, married the stepdaughter of John S. Wise. Her name was Mamie May Smith, and she was my mother."

"So the federal marshal and the outlaw became in-laws," I say. "They must have had some cozy, tension-filled conversations around the supper table."

He smiles. "I figure we McLaughlins are regular folk, you know … normal like. We play the cards we are dealt. So, there you have it, young man. That's the legend of my family's darkest skeleton. Would you like to see the cutthroat with his family?" He pages forward in the book before me on the table.

It's hard for me to swallow this tale … a story that could be a television movie. He must have seen my expression change, because he spoke.

"Check it out, David. Didn't you tell me that was your job?" He points to the photograph of parched mountains and mesas behind a dugout home with log walls and a sod roof. Two men and a woman stare at the camera lens in the sepia-toned photo. Two thin horses and a milk cow stand by the soddy on the same red clay that must have been used to construct the shabby building. Two chickens peck at the barren earth. A man squats under a scrawny cottonwood tree and rubs the ears of a lone dog, its skin stretched tent-tight over protruding rib bones.

"That one is John McLaughlin," he points to a gaunt figure standing. "Do you know the term *sooner?*"

"I saw a program on the History Channel about the land grab in Oklahoma after the Civil War. Sooners were the son-of–a-guns who cheated law-abiding folks by claiming land a day before anyone was allowed into the territory."

"I knew you must have seen that special. I saw it, too. My grandparents lived it." He shakes his head. "I always suspected Grandfather reneged on his promise to John S. Wise to obey the law. It's hard to break bad habits. Then when I saw Uncle John McLaughlin's story confirmed on a deed, I knew I was right. Here's what happened.

"A shot fired at noon on April 22, 1889 marked the opening of lands for settlement inside the Oklahoma territory. The land rush displaced American Indians that had been shuffled to the territory from other places in the country. The contestants who lined the Arkansas and Texas borders were ready to outride, overtake, or overrun their rivals to get to a parcel of unclaimed land and file for ownership with the federal government.

"The weather was perfect, dry and sunny. With the sound of the shot crowds burst westward in droves, piled inside and on top Santa Fe Railroad cars, in covered wagons and on horseback. They rode through the dust as fast as they could to get the best parcels first.

"What they found were men on foot who had already staked out the prime parcels. Nine out of every ten settlers jumped the gun, traveled before daylight in their covered wagons and claimed land before the starting shot sounded. These opportunists were dubbed *sooners*. Among the sooners were my Grandfather and his Cheyenne bride, Mary America Rogers McLaughlin. Their claims were challenged in court, but the government argued they had cleared all the squatters out well before the land rush. Sooners' claims would stand.

"The land was patented in Mary America's name but wasn't recognized as deeded to her until well after Three-fingered Jack's death in 1909. Court battles could have been responsible for the nineteen-year delay. I never found out. But, if John McLaughlin hadn't had the pluck to plan ahead and make his illegal move, Grandmother and he would have scraped out their existence on a mound of sand far from any underground springs. Instead, he chose a prime piece of flat red earth near a stream that changed, a generation later, into a dried-up backbone of a creek that refused to hold water for the spring plantings. Their garden was next to a series of small graves piled round with stones … a father's bones resting on the skulls of his son's. The graveyard was home to bats, spiders, snakes and more McLaughlin dust."

"Sounds like your grandfather lived by his own laws," I say, thinking how raw courage must run in the blood of some families, and cowardice runs in others. I turn the album sideways to take another look at the old photograph and think of my own father.

It's hard to stay alive, and harder still to make a life when the rules are stacked against you. A man must fight like that horse thief did.

"I always liked that picture," the admiral says. "I was named after my great uncle, James McLaughlin, Grandfather's younger brother. He's in the picture." The old man points to a man leaning against a tree, a skeleton petting a painfully thin hound.

"Uncle James was a major in the Union Army and a seasoned soldier. He was the acting Indian agent at the Sioux reservation in the Dakota Territory and later at a reservation in Round Valley, California. His wife was of hardy, half-Sioux and half-Scots descent. Uncle James wrote a book when he was a federal marshal in California called, *My Life Among the*

Indians. My Uncle James was involved in the death of Sitting Bull."

"Oh, come on. Don't tell me your uncle killed Sitting Bull?" I say, wondering if James H. McLaughlin is a compulsive liar.

"If you want me to explain the money trail, son, you had better not insult my namesake.

CHAPTER 11

"You depend on TV to learn about history, right?" the admiral says from his side of the booth at the Big Boy.

"Well yes, I guess I do."

"Remember the cowboy-indian shoot-em-ups?"

"The old black and white reruns?"

"That's what I'm talking about, the films where the heroes were always the cowboys who shot up the savages, the redskins. The American Indians were usually trying to scalp them and carry off their women." The old man's eyes linger on mine. "Ever see an Indian ghost dance?"

"What does that have to do with Sitting Bull's death?" I ask, or veterans fighting for compensation because the government stole their health, I wonder. "How come you know so much history?"

"I'm old," he grins, "and, I watch the History Channel too. Sitting Bull's story would never make a movie, not now, not in this country. It's too full of shame."

I'm familiar with hiding shame. "If there was enough sex and violence Hollywood would jump at the chance," I say. "The chief's name could be a big draw. If Russell Crowe was cast as Sitting Bull, the film could appeal to a young male audience where revenues are high, especially in the lucrative video aftermarket."

"Hold on! I don't know what you're talking about," the admiral says. "Unless being a strong leader in the 1860s was considered sexy, the chief had a pointless life and violent death."

"So, what killed him, this ghost dance you mentioned?"

"Yes."

The look in his eyes tells me he isn't kidding. "Did they use fire or knives?"

"They joined hands, and sidestepped left in a circle for a few days."

"There had to be more than that."

"Old Chief Sitting Bull didn't have the kind of sex appeal you young rascals look for in a movie, but he was a strong leader. The chief comes in at the tail end of the story. It started way back in the late 1860s with a vision by a Piute named Wodziwob. This man's dream had American Indians bringing back the old times with a certain step to music called a ghost dance. The idea was that when the dancers sang of future events, their world would alter, their human and animal loved ones would return to earth and all the white ones would die."

"Ouch!"

"Yes, ouch. These rituals threatened pioneers because they often led to raiding parties. The white community put pressure on Washington. It didn't take long before the federal marshal received orders to stop the ghost dance.

"Chief Sitting Bull, a Lakota, performed the Klamath Ghost Dance on the Sioux Reservation in South Dakota where my uncle James was the Indian agent. My uncle warned him to stop the dangerous practice. The chief wouldn't listen. Uncle Jim ordered Sitting Bull's arrest and rode out to the reservation with his Sioux Police to collar the chief in person. He accused Sitting Bull of trying to start an uprising and told him he had to lock him up. The chief resisted. There was a scuffle between the Sioux police and the ghost dancers and the Sitting Bull was fatally wounded."

That's quite a story. I wonder why life works out that way, that some men are lucky enough to have had decisive and powerful men in their bloodline. My line had a father who was thrown out of the Navy. My role model took the route of a coward and committed suicide instead of dealing with his problems.

"Do you think you inherited strength from the men in your family?" I ask.

"Weak men don't survive rugged or dangerous conditions," the admiral says. "Grandfather and Uncle Jim were two resilient men doing what they had to do to survive the times."

My cell phone rings. I excuse myself by saying, "This is my emergency number." I retrieve it from my shirt pocket. "Dugan."

"Davey, I'm sorry to bother you." Her voice has become loud now that she's hard of hearing. "Something smells funny in my kitchen and I'm afraid to go in there. I don't know what to do."

"Were you cooking this morning?"

"Breakfast. I made oatmeal, but I turned the burners off."

"Have her open a window," the admiral says.

I nod across the table. "Open the window in the dining room, and the one in the breakfast nook. Then check the oven. See if it's on. I'll wait."

"She should call the gas company, and have them check for a leak," he says. "Get her out of the house."

"Davey, I can't get the dining room window open, but the kitchen one works, and the oven dial is on off."

"Good. Now listen closely. Go to one of the neighbors and use their phone. Call the gas company and report a leak. Then stay away from the house. Do you understand? Get out of the house now. Hang up the phone."

I look up at the admiral. His face shows concern.

"Your mother or girlfriend?"

I can feel my blood pressure elevate as I return my cell to my shirt pocket "She has a crisis almost every day. It's my mother." I shrug. "She must have convinced someone at the agency to give her my cell phone number. It's for official business only. She must have told them she was dying. They wouldn't give my number out for a gas leak." I wipe sweat that's beading on my forehead with my shirtsleeve. "Dad gives in to her all the time. They both drive me crazy. We were talking about your relations." I want to change the subject to something safe for me. "Did the horse thief become a responsible family man?"

The old man smiles like he understands. "We McLaughlin men learned early on that if we didn't change with the times we would become obsolete and be bypassed. That was one of the hardest lessons for me after I retired from the Navy-changing with the times. It's hard to keep up. My family pointed me in the right direction, Faye and Corny and Slick."

Rudy interrupts the rhythm. "This guy behaving, Admiral?"

The old man thumps the table, and extends his hand for the breakfast check.

"Let me get that," I say.

McLaughlin stuffs the bill into his shirt pocket. "Save the government's money for the national debt. My grandson would appreciate that."

"Thanks. What was it like for you growing up, knowing you were kin to a murderer, a wanted man? Were you ashamed?"

"He was dead before I was born, but I do remember my grandmother. She had long black braids hanging over each shoulder. She didn't talk much about him. My family knew Grandfather was a bad man, like Quantrill."

"Do you know anything about your grandfather's life in the Oklahoma Territory after the Civil War? Is that a soddy he is standing by in the picture?"

"You must have read the same book by Laura Ingalls Wilder that I read to Corny when she was little. She called a sod building a soddy. We all called them that in Oklahoma."

"I'm embarrassed to say I watched *Little House on the Prairie* on …"

"… on television. That's right." The old man shakes his head and continues. "John McLaughlin met and married Mary America Rogers out there on that red earth among those ponderosa pines sometime during the sixteen years he was missing from the family. Rattlesnakes and thorny juniper trees were welcoming Native Americans into Indian Territory from all over the country at the time."

As Rudy finishes clearing the table the old man asks him to take care of the bill. He hands him the crumpled check and a twenty.

"My grandparents had four children. Their oldest son was Arthur, a redhead. The middle two died as infants. My father, Walker, was their fourth child. Years later when he had his own son, John, he told him the family history about Grandfather, but never mentioned it to any of the rest of his twelve children. My brother John was as straight as a deck seam, but he was ornery. When I was nineteen he told me all he knew about our horse-rustling ancestor, but told no one else in the family.

"The horse thief died young. Grandmother told me it was for the best. She said he would have stirred up even more trouble if he had lived. Our family would have had to sleep with the shame like George Custer's kin did."

"Do you mean General Custer, the one Native Americans killed and scalped at Wounded Knee?" This can't be fiction. I tap my fingers on the tabletop. I'll check his facts when I get within range of an Internet connection. I get the shivers connecting all this history to faces I've come to know. I can almost feel the beat of the old man's ancestral war drums.

"You still haven't told me why you transferred twenty-five dollars a month from your bank to Lawrence, Kansas."

"Have patience, son. You won't get this kind of information watching movies on TV. So, you have heard of George L. Custer?"

"Sure. He was born around here somewhere, wasn't he?"

"That was a well-researched answer, David. He's from Monroe, Michigan. In 1870 Custer rode south from Ft. Supply, Oklahoma with his cavalry. They surprised a winter encampment of Southern Cheyenne on the river bottom of the South Canadian River. Chief Black Kettle sent his people into a grove of trees for their safety. Custer found them and killed every one he caught, man, woman and babe. Then he scalped them. Imagine that, a general in the US Army scalping women and children, scalping Native Americans who would have contributed more to this country than that moron did. He was just as bad as my grandfather and I'm just …hold your fire." He looks up.

The old man waits while Rudy lays his change on the table. He says, "Thanks" without counting it, and sips some water before continuing.

"The French paid rewards for enemy scalps during the French and Indian Wars. Natives learned from the French and the US Army learned to scalp from Native Americans. The US military also learned guerilla warfare, battlefield, and maritime strategy from Native Americans.

I can't help but smile while I listen to the old man put an American Indian spin on his story. I have a hunch it is true.

"When Custer's troops finished the massacre at the river, he moved his Army on to Fort Cheyenne. They rode into the Cheyenne encampment in broad daylight and killed every Indian they saw. My wife, Faye, lost her grandparents and most of her aunts and uncles during that fool's disastrous campaign.

"Custer became a rising political star, a hero for killing Indians. People in Washington thought he was brilliant and urged him to run for president. The president, worried about his own re-election, ordered Custer into the Dakotas to battle the Sioux.

"This tribe was known to be tough fighters and fierce protectors of their lands, which included the hill called Wounded Knee. They seldom lost to the long knives."

I gasp, recalling the results of that battle. "The president of the United States planned the death of one of his own generals?"

The old skipper tips his head and gives me an exasperated look. He shuffles his shoulders and turns his attention to counting the change Rudy has left on the table. He nods the waiter over. "You having a bad day, son? Don't let the management know you're giving their money away," he says and hands it all back to him.

Rudy eyeballs the receipt and recounts the money. "Did you give me a fifty or a twenty?"

The old man holds up two fingers.

"Thanks. The boss would have taken thirty out of my pay." The young man counts out four dollars and seventy-three cents and hands it back to McLaughlin. I watch as he takes the other thirty back to the cash register, pushes the tab for the drawer to release, and stuffs the bills in the slots.

I lean towards the admiral. "Why didn't you keep the money? They wouldn't have traced the shortage to you."

"Because, Agent Dugan, you would have nailed me for stealing. I'm not going to jail for a lousy thirty bucks. If you want to help me loot Fort Knox, we should talk."

CHAPTER 12

That afternoon I report to my boss that I have sat through two hundred years of the admiral's history and have nothing incriminating to report.

"Cut an agent into the action to replace the informant," my handler coaches. "Get a professional into one of those NAAV meetings as a player. We could be halfway through this investigation and the informant might say he's had enough. He's old, the man could die before the case comes to trial." Then my senior agent reminds me that my every move must be planned in conjunction with his office and I only have a few days to wind up my case. My job is to orchestrate the game according to the bureau's rules. "Don't let the target take over the investigation. Have you checked his military records?"

"I tried, sir, but fire destroyed ..."

"Agent Dugan, you can have two things in life: reasons and results. Reasons don't count."

"Yes sir," I say, and roll my shoulders back. "In the last twenty years the informant has had cataract surgery on both eyes, basal cells removed from his head and tumors excised from his hip and arm. He has an abnormal growth on his lower legs, which may have been caused by radiation. The local dermatologist had not seen anything like it before, but gave him ointment which does nothing. He has macular degeneration in both eyes, may have upper respiratory issues, but I didn't find that in his records."

"No life-threatening diseases?"

"He's a tough old codger with a healthy outlook on life."

"That's more than I need to know. Assure me the target will live through the trial and I'll be happy. Let me see the letter you worked up for him to show the conspirators." He takes the paper from my hand, and looks it over.

"Proceed with your investigation. You may uncover some sticky lump of evidence. Find out where the safe house will be and let me know," he says. "I repeat, do not let him direct this investigation. The meeting location should come from Ortega and Gibbons, not the informant. Get what information you need, thank the guy and get him out of the way. Get McLaughlin to meet with the conspirators. Keep me in the loop. The clock is ticking, Dugan. Your orders have you in D.C. next Wednesday. He hands back my letter, and straightens his tie … a cue I recognize as a formal dismissal.

I locate a laptop in an outer office and file my daily report: "The informant has not rented a car from any Jackson County agency during the past year. His name was not listed on a manifest for an airline, train or a bus for the past two years. Storage facilities within an hour's drive of Swainsville have no records bearing his name."

I have not been able to ferret any sticky lumps of information from the Internet, even with my big nose. I arrive home to a cold Heineken and a thick folder of medical files. I search a stack of newspapers for my TV remote. It's nowhere. I recover the remote from beneath a blanket, flip past golf, an old movie and then tap the power off button with my thumb.

I wonder if I could have missed something important. I read every line in his folder again, including all his promotions. One endorsement for elevation in grade is for service aboard the USS *Rendova*, CV4 and is stamped Diego Garcia. Those two words rattle the memory chain linked to my father.

Diego Garcia appeared on my father's court-martial paperwork. Are those words the name of a person? A city? I dig out my father's folder, and the document detailing his dishonorable discharge. Diego Garcia is the last port listed before he was shipped to the main battalion for discipline. I pull out my computer to see what I can find.

I Google the port and find it is a Navy communications station located on a chain of fifty-two islands in the Indian Ocean off Madagascar. So, my father's last port was just off the coast of Africa. I wonder what the admiral was doing there. I collect his files from across the bed and shuffle them back inside his folder.

Not one private institution has refused to give me copies of the admiral's records, and not one has been pleasant about doing it. This Patriot Act is a dream for collecting information, but unpopular when I deal with the jittery public. People hate it. They call me Joe McCarthy to my face.

I retrieve my cell phone from under a pillow, and punch in my girl's number. "This is David." It's her answering machine. "I'm calling to wish you a happy birthday." Damn. She is never home. "I'd like to be with you right now." She would use a cell phone if I would pay her bill. "I miss your sweet smile, and your great body." If I tapped her phone she would be pissed when she found the bug. I shouldn't have taught her where to look. The bitch has to be out with some man, someone from work. "I adore you. Call when you get in." The cunt better not lie to me. I bet she's banging this guy while her phone is ringing. "I don't know when I'll get into the city. Call me." I need to gut-out my relationship with her parents and mine. Damn, I miss her.

I snap the cell closed, roll on my back and make shadow animals on the wall with the light from the street. My bed is a rumple of blankets, a tangle of sheets unlike the rest of this efficiency apartment and my obsessive lifestyle.

I started dating her three years ago, and have spent most free weekends at her apartment in New York. I liked that she didn't expect anything of me, and she said she never lies. She liked it when I took her to the MOMA to see the Impressionists, to Madison Square Garden to see wrestlers, and to Carnegie Hall to see Arlo Guthrie. The woman is reasonably attractive and witty. She isn't well educated, but is open minded and willing to experiment kinky sex with me.

I liked the way she stopped what she was doing when I spoke, looked into my eyes and hung on my words. She made me feel like I was the most important person in the world. This woman seemed to see past my physical shortcomings.

I will admit I have never been good with women. The barometer I still use to measure females is my overly stringent mother. Living with her was like a reverse prism. The woman sucked the light from around me until all the enjoyment of being alive withered away, disintegrated into dust. I never understood her, have stopped trying. I escaped her at the first opportunity and have kept her and the fair sex at bay … until this woman infected me with her laughter.

My parents are professionals, Mother a drab, unaffectionate bookkeeper and Mr. Dugan, my stepdad, a sharp-nosed, civil engineer and a dedicated drunk. My mother expects me to marry up. Over the years she has given me names of nice girls from nice families with nice educations.

"Just pick one and marry her," my stepdad sputters, his mouth a black line between clenched jaws. "Get your mother off my back."

I followed a few of Mother's leads, but my life on the road didn't seem to qualify, wasn't normal enough for the kind of marriage these women wanted. I always went back to the same girl.

She always seems happy to see me. She can tease me out of my dark reserve. I've never been crazy about nice girls. I've always preferred the naughty ones, the ones who like unusual sex.

I think about the last time we were together … our lips touching, tonguing her mouth open, then moving my lips down her neck to the valley of her breast. I plucked buttons off her shirt with my teeth, and then it gets better. I open another Heineken.

CHAPTER 13

Snow fills the atmosphere like a thick fog, feathering the road to Swainsville like a busted pillow in a fight. The white fluff drapes from roof gutters and sticks to tree limbs. When I inhale the crisp air the scent is soap-clean like my woman's underwear, a smell that releases unpleasant tape loops to play out in my mind.

She is having an affair. I know it. The certainty tightens my chest. Acid edges my esophagus. I could have her tailed, photographed.

A snowplow slows at the stoplight, drops its blade, and splits the silence with such a deafening screech of steel on pavement that it could vibrate graves open in the village cemetery. The vehicle flashes red and beeps a warning as ice-melting salt sprays the street from a spigot beneath the tailgate.

I drive to the next cleared road, turn left to avoid the plow and find truck tracks that scar the sheet of snow. The two-track leads to a car stuck sideways, taillights glowing red, rear tires spitting snow in sheets across the street.

I slip the gearshift into park, leave the engine idling and step into the punishing weather. The snow is deep. I tap on the steamy driver's side window offering help to a perfect stranger and consider how I am changing. My natural instinct is to be a chameleon and watch … remain neutral.

The woman mouths a *hello*, and rolls the window down a crack. "Will you give me a push?"

I nod and stomp to the front of the vehicle where the head-lights turn the snow yellow. I push. She rocks the car from drive to reverse. I push. Her tires catch. The car shoots back-wards, careening down the street, and stopping on a bare patch of pavement the snowplow has already cleared and salted. She gets out and plods towards me through drifts, her shout blown by the wind. "Hey! I thank ..."

That voice sounds familiar. I trudge in her direction, each step aerobic in the deep powder. I puff as I pull off my ski cap.

She grins. "It's you, the barefoot FBI agent who lost his gun." We both laugh. "Dad told me you had taken him out for breakfast," she shouts into the wind. "Thanks. He needs to be with people." Her volume and pitch rise to be heard above the storm. "He says he feels sorry for you." She grabs for the scarf the wind has torn from her neck and tucks one end inside her coat. "Can I buy you a cup of coffee," she asks, motioning with her arm, "at the Big Boy?" The wind blows me back to my car like a sail in a storm.

I clear my windshield and wonder why her father feels sor-ry for me. The old sailor may have changed course when he realized I am just a little fish in his pond. The man is a clever old shark. He could hurt me. I slip the lever into drive and tap the gas pedal. When the car jerks forward, I crank the steer-ing wheel and gun the gas. I can't help but grin as my car makes a perfect donut, just like in the movies. I skid sideways down Main Street, spin straight, and turn into the parking lot of what has become for me, Swainville's commissary.

"Corny, isn't it?" I say and remove my ski cap to the woman waiting just inside the door. I know all about the admiral's daughter. She is almost twice my age, is divorced and has two children. Her oldest, a son, is in the middle of a divorce. "How about some strawberry pie with that coffee?" I say. "My treat."

"Sure. The pie is especially delicious when it's blustery out-side ... reminds me of a sunny summer day."

The old man told me he had been tiptoeing around the house for weeks. He said his daughter is all worked up about how the divorce will affect her only grandchild.

"My dad named me Corny because I told stupid jokes when I was little. It stuck. The FBI doesn't need to know any more about me other than I was a US Navy WAVE, and I am a Vietnam Veteran with a three-nine security clearance."

I have an afternoon of paperwork ahead of me, and I need to make a stop at Radio Shack before they close. But running into Corny is worth working until midnight. She might give me some insight into her dad. The woman's temperament is defiant. She's definitely her father's daughter.

The place is empty except for the wait staff stuffing napkins into chrome canisters and refilling ketchup bottles. We strip off layers of scarves, gloves and coats, pile them on the bench beside us, and slide under a gray Formica tabletop. Rudy walks in from outside wearing a cheap leather jacket and nods when he sees us. He rubs his hands together, tells us they will be closing in twenty minutes, but will take our order anyway.

"Looks like you gained a cousin," I say as Rudy disappears into the kitchen. I notice her brows move from low to high on the inside by her nose, a classic example of a person with high expectations for others.

"How's that?" She blows her nose.

Rudy sets down plates of pie and steaming mugs. "Corny, watch what you say to this guy. I don't trust him."

She glances up. "Thanks, Rudy." When he is out of earshot, she says, "Does he know you're FBI?"

"The guy thinks I'm a cop. I don't know how he knows." I fork a whole strawberry into my mouth. "Where is your brother?" I mumble, still chewing.

"Slick lives in Utah. Daddy misses him. They've drifted apart, I don't know why. They haven't talked in months. Neither one of them will give me a straight answer? So, who is my new cousin?"

"Me. Your father now introduces me as David McLaughlin. It's our cover. With your security background you will understand how important it is not to blow the lid on us."

The admiral's daughter nods, and warms her hands around the cup she hasn't tasted yet. "Yes, he could get hurt. You've spent a lot of time with him. Daddy enjoys you. He needs a challenge … someone to listen to him. Has he been giving you a bad time?"

I grimace.

"He's a terrible tease." She grins. "He sounds tough, but on the inside he's as soft as one of these strawberries. His ways can set you back a few paces, that is, if you lose your sense of humor."

"Will you tell me about your mother?"

Her face lights up. "Faye? Sure." She sets her fork down. "She wasn't my birth mother. She was the woman who raised me. Mom was great. She told me when she and Daddy decided they wanted a baby they went to the orphanage where I lived and looked for the smartest and prettiest baby. Out of all the children in the orphanage they chose me. Faye was a psychiatric nurse and very good at it. That woman knew how to make my brother and I feel like we were the most important people in their world. He was adopted too. Slick is a few years younger than me. You actually look a little bit like him. Daddy adored Faye."

"Were they good parents?"

"Daddy was at sea most of the time. When he had shore duty, we traveled to his new duty stations, changed schools, and made new friends. We moved a lot."

"Thirty-two times. Your father counted it out for me," I say. "He told me he had shore duty only five of his thirty-three years in the Navy. That must have been tough for your mother.

Did I read your father's records right? Was your mother older than him?"

"Daddy always said she was the perfect woman for him. When she died she was eighty-seven. They were married forty-seven years, I think. Let's see. Dad was thirty-one when they married. She was forty. That would be right. But age was never an issue. My mother was bright and caring. I don't think I ever heard them argue. They made decisions together." Her blue eyes smile out over the black coffee in her cup.

"Daddy is a natural teacher," Corny continues. "He approaches life with a positive attitude. He was good for Mom. She worked with patients who had emotional problems. He taught her his approach to problem-solving, helping her with what he learned by leading men. Faye had an analytical mind. She helped Daddy conceive unique solutions to help his sailors."

I am fascinated to learn how a real family operates. I can't imagine a marriage with an equal distribution of emotional effort. My mother had always made all the important decisions in our lives. My stepdad went along. He said it was easier that way. Maybe she made life too hard for my real father and that's why he killed himself. Maybe it wasn't my fault, after all.

"What did your mother look like?" I say, and try to picture my woman and me after forty-seven years of marriage. I can't. I can't even bring up the image of what she looks like today.

"Mom was a heavy woman. Daddy referred to her as comfortably round and soft. He said she moved with the grace of waves at sea. Her picture is on the wall at home … the nurse. There's another one that hangs on a wall near the kitchen sink."

"Did your mother enjoy being an officer's wife?"

"She was not fond of dress uniform affairs. The Washington events were the worst. She told me she found officers' wives pretentious and humorless. I guess that's why Daddy went to the required events and Mom stayed home with us."

"I'm curious about how your father jumped from the rank of an enlisted seaman to that of an officer."

Corny smiles. "I think it was an accident. I heard him tell that story so many times I know it by heart. He claims he wasn't a hero. He said he was just trying to save his own behind. You may have noticed Daddy downplays his accomplishments." She takes a sip from her mug.

"He has never mentioned the incident to me. What happened?"

"It wasn't that Daddy didn't like President Truman. He complained about the extra work involved whenever the big chief sailed his flagship into waters Daddy thought were his personal part of the Pacific. He said the commander-in-chief was watching maneuvers from the deck of the USS *Missouri*. Truman had observed gunnery practice and was about to come aboard Daddy's ship to present Patrol Squad 47 with a safety award. The squadron was in their fifth tour patrolling the Far East and had fifty-four hundred accident-free hours.

"My father worked on the carrier's flight deck. That morning a plane was landing with a wobbling rocket under one wing. The timer fuse on the explosive was set to detonate a thousand feet after launch. The missile came loose on touchdown, and bounded across the deck towards Daddy. He jumped into a nearby pit used to store an anti-aircraft gun. He said he prayed the stray ordnance would bounce right over the top because the gun pit was loaded with live ammunition. Instead, the rocket followed him in, slid to a stop, and nestled in beside him.

"He told me he grabbed the rocket, lifted it over his head, and threw it overboard out and away from the ship. The ordnance exploded as soon as it hit the water. His superiors reported it would have blown off a good portion of the bow of the ship had Daddy hesitated a second or two. Since his ship was running parallel to the *Missouri*, the explosion could have blown a hole in the president's flagship as well.

"Truman was piped aboard by the boatswain's whistle shortly afterward. He reviewed the troops and was about to present the safety award when Daddy was called before him. The commander-in-chief awarded him a citation for bravery while the ship's band played *Anchors Aweigh*. Daddy's friends kidded him about grandstanding in front of the president, but they all knew he had saved their skins. The president gave him a spot promotion from master chief petty officer to lieutenant junior grade, a two-striper, and the opportunity to attend command school. Daddy liked Harry Truman after that."

"That's quite a story," I say. "Your dad must have been pumping pure adrenaline when he grabbed that live rocket."

"My father never looked at that as anything more than being in the wrong place at the right time. His proudest achievements came from working with his men. Has he told you about the company of forty-six misfits he was assigned at the US Naval Air Station in Corpus Christi?"

"Men from his division?"

"Em hm," she says and swallows a strawberry. "He excelled at helping troubled sailors, treated the men like they were

his own sons. I think he was a lieutenant at the time, but I could be wrong, my memory's a blur." She takes a sip of coffee. "These men had hit bottom and were on their last chance before the Navy threw them out. Dad talked to each one of them, found out what was bothering him, or her. There were maverick women in the Navy, too. He helped them all.

"His work with twin brothers from Kentucky must have filled him with the most personal satisfaction. He reported their progress to us around the supper table. They were backward new recruits, in constant trouble with nowhere to go but up. Daddy said he saw nothing wrong with the boys. One had a face full of pimples and the second fellow had freckles. They had been raised by grandparents in Kentucky's hill country, and never wore a proper pair of shoes or ate three squares a day until they joined the Navy. One of the brothers said that folks looked down on them, like they were stupid.

"Daddy treated them like equals, gave both men jobs. One drove a station wagon on the base for visiting officers, a car kept polished like it was new. I remember seeing the sailor standing at attention, saluting officers and opening and closing the door before he drove them where they needed to go. The other kid from Kentucky hauled Daddy around base in his van."

Corny finishes the last bite of her strawberry pie, lays her fork down and pushes the plate away. "I remember times when those two boys came by our house at three in the morning with a string of fish. I was pretty small and usually asleep, but they made such a racket I would get up to join in the fun. My folks would help clean the fish. Mom fried some up for an early breakfast and put the rest in the freezer. They let me watch for a while, then marched me back to bed.

"Both young men were transferred to the Naval Air Station at Barbers Point, Hawaii for duty on a crash crew that fought airplane fires, and rescued people. They got real proud of being in the service. They wrote Daddy letters long after they had transferred to other stations. He always read them aloud to us. We all rooted for them to succeed just as much as Daddy did."

"I didn't think brothers could stay together in the service," I say, and finish my pie.

"If twins asked they could be transferred together," she says. "I remember another story he told about a frustrated boy who was troubled because he couldn't get his wife pregnant." Corny daubs her mouth with a paper napkin and raises her hand for the waiter. "The young man's poor self-image turned him into a first-class troublemaker. Daddy sent him over to the hospital where they found one of his testicles had never descended. Dad arranged for the surgery and a thirty-day leave. A little later he announced his wife was pregnant. I can still see Daddy the night he found out. He came home happy, took Mom in his arms and twirled her around the kitchen floor. They danced while Slick and I watched."

"You're lucky you have him for a father." I like this woman. She is comfortable to be around, but twice my age … my bad luck.

Rudy stops at the table and looks at his watch. He fills our cups. After a brief dispute between us, he gives the bill to Corny.

"I heard Daddy tell his sea stories often enough." She counts out ten, one-dollar bills from her purse, cocks her head and gives them to Rudy. "It was part of my memory therapy," she says when he leaves the table. "He wanted me to understand that he took pride in his work, and I was to pass that ethic on to my children and grandchildren. But, he didn't tell me just about his successes.

"There was this kid from Boston. I don't remember his name. Daddy said he shouldn't have been in the service to start with. He was constantly on the bubble. One day he sent him on a job to trim some oleander bushes with a pair of hedge clippers. The kid said he grew tired, chose a sandy hill to sit and watched some ants swarm. When he missed muster that afternoon, Daddy nosed around until he found the poor sap lying on his stomach in sick bay. The company stooge had been bitten by fire ants and was in a good deal of pain. The kid told Daddy he was angry at his work crew for not warning him. He was hotter than hell because they laughed at his misfortune and furious at them for hinting he was stupid. He blamed his painful condition on them, and wanted to press charges. This kid was always on the edge of passing or failing something.

"Daddy got the picture when one of the guys confessed to taunting the kid. He said not one of them would take the time to piss in his ear if his brains caught fire. They told Daddy they had to be hard on the kid because they wanted him out of their unit before his stupidity got one of them killed.

"Some time later Daddy took our family for a cruise in his Roadmaster. He saw the same young sailor hitchhiking, and pulled over to give him a lift.

"My father had saved a long time for that Buick, a big blue bullet of a car ... you know, the pretty one with three round holes on each side of the front fenders. He usually kept his prized hunk of steel slick-shined with Turtle Wax and covered with a tarp.

"When the kid from Boston got out at his destination, he thanked Daddy, and then slammed the door so hard it broke the window glass. My father was upset at first, but then he told us he felt sorry for the kid. He never forgot that kid from Boston, and neither did we."

"Why does your father feel sorry for me?"

"He says you're a young punk and you don't know anything."

CHAPTER 14

As the wind chases away punishing snow clouds, I pull into a parking space by the admiral's condominium. It's eight o'clock. The thermometer on my dash reads six degrees above zero. I recall my case handlers' instructions from last night. "While you're having breakfast with the informant, finalize a plan to get evidence that will hold up in a court of law." I mentally run through the follow-up paperwork I will need, and plunge through a drift across the sidewalk.

It's slow going. I sink knee deep with each step. I can hear my pulse throb in my neck as I work up a sweat. I don't want to fall down or pass out in this weather, so I stop to catch my breath and glance over the ridge that slopes to the frozen lake. A lone figure lies in the snow.

The black snow boots, nylon trousers and red flannel shirt tucked under red suspenders looks familiar. "Oh my god." I hurry forward, tripping in the snow. The figure is curled into a ball, the head covered with a Navy baseball cap resting on one outstretched arm.

"I hope that's you, David," it says. "Good morning."

"What are you doing down here?" I unzip my parka, and wrap the down jacket around his shoulders.

"Counting my bones."

"How many did you get?" I slide around behind him.

"Same number as when I fell."

"Mind if we talk inside?" I boost him into a sitting position, kneel in the snow and pull his arm over my shoulders. "Can you walk?" I say, and lift. We plow up the snowy ridge with the lopsided, heavy-footed gait of injured football players leaving the playing field. One of his arms is over my shoulder, the other hangs loosely fisted at his side.

"I was watching birds from my window like Faye and I used to do," he volunteers as we move to where the wind has blown the snow clear and tough January weeds still stand guard. "Faye kept parakeets, she loved birds." A deep drift blocks our path.

"Hold your position sir, and I'll demonstrate what a good pair of boots from Meijer's can do." I kick a path through the snow while he watches. His face has a faraway look when I come back and take his arm.

"The birds touched down on the limbs of that red cedar over there," he stops at the crest of the ridge and points to a thick evergreen. "At first they puffed twice their size and preened their feathers. I watched them perch on the limb for a long time, thinking about how cold they must be, wondering how much cold they could take before they gave up and let the cold come inside. After a while I knew something was wrong when they didn't move. It seemed like I heard Faye's voice say, *Hon, they'll freeze out there.* I knew she would have wanted me to bring them inside." He moves forward again.

"But a gust of wind came through the tall trees. The breeze pitched snow to the ground. I watched the branches spring back and the birds drop." We step onto what had earlier been the shoveled sidewalk as he continues. "I reached for their shadows. That's when I slipped. I couldn't get a grip to pull myself up, so I crawled and felt with my fingertips for the birds. I was resting when you happened along."

"Did you find them?"

His lower lip drops into a deep curve. "Em hm ... as cold as death."

I gulp and change the subject. "What were you thinking while you rested?"

He clutches the porch rail and pulls himself up the steps one foot at a time. "Ha, I was dreaming up headlines for tomorrow's paper. That's what. After a story about dismantling village holiday decorations, there would be a small headline like this: *Old Geezer Freezes in Cold Breeze.* Or maybe this: *Dogs Eat Slab of Meat - Turns Out to be Sailor's Feet.*" He stops to rest and catch his breath. "The one I liked best was: *Man Found Frozen on the Berm Inching Along Like a Worm.*"

I don't laugh. "Do you hurt anywhere?"

He pulls keys from his pocket. "My sense of humor is fractured." He finds the brass one for the front door, and hands it to me with the slotted side up. Murphy watches from the window.

"I hate my brittleness. My bones will try to twist and shatter if I don't watch them." He turns his face away from the wind.

I have the front door open, and am ready to rush him into the heat, but Murphy bursts from the doorway and walks around the old man, meowing in earnest.

The admiral steps inside, slips off my jacket and hands it back to me. "Get in here Murphy. I don't want to have to hunt for you in a snow bank." He pats his leg and the cat lopes inside and rubs against his leg. "I may have skinned my knees, David." By the time he is settled in his chair, Murphy has established himself in the old man's lap and is licking snow from his paws.

I return from the bathroom with a clean towel and find the admiral has both his knees uncovered. He pokes the walking stick at the chair where I dropped my jacket. "That is one warm parka." His words make me feel great.

"That Meijer's is a pretty good store. Thanks for the tip," I say and daub the blood from his knees. The cat stands guard from his lap.

"There's a spray that kills bacteria above the sink," the old man says and points toward the bathroom with his cane.

The electronic listening device from Radio Shack is still in my coat pocket. This is the perfect time to plant the bug under his sink. He can't bend down to check even if he suspects he is under surveillance. A magnet holds the small monitor to a pipe.

The aerosol can is right where he told me it would be. I spray his knees with the antiseptic pain relief, and discover I enjoy the old man's approval much more than his discomfort. Wide gauze bandages with cartoons on them are the only dressing I can find. I hold one up.

"They'll do just fine," he says. "I use them on my grandson, tell him stories while I patch him up ... deflects from the pain."

His pant legs pull down over the bandages easily. I step back. "So, other than nearly freezing and banging up your knees, how are you?"

"I've got one foot in the grave and the other on a banana peel." He grins. "But basically I'm better than you are." Murphy jumps as he stands and reaches for his jacket. "Let's go eat." He moves toward the door and slips one arm into the sleeve. "When my father was hungry he used to say he could eat the south end out of a northbound polecat. Do you know what a polecat is, son?"

CHAPTER 15

Rudy serves the old man biscuits with sausage gravy and places a large ketchup bottle next to his plate. "Admiral, I don't know what kind of cock-and-bull story this guy is feeding you, but he's not to be trusted."

McLaughlin twists in the booth and looks up in surprise. "What do you know about David?"

The waiter looks me straight in the eye as he talks and tops up our coffee mugs. "He's investigating a guy named Hatch. I saw a file on the seat of his car yesterday when he was having coffee with your daughter. His door wasn't locked, so I looked inside. I think he's FBI."

The admiral lowers his head and looks over the top of his glasses in reproach. "Rudy?"

The young man ignores the look and bends down into my space. "Admiral McLaughlin is a friend of mine. He has plenty of friends in this village. Don't give him grief. He's already had his share." Rudy sets the pot down on the table and addresses the old man. "He's small, and he's alone, Jim. Just say the word and I'll take him outside." He pushes his sleeves up and stands with his feet planted wide.

"Don't judge a man by his size," the admiral says. "If he gets aggressive with me, I'll talk him to death." He grins. "Thanks, son."

The waiter starts to say something, but a screech of laughter interrupts him as a group of Red Hat Society ladies takes the next table. Their voices come in waves, flooding the room with confusion.

I lean over and whisper, "The man in the booth behind us yesterday was one of our agents."

The old man's eyes scan the women at the next table. Their loud slurping noises and giggles gather stares from around the restaurant. He inspects other diners in the restaurant, and his gaze comes back to rest on me.

"It's bureau policy," I say. "We almost never work alone. My backup isn't here today."

McLaughlin leans toward me and speaks from behind his mug. "What did I do so dangerous that two agents need to shadow me?" His tone is playful. "Don't tell me all those babes are federal agents, too?"

I scan the chattering females. "I don't recognize them as being with the agency."

"They could be CIA."

"How much trouble are you in?"

"Not enough for you to keep hammering me."

"We have to be certain you don't have some other reason to volunteer your services," I say, "… a hidden agenda. Taping is standard protocol with an informant until we establish credibility. We only use another agent when we're not sure of the source."

"I must have passed muster yesterday if the second agent isn't here today."

"No, he's out with the flu."

The old man hits the table with the palm of his hand, and laughs. The Red Hat ladies in the next booth turn and grin at us. One waves a greeting with a red-gloved hand. He nods politely, and whispers, "Cloak and dagger specialists don't get sick on television, David!"

"No sir, nor in James Bond movies. We federal agents are portrayed as tougher than we are. Please don't tell the bad guys."

"How sick is your partner?"

"He has diarrhea."

"Pepto-Bismol works best for me."

"Thanks. I'll drop some off. Here's an outline of suggestions for your conversation with Ortega and Gibbons. Remember you are asking them what they want you to attest to in the fake document. The idea needs to come from them." I hand him the memo my case handler has approved. "Let's go back to your place. I'll put a bug on your phone."

"You carry wiretaps with you?" the old guy asks, glancing over the document.

"You can buy a pretty good bug right here in town. It's Radio Shack technology. Attach it to the receiver, hook it up, and it works. You'd be surprised at the quality. A person would never know he was being tapped."

"Aren't those illegal unless you have permission from a judge?"

"As long as one of the people on the tap agrees to it, there's no need for a subpoena."

"Let's talk about the plan."

"Okay. After I place the concealment device in your phone, you call Ortega or Gibbons and tell them you're willing to help. Listen to their plan. The fraud has to start with them, so it's important they give their ideas first. After their idea is down on tape, you tell them what you think should go into the letter they want you to sign. Use the suggestions I just gave you. It would be better if they requested both brothers' records from St. Louis. You may need to tell them about the 1976 fire in the records warehouse."

"Every serviceman knows about that fire," he says.

"Okay. Skip that. We know they won't find any records. My boss already had them pulled. Review the where and when of the plan and tell them to put it on paper. Have them mail it via the US Postal Service so we have a document plus a recording to use as evidence."

"And then what?"

"After you compose the letter, we take it to the meeting place. We put a wire on you to record the transaction as you give them your signed letter. That will be another bit of evidence for our collection. They send the phony letter along with their doctor's diagnosis and the rest of the paperwork required to request compensation. At that point we will have done all we can do. We turn the tapes in and wait. Agreed?"

The admiral nods.

I sit straight in the booth. "So, when did you get your admiral stripes?"

The old man straightens his spine. He takes a sip of his coffee, the cup slips, and drops from his hand. Coffee spills over the table and down onto his lap. He slides from the booth smartly, brushes the hot coffee off his jeans, and pulls the denim away from his thighs. "I don't need to be scalded the same day I nearly freeze."

I signal Rudy. As he wipes the table his hand spasms, jerks and a saucer drops and shatters on the floor.

"Just a little edgy today," he says, looking up at the admiral. He has the mess cleared and the table restored in no time.

"Want to go home and change?" I ask the old man as he returns to his bench.

"Negative. Let's try a new topic." He turns to the waiter as he piles dishes on a plastic tray. "You having trouble with that table of women, son?" He winks. "Say the word and David here will throw them out."

Rudy smiles up at the old man and visibly relaxes.

"Bring me some more of that mud, will you Rudy?" he says.

"Last night I checked out Quantrill on the Internet," I say. "He was a terrible man. I find it hard to believe John McLaughlin would ride with that rogue."

James McLaughlin pulls a sheaf of papers from a worn brown envelope under his shirt, and hands them across the table. "This is a list of Quantrill's raiders. They may not mean much to you. The hooligans used assumed names. They did that so the men could return to their families without being caught by their past. You won't find John McLaughlin on the list, but below Indian Jack you will find Three-finger Jack." He watches me run my finger down the list and stop at the name. "After the war the men melted into the landscape in Indian Territory, or returned home under their family names."

As I peruse the list, he starts in on his meal. He spoons in the gravy first. The sausages are eaten next. He swallows biscuits covered with ketchup last.

"Where did you get this?"

He takes a gulp of coffee before answering. "You're not the only one who uses the Internet." He wipes his last biscuit around his plate to soak the remaining gravy. "I actually have a nephew who works on our family history. He sent the list from Oklahoma."

"I'd like to get back to my question about the transfer of funds from your bank into the widows of Lawrence, Kansas fund," I say. "What's the connection with your grandfather, the horse thief?"

"Son, I'm not proud of my grandfather's behavior. I do what I can for families of the men he killed. It helps me sleep at night."

"But you don't know for certain he was involved in that massacre or any of Quantrill's atrocities." If my grandfather had ridden with Quantrill, I think, my family would have erased his name from the family tree like he had never existed.

"My father was convinced he rode with Quantrill. That's good enough for me. Even if he didn't use his trigger finger, he was guilty by association. He shared the responsibility for killing a hundred fifty men and young boys. He must answer for eighty women who became widows and two hundred fifty children who became orphans. Some of their descendants still live in Lawrence. They had it rough for years. I know how it feels to grow up without a father. I watched my mother struggle to raise thirteen children."

I realize I have forgotten to blink when my eyes begin to sting. I understand guilt too, but, unlike this man, I don't know what disgusting deeds the men in my family committed. I sense my father inherited a malignancy from his father. Both men must have germinated from defective sperm. Neither possessed the natural courage this old man exhales like carbon dioxide. I wonder. Am I another bad seed from the same packet? I shake the thoughts from my head and move on.

"Any more horse thieves lurking in the family barn, sir? Chorus girls? Movie starlets?" I force a laugh, expecting the worst. "We better dig them out now before the prosecutor gets to them."

His glance tells me to watch my step.

CHAPTER 16

"What did you drive before the golf cart?" I ask as the old warrior and I finish breakfast.

"A Toyota Pickup. 1984. Blue."

"A blue truck?" I say, and remember my father's rusty blue pickup and the dangerous rides we took together. "What happened to it?" I close the pad of notepaper and return my ballpoint to my shirt pocket. "Did it have doors?" This interview is headed off topic like most of the others.

"Of course it had doors." He looks up from the empty plate of biscuits and gravy. "Now, that was a queer question," he says, and adds more ketchup to his empty plate. "There are doors on trucks just like there are nuclear weapons on subs and aircraft carriers. The chassis was fine, but there were transmission problems."

"Did you have it repaired?" I ask, and try to remember if my father had trouble with his truck's transmission.

"I was lucky to be able to drive it as far as Caldwell's Gas Station." He frowns. "Howard Caldwell wanted fifty-eight dollars an hour to repair the wreck." He grimaces. "I won't pay fifty-eight dollars an hour to fix anything. I gave it to Caldwell for junk."

I open my notepad and jot down that he's frugal as well as stubborn. "Admiral McLaughlin, may I ask you about your duty aboard the USS *Ranger*?" I am fishing again, this time anxious to catch something larger than a bluegill.

"What does the *Ranger* have to do with the NAAV?" he asks. "That carrier didn't take part in atomic testing."

"I'm looking for skeletons, sir. Keep talking."

His full, thick eyebrows arch. Their shape is a sign he could be courageous and generous. But right now he looks dangerous.

"Okay." He shrugs. "The *Ranger* was a large deck, attack aircraft carrier. It was a thousand forty-six feet long, and a hundred thirty feet at the beam. It drew thirty-seven feet of water, and weighed 81,101 tons at full load. Our four screws gave us a top speed of thirty knots. We carried about thirty-eight hundred men and seventy-five aircraft during our pleasure cruises. The *Ranger* could be compared in size to an eleven-story building. How am I doing?" He rubs his chin.

"Great, keep going," I say, and scribble on my pad. This worm of information is so spongy and small it wouldn't be enough bait to catch a minnow. "What was your rank?"

"A four-striper."

"What happened aboard the *Ranger*? What did you do all day?"

"Worked, sailed the ship and worked some more." He pauses and grins. "At that time we had these haughty friends from the Air Force who annoyed us with their bragging. There was

healthy competition between both branches of service, but
the Air Force was the worst, and the loudest."

"I thought you worked together."

"That was the theory until it came down to being funded
by congress. For example, we made fourteen modifications
to the A-6 Intruder to keep it flying, used it for fourteen different jobs. At the same time the Air Force mothballed a hundred thirty B-36 bombers. The flyboys got almost all of the
congressional money that year, yet the Navy was desperate
for airplanes. We could have modified every one of those
bombers and kept them flying."

He snickers and rocks his head. "We got the flyboys in the
end … made monkeys out of the Air Force. See David, the
Air Force guards the continental United States. The Navy has
four fleets to guard the coasts, two in the Atlantic and two in
the Pacific. One fleet is always out while the other stays in
port so sailors can have some semblance of family life.

"I was on assignment in Quantico, Virginia, inspecting airplanes. I stopped at the O Club to sip a draft beer with my
friend Ricco Botta. That old spaghetti-bender drank dago red.
For as long as I knew him that was his juice of choice. This
Air Force general from Texas, headquartered at Will Rogers
Field, in Oklahoma, joined old Ricco and me at the bar. He
ordered whiskey and sat there on a stool with his elbows on
the bar and these heavy horn-rimmed glasses holding down
his nose. He was all talk … nothing but a big noise with dirt
on it. That old man finished his second whiskey and started
in on how much better the Air Force was than the Navy. After
his third whiskey the Navy could do nothing right.

"Ricco winked at the old bag of wind, leaned towards the
Texan and whispered that there wasn't a place on the face
of this earth that the Navy couldn't strike with carrier planes.

"The general sat up straight and smacked his glass on the
bar. *Impossible.* His expression changed slowly from surprise
to scorn to a smirk. *Anywhere?* The old bird tried to cover
his laugh by adjusting his glasses. *You don't have the range.*

You couldn't get by my radar. After his third glass of sipping whiskey he stumbled away trailing alcohol fumes all the way out the door.

"A week later, Ricco and I were at a meeting at the Pentagon when that old blowhard came up in conversation. I notified Alfred Pride, commander of Fleet Air Pacific. He was responsible for all aviation activity west of the continental US. I told him Ricco and I planned some training exercises. He always agreed to training exercises. Ricco notified P.N.L. Bellinger, Commander of Fleet Air Atlantic, and then he returned to the Caribbean to his task force.

"The USS *Ranger* was at sea, off Long Beach, California, steaming along, fat, dumb and happy. We converted some of our A-6 attack planes to tankers and launched them with orders to orbit over Albuquerque, New Mexico. When they were out an hour, we launched the A-6 Intruders. They refueled in the air over Albuquerque and proceeded to Oklahoma City.

"Targets for training exercises were electronic boxes located in the middle of a field. The boxes emitted impulses our planes could pick up with their radios. Navy attack planes knocked them out, flew back to Albuquerque, refueled and returned to the *Ranger.*

"Scuttlebutt was that when the Air Force general was informed the target had been taken out, he was heard to say, *Where the hell did those damn Navy planes come from?* About that time Ricco's second wave hit him from the East Coast. When word came about the second strike, I went back to my cabin, laid my hand on a piece of Navy stationery with only one finger stretched out and traced around it. Ricco pulled paper from his goat locker and did the same from his cabin in the Caribbean. We dispatched them to the old wind bag in his personal mail."

"Did he ever find out it was you and Ricco?"

A few days later both of us got a message on Air Force stationary. The only words on the paper were, *You bastards!*

The old wrangler slapped his leg and roared. "We proved it could be done. That old scoundrel was still in the Navy and worked at the Pentagon with about forty-nine medals and ribbons up there on his shoulder when I retired. No man in the service could live long enough to earn all that shoulder hardware. Those birdbrains write commendations for each other. Don't mean a thing."

"Would a medal or a star for a sailor equate to an eagle feather for an Indian brave?" I say.

"What do you know about eagle feathers?"

CHAPTER 17

I lean forward on the bench seat at the restaurant and address the old bulldog across from me. "You mentioned you were part Native American."

"Yes, I was born a quarter Cheyenne." He leans forward. "Where are you going with this?" He grunts. His mood has changed from grim to grave.

"Let me see if I have this right. During a battle when a warrior kills an enemy, he must lay a hand on the body for the kill to qualify to wear an eagle feather upright in his hair."

"The Cheyenne call that counting coup," he says. His elbows are on the table, his hands cup his chin, and his brow is wrinkled.

"This gesture is supposed to be more dangerous than the actual killing of an enemy."

"That's right. The battle might still be blazing, arrows flying." His face grows reflective.

"When a fighting man approaches his foe, dead or alive," I say, "he announces he is about to perform a coup. His buddies witness the act. That is like what you and Ricco did with that Air Force general from Texas. Am I right?"

"I'm following you."

"Then you have every right to wear an eagle feather. Your friend, Ricco Botta, does too."

"I like the analogy, David," the old warhorse mugs. "So, you think the notes that Ricco and I sent the general were like scalps and his note to us our eagle feathers?"

"Em hmm." I feel cocky, pleased for being able to know some bit of history that could apply to him. I finish my glass of water and nod to Rudy for a refill. "What was it like growing up in Oklahoma, being part Native American?"

"Normal, I guess," the old man says. "Five Civilized Tribes lived in Oklahoma when I was fetched up. They called us civilized because we obeyed the white man's laws." He snickers. "Full-blooded Indians I went to school with couldn't speak their native language as well as I could."

"Do you remember any Cheyenne?"

"The word for girl is *he'ekaeskone* and the word for making love is *palm palm*. I only remember the words a young buck had reason to use."

The sound of breaking china shatters the air. Both of us look as Rudy bends down to pick even more shards of plates from the polished floor. "Sorry," he says. "Everything all right up there?" he asks, and glances at the old man.

"Everything's perfect, son. I haven't given away any state secrets … yet," he says.

The waiter's smile looks sincere. This old man has an amazing effect on people.

"I'll have this cleaned up in a minute."

We sit without speaking while Rudy fills a gray plastic bin with broken china and moves into the kitchen.

"What's the deal with that waiter? He's a bit hard on the china."

"He's been back from Fallujah for about six months. Roadside bombs took out some friends, hit his convoy, gave him a concussion and some shrapnel wounds. He was in some heavy fighting … nasty split-second decision up-close fighting. I've seen it before. Soldiers put their emotions aside, bury the memories and just keep going … doing their job … but they don't always choose well. Rudy told me he slept on the floors of abandoned houses … had to move corpses just to lay out his bedroll. That kind of experience can take its toll on any man. They sent him home after he opened fire on a car that wouldn't stop, killed some innocents. He told the review board that he had to light them up."

"Rudy did that?"

"Take it easy on him," the old man says. "He's making some progress, but he needs kindness and understanding."

I speak next to get us back on track. "Did you carry nuclear weapons aboard the *Ranger*?"

Even though the old officer's smile disappears, his eyebrows lift and hold, a sure sign he has a passion for this kind of action.

"Is this a test to see if I will divulge classified information, Agent Dugan?"

Actually, it is, but I won't let him know that. "Information classified forty years ago won't be classified anymore," I say. I know he was on the *Ranger* in the '60s, the same time the U-2 conducted high-altitude photographic reconnaissance over the Soviet Union. I'd like to worm that information out of him. "Did the ..."

"Of course we carried nuclear weapons." Not a hint of a smile crosses his face. "All carriers had them. Subs did too. But U-2's didn't carry shape. They were used for spying only." He softens. "Special weapons exercises were regularly scheduled when I was a catapult and arresting gear officer. We launched two airplanes at midnight every night sent out with Shape."

"Shape?" I am puzzled.

"Firecrackers. Big ones." His smile fades. "Shape used to be the code word for nuclear weapon. The Shape ordnances were dummies. Empty. Pilots never knew their guns weren't loaded. They understood the exercises were for training, but could be turned active should the whistle blow. The planes wouldn't get back until one the next afternoon. Can you imagine that, David? Thirteen hours unable to move."

"How did pilots go to the bathroom?"

"They used what we called a relief line."

"You mean a catheter?"

"Negative. They put their dork in a funnel," the old man says and goes on with his story. "Cook packed the pilots a box lunch. Once the plane was at altitude, pilots set the auto pilot, ate their fried chicken and went to sleep."

My eyes pop open. "They slept with nuclear weapons on board?"

"Sometimes."

CHAPTER 18

I watch my finger circle the rim of the coffee cup I have just drained. I wonder what it must have been like for sailors like my father to ride around the ocean with nuclear weapons aboard, warheads more powerful than trillions of sticks of dynamite. I had a zillion questions. Were sailors aware of the explosives they carried? Did a guy lose it when the guy in the next bunk struck a match and smoked the air blue with his cigarette? Did the daily threat of disintegration cause normal men to shake and weak men to explode? How did sailors deal with stress? "Were you ever wounded on a ship carrying a nuclear warhead?" I ask James McLaughlin across the smooth gray tabletop.

"Cracked my dome once." He rubs his temple and mugs.

"Bump your halo on an overhead pipe?"

He shakes his head. "Helicopter crash, had to get my flight time in, four hours a month to get flight pay. We were landing under reduced power. A gust caught the fuselage. The pilot couldn't bring her right. The metal rotor slammed into the deck. She shattered when she hit. Shrapnel scattered all over the flight deck. Killed nine people."

My lungs call for air. "Was the pilot killed?"

He shakes his head no.

"Did they evacuate you to a hospital?"

"Negative. Went back to work. But five days later when we hit port the doc sent for me. He ordered me first to sick bay and then to the base hospital. Those bastards kept me for five days."

"You must have had quite a concussion."

He squints at me. "That's a negative. The doctors found nothing wrong with me, just my cracked skull. The truth boils down to dollars and cents, son. Military hospitals with empty beds were closed down by Congress. I was there to hold down the sheets. Besides, I knew a crash like that wasn't the way I would die."

"Are you psychic?"

"I just know things. My mother called it a seventh sense. I was the seventh son of a seventh son."

"That large lump on your left wrist. Is that from … from shrapnel?"

The old man looks at his wrist and snorts. "I broke that riding bulls."

"You carried bulls with nuclear warheads aboard Navy ships?"

He winks at me. "I saw an elephant aboard a Navy ship once in Bangkok, but never a bull." He slumps back in the booth and sinks into his past. "I broke my wrist in Oklahoma when I was thirteen, riding my father's best breeding bull out behind the barn. He almost done me in. Almost. My wife always told me the damn Navy would kill me. She was usually right. It almost did, but I never told her about what happened out there."

"What happened?"

"In 1955 aboard the *Boxer* we lost a cable on one of our arresting gears. The steel cable that hooked planes landing on the carrier's deck was stretched and frayed. We were crippled without it. I ordered one flown in from Philadelphia to the West Coast and then on to Okinawa. An old tin can escort ship brought it out to us at sea.

"The cable arrived wound on a twelve-hundred-foot wheel. I moved to where I could spool it off perched on the forks of a lift truck. I had new cable welded to the old, then fed new in as the old was pulled out. This twisted wire rope went down under the flight deck, around curves and corners and finally came back up on deck again, a major feat on the open sea … on a good day.

"That day started out with weak coffee. Then, some damn fool on the bridge turned the ship at the wrong time. When she tipped there went the cable. The wheel flew off the lift truck, and tried to roll over the side. I was the closest man to the cable and had to hold on. I grabbed the steel-wrapped spindle and held on as we slid toward the sea. I hooked a watertight hatch with my foot to slow me down. That kept me from slipping over the edge until my men rescued me, but the strain tore my guts.

"I told the doc that I had no choice. The pilots would have hung me from a yardarm if that spool had disappeared overboard. Doc didn't write me up, but that scrape caused a good-sized hernia. After that my guts would fall out while I worked. I'd lie down on deck and stuff them back inside. The men got tired of watching me, complained to the doc, and I was sent off for surgery."

I rub my belly. "Was it always that dangerous aboard ship? Did many men die in work-related accidents?"

"Not many. It was our job to train men to work safely. Accidents happened when sailors got sloppy and didn't follow procedures."

"Have you any other wounds?"

The old man is quiet for a while. He leans forward and rubs his hip. "I was standing near an anti-aircraft gun during a training exercise and got stung by shrapnel when the blast deflector shattered."

"Stung?"

"Emm.The discharge energy was like a volcano, spattering debris twenty feet from the gun. A cast-iron shard blew me to the deck and tore into my pelvis. It stopped when it hit the tip of my hip bone. The sailor next to me got it in his breastbone. The explosion whacked the wind out of both of us, stung like an electric current."

"Was he killed?"

"We were flat-out topside after the blast. The sailor stared at the chunk of iron sticking in his chest, and said, 'Well, I'll be damned.' I watched as he felt for the shrapnel, pulled it out and said, "Must be my lucky day." Had the scrap hit any way but with the flat side down, it would have gone right through him. I was able to work the jagged piece of iron out of my hip with my fingers."

"Wasn't there a lot of blood?" I ask. "Didn't anyone come to help?"

"There wasn't much blood. We helped each other stand and wobbled side-by-side to sick bay. After we filed our accident reports, we walked down to the galley for a cup of joe."

I rub my chest. "Any other injuries?"

"Just my bark," he says.

"Is that a cough, lung congestion?"

"Negative," the admiral says and slides to the edge of his bench. He pulls down a sock and tugs his pant leg high enough to reveal a continuous deep-furrowed scab from his ankle to his knee. The gray crinkled crust has crept outward around the leg like moss. His foot is crimson below his ankle.

I lean in for a closer look as he bares the other limb. "How long have you had this skin irritation?" Both legs look like dead tree stumps. I had read about this in his medical records but had no idea how bad it looked.

"I've been growing bark for … for almost thirty years," he says and pushes his pant legs down.

"Does it hurt?" I am uncomfortable.

He shakes his head *no*, and slides back in the booth.

"What do your doctors say?" I scribble a note on my spiral notepad. The sight of his rugged stumps has stirred up images, tugged out hidden memories, caused me to sweat.

"I don't care for white coats," he wipes his nose on the back of his hand. "It's not the medical profession I dislike, son. It's the bad news they carry. Besides, my seventh sense would be here telling me if a war-related poisoning would be the cause of my death."

I am baffled by why this intelligent man would buy into hocus-pocus, and wonder what his alleged psychic power had to do with the way he would die. I'll put my money on a doctor's diagnosis of the jungle fungus creeping up his legs. My thoughts careen back to my college roommate's father who suffered after Vietnam. Doctors had no idea why he was dying. Then my roommate died after Desert Storm. The doctors were baffled by his illness, too. War doesn't end on the battlefield, it seems. Yet this old survivor sounds confident he will make a hundred.

I ponder what I would do if I were psychic. Would I see that I was doomed to die like the other men in my family? Or would I see it coming fast like in a car crash? It might be slow, like in the entrance hall of a nursing home, bent over in a pool of drool. I don't want to know.

It had been a long time since I thought about the rugged texture of that dead tree the day my father ended his life. My personal protocol is to bury bad memories when they surface, and force my mind elsewhere. That way the dark burrows deeper, and I move on with my life. But today reality reversed. The old man's bark triggered a memory of the tree trunk I crouched behind the moonlit night bats flew above our family garage.

My mother told me the old tree's umbrella had once grown tall, its shade screen reaching over the pond where spikes of new cattails cut the sunny surface. A summer hurricane had twisted the trunk like a stick of black licorice and pitched its green parasol into the swamp.

I remember seeing black bats scoop supper from the ponds surface and flap away. Earthy dampness covered my hands like dew. Where I grasped the stump, the rough bark dented my arms and made welts. The smell of used motor oil and decaying lobster traps seeped from inside our garage.

I was playing Agent Elliot Ness, the investigator from old television show reruns. He'd had a tip mobsters were holed up somewhere inside the dark building, hiding from the FBI. Ness had the stakeout that night. The bad guys had machine guns, and would use them. Ness had a piece, a smooth stick from the pond that looked like a sawed-off shotgun. I was Ness, of course, and my weapon was loaded and ready.

That garage was a gloomy building, decaying and overgrown with evergreens and wild grapevines. On one side the cattail pond undermined the corner posts, and caused the boards to lean and shift so a trained agent, like me, could slip between them. I reviewed FBI procedures for capturing gangsters while I waited to enter the darkness. Should I call for backup on the walkie-talkie hidden in the cuff of my coat? No, I thought, help would arrive too late. It was now or never.

I slipped a grape Tootsie Pop into my mouth to suck for luck, closed my eyes and squeezed through the slats. The urge was strong to get right to the chewy chocolate center, but I resisted. An FBI agent must practice restraint. Besides, the noise might give away my location.

That's when I heard the groan. Toward the corner of the garage I saw something move in the dim light, something near the workbench, something hanging that had not been hanging before. I brushed my arm through the darkness as I advanced toward the mystery, felt something soft and pushed it away. I recognized the source of the groan: a rope rubbing wood. Something heavy was swinging above me, a pendulum.

It slammed into my cheek knocking the Tootsie Pop from my mouth. Play stopped as Agent Elliot Ness fumbled on the dirt floor for his sucker. The invincible agent was suddenly replaced by me, an angry seven-year-old boy.

I rose, unsteady, and slammed the hanging shaft, then ducked when it swung back. In my fury I shoved it away again. The sound of groaning filled the garage. As I wrestled the pendulum silent, something fell among the furnace cinders on the greasy floor. I felt a shoe, a big shoe. I reached up and felt a human foot with human toes. Farther up the shaft I touched soft cloth. Leaning back and squinting I recognized my father's red shirt in a shaft of light. My eyes stung and smarted with rage.

Until now that rage was an ageless, blocked memory. But it has crawled into the light, shrieking and waving at me to pay attention. I remember being furious with my father for kicking my candy into the dirt. "I hate you," I had howled. "I hate you to hell."

I remember when I learned he was dead. I was glad because it served him right for ruining my sucker. The next day I came back to that steamy garage. I dug a hole in the dirt floor with a pick ax, buried the Tootsie Pop and this memory of him. I kicked in some cinders and stamped the grave flat. I hung the pick on the wall. No one would see where the hole had been. A little later, when I understood our sailor wouldn't be living with us anymore, I felt sad. But, anger trumped my sadness, and forgiveness never came. His unmarked grave had been forgotten, a just reward.

It takes clearing my throat several times to pull me back to the present. I force my focus on Admiral McLaughlin. "Does anyone in your family have anything like your skin irritation?"

"Negative."

"What do you think caused it?"

"Radiation. I witnessed seven bursts in the South Pacific from '46 to '52. My paperwork shows I got sixty rem of gamma radiation. At that time the military set an arbitrary standard for tolerable levels at sixty rem over two weeks. Limits set for radiation workers in 1980 were five rem over a year."

"Whoa," I say. "That amount of radiation could make a man's eyes smoke and his brain change direction. How did humans survive?"

I had seen a TV special on survivors of Hiroshima and Nagasaki living with radiation sickness. A friend of my mother's survived the blast, married an American GI and died of cancer in the prime of her life leaving a husband and two young daughters. That was horrible, but this was unthinkable. Without their consent, the old sailor and his shipmates had been fried by their employer, their own government, and then sent out to pasture as soon as they grew sick.

"How could the president allow that to happen? How could other presidents make treatment for survivors so difficult?" I ask. "Today returning soldiers barely get a handshake for risking everything. The head cases are called the 'walking wounded.' What is wrong with our system?"

"It's better now than it used to be," he says. "Technology allows us to do a better job. After Vietnam they kept records of patients dying from Agent Orange. The same thing happened after Desert Storm. Post-traumatic stress disorder, PTSD, was officially recognized as a medical condition in 1980. You'll like this treatment, David, because you're from the video game generation. Our Rudy hitches a ride to Walter Reed once a month for treatment. Ask him about it." He motions Rudy to the table. "David would like to know about the new treatment you get for PTSD in D.C."

Rudy sets the pot and muffins down. "It's not new. Twenty years after Vietnam, they came up with virtual reality headsets and a game called Virtual Vietnam. Therapists put veterans back into the thick of war. It was called immersion therapy … you know … the guy revisits and retells the trauma over and over again to rid the incident of its overwhelming power.

They tell me the idea is to disconnect the memory from the reactions to the memory.

"Why didn't you just go see a therapist?" I ask.

"Hell, I wasn't about to talk to some dude who didn't understand shit about my life, about my wife. I didn't want to be labeled a head case. I grew up with video games. Walter Reed has this experimental treatment called Virtual Iraq. I work through my combat trauma in a computer-simulated environment with a therapist. I wear a pair of video goggles, earphones and a scent-producing machine. It's kind of like that video game, Full Spectrum Warrior, only they rewrite it around each guy's trauma. My triggers are explosive noises and the scent of burning hair."

"How is it working?"

"I can drive now, and I'm okay in crowds. For a long time I was afraid to go out at night. I still prefer to be around people who have been in combat, who understand. Sleeping is still a problem, but I think I'm coming out of my depression. Don't you think I'm doing better?" he asks the admiral.

"Absolutely," the old man says. "Working here is good, too."

"Yea, but I have to pay for all the dishes I break. Sometimes my take-home isn't so great."

"You angling for a bigger tip?" the admiral winks.

"Sure," the young man grins, and moves his coffee and tray of hot muffins down the aisle.

"He's a good kid, but this is no short-term fix," the old man says. "He'll need long-term help."

I nod an understanding. "Do you have any other unexplained illnesses?"

"None that bother me." The sound of sandpaper scrubbing rough wood drifts across the table as he slides a paper napkin across his beard.

"I read your records. You have diabetes."

"Affirmative. I poke my belly twice a day and watch my sugar levels." He straightens the silverware beside his plate, and reaches to straighten mine.

I'm not surprised with his answer, not from a man strong enough to walk around for a week without complaining about his cracked skull, not from a man capable of working a jagged fragment of cast iron from his hip with his fingers, and certainly not from a man who survived sixty rem of gamma radiation. "Your legs look swollen. When did that start?"

"About the time the bark blossomed."

"Do you see a doctor?"

"They give me oxygen treatments to improve circulation."

"Your medical records list some eye surgery a few years ago, cataracts."

"Affirmative. That was serious. I could have lost my vision, missed my chance to watch all those babes on late-night TV"

CHAPTER 19

That night I bug the phone with the old man's help. Murphy plants his furry body between us, grooms his coat, and watches as I set the recorder. The tape spins around while McLaughlin dials the number.

"Melvin Gibbons?" he says. "Jim McLaughlin here. I know, it has been a long time. I had some personal problems to take care of, but I've been thinking about you. How's your health?" He pauses to listen. "So the surgery was a success. Good. Then you use oxygen all the time now? Whatever happened to Ortega? I see. Do you still need my help?" He moves the phone to his other ear. "How far along are you? Would you run your plan by me again?" He listens. "Em hm." He pauses. "Affirmative. Sounds like it may work. Yes, I'll help you. Hold on, Gibbons." He sets the phone down, pulls a red cloth handkerchief from his hip pocket, blows his nose and retrieves the receiver.

"Look Gibbons, you figure out from your records where you want me to say you've been and when. You said you remember the ships we were on during the atomic tests. Hook them together." He listens. "Do what works best for you. Send your notes to me and I'll work them into an official letter." He listens. "Yes, I can bring it into Pontiac if that would help. Still have your old paperwork? I see. Is it all in order?" Pause. "And a current doctor's diagnosis?" Pause. "Right. That should do it. Okay, as soon as I get the specifics I'll get my part done. I apologize for the long wait." Long pause. "Well, we better move on this. You're welcome." His face is sober as he slides the receiver into its cradle.

"Good job," I say, click off the tape recorder and remove the bug from the telephone receiver. "You look tired. I better go home."

The next morning Rudy is working the counter at the Big Boy. He nods toward the back of the restaurant when I come in, to where the old man is sitting beside a woman with white wavy hair.

"Sit down, David," he says nodding to her side of the booth. "You remember Pony Fuente, my old friend, and my wife if she'll have me." The woman beside him grins at the aged seaman with teasing, brown eyes, and scoots over.

Was that a marriage proposal I just heard?

"Hon, I've already had my share of men," she says and folds her arms across what I remember as a hummingbird-sucking-sap-from-the-lily-blossom tattooed breast. "I've buried too many. I'm used to living by myself."

Did I just witness this dame blowing off a US Navy admiral?

"Okay, Pony," the old man says, still trawling. "I had hoped you might have changed your mind. David, isn't she the most beautiful woman in Swainsville? Did you know she plays the piano and sings too?"

I feel my pants move. I don't care if she plays a broken set of bagpipes. This is one sexy bitch, with or without Benadryl.

Pony glances around the restaurant and signals someone behind me. Rudy appears a moment later.

"Hi, Gran. I know what you want … a large OJ, poached eggs in a cup and a side of crisp bacon."

"You got that right. Thanks, honey." She smiles up at Rudy. "You are one lucky fella, Jim McLaughlin. You ought to thank me for saving your hide. I'd have driven you nuts as a wife. Right, Rudy?" She gives me a wink. "Jim doesn't know about my passion for singing weird shit."

"You in a choir?" I ask.

"No. I'm a soloist."

"Come on, Pony," the old man says. "Sing something."

"I'm not going to marry you, even if you love my song."

"Agreed," he says.

"Okay, but only because you're almost irresistible, and almost the most handsome dude I've ever met."

The old man sits back in the booth, crosses his arms over his chest and grins. He seems to take her refusals in stride. I would have been devastated.

Pony moves over, and pats the bench signaling she wants me to move in closer to her. When I am settled, she yodels a song so soft we both lean in to hear every note. Her voice glides around the scale, skipping between octaves, and ends with the old man's and my heart hanging on a ledge somewhere high in the Rocky Mountain range. We are silent for a while when the song is over. Pony blushes, breaking our silence with an elbow in my rib and a smile across the table at the old man. She takes the old man's hand in hers and looks into his eyes. "Hon, did you ever give back this cute agent's gun?"

"Pony, don't blow his cover," he whispers. "David is now my nephew from New York."

She nods, and casts him a line. "You in trouble, hon? Maybe I can help."

"Not yet," the old man says, and winks at me.

"Are you CIA?" she whispers to me.

"You don't have a need-to-know, my wild mountain yodeler," the old man intercedes, with a certain sternness.

She glances at him, nods, and scrutinizes the side of my head. "I noticed your ears are clean. They look great. Did you rent a brush hog?"

This woman could drive a man crazy. I watch the admiral's expression after he's finished howling at my expense. His face softens as he takes her small palm in his, raises it to his lips and kisses it.

"You're a bad habit, Jim. But you're my bad habit." She squeezes his hand, pulls hers away and turns her attention to me. "Tell me about your family, David. What did your father do for a living?"

I could feel my heavy eyebrows elevate. "He was in the Navy."

"How wonderful. I bet he has some sordid stories to tell," she says. "Where does he live?"

"Ah … he's passed."

"I'm sorry, honey. Is your mom still alive?"

The old man's eyes sweep over Pony's as she speaks. She must have felt their warmth because she reaches her hand across the booth and takes his.

"Yes," I say. "She remarried and my stepdad adopted me."

"Weren't you lucky? So, Dugan isn't your birth father's name?"

"His name was Hatch," I say.

McLaughlin's head snaps my way, his eyes catch mine.

"So, my little mystery man," Pony whispers, "when did you join the FBI?" She looks at the admiral and winks. "You didn't hear that, did you?"

I glance at the old man as he nods and gives her a half smile, but his head is somewhere else. He's focused on his coffee mug. The skin on his brow has folded into three parallel lines cutting across his forehead.

Rudy appears at the table with two pots of coffee. "The cinnamon rolls just came out of the oven and look great," he says as he tops up our mugs. His smile disappears when he sees my face.

"Not for me, thanks," the old man says, and pivots on the bench to focus on Rudy. "Give this little lady one of those sweet rolls and some of your freshest battery acid. She takes extra cream." He smiles down at her. "Bring me some ketchup, too, when you get a chance." His blue-gray eyes catch hers and for a moment hold a tinge of fire.

"Why do you need ketchup? You ordered ham and eggs!" I say.

Pony answers. "Ketchup makes everything taste better. We learned that in the Navy, didn't we honey? Rudy," she winks at the waiter. "Hold the sweet roll and joe. I'm plenty wired right now."

"I didn't know Pony was your grandmother," I say to Rudy.

He smiles at the woman. "She's my grandma by choice."

Pony rubbernecks the room, wiggles in the booth, and waves to someone across the restaurant. "My ride is here, hon. Got to run or I'll be late for work. Thanks for breakfast." She turns toward me. "You're too sweet to be part of that government bureaucracy. Bail out before they ruin you."

I stand to let Pony slide out of the booth while the admiral struggles to his feet and plants a kiss on her cheek. She gives Rudy a peck, then tablehops her way across the restaurant talking all the way out the door.

"Where does she work?" I ask.

"She's done just about everything during her lifetime, but right now she volunteers at a shelter in Jackson. She cooks lunch and dinner for over a hundred people twice a week. Been doing it for years." He takes a deep breath and exhales fast. "Isn't she a babe?"

"I can't argue that," I say. I don't think I have ever considered a female a babe who was older than thirty, until Pony.

"All women are gorgeous, son, no matter how they earn a living." The old geezer's gaze pierces mine, grabs my spirit. "Some of the ugliest damn crows I've ever met had personalities that made them cute, even charming."

Now that is a useful truth I can live with. I had always reached for the best looking chicks, and never touched one. I should have focused on the wallflowers, I think, brooding over lost opportunities. At least I could have had one date in high school. "Are crows always hookers?"

"Crows are women so down on their luck that they follow the fleet to make their living. Men joke about them, say their heels have hinges on them so they can spring back for the next in line."

"Was Pony a hooker?" I ask, unable to get the woman or her tattoo from my thoughts.

The old man shakes his head. "The definition for gullible must have had you in mind. Pony's husband died a year ago. He was a good man, a big muscular guy … tall. Fuen was an attorney-turned-judge … old friend of mine from the Navy. Had a bad heart. She took care of him for ten years. You wouldn't know it from her attitude, but Pony has had a tough life.

"Her name was Hilda before she changed it. While she was a Navy WAVE she hooked up with a sailor who got her pregnant. The next time he was in port she broke the news, but he didn't take it well and had himself thrown in the brig. The creep refused to take visitors. He shipped out soon after, and she never heard from him again. Pony got a dishonorable discharge because she was pregnant, kept the child and had seven more with old Fuen.

"She keeps herself busy now that he's gone. Pony stops at my place every week to throw in a load of laundry and throw out food growing in my refrigerator she says could kill me. She's a pilot, has been since World War II. She's no crow. Pony's a woman who knows how the world works." He laughs. "The old girl likes to have fun. For her eightieth birthday, she went sky diving."

"Pony's eighty?"

He leans forward with both elbows on the table. She's half past eighty, but I didn't tell you that." He winks. "Do you treat your girl well? It's not natural for a man to be rudderless."

"My girlfriend?" I say, and come back to my reality. "Sure I treat her well." I know I should change the direction of our conversation, keep my personal life private, but I have never had a serious conversation about a woman who mattered to me with an adult whose opinion I valued. "I mean, well, I'm not sure what you mean by that." I know I need to get off dead center with her, to move our relationship forward.

"There are two kinds of women, son," the admiral says. "The rough ones that climb up on a barstool next to you and show you their tattoos, and the sweet and gentle ladies that will love you always. Tumble around with rough women and you'll wind up with the clap. Ladies are yours for life if you treat them right. Fuen treated Pony like a queen."

My shield of detachment disappears. "What exactly do you mean by treat them right?"

"Love 'em. Be affectionate. Kiss 'em and hug 'em. Every woman wants to know she's beautiful. Tell her, not just once, but often. Don't make a promise you can't keep. That's the fastest way to lose a woman's trust and wind up bunking alone." He winks. "Stay in contact with women, son, keep your voice or words before them all the time or they'll run off with some other sweet-talking sailor, or federal agent. I used to write letters. What do you do?"

The old man's sincerity disarms me. "Not much. I call and leave messages. She's not demanding." I'm feeling uneasy. I shouldn't be telling him this. I take a deep breath and make an effort to pull out, get the conversation back on track. "You lead a double life. You're flexible with women and inflexible with men."

"I was never abusive with my men," the admiral volunteers. He works the blunt end of a toothpick between his teeth. "I shared my knowledge, told them something useful in our everyday conversations or bull sessions. I took up for them when the occasion warranted, treated them like human beings, tried to be fair." He grows quiet. "I bought my wife a posy each time we walked to the central market in San Francisco because I knew that pleased her. I loved that woman. And I love my kids. It's a broken world, David. I just try to do what is right."

I can see the old man is tiring. It's 10:30 a.m., so I fight for the privilege to pay the bill. My automobile heater blows warm air by the time I pull around to the front of the restaurant and honk for him to come out. I take the back way through the snow-laced thickets to his condo complex. The hood of his daughter's car is buried in a drift. A pickup truck with a snow blade has cleared the road, and pushed the powder into mounds edging the parking lot. A couple of birds are having an argument in a nearby tree.

"Take a load off," he says when we're inside. "There's still some of Pony's meat loaf in the refrigerator for lunch."

"Thanks," I say from the door. "I have an errand to run."

He settles in his easy chair and pushes the footrest to elevate his feet. "David, are you comfortable?" His eyelids are pressed closed.

I'm not sure what he means. "Yes sir, I'm quite comfortable."

"Good. I may need to borrow some money after I take a nap."

CHAPTER 20

I check for phone messages at the same time I chew my sandwich and drive the car with my knees. I multitask well, but almost choke and lose control when I hear the admiral's voice. "Will you take time between arresting hoodlums to drive me to a meeting in Pontiac with Gibbons at three o'clock tomorrow? That would be Tuesday, January 2. I'll buy dinner at the Big Boy afterward and throw in an opportunity to trick me into spilling my guts. I may even pass along the evidence you need to hang me. That is, if you don't mind eating with a right-winged, cane-thumping, old subversive like me."

I pull off the road and dial the admiral's number.

"Top of the afternoon to you, David," he says before I can say hello.

"That was a short nap."

"Plenty of time to sleep after I'm dead."

"I'll be there tomorrow at ten," I say. "We can eat before the meeting at this little place I hear makes good soup. It's near Pontiac."

I park behind the Swainsville Library and enter the small building through the back door. The only librarian on duty is standing on a stool, shelving books. While I wait for her to finish I move to the history section, pull out a *World Almanac Library of States* and page to the index to research the word *sooner*. Satisfied the old man's facts are accurate, I check Sitting Bull in a volume of *Indians of North America*. The history does mention an Indian agent called James McLaughlin.

All the old man's facts about ghost dancing and the chief's death appear to be true. The guy's memory amazes me.

"Be right with you." The woman working the stacks steps down from a footstool and flashes me a warm smile. "Spring cleaning." She wipes her hands on the sides of her smock and says, "How can I help you?"

I flip my bifold open to expose my bronze badge.

Her smile fades. She studies the signature of Director Mueller next to my photo, and reads aloud: "Federal Bureau of Investigation, United States Department of Justice." The librarian takes a step back from the counter. Her arms fold across her chest and give the impression she is wearing bandoleers. Her eyes shrink into what seems to me to be twenty-two caliber bullets.

"I'd like some information on the reading habits of James H. McLaughlin," I say. "He lives at 123 Anchor Lane."

Her eyes look hot and ready to ignite the powder charges behind her pupils. "You're my first experience with the Patriot Act." She fires. "Where's your subpoena?"

I place the folded paper in her palm. Her look is as scorching as the old man's stare. I get relief from her heat when she glances down and reads aloud, "USA Patriot Act, Section 215." She stops reading to rub her temples, and I hear her mumble something about an acronym. "Oh, I remember," she says. "Uniting and Strengthening America by Providing Appropriate Tools Required for Intercepting and Obstructing Terrorism Act." Satisfaction colors her face. She searches through a file drawer beside the computer.

"Yes, here it is." She shoots a round of spare ammunition at me, then lowers her eyes to read from a folder. "'The FBI has unprecedented access to the communication, research, and reading habits of the American public. Section 215 allows the government to get any tangible thing via a subpoena from a library, academic institution, bank, travel company, or medical record.'" Disgust fills her eye sockets. "I recall feeling sick the first time I read this at an emergency library in-service right after September 11," she says. "It's a shame this sashayed through congress without a peep from any of our thoughtful birds on Capitol Hill." She continues reading aloud. "'The agency can demand bookstore transaction receipts and Internet use logs,'" she stops to scowl, "'and the bureau is not required to show how or why it might need the records. They need show only that they were relevant to an ongoing national security investigation. How am I doing?"

"You're getting it right."

She walks around the counter and steps into my space. "All the judge has to believe is that the subject was engaged in terrorism or another crime. I am mortified that congress gave away the rights our forefathers fought for."

I take a step back. She is a big woman.

"I hate this intrusion into the private reading habits of American citizens." Her scowl deepens.

"I bet I can tell you what you despise the most," I say to regain a foothold on my side of the counter.

Her frown pushes her skin down so I can't see her eyes. "And what is that?" She spins around and heads toward her computer.

"The Patriot forbids recipients of a Section 215 subpoena to tell anyone they received it. Am I right?"

Her eyes snap back an attack. "Why make trouble for this old man?" She rolls out a black chair and parks herself before the computer. "He's a veteran, for god's sake." Her voice is cold. "He's been wounded, has trouble walking." She pounds out his name on the keyboard, hits "enter," and leans back in her chair. "I hope he overthrows the government. Is that why you're investigating him?" She pats a few more keys and waits for the machine to do its work.

"The information I need may be related to an ongoing national security investigation. That's all I'm authorized to tell you."

"Yeh … yeh …yeh. This Patriot Act stinks. Okay, here's the secret information." She leans forward, studies the screen and brightens. "I have no record of books checked out to a James H. McLaughlin. Let's see … and no record of overdue books."

"That's all you can tell me? He has lived in this town for over twenty years. I know he uses the library. What kinds of books does he borrow?"

"Dunno. I can only give you a current list and any overdue books. Our computer system purges our customer's historical reading habits."

"That's not possible," I say. "The law …"

The librarian interrupts. "The memory on our computers is just too small to keep track of all our reader's records. I believe you will find the same lack of memory space in libraries across America." She sneers at me and closes her computer screen. "That gift to the American people is courtesy of the American Library Association." She stands and returns to the stacks, leaving me with my notebook and pencil still poised. "Is that enough to nail that helpless old man?" she calls over her shoulder.

I can hear satisfaction in her tone as I flip my notebook closed. "Thanks for your help. May I remind you that under the Patriot Act you may not tell anyone I was here, or that I asked for information on McLaughlin?"

"Get out before I throw this book at you!"

I slip the pen into my shirt pocket and hurry into the cold. The book bag I saw at the condo probably belongs to Corny. I hear a voice from behind me as I walk into the parking lot.

"Section 215 is due to expire at the end of 2006." I turn, no longer afraid of a flying book. "Then what will you do to annoy the octogenarians in Swainsville?" she shouts.

I should leave this alone. I know I should. "The president has asked congress for a permanent renewal of the expiring provisions." I wave and walk through the icy wind to my car, the heat from her eyes still searing the back of my neck.

The motor rolls over a few times before it starts. My hands shake. I switch on the wipers to remove the dusting of snow before it occurs to me. My video store in D.C. has a record of every film I have ever checked out, and that's a huge list. Libraries could keep their reader's history. That not-enough-room-in-our-computer ruse defies the Patriot Act.

She is still watching me from her window as I roar the engine to defrost the windshield. I dial the heater and blast my knees through my thin pants and freeze the hair on my legs straight out. A shiver runs all the way up to the base of my skull. "Damn Michigan winters." I slip the transmission into reverse and spin away.

CHAPTER 21

Thursday morning I arrive early. Murphy is working surveillance in the admiral's window. When my foot hits the porch, the door opens and the cat abandons his post between the drapes.

"Hello David." The old man's eyes are pink-rimmed and fatigue-glazed. "I'm ready." His voice is wheezy. He slips his arms into the sleeves of a jacket. Murphy is guarding his feet.

"Can I help you with that?" I ask, and pull his parka up his shoulders.

"Thanks. I drafted that letter, but I don't type. I've used longhand on my reports for thirty-three years. Hand written should be okay today." He pushes the brown envelope into my hand and hunches over. "Murphy! You're dismissed."

The cat turns on a dime and disappears down the hall. The old man drags his cane behind him and legs it down the sidewalk into a lead-gray day and a needle-cold wind.

"You seem a little off this morning," I shout from beside him.

"I had a bad night."

"Are you well?" I wait as he folds himself into the passenger seat.

"I'm not ailing, if that's what you mean."

I close his door and soon the car creaks and rattles down the frozen road. "I'll put off grilling you until later if you want to sneak a nap."

"Negative, I'd rather talk. It's those damn dreams. Can't sleep."

I drive around a large pothole in the pavement."What kind of dreams?"

"Bad dreams."The old sailor snaps his seatbelt."Last night I woke up shivering with a scream trapped in my throat.They crawl out like that when it's dark.Wake me.Scare me.Get me shaking."

"How long do they last?"I whip the wheel to avoid another pothole, turn onto Main Street and drive toward the highway.

"It's not the length of the horror. It's what happens after. It's hard to explain. After one of those dreams I'm so weary I feel like I've been towed across the Pacific on the end of an anchor chain. I'm too tired to sleep, too tired to eat, and too tired to watch CNN. Faye used to hold me and talk me through them."

"What would she say?"

He sighs. "Faye would tell me that I was home and they couldn't get me here."When he speaks his voice cracks. His focus suddenly switches. He leans forward and squints. His body is at full attention.

I glance through his side of the windshield, and see nothing but a wall of white snow.He is concentrating like a hunter with a squirrel in the crosshairs of his scope.The man is in another place, another time.

I drive onto the highway in silence and head east towards Pontiac.After a while I glance over and see he's asleep.Some desperate circumstance, some mind-numbing event must have crawled under the old warrior's armor and worked its way up into his head. And now when he's the most vulnerable, alone at night, without his Faye to hold him, it consumes him.

I understand. I have demons too: dreams of my father hanging limp from the rafter, gazing down at me with silent-mouthed instructions on where to hide, how to hold my baseball glove, whispering secrets to remember. Each time the dreams come I try to read his lips, try to understand his message, and wait to hear his apology for leaving me. Some dreams take me to our dark, damp garage near the empty lobster traps.

It's still cold inside the car, but I'm sweating. I can't push the dream away. Father's unable to talk, unable to reach down with a reassuring pat, unable to save me from taunting by the children on my school playground. Suddenly he's gone. I long for an attaboy from the man who has given me life, for him to hold me in his arms, for me to touch his warm back.

I tap the blinker lever, pass a semi and wipe my eyes. I motor along until I'm a good three car-lengths ahead of the truck.

Willard T. Hatch must have had demon dreams too. Either he was born in a weakened emotional condition, or the events of his life beat him down so low that all it took was one sharp gust to blow him over the edge. What makes a man like my father kill himself after a streak of bad luck? What makes a man like James McLaughlin rise above a starvation existence to become a leader, teacher, an admiral in the United States Navy?

I turn the wheel gently, cautious of my cargo, and swing back into the right lane.

This gentleman beside me has a compassionate streak. I believe he did care about the sailors under his command. I hear passion when he speaks about the future of men and women who fight in Iraq and Afghanistan. There appears to be a fraternity among these veterans, a commonality of experience that draws them to seek one another's company, regardless of rank or military branch.

My thoughts wander as I drive. I have begun to recognize people in Swainsville. I enjoy the village with its two stoplights, two restaurants and overabundance of snow. Life seems simple here: one place to take clothes for dry cleaning, one market for food, and one place to buy a car. Almost all the people in town own a Ford because the dealership covers real estate on the entire west end of town. Shopkeepers in the village address me by name. I'm accepted. I have a free pass because the old man has owned me as his nephew. I like being part of a community, of having a waiter know what I want before I order, and of being part of the old sailor. I might even like to live here, someday.

I tap the wiper lever. Snow falls and clouds the windshield. The weather doesn't bother me as much now as it once did. The smell of fresh snow invigorates me. Somehow it seems right.

"You get used to the snow," the admiral says, awake on the far side of the car. "Stay alert and stay alive. Cold kills those who sleep."

I jump at the sound of his voice, and throw him a glance. He has read my mind again.

"I've lived almost everywhere at one time or another," he says. "Every location has its compensations." He sips from the Styrofoam cup I had purchased from McDonald's drive-thru earlier this morning. "Tell me about your girlfriend. What's her name?"

"Leticia." I see, so now I'm under the light bulb. He's smooth, should have been FBI. "My woman lives in New York City," I say. "I've been seeing her for a couple of years." That should end the discussion.

"Proposed marriage yet?" The old man's energy level seems to increase as the focus of the interrogation changes to me.

"No, sir." I hesitate before I give up personal information, and turn up the blower.

"Well?"

"Ah, my ... my family pressures me, pushes me to marry a certain kind of girl, and I ... I don't feel comfortable with their choices."

"What's holding you back? Ask her."

"It's not that easy," I say. "They wouldn't approve of her."

"Your parents?"

"Em-hem. If Leticia had a big job or college degree and wasn't black, well …"

"She's Negro?"

"Black. African American." I just told him what I couldn't tell my parents. How hard was that?

The old man faces me, his eyebrows slashing ridges in his forehead. "And why is that a problem if you love her? You do love her?"

I stare at the two-track ahead, my thoughts churning. I wish it were that simple. The snow has turned the highway crisp white. "She doesn't seem to mind all my, ah, my physical irregularities."

"It looks to me like you have two legs and two arms. Plenty of hair covers the shell where your brain should fit. You thought you were smart enough to apply to the bureau. You were capable enough to graduate from the FBI Academy." A smile wipes his face.

I address his teasing eyes. "Are you implying that even monsters can get mates?" I am sweating, and feel like opening a window, but the man beside me is still cold.

"You're no monster, David."

It feels good hearing that from him. I sense I can trust this man, that he wouldn't use my secrets against me. I relax. "I've got to look at our future together," I say. "I want to have kids. She does too. But there's such intolerance for mixing races, producing half-breeds, pressure to keep the tribes segregated that I …" I stop short and look over. "I'm sorry …"

"Sorry I'm a half-breed?" His tenacity is back, braced and ready to tangle.

"No, sir."

"I'm a quarter-breed. My mother, Mamie May Smith Wise McLaughlin, was a poet. Her mother was Kate Jones Smith Embry Pardoe, a concert violist. Grandmother Roxanna

Wilfong was a Jewess. My father, Edward Walker McLaughlin was a half-breed Cheyenne. That makes me a quarter-poet, a quarter-musician, a quarter-Jew and a quarter-Cheyenne, a mix to scare the parent of any well-bred girl." He winks at me and continues.

"I married a half-breed. Faye's father was a horse trader, a cowboy from Arkansas. Her mother was full-blooded Chero-kee. Faye told me once she had a roll number that qualified her to have a little red brick government house on the Cher-okee reservation in Oklahoma." He's silent for a long time before he says, "Marry for love, David."

I wish my mother would have told me that. "Tell me about Faye. Corny mentioned she passed away eight years ago."

The old man's face loses its twinkle. Retreating to his mem-ories, his voice softens. "I started living when I married Faye." He looks out the window. "She was feisty, wouldn't take crap from anyone."

"Not even you?"

"Especially me. She knew how far she could go with me, and I knew how far I could go with her. We never had words or a fight. If we couldn't agree we dropped it."

I tap the brake to slow my speed when I see twin red lights flash farther up the road, brake lights burning a warning back at us. As we approach the conflagration, two lanes of taillights crawl along the highway until the road curves left. Stacked red ones signal danger. I come to a stop ten feet from the vehicle ahead, and slip the transmission into park.

"You warm enough, sir? Looks like we're here for a while." I'm familiar with D.C. bumper-to-bumper traffic. I'm running out of time to wrap this investigation, so I ignored checking the weather this morning. "I didn't use good judgment," I say. "I knew about this storm but thought it would miss us."

"Good judgment comes from experience," he says, "and experience comes from bad judgment."

His outlook seems natural, like an easy running stream. "You were telling me about Faye."

McLaughlin stretches his neck to see through the line of cars, then reclines in his seat. "There are days when I don't think about Faye, weeks wash by, in fact. It's been eight years since …" He is silent, appears lost in thought, or maybe he is hypnotized by the snow. "She was solid. Faye was. Whenever I needed some help, she was there.

"I remember one time when we were stationed in Corpus Christi, when one of my men went over the hill and got himself killed in a car accident. I knew the lad lived with his wife somewhere off base. That afternoon I went home and asked Faye to put Corny in the car, to go with me to find the wife and break the bad news. The woman turned out to be a teenager, a nursing mother living in a backwater shack. The only food Faye could find in her orange-crate shelves was a can of beans.

"'Grab your toothbrush and some diapers,' Faye told her. 'You're coming home with us.' She stayed three days until the base's Holy Joe could arrange a grant to pay her passage to her next of kin, a grandfather. We loaded her and the baby on a Greyhound Bus and sent them north."

The admiral takes a long sip of his decaf, makes a face, and spits it back into the cup. "Cold." He rolls down his window, slaps clear the standing wall of snow, and defiles the whiteness with brown acid. "Faye was generous," he continues and presses the control to roll the window up. "She listened to everyone's problems and tried to steer them in the right direction. She worked for hours making hummingbird cakes for friends with this pan shaped like a bird. Corny has it now. She edged the cake with candles, right out to the end of the beak. When I lit the candles for her, the cake looked like a fleeing Phoenix." He chuckles. "She prized peacocks, especially in April when their tail colors changed. A gentleman farmer who lived near us, Christman was his name, let Faye feed and water them when he took his family on vacation.

But my Cherokee bride was fondest of the fur balls. Murphy worshiped her."

He looks through the windowpane to the tiny white shavings flattened on the glass. "The patterns on these snowflakes remind me of the lacework on Faye's nightgowns." He moves his face closer and attempts to trace the design with his finger. "The structures are so intricate. I used to study them while she slept." He exhales a deep breath and straightens in his seat. "That's the kind of woman my wife was. She knew how to treat people. Taught me a lot." He touches the window where a snowflake lands and watches it melt away.

"I looked nine years for the right woman, David. I knew after we talked for three hours she was right. She told me I was off my onion when I told her I would marry her. She had never planned on another wedding because she was spoiled goods."

"Spoiled goods?"

"Faye had a tough start in life. She was one of seven and the only girl, born in a dusty reservation town. Tivan was the name. Her mother's love for her was as dry as their New Mexican desert. She preferred her sons. That happened sometimes in families. When a rich rancher from Texas took a liking to her at fourteen, her mother married her off. Back in Texas the rancher's mother was furious with her son. She took his Cherokee bride in for a routine checkup. The doctor injected something that knocked her out. When Faye opened her eyes he told her he had performed a hysterectomy. Her mother-in-law explained she wasn't about to have half-breed children inherit her family's land."

"My god. Did she inform the authorities, the law in her area?" I say.

He stares at me through eyes dulled gray by pain.

I wait while he rubs his temples. It is as if his train of thought has vanished, has been blown away with the dried tumbleweed in his memory.

"Where was I, David?"

"Faye's first husband. What was his reaction?"

"The fallout went like this. She ran away to California to her brother's wife and got a divorce. Her brother was in the service. She enrolled in nursing school at Pacific Union College, an Adventist medical school in San Francisco and earned a degree in nursing with a specialty in psychiatry. When I met her she was working at a hospital in Mt. Vernon, Washington named after the Skagit Indians. When she passed I thought my life had ended."

I watch his finger reach for another snowflake on the window, and stop when I ask, "How did she die?" His finger tenses, his hands curl into wads, and the muscles in his face tighten.

"They killed her at the home." Veins on his temples worm up his face. "Faye got dementia from those female hormones she took, and then had a stroke." His head drops. "I took care of her for almost a year until a county health nurse showed up at our door. She took her from me, put her in a nursing home, the best one I could find. She said I was too old and frail to care for her." He whispers, "I think she was smothered with a pillow."

"That's quite an accusation," I say, and turn in my seat to catch his expression. His eyes are glassy.

"Sunday she was fine when we talked: her lungs were clear, her breath normal. Monday she was dead." He clears his throat. "They took her body, had it cremated real fast." He stares out the window. "The night she died I had a dream about her maharajah birds. Those peacocks screamed and screamed. They sounded like babies howling. I bolted upright in bed at the sound of my own shriek and found myself in the center of a flutter of pillow feathers." He is silent a long while before he speaks again.

"I ran into her male nurse in a supermarket in Jackson shortly after her death. He was a big, muscular guy, used to work as a trainer for some athletic team. At the home he hoisted patients in his arms when they had to be moved. When he saw me standing in line behind him, his head dropped and he looked at the floor. 'Good afternoon,' I said.

"The big man greeted me and looked away. During our brief conversation his eyes flicked from his cart to the cashier and back to his cart. He never looked me in the eye. After an embarrassing silence, he said, 'I had nothing to do with it. I always liked Faye.'

"My wife had always been outspoken," the admiral says. "She had been a nurse her entire life and knew how hard it was to deliver quality care. I knew some staffers had found Faye difficult. She complained about the employees to their supervisors."

When I glance at McLaughlin his face seems aged. His eyes sag into slits. His jowls droop. "How would you know from his body language the male nurse thought there was foul play?" I say.

His eyes find mine. "For most of my life it was my job to know what a sailor would do before he got in a tight spot, how he would react before he hurt himself and his buddies. I could tell by the way this male nurse slouched in the checkout lane, by the awkward way he held his hands and by the uneasy blink of his eyes." The old man's chest heaves. He drags his finger across the glass, unable to melt the stubborn flakes. He looks weary, and grows silent as an unforgiving snow blankets the windshield.

"I miss her." He shivers, and pulls his collar higher. "That woman shared the finest moments of my life. I remember a time before Faye, when I spent all my time with men, when I valued women only for sensual pleasures. I had no way to measure how extraordinary married life could be. I grew as a person after we walked the plank together. Once we were married I couldn't imagine a life without her warmth. She became the best part of who I am. Now that she's gone, I feel a hole in my heart so vast I could sail a carrier through it."

THE ATOMIC SAILOR

He shivers again, tucks his hands under his arms, and continues in a stronger voice. "They gave me her remains in a fancy cardboard box. I flew what was left of my wife to the Cherokee Nation and surrendered her to a medicine man for the Great Spirit. It was a nice warm day. My beauty's ashes blew aloft on a soft breeze. They settled in an apple orchard on a mountainside that overlooked a green valley. We had been in that orchard many times. She loved the spot." His jowls sink and weld his chin to his chest. "I want my remains thrown on the same ground in the same apple orchard." His lower lip is quivering.

I look away and ask, "Are you warm enough, sir?"

His voice is soft and

A conversation with James McLaughlin

Life has never been easy for James McLaughlin, an 81-year-old resident of the Brooklyn living Center, but he is not about to start complaining now.

"I am a survivor," said McLaughlin, a 30-year veteran of the United States Navy.

While most servicemen of McLaughlin's generation readily identify with WWII or the Korean War when asked, McLaughlin said he is a veteran of the Cold War.

McLaughlin, an Oklahoma native, enlisted in the Navy in 1941 at the height of WWII, but it was work he was involved with in the nuclear testing program from 1946 through 1952 that left the most lasting impression.

McLaughlin felt the heat from eight atomic explosions on his face while aboard the USS Albemarle. "They sound like a shotgun going off," he noted. "We could not look at [the

James McLaughlin

breaks as he speaks. "A few weeks ago … as I slept in my chair, her … her presence awoke me." He continues in a whisper. "She kissed my cheek. Faye thanked me for carrying out her burial wishes. Then she kissed me on the mouth." He is quiet for a time. "I know it was her," he says turning to me. "She tasted the same." His eyelids look heavy. They collapse, and stay closed.

I grab the door handle. "I'll take a look at what's happening up front. I'll see how long we have to wait." I slip outside and blow my nose, then swallow the knot that blocks my throat.

James McLaughlin before retiring from the United States Navy.

explosion] until the flash was gone and we were given an 'all clear'." When they were allowed to look, what they saw were the signature mushroom clouds pluming into the sky from the devastating blasts.

At the time, experts did not know what the long-term effects were for those exposed to radiation. "If they had, they wouldn't have been involved," says McLaughlin with a laugh, adding that the scientists aboard the ship, including Robert Openhemier, worked on the bombs through a canvas covering.

Tucked into a photo album of awards, citations and other service-related paperwork is a piece of paper identifying him as an atmospheric nuclear test participant (there was nothing voluntary about it, he noted). The paper notes that he has assimilated .60 REM of GAMMA radiation in his body. "That is the type of radiation that does not go away," he said. As a result, McLaughlin said he has had cancer removed from three parts of his body. However, he does not know if other health related problems he is suffering from are due to exposure to radiation or mere age. "I am not that much of a scientist," he noted. "Whether it affected me or not, I don't know."

McLaughlin is proud of his service record, which includes a variety of medals and accommodations. His friends, who nicknamed him "Admiral" upon his arrival in Brooklyn, include other military men who served the United States in the armed forces.

While in the service, McLaughlin held a variety of jobs.

Besides operating a crane on the Albermarie, he has worked on flight decks and as a member of the Navy Beach Batallion.

Not all of McLaughlin's experiences with the government have been pleasant. Upon his retirement as a chief petty officer in 1972 he was denied medical benefits from the veterans hospital until Dr. Raymond Cole championed his cause by sending letters to Congressman Nick Smith, which eventually got him into the VA's door.

McLaughlin learned early that life was not easy. His grandparents settled into a sod shanty homestead in the Oklahoma homestead. His father died when he was a child, and he earned $12 a month as an adolescent in a sawmill while working his way through school.

Upon retirement from the Navy, he worked with the United States Postal Service for a dozen years.

He and his wife, Faye, adopted two children: Laura (Johnson) who works at Foote Hospital in Jackson, and Kevin, a flight instructor at Beale AFB in California.

Am I uneasy over this man's emotional display over a woman? Or am I afraid help won't arrive in time and we'll both freeze? I slog ahead through heavy snow targeting the red taillight ahead, and trace its bumper with my gloved hand until I feel a handle under the snow. I tap on what should be the driver's window. A narrow horizontal crack appears in the thick white powder. "Any news?" I ask. It's a woman behind the steering wheel rolling down the window.

"Said on the radio a semi skidded, overturned and blocked both lanes."

She's wearing a nurses' uniform.

"Freak storm … clear ahead," she says. "May be more heavy snow. Do you have enough fuel?" She thrusts her head through the open space. "I've got half a tank. If you run out, you're welcome to join me. I have a cheesecake in the back seat I was delivering to a friend. If you're hungry you can have it."

I thank her. On my way back to my car a snowmobile roars up and skids to a stop beside me. The rider warns me to return to my vehicle. Another snowmobile pulls up beside him and the two watch as I clomp toward my car through an opening in the whiteout. I watch the men spin their heavy machines, making donuts and figure eights, then shoot up the highway. I look at my watch: 12:15 p.m.

"Those men out there sashaying around on their rescue vehicles," the admiral says when I'm settled inside, "are examples of untrained reactions to a dangerous situation. They remind me of a poem my father used to chant: *When in danger or in doubt, run in circles, scream and shout.*"

CHAPTER 22

We have been snowbound on I-94 for more than an hour. My foot involuntarily taps a rhythm on the rubber floor mat, my ass naps on needles, and my positive attitude is headed south. I won't bet money on how long the heater will keep us warm on a partial tank of gas. "I'll be right back." I slip from the car.

Knee-deep drifts and blowing snow make moving slow. Sweat warms me as I struggle toward the vehicle behind our car that has drifted into a white mound. I'm breathing hard. I take a swipe at the snow at the waist-high bulge that should be a left front fender, feel for solid steel, but find nothing. I move deeper into the drift, feel lower, and to the right. Nothing. I strike out through the drift towards what I think is the outer highway lane, and manage half a dozen chest-high steps when I lose the bottom. Snow caves in over me.

Fear freezes my joints. Terror ices my chest. Panic stiffens my arms and legs. *Oh shit*, I think. *This is it.* Flashes of hazardous training principles crowd my mind. *When fear takes control, it is over.* Too late. I think I peed my pants.

I will my limbs to slash out at the cold white foam, a move to fight back my fear. They barely move. I will my joints to bend. At least my elbows bend. My breathing comes too fast. *Move! Move!* And the knees bend. I'm doing a limited breaststroke and an extremely limited frog kick with my legs. I see a flash of gray sky and blowing snow and recognize hyperventilation. My breathing has accelerated. My heart is beating way too fast. That's when I hear the blasts.

Three short beeps follow three long. They come from somewhere behind me. I listen. Three more short beats. I force my breathing to replicate the rhythm of what I know is the classic Morse code distress signal. I listen. *Breathe slower. Breathe slower. Breathe slower.* The horn bleats again. *Breathe three more long breaths,* I tell myself. I know it is him. *Breathe three short breaths.* He senses I'm in trouble. *Breathe three long ones again.*

My muscles stall under my skin. *Three short breaths.* This is a classic symptom of panic, I tell myself. I must take control of my heart rate or it will accelerate until it explodes. Willpower topples me forward. Resolve drives me to bend at the waist and undulate like a dolphin toward the sound. My muscles ache a refusal to stretch, but self-preservation and stubbornness push my limits. *I'll be damned if I will let a little snow get the best of me. I can do this. I'm an agent of the Federal Bureau of Investigation.* I breathe deeper and slower. The ligaments behind my knees loosen enough to bend while I make a tunnel through a snowdrift. Each plunge forward brings me closer to the signal.

I establish a foothold, and pull myself through the chest-deep snow to what has become a deafening honk. I find a hardened, solid mound, smooth and round, and follow its edge across a grill, a fender and finally to the driver's door. I shake my head, brush snow from my shoulders and stamp my feet.

"Find anything out there?" the admiral says when I am settled inside. "I was hoping for a blonde."

"More snow." I turn the heater higher to melt my pants frozen stiff by the cold. I had reasoned that after the gas tank was empty, the admiral might last eight hours in the latent heat inside the vehicle before his blood turned into frozen slush. Someone would discover him before he turned into ice. Out there in the open my veins wouldn't have taken that long. I'm cold.

I read somewhere that if a corpse is thawed slowly, it is possible for the heart to pump again, and brain damage to be minimal. The trick is to get to a hospital in time. McLaughlin's medical condition flashes to the front of my mind and I remember he is diabetic. "Did you happen to bring any medicine with you, in case of an emergency?"

"David, you look scared."

I squelch a denial while I rub a circle of frost from the window with my sleeve and squint through the foggy pane. "I've never been stranded on a highway in a snowstorm before," I say, and clear my throat. "I don't know what to expect."

The admiral adjusts the bill on his cap. "Snowmobiles cruise major highways like this one to assist stranded motorists with medical emergencies or those who run out of gas. If we need help, we will tie a handkerchief on the radio antenna, or close it in the top of a window. Let's see," he glances over at the dashboard, "we've got less than a quarter tank of gas. That should warm the car for a couple hours. Almost all people in cold climates keep extra blankets in the trunk and candles to burn for heat when the gas runs out." His eyes find mine.

I slouch in my seat, exhausted from my ordeal. I hadn't thought of that.

"Okay," he says. "The police advise you to stay inside your vehicle. It's easy to get lost in a whiteout and freeze solid." His words set me to shivering.

"At least we can eat snow if we get thirsty," I say, attempting to give the conversation some cheer. "There is plenty of that out there."

"Not a good idea. The calories your body would use to melt the snow into water could be better used to keep your core temperature hovering around ninety-seven point eight. It's okay to be scared, David. It's a healthy reaction to the unknown."

"How can fear be healthy?" I say, and wrap my arms around my chest. "Come on, you've never been afraid of anything in your life."

"I've tasted fear," says the old seadog. "I've learned from fear."

"What can fear teach? Tell me one thing, just one," I say, impatient with my weakness. How can this old man's stories get us out of this mess? My anxiety level soars. My throat feels dry and constricted. I have trouble getting enough air.

"It was the 1950s," he says, snuggling back in his seat and wrapping his arms around his torso. "My crew had finished work early. We were in the South Pacific and it was a beautiful, balmy summer day. We knew better than to swim off the fantail, but the water was too blue and too inviting. We stripped to our skivvies on the spot and dove in, all twelve of us. We swam around in the cool water splashing and dunking one another until someone shouted they saw the captain. The old man stood by the fantail holding a line tied to a big hook and watched us. All he had to do was nod his head and we knew we had better get aboard, now. One by one we scampered up the anchor chain and formed a line facing the CO. We were dripping all over the deck in our wet shorts.

"All the captain told us was, 'I want you to see something.' A sailor handed him a hunk of beef from the cooler. The old man slashed the roast several times with his knife until blood ran red on the deck. He slipped the hook into the beef, threw it overboard, held the line and waited. In less than a minute he had a strike. It took three of us to haul that six-foot tiger shark up the fantail and onto the deck. The captain clubbed it dead, slashed the carcass, and threw the bloody chum over the side into the water. He made us stand at the edge of the deck and watch as fifteen or twenty sharks tore it apart. Every one of us empathized with that dead fish, felt as if our own flesh was being torn from our bones and ripped into chunks. A couple of guys vomited. Another guy got faint and had to sit down. I swear I felt the planet move and it took me the rest of the day to get warm. Not one of us went swimming off that fantail again, rules or no rules."

"I'll give you that one," I say. My breathing is coming easier. "Tomorrow I'll buy candles, a blanket and a bottle of Jack Daniels. Sir, did you happen to bring insulin with you this morning?"

"I always bring my emergency pack with me when I leave home. Admiral Rickover used to tell his troops, 'The more you sweat in peace the less you bleed in war.' That was drummed into us so often during my career that preparedness became second nature. I taught my men the seven P's of prudence: proper prior planning prevents piss-poor performance."

I chuckle and mouth the seven P's for retention, counting them out on my fingers. "Are you warm enough?" I ask. "We could turn the heat up." When he doesn't answer I notice he's gazing out the window, off somewhere else.

I step outside, keep one hand on the fender, and push another two inches of snow from the windshield. I wind around behind to check the tailpipe. Suicidal souls in detective stories stuff the tailpipe and use carbon monoxide as their weapon. The pipe's clear.

"This would be an excellent opportunity for us to talk without being disturbed," I tell the old man, slide behind the wheel and slam the door closed. When I look up the admiral's watching me.

"Well done, David. You just turned a negative into a positive." He grins and winks. "What do you want to talk about, son?"

"Will you tell me about the nuclear testing? I need a clear picture of what it was like before we go to that NAAV meeting. Don't leave out a single detail." I retrieve my black overcoat from the back seat and spread it over his legs. I check my watch. It's 12:50 and still Tuesday, January 2, 2007. "Okay, I'm ready," I say and relax back into my bucket seat.

"We were aboard the *Albemarle*, near the Marshall Islands. It was July of 1946."

CHAPTER 23

"Drop your cocks. Pull on your socks. It's time to get out of your bunks, the officer of the day announced to seamen asleep below deck. He cleared his throat and spoke again into the public address system. *Now hear this. All hands topside by 0700.* The announcement crackled through speakers of the seaplane tender anchored eleven miles from ground zero, a circular spit of sand taking in less than four square miles. He told us to sit facing the Bikini Atoll with our knees pulled to our chests."

"Did people live on that atoll?" I ask.

"Sure," the admiral says. "But an advance team from Washington convinced the handful of families to leave their homes for a short time and move to an island a hundred miles away. They told them their sacrifice might make it possible to turn a great destructive force into something good for mankind. Islanders bought the government's story. A hundred and sixty natives moved from their tropical paradise."

"When was it safe for them to go back?"

"Not in their lifetimes. The name of the operation, *Crossroads,* was top secret. Only those with a need to know were familiar with that word and had an inkling of what it might represent. I had clearance, had read all I could find on nuclear fission, and had taken every shipboard course offered on surviving a nuclear blast. Our orders were to watch a bomb explode over some ships anchored in the target area."

"Why did they choose that tropical island?"

"Bikini was a ring-like coral island and reef that nearly enclosed a lagoon twenty miles long by ten miles wide. This extinct volcanic crater made a natural harbor and shelter for floating a ghost fleet of obsolete ships."

"You mean they used the bomb as an excuse to sink the Navy's old junkers?"

"The government was considering building a nuclear arsenal to be used as a standard warfare weapon. Their decision depended on the results of these tests, and they were betting the bomb would make ships obsolete."

"Did any survive the bombs?"

"All the ships eventually sunk to the bottom of a crater made by one of the bomb tests," the old sailor says. "The men were a different story. Most white hats knew about the immediate effects of radiation sickness on human beings from the strikes on Japan. No one knew the long-term effects radiation would have on them or their offspring.

"We were all told where to stand and what to do. We knew better than to question orders. We went about our business, worked, watched the explosion, and waited by those somber shores to clean up the mess."

"So what was life like down there, waiting for the bombs to detonate?"

"The temperature in the atoll rimming the volcano crater held to a steady eighty to eighty-five degrees Fahrenheit year around. Water and air temperature were about the same. During July of 1946 temperatures rose and held in the hundreds. It was hot, muggy and miserable on deck. Soldiers and sailors stripped to their shorts and T-shirts, and swam in the lagoon to stay cool. They washed clothes in seawater. The island was sprayed with DDT to protect the men from insect bites which carried disease. No precautions were made for radiation poisoning.

"Scientists with the Manhattan Project knew acceptable levels set for exposure to gamma radiation were too low, and that radiation could kill Americans sent to participate in the tests. I read a memo issued by a project scientist in 1945 admitting they may have erred on the high side when the *I Believe button* was pushed.

"The brass knew they would have personnel problems if we knew the standards of safety we worked under were questionable. They figured we would demand extra-hazardous pay, and were afraid if we knew the results of the study the number of occupational injury claims due to radiation would increase. The study could feed an army of lawyers.

"We men aboard the *Albemarle* followed orders and waited. We hung there like links on a weighted anchor chain, three feet back from the edge of the flight deck with our arms wrapped around our knees.

"*Hey Okie*, called one white hat over his knobby knees. *What medicine did your Indian grandma give you when you had diarrhea?* His arms shackled his legs just down the row from me.

"I hated it when my crewmates called me *Okie*. The only way to deal with them was to dish it right back. *No Cheyenne medicine man could cure the kind of diarrhea that comes out of your mouth, swabby.* A swale of laughter erupted along the deck. I figured the men were nervous.

"I'm serious, Mac. My brother wrote he had a bout he couldn't stop. Says he tried everything. You told me one time your grandmother cured you with some kind of Indian voo-doo. Come on, what did she use?

"Indian medicine isn't magic, you lug head, I said. It's based on nature. Listen this time and remember. Cut some suckers that grow around the trunk of a peach tree. Make sure they are at least two years old. Peel the bark and boil it in water. Drink a cup full at night before you go to sleep. Got it?

"When in hell is this show going to blow? asked a bos'n mate sitting next to me. I need to take a shit.

"Don't move and that's an order. The command came from behind the chain.

"Hey Mac, what do Cheyenne do for open wounds? asked a sailor a few links down.

"I called over my shoulder. Cut bark from a hickory tree and peel back the inner lining. Chew it into mush. Push it into the wound and bind it with tape or a piece of cloth. That will heal the wound and help fight infection. Any more medical questions I can answer for you sick bastards?

"The PA system crackled. Lay your elbows on your knees and wrap your head in your arms. It was the OD from the bridge. We did as we were ordered. The volume and frequency of our conversations decreased.

"A battleship sailed by the *Albemarle's* port side. Her sailors faced our deck in rows, as if connected by a nine-strand cable. They raised their round, white hats in unison and bowed. Our crew returned the salute, and cheered. The stench of burned fuel oil filled our nostrils long after the ship had passed.

"*Heads down*, crackled the PA.

"Eleven months earlier, B-29 bombers dropped bombs that devastated Hiroshima and Nagasaki. They served their purpose and ended the war. The scientific purpose of Operation Crossroads was to determine the effects of the same bombs on unmanned naval vessels. Eighty-five of the two hundred forty naval vessels that lay scorching in the afternoon sun were designated as target ships. These junkers represented almost all types of ships and were anchored at various distances from ground zero.

"The day before detonation, the *Albemarle* had been anchored in the atoll so the scientists aboard could direct the production. We watched crews from other ships rehearse evacuation and re-entry procedures on the fleet of clunkers ringing the bull's-eye. The Battleship *Nevada* was one of them. Launches shuttled from ship to ship, off-loading equipment and adjusting radiation measuring devices. No one could be aboard any of the ill-fated ships or on the Bikini Atoll during the test.

"The crew could hear baying as unlucky goats were left to run free on the deck of the doomed destroyer *Anderson*. They could hear the howling and yelping of dogs planted on the transport ship *Gilliam*. Pigs squealed on the flight deck of the aircraft carrier *Saratoga* when launches pulled away, as if they already knew their hocks would soon get smoked. Sheep grazed on bales of hay on the *Sakawa*, a captured Japanese cruiser. All the ships bobbed over what would soon be their watery graves.

"We watched as planes landed and cruisers moved, the operation was a circus, an organized spectacle. The *Albemarle* chugged out of the lagoon and cruised less than eleven miles away to Eniwetok Island. She waited. The B-29 called *Dave's Dream* paused beside the dock where our ship was moored while the payload was being strapped to her belly. Orders were for the seaplane tender to relieve itself of the bomb and get the hell away from the Bikini lagoon as fast as possible. All other manned vessels were ordered away as well.

"The *Albemarle* was at the heart of the operation because, as a seaplane tender, she had engine shops, propeller shops, and parachute lofts along with all equipment necessary to repair and keep the Navy's seaplanes operational. The ship had been refitted at the US Navy Yard in Boston to accommodate atomic testing. It had been turned into a floating laboratory ship. Dr. Robert Oppenheimer, the nuclear physicist, and his crew from Oakridge, Tennessee, came aboard in Long Beach along with their equipment.

"During the week-long voyage from Long Beach, scientists had climbed to the top deck for exercise and baked in the blazing sun. Their idea of keeping fit was to stand topside and pass a large leather ball around a circle. There was no throwing, no running, and no sweating. They were a cautious lot.

"*Is that how they taught you to stay fit at Harvard?* a white hat shouted from where he swabbed the deck.

"*Don't strain your gut. That ball looks heavy,* a painter jived as he secured his lifeline. *The fish ate the last scientist who got a hernia,* he shouted as he stepped over the edge and walked down the ship's side. *And then the fish died,* the grunt shouted. We could hear his convulsive laughter all the way up on the flight deck.

"*Can I bum a smoke?* asked one white hat who stood with a squad of seadogs and watched a group of scientists at work. *I'm gonna tell my grandkids about this bomb one day.*

"*These coffin nails will kill you,* his buddy told him, and pulled out a pack of Lucky Strikes rolled in the sleeve of his T-shirt. The pack was passed around the group. *You'll never have grandkids. You don't even have a woman.*

"Coils of smoke rose from a cluster of officers wearing baseball caps. They were watching the scientists assemble the explosive device they would help load aboard the B-29. None of the seamen were aware, like the sweat-streaked scientists were, that one misplaced wire, one over-tightened screw could turn the ship and crew into appetizers too small even for local sharks.

"Servicemen who wanted to go home had returned to civilian life after the last war. Shellbacks like me, with other new recruits were in the Marshall Islands because we wanted to be part of the largest, best equipped Navy in the world."

"Shellbacks?" I wonder aloud.

"You haven't read about that rite-of-passage?" The old man smiles. "That's right, you're from that television generation. Aboard Navy ships an official ceremony is held changing new recruits to shellbacks when the equator is crossed."

"Thanks. Please go on," I say.

"Both the experienced and untested sailors saw what the scientists did as important. We were proud to be a part of this history, whatever it turned out to be. The US Government tested nuclear devices because Congress wanted America to be the strongest nuclear power in the world. That's the line we bought at the time.

"Early on the day of the blast, the *Albemarle* was moored next to a finger pier on Kwajalein Island where the Air Force had built a four thousand five hundred foot landing strip from coral. Rear Admiral Deak Parsons waited on the runway next to our seaplane tender. He was the mission commander from the *Enola Gay* when it dropped *Little Boy* on Hiroshima. He was here to arm the bomb once the plane had reached altitude. The man climbed aboard the B-29 called *Dave's Dream*. He would watch the explosion from the air.

"A team of scientists rolled a four-wheel cart with soft balloon tires across the flight deck to the elevator. White coats stopped next to a fat bomb they referred to as *Gadget* that emerged from a restricted area below deck. The Atomic Energy Commission considered the name *Gadget* less terrifying than *Thermonuclear Armageddon* and instructed the scientists to use the former name. The cart's steel corner posts had cables lashed to the uprights.

"I was a crane operator specialist at the time. I clamped *Gadget* in the jaws of my crane, swung it over the side and lowered it to the finger pier. I was chosen to handle the bomb because of my top security clearance, because I knew what was in the heavy package, and because I didn't make mistakes.

"Scientists waited with open arms to guide *Gadget*. Men of all stripes watched in silence as the team hung the fat package off a rack in the plane's bomb bay. The doors closed. The plane taxied, turned and came back into the wind under full throttle.

"The *Albemarle* was well underway before the B-29 had pulled up its landing gear and passed her in the air. The ghost fleet was anchored in a circle around the target ship, the Battleship *Nevada*, which was painted lead red. In the outer circumference of the circle, the Battleship *Arkansas* was moored.

"I can't see the test animals they loaded on the ships, even with binoculars, the bell-bottom beside me said.

"We're too far from the perimeter, a sailor said. *I saw dogs climb stairways, and run across decks during the training exercise yesterday.*

"What will happen to all those animals after the explosion?

"I don't know, said the sailor, *but if that SOB Russian cook serves goat tonight, I'm not eating.*

"*Dave's Dream* turned and soared back toward the *Albemarle*. She was gaining altitude. The roar of her engines drowned the men's conversations as it glided past, then climbed back toward us, spiraling to five hundred twenty feet. The B-29 circled overhead while all manned vessels scattered.

"Forty-two thousand sailors and scientists were aboard the ships steaming away from the ghost fleet. Most of the men had no idea the exercise was to determine how atomic blasts as strong as the ones dropped on Japan would affect a fleet of ships and the men on board.

"If you start puking, lay down and cool off, I told my friends. I learned during Atomic Biological and Chemical Warfare School three-hundred rem of radiation could make you sick. Six-hundred rem could kill you on the spot.

"Bankston, a bos'n mate three, was in charge of the working grunts assigned to do whatever manual work the scientists needed. *Cover your eyes,* Bankston ordered his men.

"The first shot, code *Able,* would explode soon in the sky high above the flurry of ships. We were ordered to sit on the deck with our heads between our knees and wait for the aerial blast.

"*Mac, I would sell my woman for a bottle of whiskey tonight,* said Bankston from his position beside the rail. The sun had baked us brown on the gray deck.

"This was evolving into a classic Navy hurry up and wait. No one could be sure when the bomb would detonate. Both of us knew stories about drinking and women were needed to make a long, delay bearable. I sensed Bankston was trying to distract the men, so I said, *I once delivered twenty-eight cases of Jack Daniels to the Enterprise and put them in Admiral Halsey's cabin.*

"*Twenty-eight cases of Jack Daniels? That's four hundred forty-eight bottles of fun-loving hooch,* Bankston said.

"*Did someone say there are twenty-eight cases of whiskey on board?* a white hat down the chain from Bankston asked.

"*Did I hear there are girls on board?* another bell-bottom asked.

"Talking about drinking and women always worked. These men liked a good story and I admit I am a good storyteller.

"*No such luck getting women on this bucket of bolts,* Bankston told him. Then he asked me, *Is Bull Halsey a drinker?*

"*Admiral Halsey's a drunkard,* men whispered to one another up and down the line.

"I didn't correct the rumor, just moved on with my story. *Halsey ordered me to stack the cases of whiskey in his cabin with the labels out and readable,* I said for all to hear.

"The bos'n mate glanced up and down the line. *Keep those heads down, men. Mac, who drank the stuff?*

"I took a long drag on Bankston's cigarette before answering. *Halsey gave pilots a slug when they came back from tight missions.*

"*How did you get your hands on that much liquor?*

"*It was '43,* I told them. *I was with the Amphibs, stationed in Hawaii on duty at the receiving station. I happened to be in the work party when Halsey's ship docked and his order came in. I loaded it up, and drove it over myself.*

"*On the wall in his cabin hung a framed needlepoint poem his wife stitched that was about the size of a man's footprint. Halsey told me he carried it in his briefcase and when he got to new quarters, it was the first thing he unpacked and hung on the wall.*

"*I would have unpacked the whiskey first, if I were the Bull,* a white hat down the row said. The men broke up.

"*Quiet, shit-stain. I can't hear,* mumbled the next chink in the human chain. *Come on Mac, what did the wall hanging say?*

"I cleared my throat. *It read, The Lord gave us two ends to use: one to sit with and one to think with. The war depends upon which we choose. Heads we win and tails we lose.*

"I heard muffled laughter all along the line. *Halsey told me when a seaman deserved having his ass eaten, he would order him to his quarters, point to the framed quotation and order him to read the poem aloud. Then he'd say, now get to hell out and don't let me see you in here again.*

"Bankston grinned. *Good one, Mac.*

"*What was Bull Halsey like?* asked a sailor to my left, who stretched his legs one at a time to get the kinks out. The men were cooked medium rare by the sun by now, burned on the outside and red in the middle.

"*Bull was all business*, I said. *Eleanor Roosevelt came to Guadalcanal, an island near Australia. Halsey heard she was nosing around inspecting troops. We all knew her corpse would have made powerful propaganda for the enemy. Halsey ordered an airplane. 'Load that old bitch up,' he ordered. Haul her ass to Pearl Harbor and dump her out. You can tell her I said to get her ass back to Washington where she belongs. They called him down from Washington, made him clean up the language he used in dispatches after that one.*

"The men cheered and whistled as my story ended.

"Bankston looked up. The B-29 had stopped circling and was almost over ground zero. *Keep 'em down*, Bankston shouted. *Here she comes.* He glanced at me and gave me a wink that said job well done.

"A twenty-three-kiloton bomb was detonated two hundred fifty feet above the Bikini Atoll on July 1, 1946 at nine in the morning. The closest operating ship was eleven miles from ground zero.

CHAPTER 24

"We sailors aboard the *Albemarle* felt the heat from the explosion warm the flesh on our faces, our hands and our ankles. We felt the ship roll. We sat there in our dungarees, T-shirts and round, white sailor caps while scientists braced against the bulkhead wearing protective white suits with hoods and respirators.

"One fellow kept his eyes open so he could report on the historic blast. *Hey guys,* he said. *I can see the bones in my fingers right through my hand.*

"Bobby Wilson was a long-necked bird, close to six foot five. He walked like a heron … his thigh muscles pulling his knees toward his chest for yard-long steps while his shoulders moved down to meet them. He was a pharmacists mate aboard the USS *Albemarle,* the second closest ship to the explosion. We were eleven-and-a-half miles away. He watched from atop the forward deck crane and reported. *The fireball didn't even touch the surface of the water. The sea looks red.*

"*Bobby,* I said behind arms that still shielded my head. *What's wrong with your brain? Get down from there and cover your eyes.*

"*I watched it in my mirror, Okie,* Bobby said. *Nothing wrong. No sagebrush between my ears.*

"I thought about Bobby teasing me as I observed the most powerful man-made explosion on the planet, a terrifying destructive force that could rip across the ocean and blow us all into a haze of dust. My seventh sense screamed out over the thundering explosion. *There's no need to get your feathers ruffled. This won't be our last day.*

"I had known since childhood that my time to die would be my time to die, and I couldn't change it. Sailors around me mistook that for what they called my *easy manner*. They felt comfortable with me, trusted what I said because I never seemed to get ruffled. I was told by more than one officer I had the makings of a natural leader.

"The more serious the situation, the calmer I became. My men accused me of having iced beer running in my veins. I read in *Knight's Modern Seamanship* that when a sailor gets excited he's already lost control, and liable to lose his life and the lives of his men. Still, Bobby's remarks about my heritage needled me ... reminded me of home where I learned patience through disappointment.

"I sweated through ten years of drought growing up on the prairie flatness of Oklahoma. I struggled through dust storms that blew topsoil from my father's plowed and seeded fields. I worked the land with my family until the frustrations of farming drove us all into crippling defeat. I weathered stagnant poverty while I grew. I felt the pain of hunger gnawing at my belly, and saw no humor in that hunger. Being poor was tedious. My approach to life was good-natured, but deep in my gut I resented anyone who picked on the downtrodden.

"*All hands, you're free to look.* The order came from the CO.

"A fireball brighter than the sun dropped towards the foam flecked sea. A demon grey-green cloud three miles wide formed in the painted blue sky. Sailors aboard the ship felt a second rush of hot air. We were caught in a squall of dark wind swirling towards us. A mushroom-shaped cloak climbed above the green cloud, and rolled into itself like a whirlwind of tumbleweed on an Oklahoma prairie. The shot had exploded as planned in the air above the ghost fleet.

"*Holy mother of god*, mumbled Bobby. His gaze was riveted on the sky that had turned red and purple, the color of a fresh bruise. The fireball disappeared into the sea, leaving a mist of gurgling, tumbling, blue-violet-gray steam.

"A boom of cheers erupted from the crew. We were sitting, still hugging our knees, when the second shock wave hit and rocked the ship. The after-wind tipped the *Sakawa* on her side. Her foredeck dipped and she slipped under leaving the ocean bare, as if she had never existed. We waited as the submarine *Pilotfish* tilted toward where the *Sakawa* had been. She turtled and followed her down, her propellers disappearing last.

"Men choked as the wind carried smoke from the sinking ships across our deck. We watched the *Gilliam* and *Anderson* tip and plunge to the bottom. The majority of the eighty-five Navy ships had disappeared on initial impact. Those along the perimeter took several hours to sink. The gray ocean wilderness boiled like molten steel. Some men watched, others went about their business.

"We were in the galley eating corned beef sandwiches when the announcement came less than an hour after the blast. *Now hear this: boarding teams and salvage unit personnel may begin survey operations as soon as they have had lunch. All personnel that have been issued radiation badges are to wear them when boarding the target vessels.*

"*Bankston,* called the CO, waving him over.

"The bos'n mate hurried to a group of scientists talking among themselves, photographing the clouds, pointing and motioning, instructing the commanding officer. The mushroom cloud had dissipated overhead and the sky was gray. Men stood at the rail and watched drones fly through the purple cloud, collecting samples for the scientists. We watched as the unmanned planes land on the same finger pier where we had loaded *Gadget* into the B-29.

"Bankston barked orders. A work party was sent ashore to remove the air filters from the drones and wade out into the lagoon for water to wash down the plane's fuselages. I hoisted the radioactive equipment aboard from their launch with the same crane we used to lift seaplanes from the ocean.

"*Let's go,* Bankston called to a second crew. *Bobby, take your hands out of your pockets and drop the dinghy down with two men. The scientists need samples of all the species of dead fish you can find.*

"*Yes sir,* Bobby's look was dark. He glanced at me. I could see he was scared. *If that blast killed the fish, what will it do to us?*

"I didn't know it at the time, but Dr. Karl Z. Morgan, one of the scientists aboard the *Albemarle,* was the Atomic Energy Commission's foremost expert on the health effects of radiation. He was known as the father of the science of health physics. Morgan pioneered the radiation health effects field and worked on the Manhattan Project. During our operation, I saw the man scrutinize film badges worn by the men and the portable survey meters they used to evaluate radiation doses. I heard him complain they were inadequate. He was given a crew of men to conduct better measurements. I saw his report.... *the film badges and survey meters in use by the military during the atomic tests gave zero response to the beta dose.*

"Morgan explained to a few of us that beta rays dissipate quickly, but are still lethal in large doses. It was well known that gamma doses of radiation were an accumulative poison. Morgan saw dangerously high beta doses measured on other survey equipment. Those Beta-emitting radionuclides absorbed into the paint and tar resins on the ships, and held six hundred times the gamma dose. Sailors who slept on deck to avoid the tropical heat below in their quarters, awoke with erythema-sunburn that wasn't from the sun.

"Bobby wasn't the only sailor concerned about his future health. I put the same question to one of the scientists with whom I had struck up a friendship.

"*Look, Mac, we're as green as you are,* he said. *That's why we're out here testing. We're all damaged by now.*

"Bobby left to gather floating fish. He had trouble with the motor and radioed to be towed in. When the towboat approached, the kid piloting it rammed his launch, missed Bobby by a hair, and put a good-sized hole in the port side. I remember wondering why this numbskull had been chosen for this job. I'd had trouble with him before. Bobby stayed with the sinking speedboat and sent his men back with the rogue sailor. When the launch was finally secured beside the *Albemarle*, Bobby headed for the mess. He was frustrated with the lad's lack of seamanship, upset he had spent the better part of an afternoon bobbing in a sea of radiation, and afraid of how the dust of this destructive force would affect him.

"I had just finished a double order of fried potatoes smothered in ketchup and slurped down a mug of thick, black coffee when I saw Bobby enter. I motioned for him to join me.

"*That kid from Boston nearly drowned me,* Bobby said holding his mug with fishy fingers. *How did that useless dimwit get in the Navy?* He picked up the Silex and attempted to pour the bubbling mud into his beaker. *This black tar's cooked down since breakfast. Can we get some decent coffee over here?* he yelled at cook, then grimaced at the glass pot, and pushed it away.

"*Look, Bobby. We all know they don't know shit in Boston. Don't blame the kid. You didn't call him a dimwit to his face, did you?* I said.

"*Why not? He called me an asshole.*

"*Don't take that personally. Enlisted men often address officers as assholes in normal*

conversation…behind their backs. I grinned, but Bobby was in a dark place. I listened as he grumbled about the Navy. He needed distraction, so I told him a story.

"*I worked search and rescue out of Whidbey Island, Washington, on special duty to train attack pilots. This snipe-engineer from Minneapolis/St. Paul piloted my launch. We ran a steel-topped target boat to tow a plow-shaped spar that spewed spouts of water up from each side, a bull's eye for training dive-bombers. The spar was on a steel cable fifteen hundred feet behind us. I lay on the deck and watched the planes circle above.*

"*This a private conversation, Mac?* a white hat said.

"I patted the bench and three sailors sat down, each with a mug of battery acid. *One young pilot got carried away,* I continued. *Instead of aiming his bomb for the spar he targeted my boat. I lay there on the deck with my arms under my head, looking up, thinking about women in general and one little filly in particular. I could see the speck when it left the plane, like a tiny black dot from the end of a sentence. I knew that if it moved to either side, like a comma, I would be okay.*

"*Well, it didn't act like proper punctuation should. I sat up real fast, yelled at my snipe, Shorty Summers, to head for a hole in a hurry, then slid under the steel canopy. We could feel the bomb catch us broadside. After the concussion an expectant silence filled the air. I called to Shorty Summers to see that he was still alive, then ordered him to see if we were on fire.*

I picked up the radio, shouted 'May Day,' took the helm and waited.

"*Shorty reported that there was no fire, just a three-foot hole with bilge water pouring in. That ordnance cut the prettiest little hole through the side above the waterline ... came right through the timbers, through two thicknesses of strakes ... just missed the six-seventy-five horsepower gasoline engine.*

"I looked up from the table to see a platoon of coffee-drinking, smirk-faced, white hats surrounding Bobby and me. A sailor stepped forward and asked me if I was spinning another true story. I told him to pull up some deck. He might learn something. When the rest of the men were settled in beside him I continued.

"*I told this snipe of mine to stuff the hole with a mattress. I learned that in Ship Construction and Damage Control School. The mattresses we used then were about two inches thick and stuffed with the hair from a cow's tail. They weren't real comfortable for sleep, but they worked pretty well keeping the water out.*

"*I hollered May Day a few more times on my radio. At last the water transportation officer came over the airways and asked me what was wrong. I told him to secure operations right away. No more bombs. When he asked me why, I told him that his dumb bastards bombed me, and that was why. I informed him they tore a hole in my side and I was coming in.*

"Bobby laughed and loosened up. *Your snipe must have been from Boston.*

"*Did the pilot get in trouble?* asked one of the white hats during a lull in the laughter.

"*Trouble? Hell no. The Navy developed a new job classification for pilots who bomb their own ships. The lad was promoted. He's the pilot who dropped Gadget yesterday and sunk the whole damn junker fleet.*

"Men howled and slapped their thighs.

"How much do you want to bet the pilot of that launch-sinker ends up the next skipper on this tub? said Bobby. The men loved that one, but groaned as they climbed the ladderwell to go back to work.

"Normal duties aboard the *Albemarle* were suspended until the radiation dissipated. A few men went below to read, but almost everyone else stayed topside to observe the destruction. Some ships still floated on their sides in the sea, like bloated animal carcasses. All remaining ships were riddled with holes, blackened, charred and stripped of surface paint. Gun barrels and steel structures had slumped or melted away. As men watched fires burn, the sea turned a liquid pewter-gray.

"Radioactivity was high aboard junk ships near the center of the target fleet. The lagoon was declared safe for the return of all vessels by 1430 hours. By evening, all manned ships were anchored in temporary berths inside the lagoon. Our superior officers told us we were well outside of the area of contamination. By 1830 initial work teams boarded the junkers and found eighteen target ships clear of radioactivity.

"I overheard one of the scientists say we were all damaged by the radiation from the blast, one bell-bottom said. Word spread around ship like a prairie fire in a high wind.

"I could see Bobby in a launch off the starboard bow. He was back dipping dead fish from the lagoon with a net. Two sailors were in another craft. They used pails to scoop the floating remains into the bottom of their speedboat.

"A third launch was sent out to surviving ships to retrieve animals that were still breathing and the remains of the dead ones for the white coat's analysis. Goats, dogs and hogs with burns and lesions were loaded in cages for delivery to the San Francisco Navy Yard.

"Inspection of target vessels pedaled on the next morning under gunmetal clouds. Five of the ghost fleet had sunk as a result of the blast. By that evening, forty-seven target ships were declared safe and were boarded by all or part of their crews. That same day the islands of Bikini and Inyo were inspected and radiation levels declared within a safe range, but all swimming in the atoll was banned.

"Sailors slapped together square wooden sheds for the stoic critters. The structures were lashed to the port corner of the main deck and labeled radioactive. The test animals were tethered inside crates beside barrels of contaminated materials heading stateside. The entire village of shacks was on a lifeline that could be released with a coupling hook, and given the deep six, if sailors suddenly glowed in the dark or took to frying eggs on their foreheads. The crew was warned that nobody but Dr. Oppenheimer and his scientists had access to it.

"Seamen grew uneasy surrounded by all that radioactive material. I suggested we have a poker game to relax and kill some time. Wager results after the last blast had the card sharks excited. The air remained electrified with excitement from the day. When the men lost concentration, I cleaned everyone out, then crawled into my bunk. It was time for my next promotion, so I pulled out my course book and studied. If I passed I would be petty officer third class.

"Admiral, did you hear that? What was that noise?" I say, holding my hand flat for him to stop his chronicle. We both listen while the engine in our snowbound car chokes and misses. The rental car sputters and stops. A large lump grows in my throat. The admiral stares straight ahead. Neither one of us says a word. There is nothing we can do. We are out of fuel.

CHAPTER 25

"Men aboard the *Albemarle* were unusually quiet during the rest of July of '46." McLaughlin continues with missing a beat. "The ship was anchored off Kwajalein Island. It was hot. The next shot, code named *Baker*, was scheduled for detonation at the end of August, but went off underwater on July 25. It had been lowered ninety feet below a fleet of US Navy vessels. Days turned into endless waves of nothingness. We sailors were edgy from the waiting, anxious at not knowing what to expect. Imaginations ran into overtime.

"*Look at it this way, Joe,* one seasoned sailor said as a group of us ambled aft. He took a long draft on his cigarette and blew out three perfect white hoops. *You're already fried from radiation. What can you do? Nothing. So, stop worrying. Just do your job and stay out of trouble.*

"Joe watched as a breeze carried the circles of smoke aloft and paused near the lifeline along the edge of the deck. *I don't feel sick. How can I tell if I've been damaged?*

A crowd gathered.

"*I'm telling you, you're all right,* the lifer insisted.

"*It doesn't make sense for our government to put trained men and this entire fleet in danger,* said an officer who stopped near the anchor chain. *If anything happens to you, just remember the Navy always takes care of its own.*

"*Take a tip from the scientists, sir,* said the career sailor as he secured a canvas over a battery of anti-aircraft guns. *Did you notice what the lab rats wore during the Able shot?*

"The crowd of blues had expanded to a sprinkling of khakis and a lone sailor in whites.

"*I saw,* said Joe.

"*They don't dress like albino monkeys for nothing,* said a seaman who spat and watched until his spit hit the water.

"*You think we're guinea pigs for those sons-a-bitches?* said Joe. *You think they're monitoring us to see when our eyes light up?* Men of all stripes began to understand their roles in the tests. Innocence flowed from sailors like the ebbing tide.

"Resentment gathered like kelp abandoned at the high-water mark. Officers had orders to keep their crews busy to avoid trouble. Sailors in shorts scrubbed and mopped, scraped and painted. They sat through safety training films and learned how venereal disease could kill you. After work, the men watched organized boxing matches on the hangar deck, or a movie below deck. Some jogged topside to work off the frustration of inaction.

"I was on top, walking off my lunch when I saw men, scattered across the deck, playing football. All it took was an overthrown ball falling into the sea for tempers to flare. Fisticuffs flew next to a white hat leaning on a ladder reading John Steinbeck's *Grapes of Wrath.*

"*I hate that author,* I told him while I stood beside him ignoring the fight. Three men were down and six more were pounding them. *Can't you find something better to read? Heads up,* I yelled. *Here comes the CO.*

"*This book is an American classic,* the white hat said, lighting up a smoke.

"*That bastard was responsible for discrimination against people from Oklahoma.*

"*Sir, Steinbeck writes about the Great Depression, the poor white migrants and the Dust Bowl, and the …*

"*How do you suppose people felt after they dug themselves out of poverty and were labeled illiterate white trash, or prune-*

picking California day laborers? You think starved people want to be reminded about hunger? Have you ever starved, sailor? I mean famished for months and years, so poor you would have stolen crumbs from a mouse? Have you ever been too poor to enter a store, too poor to pay postage for a letter, too poor all you had to sell was your own cadaver?

"The white hat took a long drag on his cigarette. *Are you from Oklahoma, sir?* he said, and exhaled two thin lines of smoke from his nose.

"*That's an affirmative, sailor. And I've had to stand up to plenty of drunken Indian and illiterate Okie jokes. I don't know why Steinbeck had to pick Oklahoma for his story. Climate changed in Texas, in Kansas and in Ohio, too. Look,* I said. *When you hear the word Texas you think of wells pumping crude oil and longhorn cattle roaming the prairie, not poor white trash. When you hear the name Kansas you see blowing fields of wheat, not barren acres and sun-beaten farm buildings with clattering shutters and empty doorways. Ohio, hell, Ohio is full of buckeye trees and robust football players, not hollow-cheeked destitutes. But when you hear dust bowl your mind races to Oklahoma and you see poor families with a lifetime of possessions piled on top a Model-T truck. Steinbeck didn't write about Ohio or Texas or Kansas. His damned writing described us, me and my family in Oklahoma. We hurt and he profited from our desperate situation.*

"*Calm down, sir,* the white hat said, *John Steinbeck wrote fiction. This is only a paper story.* He smacked the book against his leg. *Your family couldn't have lost everything.*

"*You're right. Not everything. First Papa auctioned off the registered Jersey bull he bought for seven hundred dollars. The seventeen registered Jersey heifers we milked night and morning sold for ten cents on the dollar. Those animals had an expensive aroma, a scent of blue-ribbon stock. He gave a hundred dollars a head for those cows. The bank finally repossessed our farm. After the auction and Papa paid what he owed he had a hundred and ten dollars to show for a lifetime of work.*

"The sailor stood, and tucked the book into the back of his dungarees. *Mind if I walk with you? How many kids were in your family?*

"I motioned for him to come along. *Thirteen, and we were all half-starved. The pain of hunger was always here.* I rubbed my belly. *I joined the Navy for decent food, luxurious accommodations and to see the world.*

"The sailor blew a spout of smoke from the corner of his mouth, lagged behind and flipped the butt into the sea. I heard a splash, and saw Steinbeck's book float testing on a wave.

"*How did your family survive after you lost your home?*

"*Papa packed us in our Ford truck and drove us through the plowed red fields of Arkansas to lush farms where we picked fruit: strawberries for a penny a quart, green beans for a penny a pound. Every other berry we pulled from a bush went into the basket for the farmer. We returned to Oklahoma in December when the Arkansas crops were all in, a little clot of humans in a broken-down truck on a powder-dry prairie.*

"*We slept inside a drafty tent in a roadside park for two months. I swear, the chill from those nights will be in my bones until my last breath. Mama was pregnant with my youngest brother at the time. We had to get her inside. Papa and my older brothers convinced an ailing, elderly man we could take care of his farm, and all fifteen of us moved into his dilapidated farmhouse and yard overgrown with wild carrots and tumbleweed.*

"The white hat unrolled a fresh pack of cigarettes from his T-shirt sleeve, pulled the red cellophane ribbon, and tapped it on his forearm. A single white stick appeared. He offered me a smoke before he took one for himself. We turned our backs to the wind to share a light.

"*Mama pumped water from a well by the barn. I carried the water to cook and clean. She scrubbed our clothes in a galvanized washtub, gave birth to my youngest brother, and got up to hang the laundry to dry over a side-yard line. She breastfed my brother, scoured and whitewashed the old farmhouse walls, settled children's feuds and fed the chickens.*

"*Mama took care of that old man for over two years in exchange for a rusted-orange corrugated roof over our heads. Papa and the older boys worked the land, mended fences and tended the livestock. We managed to survive in that dry mud.*

"We both stopped at the edge of the deck and flicked our cigarette butts over the side. I put one foot on the hatch, leaned on my knee and squinted out at the salt waves.

"*Holding a family of thirteen together was tough for my mother. My older brothers, John, Patrick and Jack drifted away to the CCC Camps, and sent what money home they could. They finally joined the service. That was it, our childhood in Oklahoma. I dreamed of being a doctor, but joined the Navy because I needed shelter and a diet I could count on. I was through with starving.*"

"Excuse me for interrupting your story, admiral," I say from my side of our snowbound car. "I read *The Grapes of Wrath*, and that's how Steinbeck described it. The author told the truth."

The old man rubs the liver spots on his wrist with the palm of his other hand. *Some parts of the truth are better forgotten, David. They set off bad memories.* He abandons his wrinkled hands to his lap and straightens his slump.

"Where was I?" The admiral looks ten years younger when he is telling his sea stories. "Oh yes. This sailor had asked me about growing up in Oklahoma. The guy was a lot like you, with no knowledge of history. That young man wanted a Hollywood ending. He asked me about the good times, the daily life minus the unbearable heat, the dust, and the poverty. *Other than starving,* the fan of John Steinbeck said, *tell us what it was like living there, the real Oklahoma?* I heard the sound of boot soles on the deck behind us.

"Sailors crowded around the hatch cover. *Come on, Mac. Spin us one of your yarns.*

"A string-thin sailor said, *Who wants to hear about my brother's Hail Mary at the Notre Dame game?*

"*Already heard that one. It was as dull as whale shit. Let's hear Mac's.*

"I could tell the men were bored by the way they stood with their hands deep in their dungaree pockets. *All right. All right.* I said. *What do you want to know?*

"*Tell us about your folks, your parents.*

"*Mama was a little thing, four-foot-eleven inches. Papa told us dynamite came in small packages, and he was right. She was strong on discipline. This woman would put up with our foolishness until we got too wild, then grab a baseball bat and come after us screeching, 'Stop the fighting, you damn black Irishmen!' When her voice went up an octave we knew to jump out every door and window that was open. She never hit any of us with that bat, though at the time we thought she might. Jack, my older brother and I teased our sisters. It didn't make much difference where we were, Mama heard, and let us have it. She was always deaf when my sisters picked on us. That was my mama.'*

"*Papa was gone all week. He worked on the railroad. On Friday evenings Mama would have all thirteen of us lined up so Papa could give us a thrashing. She had already whipped us once with a razor strop. Papa used the same leather thong. He shredded several of those whips on our meat houses.*"

I laugh, remembering a spanking my father had given me for depositing excrement in his good dress shoes. He hung his blue dress uniform in my closet and stacked his shoes next to my toy box when he came home on leave. I was fascinated with those shoes, and could see my face in the polished toe. I played with the round black laces, and wore the shoes around my bedroom when I played sailor. My parents were arguing in our only bathroom one afternoon, and, well, I couldn't wait. The admiral was still talking and didn't notice my attention lapse.

"*... and when Papa came home from work on Friday nights, he brought a five-pound bucket of salted cod fish. Mama shushed us when we howled that we wouldn't eat the mud-caked fish no matter how she fixed them. She soaked them overnight in cold water. We had them in a pan of gravy in the morning and licked our plates clean. They were about as tasty as salty stones, but we were hungry enough to eat whatever she set out. Friday nights, the old man lined us up and gave us a dose of Epsom salts, whether we needed it or not. He told us it would keep our bowels open.* The sailors cheered and slapped their knees at that.

"I laughed with them," the admiral said, "remembering more about my family the more I told the men. *Mama gave us her affection, and held each of us as much as she could, but never had much time. That tiny woman always had someone in her arms or balanced on her hip. The bigger ones helped take care of the little ones. We learned that was the natural way, to take care of one another, to help the family. It was a lot like the Navy, but I didn't know it then.*

"*Mama never had a bottle of perfume in her life. She believed in soap and water. I remember her with one hand on my head, the other with a washrag over her finger in my ear. I'd be hollering she was hurting me. She had long, black, braided hair that fastened at the back of her head. She wore a poppy-studded church hat when she went to town. Her voice was clear and soft, except when she was mad. And then she could clear a room with one, QUIET!*

As the old man went on with his story I thought about the privileged life my father had led growing up with his doting parents, my grandparents. They had Florida vacations, chocolate ice cream and television. After he was married to my mother, after I was born, and after my grandfather died, his life turned sour.

"*Mama's mother was Jewish,*' the admiral told the sailors. '*She was a concert violinist who played her music in mining camps all through the West. She taught her daughter to write poetry. My mama kept a bookkeepers ledger full of her mother's old songs. She liked to sing and taught us the lyrics. Four of my brothers played harmonica. In the evenings our family sang a little, did our homework and went to bed.*

"Papa loved math. He worked problems in his head faster than anyone could work them with a pencil on paper. In '29 the railroad he worked for converted to diesel and my father lost his job. He bought a farm, then lost it in the drought.

I thought about how different my father's life had been from this old warrior's. Mother didn't like to talk about the men in our family. I learned from my grandmother that my grandfather died young in what my mother called an accident. Grandma said he killed himself. Grandfather was a builder. After he was gone my grandmother and father barely got by. Her family name and connections in Boston helped her find a suitable job and wife for her son, my father.

When cornered, my own mother followed family tradition and lied about my father's death. He didn't die in an accident, either.

"Are you listening, David?" the old man asks. "I told the men in 1934, Papa went to work for the Oklahoma Highway Department. Soon after he got that job, a district magistrate called and asked him to work at the WPA. The judge wanted him to manage three crews. He asked the man how come he was doing this for him. The judge told him it was because he was the only one who could read a blueprint.

"Papa worked each of the crews for nine days," the admiral continues, "then sent them home and brought in another crew so more men could earn an income. They were paid $23.10 for nine day's work.

"That works out to $2.57 a day, or $.32 an hour," a sailor said. How could a family live on that?

"It was $23.10 more than earning nothing. Those men knew they were lucky to have a job at all. I rode payday rounds in a car with Papa and saw him dish out the cash. They called him Boss McLaughlin.

"Riding next to my father was my reward for fetching water all week for the family. Papa had his men building sidewalks, dams, bridges, and schoolhouses. They dug wells and planted trees until he got sick and had to stop work. My father died of dropsy. Now they call it Bright 's disease or congestive heart and kidney failure. There was no money to pay for a doctor. Papa passed on in the town of Kansas, Oklahoma on July 2, 1936.

"How old were you then, sir?' asked a sailor on the ship.

"He left when I needed a father the worst. I developed into an obnoxious, headstrong delinquent.

"You, headstrong? the sailor said. *Impossible. Obnoxious? Well* ... The sailor socked my shoulder.

"I faked an injury and continued. *My three older brothers went to work at the CCC Camps, the Civilian Conservation Corps that President Roosevelt created to provide jobs and start the economy moving. The government required the workers to send twenty-five dollars a month home to their families. A total of seventy-five dollars a month fed, clothed and paid the rent for my mother and her ten children still at home. My older brothers had to live on five dollars a month in the camps.*

"Did you work?' asked another sailor.

"I tried to get a job in the CCC Camp but they wouldn't hire a kid without a birth certificate, I couldn't prove I was sixteen. Instead I worked in the woods logging for a dollar a day. The deputy sheriff gave me jobs in his mill because he was tired of coming after me every time I ran away from home.

"Mac, you were a juvenile delinquent before you were a petty officer? The men guffawed.

"I'm not proud of it. I'd slip out from the house at night and sleep near a service station on the highway. The next morning for five or ten cents, whatever they'd give me, I'd sweep their driveway. Then I'd buy bologna and crackers with the money and drink water and hitch down the road. The sheriff came all the way to Tulsa one time to get me. My older brother told me

the Navy was a good outfit. I ran away to get in, but found out I was too young. Each time the deputy hauled me home my mother took a crack at whacking me with that baseball bat. She was fast. I remember her yelling while she chased me. She said I was headstrong and needed a beating.

"*Did she ever catch you?* a muscular sailor said.

"I laughed and said, *Are you talking with me here?*

"The sailor was persistent. *Come on Mac. Did she ever hit you with that baseball bat?*

"*Just in the head,* I said. *That's why I joined the Navy.*"

CHAPTER 26

"Boredom enveloped the ship like a long day in a solitary confinement cell. The pall turned the men so jittery and quarrelsome, the captain ordered the cooks to add extra saltpeter to the corned beef and to replace the coffee urns with pots of soothing tea. The *Albemarle* floated beside the dock at Kwajalein Island for the rest of July, positioned for the second series of blasts, code named *Baker*.

"While we sat there doing holy work … pounding and chipping paint, with our feet hanging over the side, government scientists studied how radiation affected the animals that survived the first blast. They tracked emissions as they entered their bodies from the irradiated water, food and air. Fallout irritated the nose, throat and bronchi of the test animals. After dissecting dead dogs and goats, they determined radiation remained in the stomach and rectum of these animals longer, affecting the gastrointestinal tract severely, but also flowed into the blood and throughout the body. The scientists concluded it was possible that ulcers and perforations of the gut followed by death could be produced even without the animal experiencing any general effects from the radiation. I didn't learn this until years later because their findings were classified. I think the reason they weren't square with us was because they were not through with their guinea pigs.

"On July 25 of 1946, a twenty-three-kiloton gadget was unloaded into the water from the *Albemarle*, and lowered to the bottom of the atoll. Old *Able Mable,* our pet name for the ship, chugged nine miles away, anchored and had us on alert, waiting at the rails. The bomb detonated at 8:35 a.m.

"*Baker* rocked the ship, much like the previous bomb had. The base surge formed ten seconds after the blast and swept outward at forty-five miles an hour. The wall of water engulfed the majority of unmanned target vessels, as did its radioactive mist. *Able* had dulled us to the sights of the second burst, yet the destruction of ships was still stunning.

"*My god,* Bankston said, and checked his watch. *The Arkansas is standing straight up on its bow. Now it's sliding under. Did you see that, Mac?*

"The once great floating fortress roused from the sea and with a rush, slipped under, gaining its final fame. A hush fell over the crew, a natural salute for her accomplishments.

"Bankston glanced back at his wrist once the stern had disappeared. *One minute fifty-four seconds from the flash,* he said breaking the silence. *The old girl must have been rigged right to survive the* Able *blast.* He whistled a perfect wolf call. *Either her defense was down for the* Baker *shot or this gadget was a hell of a lot stronger than* Able.

"The *Carlisle* transport ship, the *Apogon* submarine and the *Saratoga* aircraft carrier sank without a whimper. We watched the shrinking black forms, a convoy that would never sail again.

"Drone aircraft flew by remote control through the clouds after the detonation. Unmanned boats penetrated the target area within two hours of the test.

"Another manned vessel sent divers down to view the location and destruction of sunken ships. When they surfaced the scuttle was that the *Arkansas* slept soundly on the bottom, upside down.

"The crew was not given decontamination procedures. Not one of us was required to shower or change clothes after being exposed to radiation until July 31, six days after the second of the two Bikini blasts. We just carried out our ritual holy work scrubbing the decks with buckets of sand.

"The *Albemarle* got underway after Operation Baker's work was complete. The captain set a course for Long Beach. The great ship groaned, grumbled about the fog and sliced through the tropical sea in silence. Tunneling below decks the scientists scrambled around like a swarm of ants. They studied the dead fish in the great ship's belly, tested samples of our blood and urine and drew charts and graphs.

"When we landed in Long Beach the radioactive animals were transferred to a medical lab. The building was near the hospital and had a *Classified* sign nailed above the door. Neighbors could hear the dogs bark and the goats bleat at night. They saw hospital personnel enter every day to feed the animals. Everyone else was instructed to stay away.

"The *Albemarle* embarked from Long Beach in December of '46 for the Panama Canal and on to the Navy Yard in Boston.

"It was a hell of a long rotation for me. I was one of the first to walk over the gangplank once we were moored to the pier. It was an overcast day. I remembered my mother praying for rain on days like that back in Oklahoma. I never much liked the rain. It seemed to put a damper on my plans. But, I wouldn't let superstition tarnish my mood. Freshly showered, shaved and starched, I bought Boston baked beans, sausages and sodas from a small shop near my girl's place. I let my-

self in with the key hidden behind her mailbox just as the weather hit. I checked her stocked refrigerator, hung my coat on a peg over her apron, and listened to the sound of rain bouncing off her tin roof. When I heard Carla turn her key in the lock, I was waiting on her couch, watching for the door to move.

"It blew open with such force the handle banged the inside wall. *I knew you'd be here.* She flew into my arms before I could stand. *I saw the ship dock in Charlestown Navy Yard this morning from my office window.* Both of us fell back in a full body embrace.

"I could feel every inch of her small frame melting into me. This was worth the long wait.

"When she caught her breath she said, *I couldn't concentrate. My boss told me I was no use to him so I might as well take the rest of the day off.*

"*Take it easy, little lady,* I told her. *Don't get too frisky. I've been at sea for seven months and I'm a little rusty at this.*

"*Oh, you!* she giggled and punched me in the chin. *I'll chip that rust off. Just give me two minutes.* She snuggled closer. Her arms enveloped me. *I've missed you so much. You've been on that ocean so long you must taste like saltwater. Come here. Let me have a bite.*

"*You're squashing me,* I laughed. *Slow down. Aren't you going to shut the door?*

"*I told my boss I wouldn't be in tomorrow, either. How long is your pass?*

"*Forty-eight hours.*

"*Not nearly long enough. We won't leave my bed.* She nibbled on my ear.

"*I brought lunch.*

"*Forget lunch.*"

CHAPTER 27

"We embarked from Guantanamo Bay, in Cuba, in November of '46. Admiral Holden, commander of the Atlantic Fleet, chose the *Albemarle* for his flagship to chase the Atlantic Fleet so he could observe training exercises. Holden wasn't the only big shot we reckoned with in the Caribbean that summer. Our seaplane tender had run afoul of Harry Truman twice by the time she reached Key West.

"The first time the president made life difficult for us was when the ship was docked in Norfolk, Virginia. Truman had just come back from South America on the *Missouri*. He treated that battleship, named after his home state, like it was his own private yacht. She moored beside us.

"My men were moving supplies from a barge when the order came from the bridge. 'All hands on the flight deck. Report in your dress whites and prepare to man the rails.' Sailors had to dress the ship, string flags and pennants, all because the president was on the next pier. We stood along the rails in our dress whites all afternoon enjoying the garden party until a limousine came alongside and took the commander-in-chief away. The skipper made every attempt after that fiasco to avoid waters cruised by Truman's favorite toy.

"The *Missouri* hauled heavy baggage because it was favored by Truman, and received a lot of publicity when the Japanese surrendered on the battlewagon's deck on September 2 of '45. When she ran aground in Norfolk within a hundred yards of the beach, she was the joke of the day for other lesser ships around the world."

"Excuse me, sir. Would you hold that thought? I'll be right back. I have to pee," I tell the old man, open the door and step outside. A mound of snow on top the car slides down the windshield and exposes a waning warrior with his head heavy on the headrest. I move through the whiteout, and feel my way to the back of the vehicle. After checking the tailpipe, I stand with my back to the falling snow, unzip my fly, and excrete a half a pot of coffee into a white drift.

"Still cold out there? You were telling me about Carla," I say, after I squeeze back behind the steering wheel. "You were a couple in Boston?"

"I'm getting there, David. That woman was a she-devil." The old man leans forward in his seat and continues.

"The *Albemarle's* second run-in with the commander-in-chief was when the seaplane tender sailed from Guantanamo Bay to Key West. So did President Truman. He trolled for fish not far from the Florida Keys on the presidential yacht, the *Williamsbury.* The crew stood by in their dress whites and manned the rails for the better part of another day watching the old man feed the fish. As soon as his yacht pulled away, the helmsman was ordered to plot a heading due north. We set off that same night to get out of the president's range and back to Boston."

"Carla uncoupled the chain on the door of her apartment, and surprised me before I could knock this time. She jumped into my arms and wrapped her legs around me. I carried her inside and kicked the door closed.

"Why all the extra security? I asked during a break in her kiss.

"I have a wonderful surprise, she said, and nuzzled my neck.

"Did you stick up a bank? I said, easing into a chair.

"Carla trilled a soft, rising, two-syllable *No,* and said, *stop that. What do you think you're doing?*

"*I'm looking for your weapon,* I mumbled with my nose between her breasts. *Did you buy me my very own bottle of ketchup?* I said and kissed her nipples.

"*Sailor, I'm pregnant, and we're having your baby.*

"I sat up. Naturally I was surprised, but hid my shock. I stood and twirled her around the room in my arms. *That's a wonderful surprise,* I said, set her down, tipped her chin up and looked into her eyes. Before I could say anything she told me what I needed to know.

"*Honey, when Mama and Daddy died during the Great Depression, I was the only one left in our entire family. I need this child, need a family, need to have a purpose in life larger than you and me.*

"I couldn't resist her, so I told her my career would keep me at sea for extended periods, and that if she was willing to do most of the upbringing, I would be willing to support them and help when I'm home.

"*How long is your leave?* she asked.

"*I have a twenty-four hour pass. Let's get married.*

"*We don't have time to get a license and wait three days if your ship sails tomorrow. We can do it on your next leave.* She glanced up at my expression. *Stop frowning and don't worry about me. I'll move in with Gwen. You know, my friend Gwen Thompson. I'll work as long as my doctor says I can, then just curl up and wait for you and the next president of the United States to arrive.*

"*Please, I don't need my commander-in-chief living with me. I'd have to salute him before and after I changed his diapers.* She shook with laughter. *I could smuggle you aboard the ship … and we could …*

"Carla unbuttoned my starched khaki shirt and slid it down my arms. I had a great body then, hard muscles from all the physical labor.

"*I'm trying to imagine what our son or daughter will look like,* she said, and slid her hand across my chest, like she was memorizing my contours. I carried her into the bedroom. That Carla. She was a devil."

CHAPTER 28

"Four months passed before we sailed the *Able Mable* back to the wharf in what I now called my Candy Town. I had wired Carla my ETA, estimated time of arrival in port a week before, along with a list of baby names for her to consider. I liked Matthew or Mark for a boy and Margaret or Mary if it was a girl. The ship was docked for minor repairs, so my commanding officer approved a five day leave. I rushed ashore half expecting to see my pregnant sweetheart waiting on the pier. When she wasn't there I bought some posies from a street vender and hailed a taxi. I was anxious to see my doll and tie the knot.

"I reviewed her last letter in my mind as the cab wound its way through Boston's busy streets. Carla had written the baby's ETA was less than six weeks away. That was two weeks ago. The taxi arrived at Gwen's address and I had the driver wait. Men aboard ship had cautioned me first babies were usually early. I was ready. I had big plans for the afternoon and evening and had made a flat rate deal with the cabbie. We would buy a ring and have dinner at a small Italian restaurant run by a retired Navy cook.

"No one answered the door at her apartment, yet the chimney was smoking. I left a note pinned to the cedar siding that said I could be reached aboard the *Albemarle*. The cabbie drove me to a nearby phone booth. I called Carla's work number. A surly voice informed me Carla had resigned a month ago.

"My misgivings jarred my certainties. I felt prickly all over as I got in the cab, and began to fidget. It was unusual for me to react like this. I was as healthy as a bull. My men had always described me as unflappable. I knew it wasn't nerves about the wedding. I looked forward to the small ceremony Carla had described in her letter. My mouth got dry. I had felt the same sensation the morning the last gadget had exploded in the South Pacific. Like it had then, my shirt soaked wet with sweat.

"The cabbie drove me to Massachusetts General Hospital where Carla had said she would deliver the baby. She wasn't registered. The nurse at the desk dialed two other hospitals in town. Carla wasn't on their radar screen. I was hamstrung with the lack of options, dumbfounded by where she and the baby might be, and baffled she had left without a message for me. I felt discouraged and desolate. There was one place I knew I could count on for solace, one place where I could think. The cabbie drove me back to the Navy Yard.

"I boarded the *Albemarle*, and a short, round man overtook me. He was what we called the ship's holy joe. The chaplain gave me a yellow envelope from Western Union. I ripped it open. *Dear Mac,* I read. My eyes flew to the bottom of the single sheet of paper and searched for the sender's name: *Gwen Thompson.* Oh my god, I said to myself, and wiped the sweat from my palm on the side of my pants. I felt like I was sinking in silt. Carla's posies dropped to the deck. I must have squeezed my eyes together to delay reading what I knew was bad news because the chaplain asked if I wanted him to read the contents.

"I shook my head and focused. The words leapt from the yellow paper. *Carla and baby dead.* My breath caught sideways in my chest. I couldn't exhale. My gut felt like the steel hull of a ship being ripped by reef coral. My knees buckled. The deck on the ship spun. I wiped my eyes on my shirtsleeve, staggered to grab the rail and careened close to the edge. The chaplain was beside me in an instant. He steered me to a bulkhead, and read the rest of the message to me. *Call Dr. Jamison at Massachusetts General. Stop. Sorry. Stop. I loved her too. Signed: Gwen Thompson.*

"*Son,* said the chaplain. *This is dated two weeks ago.*

"I lost the strength to stand and sagged to a stairway that led to the tower. The cartilage in my knees had become like jelly.

"*Sit down and put your head between your knees,* the chaplain ordered.

"I took my head in my hands. I was sick. I remembered Carla as healthy and full of life when I left her. I must have retched because the chaplain handed me his handkerchief to wipe my mouth. My thoughts raced. Women didn't die during childbirth in 1948. My mother had thirteen children, all born at home, and she was still alive and healthy.

"The officer put his hand on my shoulder. *You want to come below and talk?*

"I shook my head no. *I've got to get hold of that doctor.*

"*You have my permission to use the ship's phone.* The chaplain stepped aside and looked over the rail as I sat on the steel step, fighting tears. I willed my knees to hold and dragged myself across the gangplank. The ship's telephone was mounted to the pier. I dialed Jamison's number. His receptionist said to come right over, so I called for a cab. It was a short ride.

"*What?* I whirled around in the clinic when Doctor Jamison tapped my shoulder. My fists were clenched. I was a wreck. I had been pacing the doctor's small anteroom.

"*Sit down, young man,* the doctor said. *Your wife was in great shape and put up a good fight.*

"The word *shape* stuck in my mind. *You can be proud of her.* I staggered and the white coat caught my arm. He must have seen my grief. *You don't look like you're in such great shape. Why don't you take a chair?* He steered me to one. *Are you all right, son?*

"*The baby?*

"I'm sorry. The baby is dead. Your little boy was in bad shape. He wasn't in good enough shape to live. Has anyone in your family been misshapen with physical deformities?

"I shook my head no. The tide was turning and I had trouble staying focused.

"Have you been exposed to any unusual environments or chemicals? he asked.

"I thought it odd the doctor used the word *shape* so much. He used it over and over when he described Carla and my baby. The code name for nuclear weapons was *Shape.* I had a top-secret clearance. Anything having to do with *Shape* was classified. I had to avoid discussing anything associated with thermonuclear devices. *What does exposure to chemicals or unusual environments have to do with the baby or Carla?* I asked, avoiding his question.

"Your wife had a tough delivery. The baby was badly deformed.

"The baby wasn't normal? My thoughts whirled and surged. A hole opened in my heart like a well without a bottom.

"I've never seen a deformity that severe, Doctor Jamison said. *By the time the baby came your wife was weakened. Her heart gave out. After she died, the baby stopped breathing. We tried, but couldn't revive her.*

"How did this happen? Didn't she eat right? Don't you have pills for ...

"Yes, yes. She did everything right. I saw her every month. She was in great shape.

"The doctor babbled on but I didn't grasp what he was saying. I nodded absently when I thought I was expected to give a response. The scientists from Oakridge, Tennessee were right. Three rem of gamma radiation did have harmful effects on the human body and its progeny. There would be no safe harbor for sperm from servicemen involved in the nuclear tests. The atomic bomb killed more than fish and goats.

"I had learned more than I wanted to know listening to Oak Ridge scientists aboard the *Albemarle*. They were sure genetic damage could be caused by exposure to ionizing radiation. The particles of powder we inhaled aboard the ship, the thermonuclear lint that settled on our skin and in our hair, the radioactive dust in the air that landed on our food, all that unnatural soot would invade and change our cells. Sterility among sailors would be the least of our worries.

"*About your wife?* Doctor Jamison asked.

"*We weren't married.*

"*Can you give me the name of Carla's next of kin?*

"*She had no one but me.*

"I walked the streets of Boston until it grew dark. When I stepped aboard the *Albemarle* I was told the personnel officer was looking for me."

CHAPTER 29

"Admiral, are you warm enough?" It's after one o'clock. We're stuck on I-94 in what seems is the blizzard of the century with no heat.

"I'm okay," the old man says. "I don't suppose the weather is clearing." He shakes his head and continues with his tale.

"*It's time for you to dry out*, the yeoman told me. *Orders from the Pentagon have you next at Whidbey Island, Washington for a normal tour of shore duty. That's dry land for two years.* He smirked and punched my shoulder. *Don't get too comfortable and become a sand crab. After a year and a day they could transfer you.*

"I left my disappointment behind, packed my crumpled thoughts and caught an early train to Everett, Washington. A Navy station wagon met me on a Sunday morning. It took me by car ferry out to Whidbey Island in Puget Sound, off Seattle.

"I did get comfortable on that tour, real comfortable." The admiral closes his eyes, takes a deep breath and wraps his arms around his chest. He exhales enough CO_2 to steam a circle on the window beside him. A broad smile blooms amid his gray whiskers. He is remembering. The quiet presence of this dormant bear sobers me. We sit there in our snow-covered den for a long time in total silence before I become concerned and look for the next heave from his chest.

"Are you sure you aren't getting cold?" I say.

"I'm hibernating. You comfortable?"

"Quite comfortable," I say, relieved. I pull my coat collar around my ears. "Need some more money?"

"How about ten thousand until Tuesday?" His deadpan face is stifling a smile, his eyes are still closed.

"That's a piece of change, sir. Why ten big ones?" I say.

"… to bribe an FBI agent."

The whir of an engine purrs outside our windows curtained white with snow. As the vehicle draws near, the rumble becomes a deafening roar. His eyes blink open, and question mine. "Snowmobiles."

I stretch my twisted backbone straight. We have been confined too long. Our discomfort makes the diversion of conversation a necessity. Sleep is not an option. "Will you tell me the outcome of your move to the island near Seattle?"

"Might as well. Not enough room to foxtrot." He grins, and shuffles in his seat. "I became a master-at-arms on Whidbey Island. That's the Navy equivalent of sheriff."

"How old were you then?"

"Twenty-seven. My job had me patrolling the island with an old scoundrel, a captain with the National Guard. This old sea dog had a second job working on base as a civilian in the firehouse, and a third job selling cars. We worked out this arrangement where I supplied names of sailors looking for transportation, and when he made a sale, he slipped me a couple of jugs of whiskey. I squirreled the booze away, and brought it out when I went ashore for poker at the Eagles Lodge."

"You were twenty-seven and didn't drink?"

"I didn't say that. I didn't drink my fishing whiskey. This men's fraternal club met in a red brick building near the base. While the ladies gossiped upstairs in the lodge, the men retreated to the smoky basement to play poker. I uncorked a jug of my fishing bait and set it on the card table at the beginning of each game. We gambled and sucked our Lucky

Strikes down to stubs. I waited. When they were completely boiled, I cleaned them out."

Make a note, I thought: No card games with this shark.

"A soft-spoken deckhand who worked at the firehouse was at the poker game one night. He squinted through the haze and mumbled something about a rodeo the next day in Sedro and a nurse I should meet. *She could be just the woman for you,* he said.

"The guy was drunk, but I remember that moment like I remember my own name. He inhaled air through the cigarette that hung from his lips until the tip glowed red through the haze. *Come with me. I'll introduce you,* he said. The man tipped his head back and exhaled a plume of blue smoke across the table that reminded me of the exhaust on a '39 DeSoto a sailor friend of mine drove. That coupe backfired and belched fumes that left a smoke trail behind him a full block long.

"I had just been promoted to chief petty officer, and felt confident and cocky. So I began the day on July 4 of 1950 by watching the Sedro Rodeo's finest. The deckhand and I sat on the bleachers with a passel of workers from the local hospital. It was a nice sunny day. The smell of leather and animal manure permeated the air. My poker friend pointed to a woman in a group from the hospital wearing a dress the color of sunlight. We both walked over.

"*Hi!* I said to the nurse, and jettisoned the deckhand. This doll was candy to my eyes. Faye and I talked for two or three hours while the sturdy rigging of mutual attraction stretched my chest taut. We didn't notice when riders straddling bulls ass-bounced across the ring. Outside our bubble, the gyrations of broncos bucked cowboys into the dust. Over the taste of corndogs and the smell of fresh straw, I discovered the deckhand had been right: Faye was just the woman I had been looking for. She was a cook, a seamstress, a challenge to my intellect ... all the markings of a good wife. We walked to the nurse's quarters as the sun set, with me thinking she was the woman for me.

"At the door Faye told me she couldn't have children. I announced without hesitation, *That does it. I'm gonna marry you*.

"Without a cloud floating anywhere in the deep blue of her eyes, she said, *Sailor, you're nuts*, and walked through her door. I learned later Faye told her friends she had just met the hunk she would marry. I asked her to marry me each night for the next three weeks.

"Severe stomach cramps interrupted our courtship. Faye needed immediate gall bladder surgery. During the next week I went in to cheer and comfort her. I brought her a posy every day, told her sea stories and watched her laugh.

"Back at the base, Useless, the transfer yeoman, noticed me whistling while I worked. I wasn't the kind of guy that whistled while I did anything; I volunteered for the tough jobs, the responsible assignments that required concentration, the jobs that could further my career. Useless knew I was serious about getting ahead, and was curious about my unusual behavior. He suspected a woman might be responsible. He looked around and finally found me inspecting rigging on the foredeck.

"*Do you know the words to 'Anchors Aweigh?'* he asked, matching strides to keep up with mine.

"*Of course I know it*, I said and finished the inspection. *Every swabby in the Navy knows that song*. I skipped down the ladder to mess, grabbed some java and swung my leg over a bench near the reading rack. I thumbed through a magazine, and stopped every few pages to evaluate female flesh in the advertisements.

"The sailor caught up and took a seat on the bench across from me. He stirred sugar into his joe, replaced his spoon on the table, and grimaced at his first sip of the bitter brew.

"*Do you know the tune to 'Here Comes the Bride?'*

"*Everybody knows that song*, I said, and scratched the stubble on my chin. *What are you getting at, Useless?*

"*Mac, you better practice whistling 'Here Comes the Bride.'* The sailor handed me freshly typed orders from Washington, and laughed out loud. *When you finish that,* he giggled, *you can start on 'Anchors Aweigh.'*

"While the yeoman guffawed I fingered the orders. *What the hell are these?*

"*Your happy ass is going to Korea.*

CHAPTER 30

"I blamed that sailor for spilling coffee on my fresh uniform," Admiral McLaughlin says from his side of the snowbound car. I was shouting at the poor bastard and banging my fist on the table, yet I was the one who jumped and jarred the cup. *Look yeoman*, I argued as I sponged brown swill from my pants with a folded paper napkin. *I'm on shore rotation. That's shore duty*. I threw the crumpled paper on the table with such force it bounced off and hit the bulkhead. *Besides, I can't go to Korea. I'm about to get married*.

"*You've been here a year and a day*, Useless said with the authority of his job. He mopped the dark stain from his side of the table. *That's considered a tour of service and in the US Navy that means you can be transferred*.

"It was his job as yeoman to know the rules and type orders Washington wired the Navy base. I knew he was right. I rubbed my donkey-bristle crew cut so hard dandruff flecked my blue shirt. I rushed to arrange for liberty, shower and shave. I caught the first cab I hailed, and sailed up the highway to the hospital where I found my doll reading a book in her wheelchair in the sleepy hospital garden.

"*Now is the time*, I said after I'd kissed her. *I'm on my way to Korea. It's either yes or no.*"

"Faye thought for a moment. *Go get the judge*, she said.

"It didn't take long to clear the deck for a wedding. We didn't have flowers and Faye didn't have a special dress. We did have what I considered good company, a bunch of beautiful dolls, Faye's colleagues. My bride was lying in bed throughout the ceremony in her hospital gown. She had a tube hanging out of her stomach draining the infection. I was in hog heaven in that room full of nurses. I stayed with Faye on our wedding day until the hospital staff kicked me out. Then I caught a ride to my new ship, the *Cape Esperance*, CVE-88.

The name of the ship causes a shiver to run down my spine. "What does that abbreviation CVE mean?" I ask.

"Combustible, vulnerable and expendable."

When I don't return his smile he shrugs and says, *The Cape Esperance was a small aircraft carrier, a Casablanca class escort carrier. She had a hundred-thousand ton displacement, a length of five hundred twelve feet three inches and a beam of a hundred and eight feet. She was the eighty-eighth Jeep carrier out of that shipyard.*"

My father had printed *Cape Esperance* and those initials on one side of the toy ship he carved for me. On the other side he wrote another name, the *Rendova*. My skin prickles as I remember his explaining how he got his bad arm. It was during a typhoon off Torpedo Junction on the *Rendova*. That was his last ship before … my heart pounded … the last ship before something happened that resulted in his dishonorable discharge from the Navy. "Did that ship ever sail in a place called Torpedo Junction?" I say to the admiral.

The old man smiled, remembering. "That narrowing of the shipping lane off the Solomon Islands and Esparto Santo was a favorite haunt for enemy subs. Most ships en route to the Indian Ocean from the South Pacific passed that graveyard. Why? You hear that name in an old war movie?"

Slow down, I tell myself. There's plenty of time for the personal. Keep this professional. "Why would you want to marry a woman who couldn't have children?" I ask.

"Because I was damaged goods. I knew I shouldn't have children. Not after Carla."

"How long before you saw Faye again?"

"A week later the doctors turned Faye loose. I took her to see the ship. We found a place in town to live because she was still rehabilitating. We were together five days before I took her home to Mt. Vernon, Washington, where she lived before we were married. I called her from the ship every day as we refitted the *Cape Esperance*.

"A few days later Faye's sister-in-law answered her phone. My wife was back in the hospital with a relapse. I asked for an emergency family leave and was granted twelve hours. It was enough to dash up to see her. Faye would be okay, but had to stay in the hospital several more days.

"*Let me look at you,* I said when it was time for me to return to the ship. My senses were keen. I extracted every bit of information my eyes and time allowed, committing to memory the look in her eyes while I held her, and filling myself with her fragrance. *I won't see you for a long time.* I kissed her, and memorized the sweet taste of her lips. *This has to last me for a while.* I tore myself away and caught a cab back to the ship. The *Cape Esperance* embarked at midnight.

CHAPTER 31

"On July 1 of 1950, US naval forces carried out a blockade of North Korea as part of the United Nation forces," Admiral McLaughlin tells me as I adjust the steering wheel so I can move my numb leg. "The *Cape Esperance* kept her crew busy ferrying planes back and forth across the Pacific: hauling shot-up carcasses back to San Francisco, and carting new ones over. We lugged crews back and tugged crews over as far as Africa. The action in that part of the world lasted until 1953 when fighting stopped and the nuclear-fed Cold War began.

"Faye's letters came once a week. I read them over and over until the mail plane brought the next batch. I wrote what news I could. *Dear Faye, There was a mishap today that involved a loose ordnance. I was promoted to second lieutenant. I will be transferred to the Rendova. Until I hold you in my arms, I send my love. Jim*"

I hold my hand up to stop the story. I am no closer to uncovering my father's secret than when McLaughlin told me he was first assigned to his last ship. "Were you ever transferred back to the *Cape Esperance?*"

"Back and forth. Forth and back. We never knew where they would slot us or send the ship next. It seemed like we sailed on the swell of the wind," he says. "Planes catapulted from the escort carrier were spying on Russian warships off the coast of Korea. The *Rendova* sailed down the coast from Korea to the Marshall Islands. The flattop's orders were to give air cover and prevent Russian planes from spying on US operations. A few months later the floating city reversed its course and cruised up the coast of Asia and back to Korea for more espionage work.

"On this tour airplanes that my crew launched laid rockets filled with napalm on the Red Chinese, the bad guys at that time. Orders were to fly in, assault, insert and withdraw. Marine planes dumped the burning goop on North Koreans who hid below in thickets. Opposition soldiers on the ground ran out of the brush with their asses on fire, and threw themselves in the snow. The men kicked and rolled and flopped, and tried to put the fires out. Napalm would burn right through a man."

"That must have been horrible to see, horrible to be part of," I say, and grimace.

"Ever hear of Ted Williams?"

"… the baseball player?" I feel like I am on *Wheel of Fortune*. "Why?"

"He was also a fighter pilot, a major player," the old officer says. "He flew with the 223rd, the Tomcat Fighter Squadron. He was part of the horror just like I was aboard the USS *Rendova*. Pilots returned from their missions and reported what they saw."

"Did the pilots boast about burning people alive?" I ask, still distressed at the image of humans roasting and rolling in the dirt to smother sticky napalm.

"Our flyboys took no pleasure in the killing, David. None of us did. It was a nasty business. It was our job, what we had to do. You couldn't let that bother you in the service. If you let it get to you, you went to pieces, and got a one way ticket home." The former officer stretches his legs and takes a drink of cold coffee. "You learned to keep your mind elsewhere when the mission was a go, like when the pilots tried hitting the running lights aboard the *Rendova*." He scratches his white beard. "The men played this game on fly-aways to relieve tension."

"Your men destroyed government property on purpose?"

"Sure. It worked like this. A colored light was mounted two inches above the flattop on the forward corner of the flight deck, starboard side. The green light signaled oncoming ships what side of the ship they were on. We were flying F4U's, gull-winged fighters. Pilots tried to knock the signal light off with their right wheel when they took off during daylight hours. My crew on the flight deck threw five bucks apiece into a kitty to give to the first pilot to knock it off.

"I had that light repaired two or three times out of hundreds of fly-aways, then I had it lowered. When the word got out it had been moved, the flyboys became surly. I remember a lieutenant who had already spent the money he was trying to win. He called me a chicken-shitted bastard, on my good days." The old man grins. "That's the kind of distraction we needed to keep the killing off our minds." A frown forms between his eyes when he sees my expression.

"Worse than napalm were the *Lazy Dogs*. We hauled ten thousand tons down to Vietnam aboard the *Ranger* in '64 and used them on Vietnamese troop concentrations. Navy flyboys delivered them from single-engine piston slammers, the AD6 Intruders, out of the Gulf of Tonkin off the North Vietnamese coast. Those birds were the best airplanes made. They could haul heavy bomb loads with a single engine. We hung twelve *Lazy Dogs* on each plane, six under each wing."

"How could anything be worse than napalm burning people alive?" I ask.

McLaughlin exhales and his voice drops in pitch. When he speaks his words stretch flat in a monotone. "Each of those rockets carried a thousand, thirty-caliber slugs. Each slug had fins as sharp as razor blades. The weapon was inert, carried no explosives. The *Lazy Dog* broke open on impact, spun, and chewed anything in its path to pieces." He turns his head away, and stares through the snowflakes.

I can't help it. I am speechless, sickened. I visualize myself hanging below the wing of an Intruder. I am the *Lazy Dog* that twirls through the sticky, tropical heat, and bursts on impact with a banyan tree. I am the *Lazy Dog* that gives birth to thirty menacing delinquents. I am the razor blade that whirls and slices though the thatch on a roof, water buffalo, a young boy …

The old man's gaze moves back inside the car. "The Navy shared airplanes … David?" He sees me with my head down and my arms braced on the steering wheel. "Son?" He leans over and touches my shoulder.

I jump. My head snaps towards him.

"Your face is pale, David. Are you okay?" He pauses. "Your thoughts sailed someplace. Was it a woman that swept you away?"

"No. Not a woman," I say eager to come back to the safety of this bizarre snow den, back to the comfort of this Michigan freezing blizzard, back to 2007. "Keep talking."

"Okay, but you do look green around the gills. As I was saying, the Navy shared airplanes with the Marines. During the Korean War when the Air Force needed help, they called on us. The Air Force's …"

My mind slips away from his story, again. The image of a slug of polished steel chewing through a woman's thigh comes slashing and bleeding through my thoughts. The woman's thigh is my girlfriend's. I can't control the image of those razors whirling their warning, can't make them go away, and can't stop the shredding of flesh. I am having a daylight night-scare like the old man's bad dreams. I am sweating.

"… high-powered jets couldn't get low enough to bust up the tunnels, the bridges or the rail road engines. The planes moved too fast."

I sit up straight and blink. Focus, lug head, I tell myself. Calm the storm in your guts. You may miss something important, or he might clam up.

"That's when the AD6 piston slammers came in handy," he says. "We used the Intruders in Vietnam, too." The old man must have seen my distress in the driver's seat. "This too heavy for you, son?"

"No. I'm good. Did Faye write you during this time?"

"She wrote me twice a week, every week I was away from her."

The old man's look says he understands my sudden change in subject. He must know the horror is too much for me. Does he think I am weak? I wonder. Am I?

"A mail plane delivered at least once a week to ships deployed anywhere on the globe, unless the ship was on a classified operation."

"Did you write her?" I take a deep breath. I am back.

"Sure. Sometimes she recorded tapes and sent them. I could hear her voice. Corny's too. I recorded tapes for her."

"How did ..."

"I checked out a battery-powered tape recorder," the old skipper says, "and headed down to warhead storage."

"Nuclear warhead storage?"

"The hold was off limits for everyone but the few on board with the need to know. It was a small armored cubbyhole in the center of the ship where fuses for the torpedoes were kept, where no one would disturb me, where I could listen to her tapes and record mine for her.

"In the most dangerous place on board?"

CHAPTER 32

"What was it like at sea when you were aboard the *Rendova*?" I stretch, and shift in the bucket seat to get my blood moving. I feel nothing when I wiggle my toes, and my ass is numb. I'm thinking about the daily routine my father must have liked. If he was in the Navy for seven years, he must have served more than one hitch. "How did you pass the time at sea?"

"While the ship wandered around the ocean, we worked, we drank coffee, and we starved," the admiral says. "The *Rendova* was a small carrier. Refrigeration units for fresh food were limited. We would be at sea for thirty days and in for ten. After two weeks at sea all the fresh vegetables and meat were gone. We had to get along on beans and rice. I bought a can of sardines at the ship store every night, and dumped it on my rice before I ate it. When I left Faye and Corny for Korea I weighed a hundred ninety-six pounds. When I returned seven months later I weighed a hundred forty-six. Faye saw me and said, 'Ye Gods. I gave them a man and I got back a bag of bones.'

"What did the other men look like?"

"Skinny skeletons that shook and shivered." When he raises his eyebrows his cheeks pull his face into a broad grin.

Something is odd about his looks. "What's different about your mouth?"

"Like my new choppers?" he says, and turns his head left, right. He clicks them together. "Pretty good match with my original equipment. Drove my Harley over yesterday and had the bridge installed. I found a painless dentist in town. He advertises he caters to cowards."

"Did he check your spark plugs too?" I ask. The temperature in the car is dropping.

McLaughlin lowers his chin and cranks his head toward me. "David Dugan, I do believe you are growing a sense of humor. Good work, son."

"I understand you were quite a gambler," I say to change the focus back to him.

The old man glances at his outstretched hand. "I used to wear a ring right here." He rubs the middle finger on his right hand. "It belonged to my grandfather. I didn't always win. It doesn't matter that I can't pass the ring along to my son. Thanks to atomic science, the McLaughlin military tradition stops with my blood." He shifts his weight. "I haven't played poker in years. When we were at sea for long periods we played cards for amusement. A big night for me now is watching CNN. Why do you ask, David? Got some money you want to lose?"

I shake my head *no*. I had never gambled in my life. The thought of playing poker made me uncomfortable, especially on the meager salary the FBI paid a beginning agent.

"When I was your age I let myself get pulled into payday poker games for reasons other than recreational," the admiral says. "My mother still had six children at home and no source of support. Once I went home on leave and found that my younger brother, Peewee, had sold my old clothes to buy textbooks. Without books he couldn't go to high school.

"The government had a plan to help families whose breadwinners were in service during the war. The US treasury matched up to half the amount a serviceman sent home each month. My poker earnings were my spending money. Half my salary went into the bank. The other half was matched by the government and sent home to Oklahoma. That helped keep my family going for nine years. I throw the dice every day I get out of bed. FBI agents do too."

"What do you mean?"

McLaughlin nodded. "When I was twenty-one I had to sort out my career. I was furious at being washed out of flight school by a Navy surgeon because I had a deviated septum. I blamed the surgeon for my failure for the next two years. Then I got a bloody nose aboard a jet thirty thousand feet over Japan. I couldn't get the bleeding stopped. That bastard was right."

"And?"

"Washouts like me were plopped into the Amphibious Forces where the probability was high we would die. We all knew it was a risky job, but didn't have a choice.

"Amphibs teamed with Marines and Seabees. We were first to land on the Marshall Islands still under Japanese control. Marines went in first to secure the beaches. Seabees followed, brought equipment in on landing craft and built airstrips with crushed oyster shells. Amphibs followed the Seabees ashore to take care of the airplanes. We hauled fuel ashore in fifty-five gallon drums and stored it in makeshift hangars we rigged and covered with camouflage nets. When planes landed we repaired them, refueled them, and sent them back up.

"Japanese who still occupied the islands hunted us like we were ground birds. The odds of staying alive were not good. Their snipers lashed themselves to treetops. I only stopped one bullet. We joked among ourselves that the Japs welcomed us with bloody hands and hospitable graves.

"Japanese soldiers witnessed or heard about the brutality of our bombing raids on their cities. We bombed Tokyo in 1945 with jellied gasoline, creating firestorms that killed over a hundred thousand. The napalm burned out sixteen square miles of their capital. It charred and buried innocent people alive in collapsed buildings. Then the *Enola Gay* dropped the bomb on Hiroshima that killed seventy thousand. I'm not surprised they showed no mercy when they captured Americans.

"Their soldiers doubled-down the stakes on soldiers they captured. They skewered unlucky boys on green bamboo poles.They cut their privates off,stuffed them in their mouths, then planted the post in the jungle where we would find them.

"These are the memories that haunt me, David, keep me from sleeping,and give me the chills that last for days."

"What was the worst ship you ever served on?"

"No contest. I served twenty-four months on the *Boxer* ... from January of 1955. It was hands down the worst duty of my career."

"Why was that?"

"The skipper. He worked the crew long hours with little sleep.The man was lethal on morale. He would stand on the bridge watching us work while he gulped down black coffee and rolled one cigarette after another.He would smoke them down to the butt, flip them into the sea, then come down from the bridge to say terrible things about my men ... in front of them.

"The men threw dice every day they spent ashore. The *Boxer* was docked in Japan in 1955. A fine young man, a steward's mate,fell for a girl from Sapporo.He spent his leave with her up there on the island of Hokkaido.They both went to see her doctor before he left to come back to the ship.The doctor said he needed a big dose of penicillin.Do you know what Wild Root Cream Oil is,David?"

"Ah, it's a hair dressing,gives a slicked down,greasy look. I think my stepdad uses it."

"Do you know what it looks like,David?"

"Sure. It's white,like a lotion."

"Right. Well, her family's Japanese doctor gave him a big dose of Wild Root Cream Oil instead of penicillin."

"A doctor did that?" I flinch, and remember my stepdad's strong scent. "Did it kill him?" The inhumanity of the doctor's revenge sickens me. And the smell of my dad will never be the same.

"They brought his body back to the ship." The old man clears his throat. "My friend, the ship's doctor, did the autopsy and confirmed the cause of his death."

"Excuse me." I scramble to get the door open, and barely have my head out when I vomit. I rinse my face with cool snow, and wonder if I'll be able to sleep tonight.

"You don't have much of a stomach for violence for an FBI agent," he says after I settle back inside. "That's a good thing. That Japanese doctor wasn't alone in injecting deadly chemicals into American sailors while the world was at peace.

"Hazel O'Leary, from the US Department of Energy, came clean during a press conference on December 7, 1993. She announced that human experiments had occurred in which the Department of Defense injected plutonium into its service men and women."

CHAPTER 33

"My grandmother told me stories about how they planned to survive during the Cold War when the Russians bombed us," I tell the admiral. The temperature inside the car is tolerable, as long as we stay bundled in our coats. We have been stranded here on I-94 for over three hours, a half-hour without heat. If the plows don't free us soon, the old warrior and I will freeze. "While you loaded nuclear warheads aboard … what was the plane's name?"

"The B29 was called *Big Stink*, but in 1946 when it was assigned to Operation Crossroads, they renamed it *Dave's Dream*."

"That's funny. While you were blowing islands into nuclear dust in the South Pacific, my grandmother built a bomb shelter in Boston, Massachusetts. While you watched mushroom clouds, my stepdad helped stock a six-month supply of canned food along the shelves of their reinforced and enlarged backyard root cellar. While you were being fried by radiation, he shook out moths and aired blankets, performed a monthly check on the shelter's flashlight batteries, and wrote long letters to his father. My step-grandfather was out on a ship somewhere, but on the other side of the world. Grandma told me my father's school had atomic bomb drills. The whole nation lived in perpetual fear."

"That hasn't changed," the admiral says. "But the way we fight war has changed. It had to after WWII and Vietnam's body counts.

"Protests pressured Washington to find another way. During Desert Storm we fought a war by remote control, like one of those electronic games my grandson plays with his thumbs. We watched the killing on TV. Then the enemy changed.

"In Afghanistan they fought our technology successfully with rifles from mountain caves. The opposition changed into extremists who learned our weaknesses, then exploited them. It's not one country's democracy versus another's communism anymore. It's radical Islam against the world. These tribal nations have suddenly become oil rich. Their governments are dysfunctional. It's a place where monarchs, bloated with wealth, rule a population that is thirty percent unemployed. And they're hot as hell. It's the mullahs who pull the culture backwards as the Internet and the information age push it forward. They train murderers to use suicide as the weapon of choice against innocents.

"The rules by which we fought wars are obsolete. What hasn't changed is the threat of nuclear holocaust."

I shift in the car so I can see the old man's face. "My grandma told me when she was in school atomic bomb drills were like training for a fire evacuation, only the children stayed in their classrooms. The teachers had them sit under school desks and cover their heads with their arms. I wonder what they tell kids these days."

His face is expressionless. "Young people know after the first nuclear explosion we will all die. I think they see it as inevitable. Life has become cheap. These kids shoot fellow students while they study in school libraries or go to movies."

I stroke my jaw. Governments are like families when it comes to leveling, to telling the truth and dealing with reality. When the facts are out on the table, the comfortable world of disbelief disappears. My mother stopped talking about my father after his death, it was like she rubbed him from her memory with one of those soft gum erasers I used in school.

"David, are you still with me?" the old man says. "Don't fall asleep on me. You'll freeze."

"My blood-caffeine level is too high for sleep. I'm all ears."

"During the Cold War the Department of Defense readjusted the public's focus so they wouldn't think about the terror. They kept the reality of an attack quiet, and didn't announce that if we were nuked, the people in the target zone would have a quick death from the concussion, and those a few miles away would have a slow death from the radiation. Instead, they told Americans they needed more tax money to build mega-weapons to protect them. Fear of a nuclear attack haunted our country. People needed to be convinced there was hope, so they listened and believed the lies. The government's public relations people were brilliant.

"Scientists saw death from radiation as inevitable for us all if we were hit, yet they didn't know how soon death would come, or, in some cases how painfully slow. That's why the Atomic Energy Commission got congress to fund experiments on the healthiest lab rats they could find: young, healthy men and women serving their country. Testing would be done far away from large concentrations of population on ships in the South Pacific.

"After a while congress complained about the transportation expense to the other side of the world. The Department of Defense moved the tests to Nevada, Arizona, New Mexico and Utah. People trusted their leaders in those days."

One lie collects another. I remember the day of my father's funeral. A white worm curled through the flesh of a fish I found at the edge of the pond. More pale coils crawled from the mud and spiraled into the untouched flesh on the fish head as I watched.

Buried memories wriggle from pods deep inside my mind, poking my reality. The entire day of my father's funeral should have been sucked up in a time warp and no one would have missed it. When we returned from the mortuary, adults stood whispering in our front room. I remember being confused about why they had to whisper, and wondered what the big secret was. They all knew my father was dead.

My parent's egg-shell-white friends watched my every move while they stuffed their mouths with pink ham layered thick on soft white bread. Pity emptied from their eyes while they sucked down curled white macaroni heaped on paper plates and stared vacantly at one another. Complete strangers tiptoed through the kitchen, eating molded Jell-O salad with bloated marshmallows until their cheeks bulged. They held conversations that hushed as soon as my mother or I appeared. My stomach churns now just remembering.

I recall the feeling that I couldn't take one more silent hug or poison pat on my head. I remember running past the screen door into the dusty sunset to escape the silence. The door slapped hard against the clapboard siding. The sound caused long lines of dust to puff from cracks between the boards. The clap caused stirring and then movement from the crowd.

People droned on among themselves in hushed tones as they cleared out, but became animated as soon as they left the porch and padded into the darkness. Conversations exploded, grew raucous. I heard laughter on the gravel road not three feet from where I hid behind the cattails. The din faded when the chattering stopped and a vacuum of silence formed. The calm was replaced by the sawing sounds of katydids. Lightning bugs blinked a natural peace. Lamps in my bedroom beamed light through my window. Between slender stalks I stared at my mother through her bedroom window. She was looking at her bureau mirror while she brushed her hair.

A familiar dragging sound on the road broke the hush of nature's music. A bowed, withered woman emerged from the shadows, my nursemaid. She inched up our steps, her lame foot lagging, then tapped on the sash. I heard our screen door scrape open, and Mother's footstep on the porch. When she called for me I crept through the cattails toward my one remaining parent.

At the doorway I thought of the words men had used to describe her at the funeral ... a real babe, a nice piece of ass, and a lonely widow that could use some comfort. I wondered what they meant. Mother's cheerful energy was missing, sucked empty by the maggots that had just left. She instructed my caregiver, finished tying her apron behind her back, and nodded to me.

"I'll be home after work, Davey," she said as though this day was like any other. "Do your homework and brush your teeth before bed."

All that was left in that silent house was the smell her starched apron left on the ironing board, the buzz of the refrigerator cooling Jell-O leftovers, and the brittle creaking of the old lady's bones. That day made up the first film of lies that would become, over time, thick layers of family deceptions.

I laugh to myself when I think about how naturally my mother's training channeled my future into the counterespionage field. Colleagues at the agency refer to themselves as a wilderness of mirrors. I understand.

"Our fleet made a big show of working with United Nation forces in the Northern Hemisphere," the admiral says, as his story spins on like the screws on his ships. "We continued to test bombs in the Marshall Islands. I worked with the patrol squadrons of VP-47s that flew off the beach in Iwakuni, Japan, and off the aircraft carrier the USS *Rendova*. Our planes photographed Russian warships. We weren't told why. We figured they were looking for a buildup of the Russian fleet, expanded missile capabilities or Russian nuclear submarines.

"We worked together on the flight deck for seven months and two days catapulting the VP-47s airborne, guiding them home with the ship's radar, and catching them with the arresting gear to prevent their dumping in the black waters off the coast of Korea.

"The *Rendova* received orders from Washington in '51 to leave the Asian peninsula and head for Long Beach to load a special package. We would be gone a month. The topic was classified, but we deduced the package waiting for us in

Long Beach would be another platoon of scientists in white coats complete with pocket protectors, and another fat gadget, filled to overflowing with enough explosives to blow us all to kingdom come."

My thoughts career from the admiral's story and ricochet off the walls of my childhood memories. I recall the feel of riding astride impending disaster, only mine wasn't at sea and it lasted a lot longer than a month.

I waited for the explosion all through junior high and high school. The buildup started after the last of the funeral flowers were thrown into the trash behind the garage and my mother had retreated to her room. I was quiet for a while puzzled by her grief. Whenever I entered a room, she rose and retreated to her private space.

I became caught up in her reactions, felt scared, guilty and developed an occasional tic in my left eye. My stomach grew fragile. Endless afternoons alone sapped my energy. I yawned like crazy. I thought these bouts of heavy fatigue and fear might go away one day, but they grew worse. A weary pain throbbed through the external parts of my ears. I was miserable. More than anything I wanted to get away from Mother.

"What's biting you, Davey?" she asked.

That afternoon I threw stones and broke every window in our garage. When she saw the wreck I'd made she hauled me out of bed, screaming. It was always about money. She said more than she needed to say and then my only wish was that she or I would disappear. I ran from the house, and slammed the screen door so hard I broke the closer. I hid in the cattails by the pond where I had a terrifying fantasy she would hang herself beside my father and I would never see her again. I remember my knees shaking and feeling dizzy.

Later that afternoon I made my way up through the scrub and found her counting change at the kitchen table. She still had her apron tied around her. It was stained, wilted and had sagged. I told her I was sorry I broke the windows. I apologized for slamming the screen door, for leaving Dad's funeral party, and for playing outside while he was killing himself inside the garage.

There was a moment of deafening silence. I felt as if I had stabbed her with a dagger. Then her voice came back, familiar and angry. It was like she had not heard. She spoke at length about this and that, but never again about my father. I never mentioned my feelings of guilt after that. But my heart grew another layer of hardened skin, like the callus on the side of my big toe.

"David?" the admiral says.

"Yes"

"You're dozing. Are you giving up?"

"No. I'm listening."

"Scientists from Los Alamos boarded the ship in Long Beach. Crates marked with purple circles were loaded aboard the *Rendova* and lashed to the hangar deck. Symbols marked the crates as radioactive materials. No one needed to tell the helmsman the new heading would be south by southwest. We scythed our way through the sea toward the Republic of Marshall Islands, a spray of twenty-three islands, twenty-five hundred miles north of New Zealand. The ship would join a task force at Eniwetok Atoll to witness two simultaneous atomic blasts: one to detonate three hundred feet in the air off a tower, a second to blast-off ninety feet underwater. Many of the men had witnessed earlier shots in '46 and '48 and thought they knew what to expect.

"*Strap your belt to an upright*, the officer of the deck ordered from under the long bill of his cap. *There's no way of telling when or how the wave surge will hit us.* The bomb, code named *Dog*, exploded on April 7 of 1951.

"*I expected a quick flash,* a sailor beside me said, *but the white light filled the sky. Something must have gone wrong. It looks like the whole world has gone up in flames.*

"The tower shot didn't snap and boom until a full minute-and-a-half after the burst. Then we heard an enormous crack that vibrated our inner ears. The sound was followed by the terrifying rumbling of what had to be man-made thunder.

"*Hold on for your life,* I warned the sailor next to me. The water wrinkled. A gush of hot air hit the ship, heating the steel plates. Warmth from the blast was intense. We danced on deck to keep our feet from burning, and covered our faces to protect our eyes.

"The eighty-one-kiloton underwater blast snapped and growled low like an angry grizzly. Walls of water circling ground zero came at us with a vengeance. The sea chopped and pitched the ship starboard. We could see a low roaring eddy edge towards us. The water was an odd color. White light emerged from somewhere below and we could see pieces of coral underwater, pulverizing as the vibrations ripped outward. The postcard blue sea grew gray. The *Rendova* sped ahead at top speed, her heart-sucking engine racing without rest. A second surge overtook us, lifting the aft deck until the screws came out of the water, rocking her in her own wake.

"Men watched and pointed as winds unexpectedly shifted. A brilliant, tumbling purple cloud, black with radioactive dust, headed for us. We were downwind from the mass, crashing through choppy seas.

"*Hard right two four zero* shouted the skipper in an attempt to escape. *Correct course, two six zero.* The helmsman checked the compass and whirled the wheel. *No good. The cloud is catching us. Can you get any more speed out of this tug?* he shouted.

"Top speed wasn't good enough and the churning gray cloud overtook us nine miles off shore, blocking the sun and covering the ship in gritty, gray ash, and small broken bits of white coral. After five seconds the darkness lifted and the sky and air were filled with a purple glow. The tower shot hauled an estimated two hundred fifty tons of Eniwetok soil to an altitude of thirty-five thousand feet. We were showered with radioactive fallout.

"*That was the greatest thing I've ever seen,* said a sailor standing near me. He was covered in ash, and bent to retrieve a souvenir stone. He fingered it in his palm before slipping it into his pants pocket.

"*Clean up this mess,* ordered the skipper through teeth clenching a stubby cigar.

"*Break out the hoses. Douse this dirt off the deck,* ordered the second officer.

"*Drop that stone,* I told the sailor. *Don't you know what a radioactive hazard is?*

"*No, sir,* he said. The young man felt around for the piece of coral in his pocket, and pitched it into the sea.

"The cloud tumbled over other ships, pelted them with stones, and blackened their decks with dust. Officers had learned from earlier tests and ordered their men to shower and change clothes to prevent radiation sickness.

"Even after we had washed down the decks, we were swimming in radiation. Most of the radioactive particles were so small they could be inhaled or swallowed without a person knowing. We walked around with fallout in our hair. Radiation came down on the food as we stood in the mess line. What we didn't know until years later was that the official government policy was not to warn personnel to protect ourselves."

The admiral's image of those hungry men as they stood in line, waiting for a generous helping of what would eventually kill them, reminded me of a food line in Boston not long after my father's funeral.

I remembered the stuffed shrimp at my mother's second wedding. I hated Mr. Dugan, her new husband. He made such a big deal over me ... wanting me to play golf with him, playing catch in a park, taking me along with Mother and him to the movies, to dinner. He was fattening me up for the kill.

I was highly suspicious and certain my food was sprinkled with poison. I refused to eat the plate that stared at me from where I was seated at the head table at their wedding reception.

When dessert came, I switched cake plates with Mr. Dugan, and waited for the poison to work. For this man who had so easily won the attention of my mother, to feel a sudden pain tweak his stomach, for this person who was to be my new father, to collapse in his own wedding cake, face down, for this man I felt no compassion. His funeral would be large because he was important. I would laugh and joke with everyone, console my mother and assure her she could depend on me to take care of her. It would be just the two of us again. If only ...

I remember Mother interrupting me as I forked my cake around on my plate. *Davey, you're smiling. Having a good time, honey?* She rubbed my back. *Your new father and I leave tonight for a trip.* I set the fork down and gave her my full attention. A more complicated life was erupting around me. *Let's go for a walk.*

"*Your caretaker will stay with you until we get home*, she said as we passed through the door. *Then we will move to a proper house with a nice yard.* She smiled. *I want you to forget about playing by that stagnant pond, and that dilapidated garage. You will go to a new school where everyone will know you as David Dugan because your new dad is adopting you. He has always wanted a son of his own. Soon you will be his legal heir. Isn't that wonderful?*

It was around that time that I began to understand I was a separate and different person from my mother, with my own unique way of being in the world. I liked hiding in the cattails. I liked being alone in the dark garage. Well, she could change my name and my address. She could move me to one of those neighborhoods she always talked about, one of those pristine places where in the summer heat sprinklers arched the same rainbows in yard after yard and everybody said *Good morning*. She could distance me from all that I had been until then, all my unseemly influences, but, she couldn't change me.

"Does that make you happy? she said. I listened because I thought it was what she wanted, but didn't answer. *It makes me happy,* she said after a long pause. Her face grew sober. *You will not die in a rundown garage like your father. You will not die in a blood-spattered bedroom like your grandfather. You will have a decent man to pattern your life after, by god. You will have a chance.* I didn't question or contradict her, nor did I fight back. But I remembered this new information. My granddad had blown his brains out. The men in my family kill themselves.

"Gadgets exploded from forty-five to two hundred twenty-five kilotons over the next three months," the admiral says from his side of the cold car, his mind in the warm South Pacific. "The bursts were treated like normal Fourth of July fireworks by the men. They compared the height of the mushroom shaped clouds and the wave surges. They were annoyed when debris dropped on the ship because it meant extra work.

"Radio-controlled drones flew through every mushroom cloud from Operation Greenhouse. They landed on island runways where the plane's air filters were removed for tests by the scientists, then washed down with water from the lagoon by sailors from other ships. Filters were replaced and planes were strapped to a barge. The flatboat was towed to the *Rendova.* I hoisted the unmanned airplanes aboard with the crane and secured them on the port corner of the foredeck. Orders were to stay clear of the target area. The scientists were aboard, again. We cruised back to Long Beach, then holidayed off the coast of Korea until late October of 1952.

"The first test used the boosting principle. It was to be exploded on November 1 of 1952, back in the warm waters of Eniwetok Atoll. The *Rendova* was invited to the party, code named Operation Ivy, where the entertainment was a ten point four megaton thermonuclear explosion. The fusion bomb furnished a thousand times more power than the fission bomb and was witnessed by nine thousand three hundred fifty military and twenty-three hundred civilian personnel.

The old man explains how bombs created craters over a mile across. "The last one vaporized an entire island. Between July of 1945 and September of 1992, the US detonated one thousand thirty-two atomic and hydrogen bombs over or under five states, two oceans and one foreign nation during wartime ... Japan. The bombs were exploded under water, in underground tunnels, on the ground, in the air, and as they hung from balloons. They were even rocketed into outer space. Atmospheric tests ended in 1962 and were prohibited by the Limited Test Ban Treaty of 1963. Scientists had tested the bomb and its effects on soldiers, weapons, animals, tanks, bunkers, and ships."

The admiral's face is ashen. Exhaustion and the cold grayed him. He rests his head on the seat back as a pack of snowmobiles roar by. One slows and stops near our stranded vehicle, by then just another drift of snow on the westbound lane. A gloved hand sweeps his window clear and motions for him to lower it.

"Hot coffee and sandwiches coming through," says the hooded figure behind goggles that cover its eyes. Before we can respond two brown paper sacks are pressed inside. "Careful with this one. All she had to put hot coffee in was a Mason jar. I'll be back with fuel."

"Thanks, but who do we ... ?"

"Farm family up on the hill ... heard it on the radio ... motorists stranded."

"What happened?"

"Semi slid sideways ... blocked both lanes ... wreckers working."

CHAPTER 34

I am so engrossed in his tale I forget my feet are freezing. The old man hasn't once mentioned the cold in all the while we've been sitting in this stalled car. He just spins another of his sea sagas.

"What happened to all those men who witnessed the bombs exploding? Are they part of this class action suit filed against the government by the NAAV? What do you know about it?" I ask as I fill his empty cup with fresh coffee from the farm up the hill. I screw the lid on the Mason jar and replace it on the floor mat. "What happened to all those men?"

The old man stretches his legs and wedges his torso into the narrow bucket seat. "I'll give you twenty dollars cash for this seat when we get home. It fits my fanny, and I finally got it warm." He settles his feet and begins. "It's not a pretty story, David. Are you sure you want to hear?"

"I'm surviving the cold, I can survive the truth."

"Match point." His smile dissolves. "Atomic veterans have been fighting a second war with our government for the last sixty years, battling your employer and mine, have been mixing it up with the men and women we elected to congress to make laws that were to be ethically right, and with judges to interpret those laws with justice." The admiral takes a sip of the hot liquid. "Ah," he says, and his expression lightens. "I needed a caffeine transfusion."

His face sobers. "David, we've been twisted and turned, cranked and shafted by our government. We've been swindled by our own system." He closes his eyes, takes a long drink and holds it in his mouth a while. He swallows it slowly like it may be his final ration of rum on an endless sea voyage.

"It all started with Orville Kelly, an Army sergeant in charge of Japtan Island during Operation Hardtack. It was 1954. His job was to record radiation levels in pools of water on the island, a short distance from the Bikini Atoll. Kelly's orders were to muster his men before dawn on the lagoon side of the island, the side five miles from the target fleet, and have them watch each of the three blasts. They were closer to the white light and the unearthly bright purple hovering cloud than any manned vessels were allowed. The men were issued protective goggles to watch the rising mushroom clouds. The heat from the blast was intense.

"My story jumps ahead twenty years to 1974 when Kelly's doctors told him he had an advanced stage of cancer of the lymph nodes. It took the next seven years of his life and almost all of his savings to prove to the Veterans Administration that his disability was related to radiation from Japtan Island.

"He and his wife, Wanda, were the force behind the formation of the NAAV in 1979. The organization was an atomic test information clearinghouse for use by other veterans. The purpose was to save them from laboring through the same bureaucratic battles Orville and Wanda had already fought."

I hand McLaughlin one of the sandwiches.

He sets it on his lap and continues talking. "Those two published a monthly newsletter to inform their fellow Atomic Veterans how to get hard-to-find government documents from the Nuclear Defense Agency. They organized volunteers to help men get VA health care and financial assistance. They directed their efforts at the three hundred eighty-two thousand Americans who were used by the Atomic Energy Commission and the Department of Defense for human testing to learn how this advanced weaponry would affect a soldier's performance. They helped organize chapters in each state to locate Atomic Vets ridden with cancers and strange deformities. Local groups reported they found vets holed up, sick and unable to pay their growing medical bills. The organization helped them fill out and file claims. Veterans lobbied Congress for over thirty years before our government came to recognize twenty-two different cancers as possibly being service related.

"Even then there were a few brave souls who saw through the propaganda and spoke out against it. I remember Bob Hope landed on our carrier in the South Pacific between explosions with his USO troop. *As soon as the war ended,* he said to us, *we located the one beautiful spot on earth that hadn't been touched by war and blew it to hell.* No one laughed, not even Red Foxx who hosted the Christmas stage with him."

The old man stops to chew the corner of his sandwich and take a long drink. "Since the tests ended in 1963 there hasn't been any government sponsored medical surveillance of the men involved in the atomic and nuclear tests, nor efforts to locate people to warn them of potential health risks. The NAAV found veterans with unusual health problems that stumped the civilian medical community, like the bark on my legs did with my doctors. They don't know what to do with us.

"Orville Kelly's claim to the VA for service-connected benefits was eventually granted, but the government admitted no connection between his disease and radiation exposure. He died from lymphoma just seven months after winning a hundred percent service-connected disability from the VA Board of Appeals.

"The NAAV legal coordinator sent a form to all of us and recommended we fill out an official claim for damage or injury. The purpose was to register with the VA to keep the statutes of limitations from running out. Then, if any of the men got cancer, their recorded claim for damage would give them the right to sue. He suggested a class action suit might be appropriate."

The admiral takes another bite. "I filled out my form." He chews and swallows. "Studies came in at the NAAV office showing the average life span for Atomic Vets was fifty-seven. I was sixty-one, and felt okay.

"Look David. I am damn lucky to be healthy enough to support my family after retiring from the Navy. Plenty of guys were so sick they couldn't work. They watched TV and drank for the rest of their lives while their wives worked. Faye and I were fortunate we adopted Corny and Slick, we didn't have to watch our offspring struggle with radiation sickness. I don't want any special favors from the federal government. I want justice.

"Listen to this." The old man removes a folded piece of yellowed paper from his jacket pocket. "This letter is dated 4 March of 1983. I brought it for you to see. It's from the Navy's legal department. It says the claim which would exempt me from the statute of limitations is invalid because I didn't have cancer. Hold that thought, because it gets a bit confusing from here on in.

"If I had been unlucky enough to catch cancer, and lucky enough for it to be on the government list of twenty-two approved for compensation, it would be invalid because the cancer didn't occur within two years of the incident that supposedly triggered it. That statute of limitations bites vets in the ass every time they bend over. The government set an arbitrary deadline for Atomic Veterans to catch a lethal disease. If this wasn't so serious, it would be laughable. It is like that book, '*Catch 22*'." He rubs the back of his neck.

"Our government used every tactic they could to weasel out of taking care of their own. That goes against everything I learned growing up during the Great Depression. We survived that tragedy because we took care of one another.

"A year after this letter," he shakes the paper, "I got another one from the same guy, an Admiral Lofgren from the Navy's legal department. In effect he told me to quit crying, that my exposure to six nuclear explosions was slight.

"After that I got the bad news about Bankston. He was the kid in charge of the work party that did the grunt work for the scientists aboard the *Albemarle*. He died of lung cancer.

"I couldn't weigh anchor, watch my men die and their families thrash around in a sea of medical bills. Strange new sicknesses picked them off like the Japanese snipers did from trees in the Pacific Islands.

"Paperwork churned like the salt water spinning through the screws on our ships. We were given hope, had the hope dashed, and then were jerked around again. Out of the twenty-five hundred vets that claimed radiation related injuries by 1985, twenty were approved and waited to receive compensation. The Department of Defense secretly warned the country's leaders that if claims sent to the General Accounting Office were allowed to stand, it could signal a stampede of applicants. Two hundred twenty thousand servicemen and civilians participated in atmospheric nuclear tests. Politicians could see, aside from treatment in VA hospitals, the government might have to provide millions in disability payments. Instead of help, Congress cut two hundred eight million from the VA's 1986 budget.

"When Orville Kelly died, Wanda took over the NAAV. She sent Joe Ortega to help organize vets in Michigan. Richard Hauschild agreed to lead the effort. I was in line to take over after Richard. We were busy developing our membership when Richard told me to proceed with caution. He said the FBI had questioned him about the NAAV, had labeled the organization subversive."

"Why did we think you were subversive?"

"We were working on a class action suit against the US government," he says. "Not long after that was underway, I received a letter from the attorney general that advised me the Feres doctrine had been sanctioned by the Supreme Court. It prohibited those who worked for the government from suing the government for anything that happened while in their employ. I backpedaled and didn't go to any more meetings. I had enough."

"You gave up?"

"I couldn't see any future in the fight for an old lag like me. I sat around home for a few years. Then Richard called and said he needed my help. So, I sat around at the bimonthly meetings where I was approached by Joe Ortega and Melvin Gibbons. That's when I called my old friend who had retired from the bureau. But that was a long time ago, maybe five years. I thought the FBI had checked it out and flushed my letter down a dark hole. How did you get involved?"

"I'm curious. Would you tell me why you informed on Ortega and Gibbons? I would expect after the government jerked veterans around, you would do whatever you could for these men."

The admiral drops his chin and frowns. "You can't pick and choose which laws to obey, David. What they were doing wasn't right, even if they deserved the compensation. Joe Ortega and Melvin Gibbons will go to jail, won't they?"

"This could be big-time fraud."

CHAPTER 35

A thunder of snowmobiles flies by. One slides to a stop beside the car trapped in front of us, talks to the driver and whirs away. A bundled figure emerges, migrates toward our vehicle, and bangs on my window. "Half an hour more," a woman says as a gust of snow blows the rest of her message away. I thank her, but she is already plodding toward the truck behind us.

My curiosity piques. "The dreams you have, sir. Are they caused from the stress of your old job, or from a traumatic incident etched in your subconscious mind?" I have always wondered about the source of nightmares. I remember hearing my father scream during the nights he was home on leave. Mother's explanation the next morning was that he had had a frightening dream.

"They used to call it shell shock," the admiral says. "A night shadow I had yesterday brought back a memory from more than sixty years ago."

I glance at the old gentleman. He seems smaller hunched forward in his seat beside me. His spine appears to have lost out to the weight on his shoulders. His spark is gone. "Can you tell me about that dream?"

"Faye always told me the demons would go away faster if I talked about them." He clears his throat. "I'll try, David." He takes a sip of coffee. "It was after I enlisted up on Kodiak Island, a bit of land that pushed up and swelled into an island when the Anchorage plate was raised fifteen foot by an earthquake. I was out in the magazine area, the place where we stored torpedoes and other ordnances at the edge of the base. I worked with a bulldozer. We were clearing snow for a road when I saw two Army boots stuck in a snow bank.

"I cracked the frozen snow around them and found a body attached. I dug that doggie out as fast as I could with my bare hands, but the man was frozen like a slab of beef. That boy and I were about the same age. I reported the incident at once. They took the dogface away and that's the last I heard of him. I didn't learn how he'd died, how long he'd been there, or his name.

"What chills me even now about that incident is that my seventh sense tells me I will be cold like that just before I die." He looks down at his cold feet. "Those boots I saw in my dream could be mine."

The old man swallows with some effort, takes a deep breath and looks at me. "You think I'm paranoid, don't you? You think my brain cells are wrinkled and shriveled like the rest of me?"

"You seem to know what I think before the notion pops into my mind," I say. "Sometimes I feel like you're walking barefoot through my thoughts."

McLaughlin chuckles. He appears pleased to get on a lighter topic. "My mother always told me her seventh son had psychic powers. I don't deny I've had some help staying alive all these years." He raises his finger to stop my next question. "I was shot by a Jap. He pinned me down on the seashore of Samara in the Philippines."

"Where did he hit you?"

"Got me in the leg. I was with the Amphibious Corps, building air stations in the Pacific at the time. A medic saw the hit and made his way across the beach. While this kid from Spokane, Washington cut my pants up the leg with a scissor, shots circled us, splattering sand as they hit. The young man had a tough time cleaning my wound while the slugs thudded around us. He worked the bullet out with his fingers, and packed the hole full of sulfa drugs. I remember his kind eyes. He offered to help me back to an ambulance Jeep, but I told him I had to keep going. I knew I couldn't stop because that's how sailors got killed out there. The medic secured the powder inside the bullet hole with a four-by-four bandage and wished me luck. The boy had more pluck than luck. I've always had a feeling when I should get out of a place, or get my men out. That hospital corpsman was killed later that day."

A snowmobile roars up. I step outside and wipe the snow on the windshield to the pavement, sweep the hood vents clear and brush the headlamps free. "You win two gallons," the snowmobiler says.

I pull the gas tank lever, and hear a scraping and gurgling sound near the rear tire. The snowmobiler appears at the window and motions to crank the engine. I switch on the ignition and pump the gas pedal. The engine roars.

"There's a wrecker a few cars in front of you," says the man, "and a pickup with a snow blade pushing the loose snow into the ditch. As soon as he opens a path, get moving."

I learn more about the freak storm from passengers in the cars ahead. The highway is suddenly full of figures brushing clean their car roofs and fenders, forming mounds of white. This section of the eastbound lane had been hit by a fast-moving front, heading due south. The highway is clear and dry ahead. Behind is a swatch of bad weather. It takes five minutes before our car can chug forward. Forty minutes later we are rejuvenated and sailing down a side street in Pontiac, still with time to spare before our four o'clock meeting.

"This is the place with the tasty soups and the grilled cheese sandwiches. They'll be easy on your teeth." I pull into the restaurant's parking lot. "We'll put your wire on and fill the car with gas after lunch."

"A wire?"

CHAPTER 36

"How big is this recording device?" he says from his side of the table at the diner near Pontiac. "Do I need to talk into my sleeve?"

"This new mike is so powerful it can pick up a conversation through two layers of clothing," I say. "The transmitter's the size of a pack of cigarettes. I'll bury it under your T-shirt, tape it to the skin on the small of your back and bring the wire around to your chest. Nothing will be visible. It makes no sound. It's the best model I could buy from Radio Shack."

"You bought a cloak and dagger gadget like that at Radio Shack? In Swainsville?" says Admiral McLaughlin

"No. Jackson. Ironic, isn't it, technology available to the general public is as good as equipment issued by our federal government." We both order soup and wait for the waiter to leave before we speak. "Your conversation will be recorded by a receiver in a van parked down the street from the meeting."

We arrive at the meeting location in Keego Harbor by three o'clock. The admiral is wired and ready to record. I see an unmarked FBI van park beside the VFW hall on Duck Lake Road as we pull into the parking lot. We are early.

Two men play bumper pool at the far end of the meeting room under a decaying cork dartboard. A third man balances on a stool beside them. Bare fluorescent bulbs bounce light off a concrete floor painted ship deck gray, and expose a bar on the far side. The room is empty, just a few folding chairs and tables, and the green felt-covered slab. The odor is of paste wax and stale beer. When the pool players see us enter, they stop shooting, fidget, and watch as we cross the room.

I hear a chuckle, turn and see a bemused grin on the admiral's lips, the same shrunken smirk he wears when he teases me. He is enjoying our grand entrance.

"See that," he says from the side of his mouth as we walk. "They're scared. Look how their postures are crouched. They expected only me. You've frightened them. They don't know you're a television-taught, police-crusader turned FBI agent, so it must be the way you swagger that has their sphincters tightened down." He slows his step to a full stop. "Did you see that, the way the guy on the left looks over his shoulder? These revolutionaries may have second thoughts about overthrowing your government."

"Did your seventh sense tell you that?" I ask. "And, it's our government. Come on." I keep my focus straight ahead as I lead the admiral across the floor. I can't help but gawk at one man's face. It looks like raw chicken. When my eyes stop stinging, I look away and blink.

"Burn scars don't age well, unlike well-cured beef," McLaughlin mumbles from the side of his mouth.

Our footsteps click a slow rhythm as we advance to the pool table. I check for small, self-centered eyes among the men, prominent, controlling brow bones protruding from practical low foreheads and cheekbones that are too confidently high. I measure spacing between eyes for ego that is too great and run the data through my memory of the Chinese principles of Mien Shiang. I trust my conclusions about the physical attributes of criminals. The old man is right. These men are nervous. Will they bolt? I extend my hand as we draw near.

"Ortega? Are you Joe Ortega?" the admiral asks before I can say a thing.

The pool player with the chopped chicken face shakes his head and steps back.

"Are you Gibbons?" he asks the second man, a big guy without a neck, with red cheeks and nose, and muscular arms that rest on a distended abdomen. He looks the part of a long-time alcoholic.

"I'm Melvin Gibbons," says a third man from his chair. When he stands he bends stoop-backed. He has a small, weak chin. Clear plastic tubes run from a bag slung over his shoulder. His plumbing runs up and around his head and hooks into his nostrils. He stretches out his hand. "Are you James McLaughlin?"

The admiral takes his hand. "Where's Ortega?"

Gibbons shrugs and sits back on the stool. "Didn't make it, sir. Died of brain cancer last year."

"Sorry to hear that." The old man grimaces. "Meet my nephew, my driver. David McLaughlin, this is Melvin Gibbons."

Gibbons inspects me, and takes the hand I offer. His grip is limp and damp. This man is unsure of the situation.

The admiral touches the folded letter tucked inside his shirt pocket, and motions toward an empty table near the bar.

Gibbons gives a nod, and follows as we take our seats.

The old seafarer places the papers on the table, and clamps his hand over the four copies he has fanned out. "The US Navy always requires duplicates," he says. "And you'll need backup copies for when the bureaucrats lose the duplicates."

Gibbons grins and shifts his weight. "I appreciate this, sir. My family will remember you kindly in their prayers long after I'm gone." He extends his hand for the letter.

The admiral offers nothing, his hand remains unyielding.

That instant touches off a memory. I scroll back through our conversations, search for the moment, and find the scene when he found my gun. It was the first time I met him at his condo by the frozen lake. He didn't give my weapon back until he was good and ready, no matter what I threatened. That was four days ago. It seems like a lifetime. The admiral's hand controls these documents the same way.

"Let's make certain the spelling of your name is correct," he says. "Is it G-I-B-B-O-N-S?"

"Yes sir," Melvin Gibbons says and reaches for the copies.

McLaughlin's grip doesn't budge. Could he be teasing? It's clear to me that Gibbons is incapable of standing up to anyone who opposes him.

"And your brother's name was ..."

Aha, I think, and hold back my smile of admiration. Now I see what he's doing.

"Alex. His name was Alex Gibbons." The man pulls his hand back, adjusts his oxygen tube, and listens with an exasperated show of patience. He looks behind him, like he's making an exit plan. The corners of his mouth draw back, pulling his lips into a thin, tightly pressed line, like he doesn't want anything to leak out.

"And you want Melvin Gibbons listed on the duty roster of the *Cape Esperance* in 1950 instead of Alex Gibbons?"

"Yes sir," he says. "That would be right." He pushes his hands deep down into his jacket pockets.

Gibbons has no idea he has just confessed to attempted fraud. Textbook perfect, I think. Now we have the entire intrigue on tape.

The old man pushes all four copies across the table.

Gibbons grabs the papers. He shakes the old man's hand, and sits down on a folding chair to read the letter. Men are beginning to straggle in for the NAAV meeting.

"Excuse us, Gibbons," the admiral says with that little curve of a lip that serves him for a smile. "I want to introduce my nephew to some old cronies."

I follow as he signals to a man across the room, struggles to his feet and walks toward some folding chairs near the door. "Nice going," I say. "He identified himself on tape."

The admiral barely glances at me. "How long do you want to stay?"

"Why don't you get tired in about fifteen minutes?" I say.

"I'm tired now."

A voice from behind him calls out, "Jim McLaughlin!"

The admiral twists toward the sound. "Why, it's Richard Hauschild. You old SOB. You're still alive." He faces a short man with deep facial lines carved into a leathery tan. He has a jutting, strong-willed chin. "Richard Hauschild, meet my nephew, David. He's my driver today."

Hauschild shakes my hand with both of his. "Thanks for dragging in this old bag-a-bones, David." Hauschild extends his hand to McLaughlin, "You look good for an old warhorse. I was worried when I didn't hear from you. Feeling all right?"

"The same, Richard, still growing bark. I keep the Navy informed of my whereabouts. How are you doing?"

"Hah!" Richard says. "I'm scheduled to have my appendix cut out. I feel like a kid. Next thing they'll go after are my tonsils."

The admiral grins. "When's your surgery?"

"Next week." Hauschild shrugs. "Thanks for asking. I noticed your name listed on the NAAV website with the other atomic sailors. Did you know the class action suit is back on the docket?"

"I heard it was close at the meeting two months ago. I give you credit for your persistence. I would have sworn it was over in 1957 after that Navy JAG decided to invoke that damn Feres Doctrine."

"We found a loophole."

The old man's eyebrows confirm a job well done.

"Sit down, Mac," Richard says and moves a folding chair.

"Did you know Bobby Mandell?" Richard motions for me to get my own chair.

"Hell yes. We served on the *Albemarle* together, in 1946. How is old Bobby? I keep up with him every few months through his daughter."

Hauschild looks down, shuffles his feet, and says, "He coiled up his lines for the last time last week at the Veteran's Hospital in Ann Arbor."

The admiral grimaces, and puts his hand on Hauschild's shoulder. "I saw Bobby bucketing hot fish into the bottom of a launch after one of the blasts. He splashed around in that scorching radioactive rain. Poor fellow fought cancer for years. He was a good man." He draws the back of his arm across his forehead.

"I was trained to fight and kill just like you, Mac," Hauschild says. He braces both elbows on his knees and stares at the floor. "But the older I get the more senseless and stupid war seems to me. I'm glad you're back with us. My job's still open for you when I retire."

"Richard, I'm tired. Let the young vets fight this battle."

"The young people are dying too," he says, "... of Agent Orange, of Gulf War gas, of ..."

"What about this loophole you found, Mr. Hauschild?" I ask. "Could my uncle qualify somehow to be included in this class action suit?"

The admiral squints at me. It is clear he doesn't like me taking over the interview.

"Tell me about the bark you grow, Mac," Hauschild says. "It first appeared when?"

McLaughlin pulls up his pant leg. "The skin condition started in 1959, the year I retired the first time. The stuff grew aggressively in Vietnam during my tour there, and subsided for a few years. For the last ten years it's been active again. My skin doctor said he never saw anything like it."

"Looks like the crust of a rhinoceros. Has the skin irritation affected both legs?"

The admiral pulls up his other pant leg.

"This one looks worse than a rhino's skin. Is it painful?"

"The top of the skin dries and peels off. Doesn't hurt. It itches."

"Did you wear protective clothing during the nuclear blasts?"

"One time we wore special gear, once out of eleven blasts. Our ships were ordered closer to ground zero with each explosion. The temperature was muggy down there. We had to be dressed in long pants and long sleeves on the bridge. That order probably saved my life. My men wore Bermuda shorts and T-shirts."

"What did you experience at the time of the blast?" Hauschild says.

"I was on deck when the explosions cracked like shotgun blasts." He pauses. "I remember the sound stung my ears. I know that sounds odd, but it vibrated inside my ears. I had to shake it out. And the feel of the ship as it heaved under me, wow. I can still feel the wave surge hit the ship with that first blast of heat. My face and hands got hot." He rubs his cheeks. "It felt like long, flat snakes in the air, flapping against me, shock waves slapping me again and again. I remember the sensation like it was yesterday."

"Were you present when hydrogen weapons were deployed?" Hauschild says.

"I was on the *Rendova* near Christmas Island where they had multiple blasts. When it was over all they had was a hole in the water half a mile deep and three miles across where the island had been. I don't know what all those tests proved.

The government incinerated three entire islands, blew them off the face of the earth."

"They proved we shouldn't be fooling around with nuclear weapons. The government will never go along with your skin disorder as being presumptive. But the condition may qualify you for our class action suit against the government. I'll plug your record in and see what we can do for you. How old are you?"

"Eighty-five. I plan to make a hundred."

The words of the senior operative at the FBI office in Ann Arbor tug at my memory. Cut the informant out. My case officer had insisted I get a professional in position to deal with Hauschild. "Mr. Hauschild," I say. "I'll drive Uncle Jim to the next meeting if he feels up to it. But, if he's not feeling well, may I come as his surrogate?"

"He already has power of attorney over my affairs, Richard," McLaughlin says with a wink.

Nice touch by the old man, and quick too, I think. "I'm his attorney and his biographer, but I don't do laundry," I say. I notice the admiral's quick grin, but he doesn't glance my way.

"David," Hauschild says, "would you mind if I had a word with your uncle in private?"

Red alert! My mind reels as my laughter merges with fear. Keep calm. Keep cool. Answer the man, I tell myself. "Certainly not, Mr. Hauschild. I'll do whatever Uncle Jim wants." I feel sweat erupt on my forehead, and droplets run down my spine. I seek some kind of a sign from the old man's eyes.

The admiral gives a uniform nod to Hauschild, but I see a hint of a twinkle in his eye. A novice would notice nothing. His expression is that of an experienced poker player who has just been dealt four aces. I begin to understand the old coot. He finds amusement at the oddest times, and at the expense of some higher authority. It is like he knows a secret and is winking at the world.

My stomach makes an involuntary noise, like a toilet flushing. "I'll be just inside the bar, Uncle Jim," I say and rub the sharp pain boiling in my belly.

"Call me when you're ready to go." I find a roll of Rolaids in my pocket, skin back the paper as I walk, and pop two inside my mouth. It occurs to me that I have become one of those stomach-growling kind of men, like my stepdad.

Leticia told me this would happen if I covered my real thoughts and feelings. My gut growls a second warning. My body has lost its objectivity. My head is still a hundred percent business but my bowels resist. I head toward the toilet.

A grin lifts the old man's cheeks as he pushes into the bar to find me later. He turns to shake Hauschild's hand. The two old veterans are connected by more than this handshake. "I'll follow up with you as soon as my surgery is over," Hauschild says.

On the way out of the hall I see a van pull away. FBI, I think. I wait until we are on the highway to speak. "What did Hauschild talk to you about?"

"He says he suspects you of being FBI."

CHAPTER 37

His words scald me. I gasp for air, and cough it out. It is nearly six o'clock and getting dark. The car swerves into the loose slush beside the roadway. The front tire catches and pulls the car deep into the snow banked on the shoulder. It takes all the strength I have to muscle the wheels back onto the pavement.

McLaughlin is quiet while I fight the elements outside and inside. The cavity above my gut churns. My career is over. Damn. The entire meeting has been taped. I feel sick. What tipped him off? My hands would have shaken had I released my grip on the wheel. The rest of my career will be behind a desk after this fiasco. The sweat beads on my forehead drip from my chin.

As we sail down the highway the admiral says, "Good recovery. That was a close call. Don't you know by now when I'm teasing?"

I flash him a look. Damn, I could have killed us both. I grip the wheel, clench my teeth and stare ahead.

McLaughlin is quiet for a long stretch of road before he speaks. "I'm serious about trying to reach a hundred, David. Will you slow down and keep all four tires on the pavement?" He checks his safety belt and grips the armrest on the door. "Hauschild thought I should know family members often offer their help if they think there's a big payoff."

"Is there?" I ask, and keep my eyes trained on the gray ribbon ahead.

The old man glances over. "Your pallid complexion is pinking up nicely, David," he says. "It must be the payout. Could be as much as seventy-five grand."

I can feel my eyebrows elevate. "What agreement did you two make about my participation?" I am serious.

"You don't get any of the green." The old man snickers.

"You know what I mean. Am I in for the meetings?"

"Damn it, David. Don't give me that face. You're family. Of course you will be trusted by Hauschild. I instructed them to accept you as my surrogate."

I cluck with dumb joy, relieved I hadn't blown it after all.

McLaughlin's smile broadens. "Why do you want to deal with Hauschild instead of me?"

"Save you from testifying."

"Your superiors wouldn't trust my testimony?"

"When your name first appeared on the case file I did a national agency check on you. Since your first top shelf clearance in '41 you have been investigated every five years for anything that might compromise national security. That stopped when you retired. No one knows what kind of trouble you may have stirred up since then. My assignment is to uncover any criminal or subversive activity you've been involved in during the last thirty years."

"So that's it." The old man whistles. He looks at me and deadpans grandly. "Find anything?"

"Your last thirty years have been rather bland, not exactly material for a movie."

The old man rubs his chin. "David, we did a good job today, didn't we?" He is flush with good feeling.

I am tired, and my humor turns dark. "I feel like we just robbed a bank and got away with it."

"David H. McLaughlin?" the old man laughs. "You would never rob a bank. The paperwork trail would be too long and you're the kind of guy who would track the robber."

"How do you know how much paperwork I do?"

"I worked for the Naval Investigative Service. The NIS is comparable to the FBI on a localized scale."

I glance over at the man beside me and then back at the highway. "I should have figured you were NIS." I pass a slow moving vehicle. "When will Hauschild contact you?"

"That's a Michigan State Police car you just passed," the old man says. He turns in his seat and watches for a flashing light. "I don't know, David." His attention is glued to his side mirror. "He says he'll plug me in and see what he can do." He watches the police car buzz by, its sirens screaming. It is after someone else. "Don't worry," he says, and returns his attention to our conversation. "I'll pass on any communications as long as you drive up from D.C. and take me out for breakfast once in a while. Agreed?"

"That's blackmail," I say and smile.

The investigation has moved along procedurally perfectly. I am well on my way to a wrap. I still have one unresolved personal item to discuss with this retired officer. I have to find out what he remembers about my father.

I pull into a rest stop, park and look over at the man. "Let's take those wires off." I remove the listening device, wind the wires and set them on the floor. "Sir, may we talk about something … off the record?"

CHAPTER 38

I buy coffee and Payday bars from the vending machine alongside the convenience center. I'm thinking about the meeting with Gibbons as we lean against the fender and sip hot water the color of urine.

"Tell me about your father, not your stepdad?"

He's reading my thoughts. The old man throws his cup in the trash, climbs aboard, and we head west on I-94.

"You mentioned the USS *Rendova*," I say, remembering one of the names on the toy ship my father had carved for me.

"Sure, that was the small attack carrier that survived Typhoon Marge. I had four tours on her."

"What was the ship's mission early in the seventies?" I ask.

"That would have been on my last tour with her, around the time the US moved our naval bases out of the Philippines? The *Rendova* was a transport carrier. We hauled airplanes. I remember it was right after a big earthquake. We ran aground on the top of a submerged peak that had been pushed up by the quake. It wasn't on the charts. Tore a screw right off. But what does the *Rendova* have to do with your father?"

"Do you remember a Navy base called Diego Garcia?" I ask.

"Sure, it's a Navy support facility in the Indian Ocean, a hell of a long way from home, on an island just off the coast of Africa. We hauled planes there too. Diego Garcia is a base we use now for forays into Iraq and Afghanistan. It's a Navy computer and telecommunications station.

"My friend Spud Monahan was promoted off the USS *Vernon County* to skipper the *Rendova* during that tour. He liked to walk around his quarters on his hands … said it saved on shoe leather, but I think he always wanted to be in the circus. He had this parakeet. Spud was crazy about that little bird. One day it got out, flew into a fan and was chopped to smithereens. Spud put what was left in a cardboard matchbox. The next time we were in port he took it to his big house inland and buried it in his garden. Spud retired before I did."

I search my memory for the names on my father's court-martial paper. "What rank did he retire as?"

"They bumped him up a rank to rear admiral so he could have a decent living for his remaining years, but he stayed on fleet reserve for another ten years. It was called a *tombstone promotion* and meant that he could be called back to active duty if they needed him. I knew a guy the Department of Defense kept working in Washington until he was eighty-five. The Navy offered that package to men who kept their noses clean, did their jobs as they worked their way up in rank, and served in active duty during WWII. The Department of Defense discontinued the program around the time Spud and I retired."

"Since your best friend was Captain of the *Rendova*, you two must have talked about what went on aboard," I say, feeling lucky. The old man is in a great frame of mind and doesn't appear tired even after our long day. It's time to learn the truth. I lean forward. "Can we talk about the court-martial?"

CHAPTER 39

The old man's chest heaves and his head bends over. "My second court-martial was dismissed." He hesitates. "My first, well, I pled guilty, and endured it with fortitude and phlegm."

Surprised at the unexpected information of a second offense, I smile to myself. It is dark now, and the roads are clear as I drive toward Swainsville. I want details of my father's court-martial, not his. So the man has two counts against him. I am intrigued by how layers of truth, wound tight for so long, wait for the right time to burst and expose their seeds. It reminds me of the furry casings on the cattails in the swamp beside our house. "How did fortitude and phlegm get you through a court-martial?" I say.

"We were underway on that damn flattop, the USS *Boxer*," the admiral says, "far out in the gray waters of the Pacific. A spare-gear feather-merchant came aboard for duty." He must have noticed my wrinkled brow from his side of the car. "That's Navy slang for reserve officer. The sailor came aboard and wanted to be the catapult and arresting gear officer. That was my job, but he outranked me. I was a senior chief at the time.

"Pilots aboard carriers spoke an abbreviated and prescribed language when they talked on their radios. This position had to be filled by a flyboy because he had to be able to understand and talk with the pilots. I had flight training. The reserve officer didn't. The air boss gave him a negative on the slot but said he could be a safety man to back me up. He was not happy that a non-com held the job he wanted, and told me, 'Don't let my star flash in your eyes. I just might whip your ass yet.'

"One morning as planes lined up on the flight deck to warm their engines before takeoff, a float valve stuck in the transfer pump on a plane near the bridge where I stood. This was a rare occurrence. The spare-gear feather-merchant working safety didn't see it. The air boss didn't see it. JP4 high-grade kerosene jet fuel flowed from the wings to the main fuel cell when the pump stuck. It drained into the bottom of the fuselage and leaked out in a puddle on the deck.

"The pilot was ready to launch. He had his eyes fastened on the safety officer standing on the bridge for his signal and didn't notice his gas gauge move. He watched for the three-finger turn up, the okay to turn his engines up full bore. That's when I noticed the puddle under the plane. I leaned down and looked closer. I saw fuel pouring out, spilling from the fuselage. I heard of this happening once before on another ship. Nine people were killed in the explosion and fire.

"I glanced around at the spare-gear feather-merchant turned safety officer. Three fingers turned up at the end of his arm. I gave his arm a hard knock with my forearm. Every second at a time like that was valuable. I turned and gave the pilot the sign to cut his engine by drawing my finger across my throat. I gave him the signal to fall away, and do it fast. Twenty to thirty knots of wind blew down the deck, and evaporated his fuel as fast as it poured out of the plane.

"He shut his engines down at once, and jumped free of the plane. I gave the push back signal to the ground crew by hanging my hands at my sides and pushing forward with my palms. They pushed his plane back to the elevator at the edge of the deck and left it there. Traffic was blocked. The day's exercise was stalled.

"The fuel infused airplane was a bomb waiting to blow, and it held up important traffic. The air crew couldn't get the plane down the elevator without folding its wings. The wings wouldn't fold unless the plane was under power. The pilot couldn't fire up the engines until the valve was fixed and the fuel washed away.

"Officers were graded on these exercises for time and efficiency. The brains up on the bridge were unhappy the exercise had been stopped under their watch, unhappy the rescheduling would be noted on their records, and unhappy with me because I didn't have the pilot take time to fold the wings before he cut the power. They said they would tie a can on me, see that I got kicked out of the Navy.

"The pilot came up on the bridge after the aborted launch, threw his arms around my neck and hugged me. Then he shook my hand and thanked me for saving his life.

"Two or three days later we pulled into Hong Kong Harbor. I was on liberty on the beach, looking for a sewing machine for Faye. I stopped at a cafeteria for lunch and was playing with my chopsticks, attempting to move food from a wooden bowl to my mouth, when I felt a tap on my shoulder.

"*Mind if we join you, chief?* asked the executive officer and the commander of the air group. I struggled to my feet, and saluted my superior officers. The men were on liberty too. While they waited for their food, they asked me to explain what happened on the carrier's flight deck. They had already reviewed the charges filed against me.

"*You did exactly right*, the commander said after I had explained the sequence of events. *If any of those assholes say a word to you about this, you let me know. I'll have some dire punishment waiting for them.*

"What kind of punishment was he talking about?" I say.

"The CAG could give any bridge officer a bum fitness report and they'd be through, career over. Any officer would turn backflips to keep from getting a bum fitness report."

"Did it come to a court-martial?"

"Not that time. The charges were dropped."

"Your paperwork shows that in 1944 you did receive a court-martial," I say. "Your records show you pleaded guilty to being drunk and unable to go on duty while the United States was at war. You were found guilty, spent five days in the brig, and lost your first chance for a good conduct medal. Would you fill me in on the circumstances?"

The old man smiles. "Well done. You did your homework. This one involved a woman, David, long before I met Faye." He is silent for a while.

I imagine his brain working, its long tentacles plucking memories stuck to the filaments inside his head, and me, like the spider, claiming the flies caught up in its web.

"Women have always been my weakness." He rakes his fingers through his hair. "I was on leave in November of '44, hanging out at a slop-chute called Tailgate Annie's sipping beer by the quart and working skirt patrol. The bar was an old Navy and Marine hangout on Sixth Street in San Francisco. This canary was flitting from table to table, flirting with sailors. I didn't know at the time she was just trying to make her husband jealous.

"Joseph Francis Michael Patrick Dunleavy, this redheaded Irish friend of mine, had the best pickup lines of any sailor I knew. I decided to use one of his finest and test the water.

"When she sat down at my table I leaned in and said, *Are you going to shack up with me or be a darn fool and miss out?* She got up, walked over and told her husband what I had said. Her old man came up behind me and hit me over the head with a beer bottle. I stood up and smacked him with the schooner I'd just emptied. It didn't even make a dent in his head, so I cold-cocked him, right in the nose. He fell. His nose bled. I was on the floor sitting on him, beating his face in with my fist when I felt myself being elevated.

"Shore patrolmen on each side got me under my arms and picked me straight up in the air. They were tall military policemen. I remember stretching my feet, feeling for the deck, and trying to stand. There was nothing to stand on. They carried me outside and gave me a ride back to the ship where I was thrown into the brig.

"The court-martial officer, my defense attorney, told me if I pled guilty to an offense on a lesser degree he could get me off. I agreed and pled guilty to being drunk and unable to go on duty while the US was in a state of war. The judge found me guilty. I was in jail for disorderly conduct for five days total. The first day I gagged on phlegm with my head in the can. Aspirin didn't touch the pain in my head for the remainder of my confinement. I went back on the beach after they turned me loose but always stayed out of Tailgate Annie's."

I can't help it. I break into laughter. He joins me. After a while I say, "What did Faye do with her time when you were at sea?"

"You are a nosy little bastard, aren't you," the old man turns to me and chuckles. "She worked at the hospital and fooled around."

"Fooled around? Do you mean with men?"

"No."

I gasp. "Your wife was a lesbian?"

"She went both ways. I'm told that's not uncommon with military women."

"Were you devastated?"

"Can't you even pretend you're professional with this line of questioning?" he says grinning. "You are one meddlesome snoop. Must get a thrill from digging out family secrets." He blows his nose, and stuffs his handkerchief into his pocket.

"I'll tell you this, but I won't tell you the numbers on my Swiss Bank account. Agreed?"

"Deal," I say.

He pauses, and looks out the window. "Faye stopped when I came home."

"Did you ever have an affair with another woman while you were married to Faye?"

He deadpans. "Okay. I'll tell you this, but I

won't tell you how I swindle our government on my income tax. Agree?"

"Deal." I say, and smile.

"There was Yoko, in Japan. She always had a hot bath waiting for me when I came home, gave great massages. She was good in bed and treated me with respect, made me feel I was the last man left on earth."

"Why Yoko?"

"The routine of marriage kills desire, son. You'll find out after you walk the plank. Staying married is an unending battle to keep life from becoming routine. Besides, I wouldn't see my wife for months and months."

I notice his foot twitch. "How did you meet Yoko?"

"She lived off base with a friend of mine. He shipped out. So I moved in."

"So she was a whore?"

"It wasn't like that. I gave her money for rent and for abortions. I knew she gave the money to her family. She worked to feed her family."

"She was a whore." I say with a nasty snigger.

The admiral dismisses me with a gesture. "You spent too much time with those tight-assed Bostonians, son. When we dropped anchor off Japan, the captain sent the chaplain into port on his private jig. He came back with a girl who spent two days locked in the captain's cabin. Can you imagine that? Sending the chaplain?"

"Women," I say. "You can't tell what they want or what they're thinking. I'm surprised you ever got married." My thoughts go back to the woman I have spent most of my life with. I've never been able to figure my mother out. I get along with her now that I keep a physical and emotional distance.

"Women scare me, too." He leans in and lowers his voice. "My wife met me at the door late one night with a butcher knife."

I move in to hear. "I didn't think she was a violent woman."

"Me either. Anyway, this little filly caught my attention around the time my wife lost interest in doing her homework. Faye was a little older than me, and I suppose it's only natural for women at a certain age. Let's just say this doll was a delightful diversion from the mundane. The night Faye greeted me at the kitchen door, she told me if I was seeing someone else, she would cut my head off while I slept. Faye was direct. I respected that in her. I denied everything, of course, and ended the affair the next day."

"You lied to your wife?"

He handkerchiefs his brow. "You betcha. She knew how to use that knife."

"At least you knew what Faye thought. Leticia won't give me an answer. I'm not sure she wants to marry me. I guess I prefer directness too."

"Want me to send her Faye's butcher knife?"

I flatten both palms before him and shake my head. We both roar.

"If she won't marry you, it's not the end of the world," the old man says. "That little filly I introduced you to at breakfast says she won't marry me every time I propose. But, I still ask." He grins. "The asking part makes for some nice intimate conversation."

"You say women were your downfall. What was your worst experience with a woman?" I know this question is out of line, but I'm curious about the extremes of the old man's character and enjoy his tall tales of women as much as his sea stories. "I'm willing to hold off asking about your weapons cache," I offer as a carrot.

He's quiet for a time, then nods as if he has decided something serious. "Son, you already know a man can have a dark side." He draws a deep breath before continuing. "She was a seagull, a whore who followed the fleet around from port to port. It all started with a zip-less screw in a dirty grind of a bar." He stops talking, seems listless and distracted.

I move closer, curious to hear the lurid details.

He takes a drink. "I awoke in a hotel room to her rifling though my uniform pockets, looting me and stuffing my money into her brassiere." The man looks miserable with what I take to be shame. "I acted out of anger when I grabbed hold of her. I slapped her so hard she flew across the room, then I dragged her to the bed and sodomized her. I regretted it as soon as my anger cooled. I don't reckon I hurt her. She was too scared to say I did." His voice breaks. "She was weeping when she left."

CHAPTER 40

"I'm not proud of abusing a woman." The admiral's voice is humble. He swallows hard, like he still holds the aftertaste of that shame. He looks fogged as he cradles his untouched candy bar in his long-fingered hand. "It was the action of a bully. David, there's a thin line between being a bully and being a coward." He peels back the paper and takes a bite, chews the nuts and throws his head back to swallow it like it had a whiskey punch. "Yes, that's one grudge fuck I regret."

"How did the Navy handle cowards?" I ask a while later as I pull the car next to the Big Boy entrance. "You still buying dinner?" By the time I park the car and walk inside he is seated and already talking to Rudy. The waiter walks away when he sees me.

McLaughlin crosses his arms over his chest and leans back once we have ordered the spaghetti and meatball special. "There is no official policy for handling cowardice, son. I can tell you how I tolerated a sad specimen of a sailor who refused my order to go aloft. He was an inept, fat kid out of Massachusetts."

My neck prickles.

"His reasons for not climbing were unclear. I figured he was afraid of heights. He was a small man. Stronger men intimidated him. He worked well under constant supervision and when he was cornered like a rat in a trap, but lacked all prospects for promotion. I felt sorry for this sailor, tried to work with him, tried to get the man to stand up for himself."

My mind floats back to my own childhood in Boston, to my mother's words when she fought with my father. She had been called from work by my teacher earlier that day to pick me up from kindergarten because I was sick. The teacher had found me cowering in a corner of the playground complaining of a bellyache.

Mother put her arm around my shoulders and asked me what happened in a voice so gentle it released the tears I'd been struggling to conceal. I blubbered to her that a boy had called me *fatty*, and now my classmates called me *fatty-retard* and refused to play with me. Mother reported the bullying episode to a man who must have been the principal and we left the playground. I remember all this so clearly.

My father was home on leave at the time, reading on the porch. Mother had to go back to work, so she left me with him to look after. I climbed a tree behind our house because I remember being mad at everyone. When I wouldn't come down, he came up the tree to get me. He crawled slowly, uncertain of where to place his hands and feet. I could tell he was scared. He kept looking down.

Then he told me he was stuck. I think he was just scared to move. We both had to stay up there until it grew dark and Mother came home from work. She had to call the fire department to get us down.

I heard a fireman say to my father that he must have been born in a stupid tree and hit every branch on the way down. I know Mother heard him. She laughed. I thought that must have been the reason my father was frightened. He was afraid to fall out of the stupid tree again.

I always felt spineless in Mother's presence. I guess he must have felt the same. I wonder why she bullied him about his fear of heights, about being short, and why she called him *stupid*. Why would she tell me I was built like him?

"Some time later during a fire fighting school," the admiral says, "that same sailor and I were put on the same hose for a demonstration of how to fight an oil fire. There was a big vat of black oil out on the flight deck, burning something fierce. It was hot. I demonstrated on the nozzle end of a two-person hose that would push a hundred and ten pounds of water pressure to keep a wall between me and the flames.

"I put the kid behind me on the hose and ordered it active. Plumes from the fire licked the sky. The sailor must have got scared because he turned the hose loose and ran like a rat from a sinking ship. He left me alone holding a pressurized hosepipe that acted like my father's prize bull on a good day. That hose snaked around, jerked my feet from under me, whipped me back and almost threw me into the fire.

"That put the lid on it for me. I didn't just think he was a coward, I knew it. Funny thing, he came up to me later that same shift and apologized. He asked if we could put all this behind us and begin again as friends. His naiveté astounded me. It was like the lad set low personal standards and then consistently failed to achieve them."

"What did officers do with gutless guys?" I ask, pushing away my plate of pasta.

"I found something else for them to do," he says and raises his cup for a refill. "I think bravery comes from the gut. It's an attitude, not something that can be taught."

"If you backed a coward into a corner, would he fight? Would it be possible for a person to learn courage?"

"I think everyone is born with the potential for courage, for standing up for what is right. I've seen young men who have been cowed in their youth, knocked down by a parent, by another adult or by a terrible experience. Those men have it harder, and are way behind the sailors who were taught ethics in their parent's home. A man can do anything he sets his mind to do. It does help if he's brighter than the December sun in Alaska."

That's enough with the trawling, I think. It's time to pull in the line. "Do you recall a Willie Hatch?"

"Of course I remember him. He was the coward from Boston I just told you about."

I gulp air. Time stops. My father was that coward? My eyes, mouth and throat feel as dry as sand. My father let go of a fire hose and ran in fear like a rat? I swallow hard, and pull a folded paper from my pocket. "It says here in '73, the US Navy held a court-martial for Seaman W.T. Hatch. You are listed as a witness." I tip the paper up and point to his name so he won't see my eyes. "Hatch got a section eight, a discharge at the convenience of the government." I tap the paper. I can feel my face flush. "Will you fill me in on the details?" I watch him stare at his unfinished pasta as he moves his fork around on the plate.

"Willie Hatch," he says as if he is pulling his face from a group photo. His eyes check mine. His expression is blank, his composure as cool.

I blink and glance away. I won't let him penetrate my thoughts.

He sets the fork flat on the plate, pushes it away and leans forward with his elbows on the table. "Hatch," he murmurs and holds his coffee mug in the air, a signal for Rudy, again. "Hatch was given a trial and found unfit for duty before a judge. What more do you want to know?"

I can feel my molars grinding. "I want the details," I say. My jaw locks down, my face muscles tighten.

"What have you dug up on old Willie?"

"I'd like to hear the circumstances that led to the proceeding." My voice is low and rumbles across the table.

The old man's eyes follow my every move, like he must have done with thousands of men during his thirty-three years aboard US Navy vessels. His pupils are flat black pellets.

I forget my training. My head is in a different place, unaware of the messages my body sends. My shoulders pitch forward. My round chest is tucked concave. My neck is drawn in, like a snake waiting for the precise moment to strike.

"David, I've seen your look before." The skin across the admiral's forehead folds, like a paper fan. "You're ready for battle?" he says, his voice elastic. "Take it easy, son." He slows his speech. "Breathe." He pauses. "That's right. Deep breaths," he whispers.

His voice releases the tension behind my brow. My god, he's a hypnotist too. I fight his powerful will.

"I'll tell you everything just as it happened. Okay?" He nods agreement for me and softens his voice further.

I had learned this same technique for calming an irate person at FBI boot camp.

"Willie Hatch somehow got through the shrinks in the recruiting process," McLaughlin says, staring at his plate. "He shouldn't have passed his physical. He was a head-case and an outsider. I never saw him with a buddy."

I feel my head nod with his. I stare at his platter of unfinished meatballs. So, my father didn't have friends, either.

"I thought at the time Hatch may have been some rich man's spoiled kid or politician's son. It's not uncommon for parents to tuck a boy away for a few years and let the Navy make a man out of him. Trouble followed that kid. He was with me on the *Rendova* and the *Cape Esperance*. He didn't appear to be the intelligence star of his class, but he wasn't dim-witted, either.

"He tried to make friends, tried too hard. He just didn't catch on. One sailor told me he faked being thick-skulled to get out of work. Another said if you stood close enough to him, you could hear the ocean. Either way, he didn't belong aboard a Navy ship. He was weak, a man without a beam."

I take a deep breath to relax the knot tying my throat. I wonder if I lack a beam, too. Mother said I have my father's stature, his genes. "Go on," I say.

"When we landed the *Cape Esperance* and secured her to the wharf in San Francisco, we followed standard Navy procedure, doubled all lines and put on the rat guards. Rodents came aboard all ships in port. That's why we used split cones slipped over the mooring hawsers. I ordered Hatch to put the rat cones on as we came into port.

"*I'm afraid to go out there. I don't want to leave the deck of the ship,* he said.

"I remembered then he had told me once before he was afraid to go aloft. This wasn't an unreasonable fear. Lots of young men were afraid of heights. Then I recalled the incident with the high-pressure fire hose. I sent Hatch down to the doctor for an official medical opinion. He came back with a negative report, so I reassigned him first to chip paint, and later to clean berthing compartments.

"Standard procedure was to keep that job three months and then we'd rotate him, cross train him to do something else." The old man rubs the stubble on his chin. Pellets from his eyes fire steadily at mine.

"I had some complaints Willie wasn't working, so I called him to the bridge. *Why aren't you cleaning the berthing compartments?*

"*I won't clean another man's shit.* I could sense his rage. He was about to lose it, so I tried to reason with him.

"*Hatch, I reassigned you below. You have another two-and-a-half months before you are eligible to rotate. Make it though and I'll get you a job topside. For now, if I tell you to clean shit, you will clean shit.*

"Willie's face steamed red. I saw his fists clench. He pulled on the neck of his T-shirt until it ripped and exposed a chest thick with black hair. I remember hearing him grind his teeth just like you were doing a few minutes ago, David."

I push for control. I want to hear the rest.

"The sailor had my full attention after he told me to go to hell." The old man shook his head in disgust. "Insubordinate. Didn't learn a damn thing in boot camp. I could see he was ready to ignite, so I kept an eye on him. He didn't have a clue how much trouble he was in when he called me a SOB. He was ready to go to the mat. I gave the sailor another chance, and asked him, *Are you sure you want to disobey a direct order, son?*

"*You bet your sweet ass I do, sir,* he said, just a touch patronizing. He pulled his arm back, but not before I landed my square fist deep in his soft, round belly. Willie was hunched over recovering when he tipped his head up and said, *You can't get away with this. I'll report you.*

"*Go ahead,* I said. *Next time you disobey a direct order your treatment will be worse.* This man was depriving a village somewhere of its idiot. Hatch stood straight, his fists at the ready, he wouldn't back down. I gave him another chance. *Willie, Willie, Willie. Are you sure you want to fight an officer?* I tried to sway the kid's intentions, told him to think about it. He wasn't much of a fighter. I stepped aside and watched as his punch passed my shoulder. With one arm I caught him off balance and pushed him down the ladder." The admiral stirs a spoon in his coffee cup after he tells the story.

I cover his hand with mine to interrupt. His chin shoots up. "What?"

I jerk my hand away. "Was it your intention to push one of your men down a ladder?" I'm defending my dead father? He didn't protect me when he was alive. "You could have killed Willie Hatch."

He nods yes. "This sailor would have been out of his depth in a car park puddle."

I fold my arms across my chest and lean back. "Wouldn't you say the punishment was rather harsh?" I'm beginning to understand what the Navy considers to be a reasonable way to correct a man's behavior.

"No, it was quite common. I couldn't smash him in the face. That would have left a mark. The kid had to know I meant business. I had to make it look like an accident, but feel like a beating. Men who don't respond to reason respond to brute force."

My stomach burns. I can taste the bile climbing my throat.

"That afternoon I got word the skipper wanted to see me in his quarters. Willie was standing there with a bandage over his eye when I arrived. *McLaughlin, this sailor says you shoved him down the ladder. Is that true?*

"Willie had to be one neuron short of a synapse to see the skipper. I looked at the kid, then at the skipper. *Sir, I can't help it if the guy is so damn awkward he fell down the ladder.*

"*Case dismissed*, the skipper said. *Hatch, an apology is due this officer for the way you've behaved.* Hatch mumbled something, and the captain said, *You're free to go, McLaughlin.* He turned to Willie and said, *Report to the brig, seaman. You've got three days on piss and punk before you report to the chaplain. Think the next time before you decide to fink on one of your superior officers. Your future in the Navy may depend on it.*

James McLaughlin stops talking while Rudy fills our water glasses and tops our mugs. "Be careful what you say about Hatch, Jim," he says and glances at me. He moves to the next table without saying another word.

The old man's eyebrows question Rudy when he looks up. He straightens in the booth and continues with his story. "I wasn't pleased as I left the skipper's cabin. Eating bread and water for three days wouldn't put Willie in a better frame of mind. The kid had to learn how to behave to last in the Navy. I tried with the kid, counseled him, advised him. He listened but couldn't change. Hell, it was out of my hands. From then on Willie Hatch was the brunt of a lot of the men's jokes and pranks. No one on board liked a coward or a fink.

"Later that same tour of duty, we were out of Diego Garcia, the base in the Indian Ocean you asked about. We had been at sea for a week off the coast of Africa when the crew started to get short tempered and quarrelsome, fought and argued with each other. They slacked off on their work. I went to the skipper and requested liberty for the men. The navigator located a small island, large enough for the men to have some entertainment, play softball, throw horseshoes and run around. We changed course and headed for this bit of jungle resting on a bed of stones and sand. Seabees had built a seaplane ramp on the island during WWII. I remembered it from being there another time.

"I discovered later Willie Hatch had stolen two cases of beer from the chaplain and smuggled them aboard the landing craft that ferried the crew to the island. Four men missed muster that night after all sailors from the island had been transported back to the *Cape Esperance*. The CO ordered a search and rescue party for daybreak."

I lean in to listen.

"As the sun crested the horizon we launched a large open lifeboat. I was in charge of the boarding party. We hauled her up to the former seaplane ramp and were climbing out when Willie Hatch bore down on us, bleating, *They buggered me. The sons-a-bitches sodomized me.* He hollered and screamed and cried. I couldn't tell if he was having a baby or dying. He was creased and rumpled. His finger pointed at the three men coming out of the jungle behind him. Hatch dragged his arm across his face and wiped away the snot and tears. His voice cracked when he told me. *They fucked my ass.*

I gasp, nauseated.

"I told the sailors I didn't want to hear another word from any of them. *You're all stepping in shit. Get on board the launch.* Three sailors followed Hatch into the lifeboat. The sun seared the backs of our necks as we rode the waves back to the ship in silence. I broke the forced calm and ordered Hatch off the launch and up the steep gangway ladder first. I told him to wait for me on deck.

"Lines were dropped and as the other sailors secured the lifeboat, I climbed onto the wooden grill and spoke to them. These sailors were all good workers. I asked one sailor if Hatch's accusation was true. He lowered his head. *Those guys fucked the kid. I watched.*

"The other two didn't comment. They climbed onto the gangway. Before they began their ascent, I ordered them to deny anything had happened. The lifeboat was hoisted aboard beside us as we scaled the ladder. The guy chains were still jingling when I hit the deck and ordered Hatch locked in the brig for his own protection.

"All four sailors had screwed the pooch this time. Serious charges were waiting for all of them that afternoon at Captain's Mast. Hatch stood before the captain and accused the men of sexually assaulting him. Each starched seamen denied his accusation. Old Spud Monahan walked back and forth and locked eyes with each sailor, sizing him up.

"*I'm going to give you men the benefit of the doubt,* he said, *but if any of you even look cross-eyed on this ship again, your ass will go to Portsmouth, our Navy's finest prison.* The skipper dismissed them and said to Hatch, *I'm not through with you.* He walked over to a phone and ordered a plane to take Hatch off as soon as possible, back to the main battalion for discipline.

"Willie looked across the captain's cabin at me with sad eyes.

"*Dry your eyes. Act like a man, son,* I told him. *Don't fight it. You'll be back on dry land, soon.*

"*Mac,* the captain said, *you will accompany the prisoner as far as the Rendova. Your orders came in early this morning.*

CHAPTER 41

"This coffee is bitter." The admiral holds his cup high to get Rudy's attention. "Reminds me of cook's morning coffee on the worst day of my life."

"You think bitter coffee is a bad omen?" I laugh.

He doesn't. "It was the end of summer," the old man says from his side of the booth at the Big Boy. "Every moment of that week is etched in the folds of my brain. That first morning burst open with the ocean calm and the sky red, and the worst coffee I've ever tasted." Admiral McLaughlin seems to grow stronger and taller in his seat as his story grows longer. "Bad coffee. Bad luck."

Something about the color red stirs my memory, a maritime ditty my father chanted when I was little. *Red sky in the morning, sailors take warning.* I can't remember the rest.

"My new assignment was chief petty officer on the *Rendova*," the old man continues. "She was on her way home from Korea when the plane set Willie Hatch and me down on her flat deck. Warm sea breezes became cool winds, and the barometer began to fall. I was on the superstructure, leaning on the rail, dragging nicotine from a fag.

"The officer on duty in the wheelhouse, Cal Bradley, emptied his coffee mug over the side, and turned to me. *Can you feel it, Mac?* he said. *It's getting cold.* He stepped inside and told the weatherman to check the barometer, then returned to the rail and lit his cigarette from the tip of mine. Deep swells buffeted the hull. *I'm afraid we're in for some rough weather. I've cancelled your prisoner's plane. He will have to wait until after the blow.*

"The metal door squealed open and the weatherman appeared looking worried. *Barometer's dropping, sir.* He glanced out over the gloomy Pacific afternoon. *Ocean's crawling with nasty weather. I've been in the charthouse plotting warnings all morning.*

"Bradley stood by the signal shack scanning the sea through mounted binoculars. I stood beside him. *Dirty weather usually swirls around the edges of typhoons,* Bradley told me and braced his hip on the rail. He stopped short, retracing his view along the horizon. *There it is,* he said, stepping away from the glasses and pointing the direction for me.

"I saw a long, low swell traveling towards us on the ocean about fifteen miles to port. Bradley spun the binoculars for me and pointed out the telltale feathery plumes of cirrus clouds radiating from a point on the horizon marked by a whitish arc. *That has all the signs of a typhoon,* I said, and spun the powerful glasses to the sharp eyes of the helmsman who was lurking behind us in the bridge house doorway. *Take a look.*

"*Alert the skipper,* Bradley ordered after the helmsman agreed on the cloud formation. *We're in for some waves.*

"*Could it be a typhoon?* the helmsman asked, checking the horizon fore and aft. *Looks like the storm is closing its throat around us.*

"*The weatherman would have warned us by now if it was,* Bradley said.

"Shellbacks who worked on deck kept a watch on the hazy sky from sunrise to sunset, and sunset to sunrise. Most of these men were experienced sailors and had ridden through rough storms before. The sky turned from red at dawn to violet at dusk as the barometer dropped. The air became heavy, hot and moist.

"*Look over there,* pointed a storm-smart lifer. L*ooks like a typhoon halo.*

"*I see land,* pointed an excited crewman reporting for the night watch.

"*That's a bank of clouds, sailor,* I corrected him, *storm clouds.*

"*You sure, sir?* He squinted under the shadow of his hand. *Looks like the Rocky Mountains look to me.* His eyes remained trained over the windward side towards the weather, and stayed there, on alert, over the long, cloud-swollen night.

"*Catch a look at your sweet mountains now,* said the weatherman, handing the heavy-eyed crewman a mug of coffee along with his binoculars. *See how the squalls break off, float from your snow-covered peaks?*

"*You're wanted on the tower,* I said to the weatherman, who retrieved his glasses from the crewman and climbed the ladder two steps at a time.

"*What causes these big blows, chief?* the crewman said, and walked with me toward the bridge ladder. *Have you been caught in a hurricane before? What's it like?*

"*Slow down, son. One question at a time,* I said. *Yes, I have been in a big blow. It felt like a ride in an amusement park.* I winked at the frightened crewman. *In the southern hemisphere hurricanes are called typhoons.*

"*They are caused by a collision of warm air with cold air. The warm air rises like a bubble in water and the cold air rushes into the void.* I spoke from where I stood at the base of the ladder. *The trick is to avoid being sucked inside the swirl. A twist in the air caused by the earth's rotation triggers the storm to move in opposite directions in the northern and southern hemispheres.*

"*I heard that turds in a toilet move clockwise down the drain in the warm waters of the South Pacific like typhoons, and counter-clockwise in the northern hemisphere like hurricanes. Is that true?* asked the young crewman.

"I had to laugh. *You tell the sailor who told you he's right about the typhoons and hurricanes. That's called the Coriolis Force. But his toilet theory stinks. Water flows in the same direction in a toilet no matter where on earth you use it. That's called plumbing.*

"I heard the officer of the deck speak to the weatherman when I got to the tower. *How's the barometer, son?* he asked.

"Falling, sir.

"Most of the crew knew from experience they were in for more serious weather than just a traveling disturbance. It was November. The nastiest winds usually occurred during autumn. Men watched at the rail as the dusky air thickened and shadows engorged the ship. Darkness took over the last calm day.

"*Engage your foul weather-eyes,* I told my men who gaped by the rail the next morning. *Watch for the tell-tales. It could get choppy real fast and you may need to take typhoon positions.* Before we went down for lunch a fine misting rain grew out of the atmosphere. By the time we returned to the flight deck, twenty mile-an-hour winds gusted over the ship's port side. In no time at all foam boiled along the deck, piled against the bridge house and sloshed over the side.

"No one could have been ready for what happened next. The bow of the *Rendova* pitched up, paused, and shuddered on the crest of a large swell. When she dropped, it was with a jarring splash into a trough that sliced the ocean wide open. The young crewman's face was white, his mouth open, but wordless.

"*I suppose you want to go surfing. Is that it, sailor?* I asked, and pulled open a hatch to go below. The wind was howling like a hungry wolf.

"*Where ya going?* The man reached for a life raft bracket.

"*Wherever I end up,* I told him. *I'll let you know.*

"Excuse me, admiral, but that sailor sounded scared. Were you always this tactless in dealing with frightened sailors? Were other officers this rough on their men?"

"Look David. We were not their mothers. A leader couldn't treat his men like scared little boys. He had to treat them like seasoned sailors and hope they lived up to those standards. I wasn't a bully. Enlisted men treated each other like that, too."

"What happened if a man cracked under pressure?"

"I sent the head cases down to the doc for psychological testing. It was up to him to return them to duty or make them walk the plank." He lowers his head and glanced over at me. "Just kidding. We stopped doing that a few years ago. Now we send them out on the evening tide toward shore. Look, David. It's not a perfect world out there. FBI training must be about the same."

"The bureau screens head cases before they set foot in boot camp," I say, and think, except if applicants lie about an insanity gene in their family. "Please go on. The *Rendova* was being exposed to a severe storm at sea."

"I went below to check my men," he says. "The heavy cross-sea jolted the crew below in their bunks, upset unsecured gear and spilled coffee in the mess. I caught that shallow-brained Hatch stirring up the crew, trying to be a big shot. I was standing behind him when he said he didn't personally believe in omens, but that morning he had seen sharks in the water, circling the ship. The men didn't need this kind of talk, so I told him to zip it, threatened him with the brig, and climbed topside to report. He was a magnet for trouble.

"Outside the wheelhouse I drank bitter coffee and watched as the captain climbed the ladder to the bridge.

"*How are you doing today,* chief?

I saluted the portly officer and said, *Living the dream, Captain Hartman. Living the dream.* He was the only person aboard allowed to wear reflective sunglasses. We rarely saw the old cuss's eyes.

"*How's the barometer?* the captain asked as he entered the narrow room surrounded by windows.

"*Falling fast and unstable, sir,* reported the OD, Cal Bradley.

"I had read in '*Knights Modern Seamanship*' these violent sea storms could vary in size from a few miles in diameter to up to several hundred miles in width.

"*What's the bearing and distance of the center?* the captain asked.

"This storm was ten to twelve compass points right from the direction of the wind. The wind was at 240 and out of the west. That put dangerously strong winds coming from 250 or 252 degrees. The direction of the long swell was 230 degrees. We took turns observing the disturbance in the distance and scanning the horizon with the binoculars. By the book this could be a typhoon, and only the barometer could indicate how long we had to maneuver the ship into position.

"*On what track is the typhoon moving?* said the captain.

"Both Bradley and the helmsmen snapped a look at Hartman in disbelief. *Typhoon, sir?* they said at the same time.

"*The weatherman didn't report the storm would be that severe,* I said, and felt dread flood through me. I took a big gulp of coffee to swallow the lump forming in my throat.

"*I told him to squelch it,* said Hartman. *We will be out of its path before it hits. I want to be back in San Francisco on schedule.*

"That was a strange order from a trained naval officer I thought, and wondered if he misspoke. *You want to outrun a typhoon, sir?* I asked to confirm his intentions.

"*You heard me, chief,* said Hartman. *Weatherman, give me the direction of the wind.*

"*With respect, sir,* Cal Bradley said, *uniform safety procedures dictate …*

"*Mister,* the captain said to Bradley. *There are four ways to do things aboard this ship: the right way, the wrong way, the Navy way and my way. We will outrun this storm.*

"We were familiar with standard safety procedures for this kind of storm at sea. The captain would order the helmsman to head into the violent circling blow and keep the wind coming over the bow. When the ship had sailed a full hundred eighty degrees around to the other side of the swirling mass, the helmsman would be ordered to turn the ship away from the fuss and feathers. The carrier would break from the storm and she would steam ahead into safe seas, correct her course and proceed on her mission. I hoped the sarcastic comments on the mental limitations of this old canker we made in private would prove untrue. Standard procedures never included outrunning a storm.

"We tried to hide our fear. A commanding officer's orders were final and not open to discussion, even if he was wrong.

"The helmsman shifted into automatic storm mode, acting like he had salt water barnacles between his ears. He did what he needed to do, what he had done for fifteen years, and what he could do in his sleep without thinking. He had to heave-to and watch for changes in the bearing of the storm center while keeping his eye on the falling barometer. That would give him the storm's track. *"Permission to heave-to, sir?* the helmsman recited from rote.

"My eyes bonded to the barometer, watching for the slightest blip.

"*Heave-to,* the captain roared and steadied himself on a stanchion.

"*Barometer is still falling, sir,* I reported. The winds gusted stronger.

"The helmsman followed orders. On a pad he kept in his shirt pocket he noted changes in the bearing and the further drop of the barometer in five minute increments. *We're in for a ride, sir,* the sailor managed a sick grin as he pulled a safety cable from the wheel mount, lashed it through his belt, and strapped his skeletal white frame to the wheel.

"Foamy seas filled the view through the wheelhouse windows. The ship groaned like a wounded bear. Swells grew deeper with thirty-foot walls. The *Rendova* met the fury of what the captain revealed was Typhoon Marge. The first frontal wave tossed the attack carrier around like a fishing float. The inclinometer on the tower dipped to twenty-five degrees."

CHAPTER 42

"Most sailors learned in basic seamanship that Northern Hemisphere storms circulate counter-clockwise," the old man continues without missing a beat. "They knew the ship had to turn to port, into the weather to ride it out. They had seen flocks of seagulls ride out a freak storm, their beaks by instinct pointed into the wind. The men could tell from the direction of the wind they would soon be in the most dangerous part of the storm. Below deck sailors braced for the ship to turn. Their bare feet felt for the shift to port at any moment. They waited to feel the surge of wind coming at us over the bow.

"*Turn her starboard. Run away from this weather,* ordered the captain.

"I winced. The helmsman and officer of the deck grimaced. I heard what must have been their teeth grind over the sound of the sea. *Come again, sir?* Bradley said.

"I leaned toward the man responsible for the safety of the *Rendova* and her crew, the man who was playing god, junior-grade. I cupped my ear to hear him. This order could spell disaster.

Captain Hartman glared at the helmsman. He watched for him to move. *I repeat, run for sheltered water. That is an order, mister.* He eyed each of the officers on deck.

"What the hell was the old man doing, I wondered, as my stomach rolled over?

"The helmsman knew from experience a sea this rough could break an aircraft carrier in half. He stared at Bradley, as if to pass, in the split second between blinks, a frightful message to a secret co-conspirator. He gulped, begged for help, and watched the color drain from Bradley's face.

"The officer of the deck took a deep breath and nodded to Captain Hartman. I saw muscles tighten down his neck, his jaw clamp shut and his lips freeze in place. Bradley's tense stare told the helmsman a captain's order was a captain's order, no matter how stupid it sounded. He would not buck the system.

"*Turn the damn ship now,* Captain Hartman shouted, his short fuse ignited, his eyes searing with rage. He was an Annapolis graduate who expected his orders to be followed in an expeditious manner. He spread his feet to keep balance and crossed his arms over his chest.

"Cal Bradley swallowed hard and repeated the captain's order. *Turn the ship, sailor.* You could see in his eyes he knew this was wrong.

"The helmsman caught the look, and began to squirm. I knew that move. I had to pee when I got scared, too. *Affirmative, sir,* he said and nodded, numbly. The man focused, and spun the wheel.

"Damn state of affairs this is, I thought. Three of us are petrified and the other one's off his onion. Together we controlled the fate of a multi-million dollar ship and over five hundred lives. I watched the helmsman struggle with the wheel. His eyes bugged wide and aimed straight ahead. His lips were drawn tight across his teeth as he held the new course. During a couple of steep rolls I could see flickers of panic spark from his eyes.

"The OD tossed me a questioning glance and ordered me below to see to the men. Before I could move, a wave caught the ship part way into the flawed turn and eased her sideways. The crest of the swell held her amidships. The carrier hogged. Expansion joints squawked and squealed. Bare metal rubbed against bare metal with uneasy screeches.

Both ends of the ship sagged. Her screws came out of the water. She lost power.

"We were breathless as the ship balanced on the hip of the wave. We knew she was helpless. She tipped. Overhead lights operated by battery flickered, but stayed bright long enough for me to see the inclinometer on the tower. Thirty degrees.

"The captain slid across the lopsided wheelhouse, grabbed a rail and pulled himself upright. Cal Bradley held on to the wheel strut. A dark look clouded his face. No one said a word.

"The helmsman stood with his feet apart, his torso braced against the helm. He fought the wheel to hold his course. The next wave laid her up on her side, forty-five degrees.

"Even sailors on their first tour at sea were afraid. They had watched the sea run in long parallel waves, and knew it was common sense for the bow of the ship to cut into the waves instead of running between them. Experience and intuition flagged disaster to the men. I saw the inclinometer on the tower was at thirty-five degrees before I left the wheelhouse and moved down the ladder to check my men. I crawled down the metal stairway with one hand braced on each side rail.

"It happened too fast for the men on the flight deck and those below decks. None of us were prepared for the sudden tip and jolt as waves slapped the ship's vulnerable side. I had made it down the ladder to the hangar deck when I saw the sea wash the lifeboats adrift, a sobering moment.

"I pulled myself behind the stairs and wedged my body between the ladder and a bulkhead. The wind was so strong it pulled at my eyelids. The salt water needled my face. My feet felt the engines slow, the screws were out of the water again, but the propellers restarted when she dipped into the next wave. And then the mechanical pulsing stopped. The sea would win if we permanently lost power. A drifting steel hulk wouldn't float like a wooden hulled ship. Deprived of forward movement if caught in a trough in a rough sea, the carrier would capsize or fill with water and sink.

"Ragged waves reared and tossed as high as the ship's mast. The superstructure lay parallel to the sea, then whipped like the blade on a windshield wiper as the ship righted and tipped to port. The screws caught with a jolt and we surged ahead.

"Water swept around the bridge house and pulled me awash. A wave took my hat down the deck and into the drink. I groped for a support to stop from being swept after it. A ventilator bracket offered me a grip until it broke. I coughed, spat salt water and held on for my life. Swirling water caught me. I gasped for air. I was headed over the side when my hand caught a hatch cover. My fingers curled around the slippery metal and held like steel hooks. Waves washed past me. Waves dragged me. Waves pummeled me against that open hatch. I flopped on the deck like a soggy, stuffed doll with a pucker factor on high alert.

"I watched a massive wall of water crash into the roller doors on the hangars, then cave them in. During a reprieve from the churning water I scrambled through the hatch, slipped and slid down the ladder. Water washed in with me and streamed below through the second deck hatches.

"Below decks the men moved on instinct as they felt the *Rendova* tip. Men grabbed stanchions to hold themselves from being tossed about. They braced themselves inside their bunks with their knees and the soles of their shoes. They protected their heads with elbows and pillows against flying debris. A pair of dungarees that hung from a hook swayed back and forth with each groaning roll of the ship. When the ship tipped, they stuck out at an odd angle as if blown by a strong wind. Sailors who had not yet vomited breakfast ripped the Phenobarbital tablets taped on the overhead, and swallowed them without water.

"Sick bay was in shambles. Men had been thrown from their bunks. Seamen were drenched. They tried to stand, to run, to climb topside. We were wading waist deep in seawater. Men floated in the flood, struck unconscious from unsecured spare gear. The vessel wallowed broadside.

"*Get these sailors secured,* I ordered the men who were capable.

"*Help me,* cried a pop-eyed white hat in a wild voice. It was that damn, helpless Hatch. He held his arms like broken wings. *Someone help me.* A sailor appeared from nowhere, threaded his busted arms through a life vest and steered him forward toward an open hatch and ladder that led up.

"Down on the mess deck, boiling-hot soup slopped over the tops of the copper cookers, scalding the cooks scrambling around the flooded galley floor.

"Sailors aboard the *Rendova* knew rough weather drills without their chief saying a word. Those who could move closed hatches, and assisted those who couldn't. Men wearing yellow life vests climbed ladders to get out.

"*We're going down,* shrieked a young sailor as the ship was flung skyward. His nostrils were dilated. His eyes bulged. *I don't want to drown! I don't want to die.*

"*Take some deep breaths and count to ten.* I grabbed him by the shoulders, and strung his arms through his life vest. *She's not going to sink. I've got you.* I turned the man around, buckled his vest, and shoved him toward the forward hatch.

"When I made it back up to the hangar deck I saw the black, ragged sea climb toward the sky with each roll. I looked to the heavens. There were no stars.

"I scrambled up to the bridge house as the ship yawed. The compass heading read one-eighty degrees. We had held our course for a couple of minutes when a swell, a wave and a gust of wind hit together. The aircraft carrier was flung on its beam ends to port.

"The helmsman reeled, banged against the wheel, and fell to his knees. He grasped for the wheel spokes to stand. Blood stained his whites at his knees, and urine stained his pants higher up. The odor of fresh shit permeated the wheelhouse.

"Cal Bradley's eyes were on the gyrocompass. *We're okay,* he shouted, feigning calm. *We'll all be back chipping paint in a few hours.*

"The crashing didn't last long, but it was the longest five minutes my men and I had ever experienced at sea. All decks were chaos. The crew responded during the reprieve, and did their best to position themselves for the next onslaught. It was commotion whipped into organized confusion.

"The ship stirred and shuddered. A moment later she lay over on her port side at forty-two degrees. The helmsman, protected from the waves in the wheelhouse, had a firm hold on the wheel and kept his course steady. The captain was at his side. The next swell brought her upright. Without a pause she rolled to starboard twenty-five degrees. I held my breath. The wind held her from tipping farther. The steel coffin creaked. Thumping sounds from all directions signaled unsecured supplies and gear were still loose.

"The *Rendova* groaned. When we heard welds snap and splinter loose from the frame, the crew in the wheelhouse grew silent. The radio buzzed and sputtered amid the wreckage. The weatherman found the receiver and held it out for the captain to hear.

"A crackling voice reported, *Five-hundred men down here have dropped to their knees in one motion to pray. Is this it, Captain? Is she breaking up, sir?*

"Squealing sounds erupted from below. A sudden sea surge jerked the phone from the weatherman's hand. The black cord snaked across the wheelhouse floor and wrapped around my ankle. I reached down to free my foot and was stunned by the view on deck. Inch thick steel expansion plates were tearing like tissue paper from where they were welded and riveted to the hull. They came loose and slid into the sea. The bounding bar sheared clear. An eight-by-four foot steel strip whined and squawked as it ground into the bare metal of the broken expansion plate. I could feel the propeller come out of the water. The screws stopped again. The entire ship shimmied and moaned. Gusts up to a hundred fifty knots fed the storm. A surging sea swished by the weakened hull, unaware of the scrambling sailors inside.

CHAPTER 43

"Was anyone lost overboard?" I ask Admiral McLaughlin from my side of the booth where my butt and feet have fallen asleep. I feel like concrete setting up. I need to move.

"We lost no men from the *Rendova*, but two Navy ships disappeared during Typhoon Marge."

"Including their crews?" The question escapes my lips before I think.

His look told me there were no survivors.

Admiral McLaughlin stretches his legs into the aisle and continues. "A heavy cross-current spit the sea as the *Rendova* rolled to port. The helmsman held his course. It seemed like an eternity before the ship slid from the swirling mass and emerged into the relief of medium seas. The ocean was a maudlin umber and ochre with kelp trawling behind in the ship's wake.

"The old girl had sustained serious damage, and the crew was badly shaken. Men made their way on deck and heaved at the rail until their insides were scooped clean. Eventually the crew put their backs into their work. Sailors pumped seawater from below decks without complaint, elated they weren't thrashing around with the sharks. They repaired and cleaned the ship with an adrenaline rush, thrilled to be alive. That night it seemed like everyone was up on the flight deck watching the most beautiful sunset anyone had ever witnessed."

I remember the rest of the ditty my father used to chant when I was a little boy: *Red sky in the morning, sailors take warning. Red sky at night, sailors delight.* It made sense to me now.

"Anger surfaced next," McLaughlin says. "Sailors aboard the seaplane tender had become experienced seamen. The encounter with Typhoon Marge had stripped the spit shine from their training and added the patina of wisdom that comes from firsthand experience. Many of them had been taking classes, had read '*Knight's Modern Seamanship*' and knew rough weather drills.

"After the storm the crew refused to address the captain as anything but *Hartman* except to his face. The men had lost respect for him. I listened to their complaints. In the sailors' eyes the old man didn't deserve the rank he held. Most of the veteran sailors on board considered a man's station in life connected to the cut of his jib. The way he behaved and treated his people was key, not how close he ranked to the top of his graduating class at officer's training school.

"They agreed the captain of this shipwreck should walk the plank for giving the order to run from the storm. We were all biting angry at the bastard. Our heads could house thoughts of retribution, but those thoughts were not allowed to pass our lips. Sailors wore paperclips on the pockets of their blue overhauls indicating their level of disgruntlement. The acronym, PAPERCLIPS, stood for *People Against People Ever Reenlisting. Civilian Life is Preferable*.

"When the rolling seas of the North Pacific allowed, Captain Hartman disappeared inside his cabin and didn't come out for a week. His steward reported he sank into the comfort of a chair after the storm. At week's end he hauled out an empty case of Jack Daniel's Tennessee Whiskey.

"Skulking away from the still raging Typhoon Marge, the *Rendova* cut a new course for the West Coast of North America. Anyone capable of welding was put to work tacking the ship back together. Marge finally blew by and was replaced by a gray drizzle and a sea the color of red wine. Our bucket of broken bolts steamed through rain, gusty winds and cross-swelling seas in the backwash of the storm. Our heading was the shipyard in San Francisco.

"The rolling and plunging had smashed dishes, chairs, and bottles. Water sloshed in the passageways and antennas were down. No hot food could be served until the third day out, no coffee at all. Makeshift splints and bandages confined the wounded to their bunks.

"Human hands working together repaired the ship while she limped and clanked along the whale road toward home. It would take an extra two weeks to get to San Francisco because our engines had been compromised during the storm.

"A young man welding a popped door looked up while I inspected his work and asked. *Do they call the Rendova a Kaiser coffin because bad weather could sink her?*

"*This ship is no Kaiser coffin as you damn near found out,* I said, ribbing the kid and thinking we had all nearly died. *Remember this, son. The USS Rendova, CVE-114, was built by the Todd-Pacific Shipyard in '44.*

"*Fifty Liberty Ships were made by a company called Kaiser Shipbuilding out of Vancouver, Washington,* I told the sailor. *They were built in a hurry after Pearl Harbor, slapped together to ferry troops and equipment to ports along the fronts. They are still seaworthy, and this one will be too if you do a good job and tack her back together. Rosie the Riveter worked for Kaiser.*

"*Who is Rosie the Riveter?*" he said.

"I took a deep breath and inspected his welds on the door hinge. I nodded to a joint that needed another patch and whispered, *Never tell a woman you've never heard of Rosie.*

"Within the confines of a ship, rage can make the smallest discomfort seem gigantic. The carrier chugged along, scarcely faster than the pod of dolphins that surfed the waves beside us. Anxiety swayed to boredom and back as we sailed toward the naval repair yard. Bare metal grew a ruddy fur of rust from the salt air. After the patchwork was done and the ship secured, we decided she was too broken to have the men resume normal work details.

"Sailors sat with their feet over the side, watching the sea spray and the shadow of the ship cutting through the swells. Some days were static and windless with only the steady scorch of the sun to mark the time. Beneath the flight deck men played cards. No one won.

"I was reading when Lieutenant Kolinkar, the legal officer, came into the bunkroom we shared with thirty-two other officers. Karl was uncommonly quiet. He sat on the side of his bed and unlaced his shoes.

"*I thought you were officer of the watch tonight?* I closed my book. Kolinkar didn't answer. *You all right, Karl?* I said.

"*I'm confined to quarters for five days.*

"*You caught stealing heartless Hartman's booze?* the gun boss said from a bunk across the passageway.

"*Lay off,* I said. *What's the fallout, Karl?*

"Lieutenant Kolinkar dropped to his bunk, swung his feet up and braced them on the bulkhead. He clasped his hands behind his head before he answered. *I was on duty on the tower, halfway through my four hour watch. Nothing had happened but salt water fore and aft. I had some change in my pocket and was jingling it around with my hand when Hartman climbed up on the bridge.*

"*You stupid bastard,* the gunnery chief said. *You know the old man can't stand noise of any kind.* He grimaced. *What were you thinking?*

"*I wasn't thinking and didn't expect the albatross to be on the bridge that late. The old bird fixed on me with his dark accusing eyes. He told me when I'm on watch I don't have use for coins in my pockets. He relieved me and sent me to my cabin to stay for five days.*

"The gun boss moaned. *That man's brain is a size nine and a half, I'd gauge.*

"*How much longer do we put up with that SOB?* Kolinkar spat out the tired song we all had sung.

"*Steady as you go, lieutenant. Follow procedures. Write the captain up,* I said. *Date and sign it.*

"*Come on Mac, what's the use of polishing another cannonball?*

"Lieutenant Kolinkar scowled. *Pigs in a bucket. Fuck it.* He thumped his foot against the bulkhead, and stared at a rivet in the overhead.

"The old man sent for me during dinner two days later. The messenger told me an expansion joint in the overhead of his sea quarters squeaked. I finished the last few bites of food before I responded. When I arrived at his cabin, the captain stubbed his cigarette in his ashtray and shouted, *Damn you, Chief. When you get a message I sent for you, don't resume feeding your face. You will proceed to me at once.*

"I stood at attention while he spoke. *Yes, sir.* I would give the old bird a chance. *Captain Hartman, the men are tired, and I know you mean well, but ...*

"*Don't mistake me for someone who gives a shit.* His eyes looked empty. He swatted me away like I was a housefly. *I have no loyalty and I have no pride. I'm doing my job.*" He lit a fresh Camel and took a long draw before flipping it through a porthole. *Do you have something to report to me, chief?*

"*No, sir.* I returned to the mess and fixed myself a big bowl of vanilla ice cream. I poured on chocolate syrup, grabbed a cup of joe, and sat down to relax while the sea pushed past.

"Our ruptured bucket with its broken crew approached the Farallon Islands that marked the entrance to San Francisco Bay. The men were weary from the hard blows behind us. They watched the steep headlands of rock at the opening to the inlet bristling with white caps and were relieved when we picked up a pilot boat. Dark splotches of kelp marked the shoals. The helmsman steered the keel around them into the sheltered waters of the channel. We chugged behind the small tug into the bay to a private dock.

"Twelve ambulances came alongside to haul the injured away as soon as the cleats had her moored to the dock. Men had broken bones, concussions, and open wounds all because the captain ignored typhoon safety procedures.

"The first thing Captain Hartman did ashore was to call a press conference. *The Pacific Fleet*, he told the reporters, *is responsible for the safety of a hundred and two million square miles. That's fifty-two percent of the globe's surface. It is hard work in all kinds of weather. But, this last passage was the wildest time I've seen at sea in twenty-eight Pacific crossings.* Hartman made himself out to be a big hero. He talked like he saved the ship. We couldn't believe it. Sure couldn't digest it.

"Dockside repair was a whirlwind of activity. Men were rotated on one day off the next, just long enough for a sailor to go out and get drunk. A private contractor worked around the clock and had the *Rendova* underway in twelve days. The skeleton crew left aboard spent time flaking the lines into neat figure eights so when we arrived in San Diego we could uncoil them fast without snagging.

"A yeoman from the ship's personnel office approached and handed me a yellow slip of paper as we embarked on our shakedown cruise. I will never forget that happy moment. We were under the Golden Gate Bridge when I read I had been transferred back to the *Cape Esperance* upon arrival in San Diego for further transfer to Pennsylvania. I had been accepted for seventeen weeks of Catapult and Arresting Gear School at the Naval Air Materials Center. This set of orders allowed me to leave the noxious memories of serving under Hartman bubbling in my wake.

"Work on the flight deck with planes coming and going twenty-four-seven was a dangerous job, but offered hazardous duty pay, a plus for my wife and the baby we had adopted.

ilot's life depended on the skills of the flight deck hese planes were shot from the deck like cannonballs piercing the sky. The crews guided planes home in all kinds of weather to our bobbing runway at sea. If a plane came in too low, it could hit the side of the ship below the runway and explode. If the pilot wasn't advised of a crosswind, the plane could be blown into the bridge or flip on the deck and burst into flames. It was a responsible job, and I was a responsible candidate.

"*I thought you had given up on that school*, said the personnel yeoman before I slapped him on the back. *Are you sure you want to ease away from the great Rendova,* the sailor snickered.

"*You SOBs are going to have to take some responsibility for your own amusement when I'm gone,* I said as I crouched like a prize fighter, popping a few punches his way. He moved out of range. We both walked to the rail and gazed at the moon's pull on the night tides.

"Seventeen weeks later I had had enough of solid ground and flapping bed sheets on the backyard clothes line. Philadelphia had been good for my little family, but I was losing my sea legs. I stood outside at night to scan the sky. I couldn't see stars or feel the rocking ocean. My allergies were in full bloom. I always felt healthier at sea where the air smelled nice and clean. I breathed better without the toxic carbon monoxide of an inland city, and the ragweed of the Midwest. At night I dreamed of standing by the ship's rail in a heavy sea. Without water I felt like god was gone. When I had completed my course I reported for duty in San Francisco where the *Rendova* was readying to embark for Korea.

CHAPTER 44

"The last time I saw Willie Hatch was the day we landed in San Francisco after the typhoon. He was standing on deck about to disembark. We had already parted ways, but he turned back and looked up at the bridge. For a long time we stood there. His cap was gathered in a fist held to his chest. He raised his hand, saluted with his middle finger extended, and smiled. Then he pulled his cap down over his eyes, turned, and disappeared with his military escort.

"I was still at sea when Willie sat for his court-martial in San Francisco. I had submitted my testimony in writing. *I saw no evidence to substantiate Hatch's claim.*"

I feel hot. My emotions are all over the place ... confused, aghast, furious. I pull the collar of my shirt from my neck. "The man was raped by the other seamen," I say. The ice rattles as I down my tumbler of water.

"Yes, I'm sure of it," he says, and drains his glass.

"Why didn't you stand up for him? He was weak."

"I didn't think Willie thought his career was worth fighting for. Besides, I couldn't afford to lose three good men for one incompetent. We needed the other three for operations. Hatch was no good under pressure. He knew it. We knew it."

"You covered for your friend." I stiffen.

"I suppose I did," he says.

The admiral is unaware of the memory he evokes in me of a playground bully from my elementary school. My lips twitch. "You iron-handed, son-of-a-bitch. You should be horsewhipped." My fists clench at my thighs. I stand abruptly. Spaghetti-stained plates and empty mugs scatter on the floor as my knees hit and tip the table. The echo of shattered china churns the air as I rush from the restaurant, kicking snowdrifts and stomping along the roadway to no place in particular.

I find myself at the Overlook, just off the village square, and order a whiskey. "Make the next one a double," I say after chugging the first. I walk to the restroom. A moment later my fist hurts and there's a hole in the plaster on the men's room wall.

CHAPTER 45

Images pierce my thoughts with possible scenarios. The picture always starts with a pile of faded denims heaped on the jungle floor. Over and over I see Willard T. Hatch pushed prone, pinned to the black jungle loam. One sailor twists his arm, bending his hand flat to his back. The second man stands with a foot on the downed man's neck. Kneeling behind him a third sailor unzips his dungarees, and drops his underwear. The rapists take turns. Buttock muscles clenching and relaxing as their hips thrust forward and back. And then the jungle is silent.

The pictures burn my mind and make me physically sick. I vomit until I'm empty, gag and hold my convulsing stomach. When the dry heaves subside, anger and a passion for vengeance fill me. The load of revenge is so heavy my thoughts roll to pity and then to revulsion. In the end I want to open my veins and drain my father's shame from me.

I sit by my window, more lonely than I have ever been in my life. I call my woman. She's not home, she's never home. I gaze through a gloomy darkness, stare at a streetlight, and try to make sense of it all. The vomiting comes back, then the anger returns. My emotions boil to such a pitch I drink a full six pack of Heineken.

I lay tangled in sheets while my thoughts burst into a series of twisted knots. McLaughlin's generation had a raw deal. None of it was fair for him … not growing up poor and fatherless during the depression, and not being a forgotten guinea pig for the Department of Defense. But he lived with it, lived through it and moved on. He even fought to change the system, to correct his government's mistakes. Yet, he was a liar.

My father, weak and vulnerable, was compromised on that tropical island. His treatment wasn't fair … not the rape by his shipmates, not the denial by the three men who sodomized him and not by the trumped-up charges that ordered him dismissed in disgrace. Why didn't he have the inherent wisdom to keep his mouth shut, forget the incident and move on? Why couldn't he come to terms with the mistreatment the Navy dished out and move past the rape? Why didn't he learn to control his rage? Why didn't he refuse to talk about what happened like so many other veterans? Why didn't he lie to my mother?

When compassion for my father had run its course, hate took its turn. Why didn't he hang himself in her bedroom where I wouldn't find him? Willard Hatch had picked the garage. That bastard must have known that's where I played. He must have known I'd be the one to find him, that his decision to end his life would forever mark mine.

I remember wondering back then, if his suicide was my fault, if killing himself was his way of punishing me. Now that I know his father killed himself, I wonder if suicide runs in Hatch genes. I drink another beer to get past that fear.

It takes still another beer for me to accept that Willard Hatch was incapable of thinking past himself. Suicide is the act of a sick man or the selfish act of a coward. Either way, Hatch burned and scarred the lives of his family. His inheritance to me was like a rem of atomic radiation, to carry, to wait and to worry about for life. Is my destiny defined? Will I kill myself and abandon my son? I roll around the mattress looking for answers.

Why didn't the Navy support the weaker men? Why didn't congress take responsibility for the damaged soldiers they knowingly sent into harm's way? Why didn't our nation insist we take care of our own, like McLaughlin's family did to survive the Great Depression?

I'm angry with the Department of Defense. I'm angry with the commander-in-chief. My head hurts. I long for the escape of sleep.

I roll over and open my laptop. My resentment smolders as I read the history of the Manhattan Project on the Internet. In 1947 the name was changed to the Atomic Energy Commission, but the mission remained the same, building and testing earth-shaking, planet-breaking weapons.

Our government is still sucking fearful Americans into an endless race for the biggest and most destructive weapons. Maybe the nefarious old man was right when he pushed my father down the ladder. McLaughlin's decision to discard the life of a wanton misfit may have been justified.

Willie Hatch was a man who could not be counted on to hold his own on a two-man fire hose, a man who was frightened of going aloft, and a man who wouldn't follow a direct order. This maverick chose to fight a superior officer. In the end, he chose suicide.

The admiral told me that sometimes the only way to change direction is with violence and force. Maybe he's right. He is an experienced military officer. My father just didn't get it, and this officer must have seen that.

I'm weary. Confusion has drained my judgment. My thoughts are blurred dim by this unending, sleepless night.

CHAPTER 46

"I'd like to buy you breakfast," I say into the telephone receiver, "at 7:00 a.m. on Friday."

"You wouldn't poison me, would you?" the admiral asks.

"The FBI would fire me if I poisoned an informant ... without permission." I need to clear the air in order to close the case. "Sorry I left in a huff."

After a pause he says, "I know the incident with Willie sounds heavy-handed. That kid just couldn't get it." Another pause. "You still there?"

"I'll pick you up at eight," I say, and click off.

Snow falls through the powdery morning light as I make my way to the village. Chunky snowflakes glint like glass beads, and pop as they hit the windshield. At the restaurant I pick up a *Detroit Free Press* from the pile near the door, order ham and eggs and read the paper while the admiral talks to the waiter about an advanced degree and a teaching career in college.

"Two more years working for a degree," Rudy says. "I don't know if I can handle a commitment that long."

"Commitment is different for everyone," the retired admiral says and looks down at his plate of ham, eggs, and ketchup. "These eggs were a day's work for the hen, while this ham was a lifetime commitment for the pig."

Rudy feigns disgust, and pushes into the kitchen with a grin on his face.

"Listen to this," I read. *Leader of Atomic Veterans Dies.* I fold the paper in half so I can watch the old man's expression as he listens. McLaughlin looks stunned as I read the article.

"I need to use your telephone. You dial." He spits out the number from memory.

I fumble in my jacket and produce my compact silver cell. "How in the world do you remember all these details?" I ask handing the phone to him. "You'll have to wait for the party to answer."

"Total recall can be a curse." He listens with the phone flat against his ear. "Is this Minnie?" He pauses. "I just read about Richard in the *Detroit Free Press*. What happened? Em hmm," he says and adjusts the phone on his ear. "Yes." He leans forward, his eyes fixed on his empty breakfast plate. "I'm so sorry, Minnie. Richard was a solid man, a fine man. You can be proud of him. He must have accomplished what he was supposed to do on this earth and now the Lord has called him home." He pauses, and listens. "What's the JAG officer's name?" His eyes meet mine. "Then, it is official." The old veteran puts his spare hand on his forehead and listens. "Do you have my number?" He pauses. "That's right. You know I would. Goodbye, Minnie." He folds the phone closed and hands it back to me.

"Richard Hauschild's appendix burst and the infection took hold before he was put on the operating table. His blood pressure dropped when they opened him up and his insides were eaten away. Cancer," Admiral McLaughlin says. "His heart stopped, they tried but couldn't revive him. It was over." His voice cracks. His face wrinkles. He looks away.

The old skipper continues reporting through his grief. "The day before he went in the hospital he received a letter from a JAG officer at the Veterans Administration. The class action suit had been dropped because of the Feres doctrine. Remember I told you about it … no serviceman can sue the government for anything that happened during the time he worked for the government. Sounds like the loophole

Hauschild thought they might have is a slipknot. All of us involved with the nuclear testing are either dead or dying. Our numbers have dwindled dramatically." McLaughlin's eyes seek mine. A smile forces its way across his face. "Our work together is at a dead end, David, it's time to coil up the lines."

I ride with his pain, envying his ease of resolve. "We still have the trial for Gibbons," I say, and make an attempt to be positive. "The prosecutor will put me on the stand, save you the torture of testifying."

The admiral stares at the table, his face reflects in the gray surface.

"Thanks to your cooperation and the evidence you gave the government, we should be able to nail him." I smile when he lifts his eyes. "We wouldn't have had a case without you." McLaughlin is right. The investigation is over. Neither of us celebrate or laugh aloud. Our breakfast meetings have ended.

We sit across the hard surface from one another camouflaging our feelings. Our conversation has lost its edge. With my elbows resting on the table, I say, "Guys like me will keep enforcing laws like the Feres doctrine."

"I worked enforcing those laws, too," the old man says and leans back on his bench. "If I still smoked, I'd light up right now." He mimics a cigarette between his fingers, takes a deep draw, and blows white circles of imaginary smoke.

"What happens to the new batch of veterans who get sick from unknown diseases?"

"They'll suffer like all the rest of us did." He pauses. "David?" McLaughlin's voice is low and halting. "I'm sorry about your father."

I stare at my coffee cup. My jaw tightens. "How did you know?" Before the admiral can answer, I say, "Was it your seventh sense?" I see him nod.

"What happened to Hatch after he left the service?" he asks.

"He came back to Boston and got into trouble, became an embarrassment to our family. I was seven when he hung himself in the garage."

The old man's eyes tell it all. I see his pain at my losing the chance for warmth from a father. I see his grief revisited at losing his own father when he needed him the most. I see his anguish at not being able to procreate and sustain the McLaughlin bloodline. I see he misses his adopted son Slick. This warrior understands the importance for a boy to have a father, and for a father to have a son.

"How did you find me?" the old man whispers. He looks drained.

"When the NAAV case surfaced, I was working in research. I ordered my father's file from St. Louis around the same time I ordered yours. I had always been curious about his service record. I knew the name of his ships because he carved me a toy ship for a gift and printed the names on the side. When I saw you had served on the *Cape Esperance* and the *Rendova* I became even more interested in your file. There were eight sailors with the same name as yours in the Navy during the time my father served. I just got lucky with you. My favorite toy, a seaplane tender connected us. That and the Navy."

"Lots of men carved ships from wood in their spare time at sea," he says.

"My mother refused to talk about her first husband," I tell him. "I thought his death was my fault. I couldn't figure out what I had done or said to him that would cause him to bail out like that, cause us so much unhappiness. I thought my mother was protecting me with her silence. When I read in his service record that the results of a military trial led to his undesirable discharge, I wanted to know the charges against him. It was pure serendipity that your name appeared as a witness on his paperwork the same day I saw your name listed on the bureau's upcoming work assignments." There, I think I made it through one wave without drowning.

The admiral is quiet.

"My father had many weaknesses and led a troubled life. He was screwed up just like me. It may have been his destiny to die that way, and his father's fate before him."

McLaughlin's eyes snap open. "Your grandfather committed suicide, too?"

"Blew his brains out." My chest grows lighter after the terrible secret is squeezed clean.

"Destiny is not a matter of chance, son," the old man says. "It's a matter of choice. Don't ever forget that. It's not to be waited for. It's something to be achieved."

"I don't know anymore," I say. "Maybe I'm weak like him. I learned at the academy about patterns of criminal behavior that repeat. I wonder if…"

"Only crazy people never have doubts," the old man says. "I'm always disappointed by those who see people who change their opinions as a sign of weakness. It seems to me to be a sign of their sanity."

I swallow hard and the knot growing in my throat dissolves. I feel freed of one protective layer around my heart. "I'll finish your paperwork today, and then go into New York for the weekend."

"Will you see your girl?"

"There you go again. You're reading my mind. I think I'd like to bring her here to meet you. Would that be okay? Maybe you could use your seventh sense on her. I'd like to know if our marriage will work before I take the plunge."

The old man brightens and sits upright. "That might be a mistake, David. Women still consider me a hunk."

CHAPTER 47

My fingertips rap a tabletop rhythm as I wait in Leticia's Brooklyn flat on Saturday afternoon, anxious to take her out for dinner. When she arrives and finds me sprawled on her bed watching TV she's mildly happy to see me but looks exhausted. I'm surprised to learn she has been taking classes at NYU after work and on weekends.

"Of course I'm glad to see you. It's just that … I'm tired. Can you come up to the city next weekend?" she asks as we walk to her favorite diner. "It's my semester break and I can spend four entire days with you. I've got a big project due, and as much as I'd like to, I can't see you this week at all. I lose focus when I'm with you." She takes a few steps, stops, and turns. "What's different about you?"

"New shoes." I grin, pleased she noticed.

She glances down and raises her eyebrows to acknowledge the footwear. "Somehow you look shorter. Maybe it's my new heels." She wraps her arms around me. "We fit each other, don't we?"

I kiss her nose and we continue walking.

"Good evening," says an elderly man walking alone in the other direction.

"Hello," I say.

"Top of the evening to you," says a drunk, tipping a hat with a greasy brim to us as he emerges from an alley.

"Hello," I say.

Two men laughing on the corner smile at us. "Hello."

"Piss off," I say, pulling my woman closer to me.

She stops and crosses her arms over her generous chest. "No silly, that's not it. Something else is different. You seem mellow." She shrugs. "No, that's not it, either. I don't know why I brought it up. It doesn't matter. So, can you come up next weekend?" She takes my arm and we continue walking.

"I like that … that thing you're wearing. You look beautiful tonight," I say after we occupy the last two stools at the counter. "Come to Michigan with me next weekend."

A surly waiter in a dirty white apron steps in front of Leticia. "What's it gonna be, honey?"

After we order the burger special, I say, "I want you to meet this old man in Michigan. I wish my father would have been more like him. I know it sounds crazy, but in just one week we have developed this … this friendship. We can talk about anything. He tells great stories and has total recall. He is absolutely awesome. What's insane is that we're both in an investigation involving him."

I steal a hot French fry from the plate the waiter slams on the counter between us and continue talking while I chew. "I guess you could call him my mentor. I told him about you. He wants to meet you."

I swallow, and snatch another thin golden stick. "He's a quarter Cheyenne." I smile and give her a hug. "Say yes. Besides meeting him, I could use your help packing my apartment. I'll be moving back to D.C."

Steaming plates of burgers slide down the bar and land precisely in front of each of us. Leticia works at squeezing ketchup over hers until I take the bottle from her and tap it soundly on the bottom with the base of my hand. Thick red sauce shoots out, covers her burger and oozes down the sides.

"So, David wants to take a trip with me?" she smiles and motions for me to pour ketchup over her fries. She snakes one through the red sauce, licks the slender stick clean with her long pink tongue, then sucks the fry inside. "You want me to meet someone important in your life?"

She licks red sauce from her fingers and dabs her mouth with a paper napkin. "Sounds like a serious invitation, Dave." Leticia fingers another fried potato. "You've never taken me anywhere important before." She holds the fry next to my mouth and says, "Open."

"It is serious, and, I am serious," I say, opening my mouth for the fry. I get off my stool, take her hand and kneel on the scruffy tile floor. "I love you, Leticia. Will you marry me?"

"David Dugan, where did this come from?" she asks, stiffening. "I thought you liked the status quo ... your space, my space, the freedom to walk at any time."

"Changed my mind," I say, and eye my burger.

"Marriage is a different matter," she says. "I don't think you have a clue ..." She is distracted.

"Leticia, my knee is stiff."

She pays no attention and goes into a stream-of-consciousness conversation with herself. "I'll have to give this some thought ... I do want to get married some day, but you don't know how to be intimate. You don't treat women well ... your mother, or me. I don't know if we're right for one another."

"We have great sex." I change knees but keep hold of her hand.

"That has nothing to do with intimacy or respect. You don't trust me."

"Why would you think that?"

"You call me two or three times a day to check on me, to see what I'm doing. What is that about if not lack of trust? You get all jazzed up with jealousy. You claw at me."

"Honey, I told you I love you. I just want to talk to you, marry you and be with you always." I rub my knee.

"David, you haven't introduced me to your parents. When did you plan to do that?"

"You're right. I'm wrong. I have it on good authority it's all right to change your mind, it's not a sign of weakness. It's just that I've always worked hard to please them and show them that ..."

"... show them you're not a failure like your father," she says.

"My father? What do you know about my father?"

"Look David, I know you feel guilty about your father's suicide."

"How do you know about ..."

"You talk in your sleep, and, I spoke to your mother."

"You called my mother?"

"I phoned her office. She was very sweet."

"Jesus, honey, stay away from her. The woman is a cannibal. She's capable of ripping your heart out and serving it back to you as an appetizer." I take both of her hands in mine. "Leticia, please marry me."

"I ... I ... don't think so. I'd have to sell you to my parents. All they know is that your name is Dave. When I tell them you're FBI they won't be pleased, but they would accept you. Black folks never turn their backs on family no matter what."

I move up to my stool. "I love you, Leticia. Marry me and we'll make it work." I wrap my arm around her and kiss her cheek while she picks up a fry and swims it through the ketchup. "As long as we love each other we can make it work." I keep one arm around her and dive into my burger.

"This is so unlike you," she says. "Have you thought this through? I want more than kinky sex. What about children and the hassles they would face because they'd be ..."

"Half-breeds?"

"Yes, you could call them that. I don't think so, Dave. I'm not sure marriage would work for us, and, I don't want to end up a single parent working my ass off raising my kids while my old man is off screwing somebody else."

"Will you at least come to Michigan with me this weekend?"

Leticia pushes her plate away, turns and gazes into my eyes.

"Want some dessert?" I ask, grab her arm and exit the diner. The click of her heels echoes in the empty streets as we walk back to her tiny flat.

On Sunday morning I call the admiral and ask if he would be around the following weekend to meet my woman and to sign off on a few reports for the Ann Arbor field office.

"You get serious with your woman, Agent Dugan?" the old man cackles into the phone. "Done a background check?" He laughs into the mouthpiece. "Of course I'd like to meet her. Bring her along. I'll buy you both a decent meal at the Big Boy."

CHAPTER 48

Monday morning I sit through a refresher course on new weapons at Quantico and pull the early shift guarding hotel hallways for presidential candidates. I squeeze out one evening to tell my mother and stepdad in Boston about my plans. My mother smothers me in melodrama and freaks when she learns Leticia is black. I don't know why but I am surprised she is this uptight. I should know to expect the worst from her. My chest burns from stomach bile as I walk out to my car.

FBI training critiques run all day Saturday which leaves me with little time to pack or buy a new battery for my cell phone. Our Sunday flight to Detroit is problematic with false starts and delays. We have a tight connection ahead on the return trip because Leticia has an early class. The only car left to rent is an antique hatchback which we drive into Swainsville at five on Sunday afternoon. It feels good to have my woman next to me, yet I am looking forward to some verbal sparring with the old warrior.

"He's an eccentric old coot with an amazing memory," I say and steer toward his frozen lake. "He'll want to tell you sea stories," I say and power over the hard packed snow. The parking lot is crusted a dirty gray, and is pocked here and there by icy footprints. "We'll take him out to dinner at the restaurant I told you about." As I switch off the ignition music from a chickadee fills the air.

"You mean dinner at the diner that serves awesome strawberry pie?" she says.

"Emm, but it's not like our diner in the city." As we walk the sidewalk together, wild winds sweep over the frozen water and blanket us in a fine layer of frosty snow. "Waiters are courteous in Swainsville," I say, brushing the cold powder from her startled face. "Your lips are turning blue."

Sunshine bursts from behind a dark cloud. The sky turns turquoise. "Old men here propose to women just to make conversation," I tell her. The wind stops. When I inhale, I notice a lack of moisture in the air, which leaves a drying-out, breaking-down cold that freezes the hair inside my nose. I wrap my arm around my woman and pound on his front door with my knuckles. A holly wreath with a large black bow hangs from the brass knocker. I didn't notice that wreath on his door the last time I was …

"Dave, what are you doing here?" Corny says as she pulls the door open.

"Hi. I came to see the admiral. He's expecting me. I called last week. Corny, this is my fiancée, Leticia."

"You better come in." The admiral's daughter steps aside as we walk into his condo. Murphy runs from the bedroom, snarls when he sees me, and plants his claws in the carpet next to Corny. The old man's recliner is missing. The sofa has been moved. A tri-folded American flag rests on the bookcase under the picture of Faye.

"Daddy died early Friday morning."

My heart twists inside my chest, and pushes my breath away. My knees fold. I collapse into the sofa. "Died?" My elbows rest on my knees. My head is in my hands.

"David?" I hear Leticia's voice from the door, then she appears at my side and slides an arm around me.

"He was fine last week when I left him," I manage to say, suddenly cold. "What happened?"

"Tuesday night he asked to go to the hospital."

"He asked? He must have felt lousy. He hated hospitals. He hated doctors. He actually asked?" I say, disbelieving his own daughter's words while I rub my shivering arms. I'm stunned. Emotions block my mind from processing real time information. He had told me his aim was to live for a century, and I believed him. A man with a will as strong as his could do whatever he set out to do.

My brain bumps back to memories of his sense of fun. Could this be another one of his practical jokes? When I look up, the pained expression haunting Corny's face assures me it is not. I rub the back of my neck but can't make reality disappear.

So, James H. McLaughlin has left his final mark. Tears stain my cheeks as I think about life without my mentor. Will I remember I am the one who determines my fate? Can I remove the calluses that strangle my heart, the scar tissue that keeps me from loving a woman? Will I be able to trust a woman enough to start a family and then maintain that target as the focus for my life? Will I be the kind of father who is there when my son needs me? Will I be wise enough to hold the vision he helped me see of what my life can be. Will I find the courage to set my own marks?

"I know, I was shocked too," Corny says, sensing my grief. "So I drove him to the emergency room. His blood work indicated he had or was having a heart attack. They ambulanced him to the University of Michigan Hospital in Ann Arbor to check for damage the next day."

Murphy stands a solemn sentry at her feet.

"The heart catheter showed the aorta valve had blown open and was beyond repair. The doctor told Dad he wasn't a candidate for a transplant. Dad told the doctor he was going to beat this with positive visualization. He said he had every intention of living to a hundred and insisted they check him out immediately so he could get to work on it. He had made up his mind, so I took him home."

"Why didn't you call me? I still have some questions about…"

"Didn't he call you?" Corny interrupts. "Daddy made a number of phone calls last week. I overheard him laughing with Pony. He asked her to marry him again." She giggles. "Can you believe that, a man his age? But, I'm surprised he didn't call you." She turns to Leticia. "Daddy liked David."

Corny eases herself into an armchair. "Thursday night we watched the news before I went to bed." The cat coils into her lap. Her hand strokes him mechanically. "Daddy had been sleeping in his recliner. I was awakened about one o'clock by a heavy thud and Murphy's caterwaul." She looks down and scrubs the cat's fur with her fingers. "I found Daddy face down on the floor in front of the linen closet." Her voice breaks and she begins to tremble. "When I rolled him over he was clutching a heavy woolen blanket. That surprised me. He never used blankets. I dialed 911. They talked me through reviving procedures." She wipes a tear with a knuckle and clears her throat. "The EMT people took over the CPR, worked on him for another half hour, but, he was gone." She fumbles in her pocket for a tissue and blows her nose. "He must have been cold."

He knew it was the end, I thought. His seventh sense had told him he would be cold. "How's Murphy taking it?" I ask, sniffing.

"That cat curled up in Daddy's chair and wouldn't move. When I had them take the chair away, he hid in Daddy's closet. This is the first time he's been out. He must like you."

"I don't think so. When's the funeral?"

"No funeral, Dave. He wanted to be cremated."

"When's the memorial service? He should have a military honor guard and a twenty-one gun …"

"No memorial service. No fuss. He wants his ashes …"

"… taken to the Cherokee Nation and given to an Indian medicine man to be delivered into the hands of the Great

Spirit," I say. "He told me he wanted his remains carried on a soft breeze to settle in a mountainside apple orchard. He wants to look over the green valley with your mother. He said they chose that spot so they could listen together to their ancestors talk in the language of the wind." My voice breaks into a sob.

Leticia's face shows surprise.

Corny weeps from her chair. "That's right. They both loved that orchard. I will honor his wishes."

How raw everything feels. "Where is the admiral's body?" I ask.

"Daddy's at the funeral parlor just up the hill. If you want to say goodbye you'd better see him today." She pauses and looks into my eyes. "David, you do know Daddy wasn't a real admiral."

"What?" I am stunned.

"That's just a nickname used for lifers in the Navy. We called him that. Everyone called him that."

My mind whirls. I stand to look out his window. Crumbs of light sparkle on the snow like the twinkle I recall from his eyes when he teased me. He was a master at head games. Was he expecting me to figure out he was fabricating all those stories? And, if he made up his rank did he also lie about what happened to my father? My mother's last words to my father echoed in a tunnel inside my head. *You are a liar. I can't love a liar.*

Was Mother right? Could one lie destroy the remaining truth? What was the truth? I turned to Corny. "But he told me the ..."

She frowned. "Did Daddy tell you he was an admiral?"

My thoughts race back over our conversations. We had talked about his rank and around his rank. I couldn't remember the old man ever claiming to have attained the rank of admiral. I do recall asking him at the Big Boy, then the coffee spilled and we segued into another topic. I may have made a mistake when I assumed his rank from the family picture. Or did he deliberately evade the question not willing to correct me? I didn't get his game, just like my father didn't get how to survive aboard a Navy vessel.

"Did your father ever mention he took a tombstone promotion when he retired?" I feel betrayed.

"Maybe. I don't remember," she says. "I do remember my mother being upset when they called him back to active duty and they talked and talked."

"Yes, he told me about that."

"He was gone so much. Mom missed him, and she needed help with Slick and me. We weren't easy children. I remember hearing Daddy tell her he would fix it somehow when he came home from Vietnam."

When in doubt, review the facts. That's what the FBI taught us in boot camp. The only record I have on James H. McLaughlin shows he retired for the first time in 1959. An idea strikes me. "Corny, did your father keep any Navy records?"

"His fireproof box is in his closet. I'll get it for you." She disappears, and I hear a door open and close. When she returns she carries a small metal box. "I planned on looking through them, eventually. Daddy had some medals, too. They hung in a frame on his bedroom wall. Do you want to see them? He's missing a few. His grandson took them to school for show and tell and lost them."

"Was he upset with him?" I ask, holding my arms out for the records.

"Yes, at first." She hands me the box. "He loved that little boy, so when he cried and told him he was sorry, Daddy told him it didn't matter."

I pull a file and peruse the forms. "It says here he had a permanent appointment to chief aviation boatswain's mate and retired as a master chief petty officer. That's the highest enlisted rank he held, according to these documents. What about President Truman's citation?"

"Dad had a presidential citation?"

"Corny, you told me about that over strawberry pie at the Big Boy."

"I did? I'm sorry, Dave. I forget things. My memory comes and goes."

"Do you remember if your father attended the Navy Command School at Annapolis?"

"I don't remember. Sorry." Corny rubs the back of her head with her hand. "He may have. I think we lived in Maryland for a while." She frowns.

"Are you all right?"

She nods. "When I was a little girl I was in a riding accident at a stable. It was my eighth birthday party. I hit my head hard on a curb. My parents told me they were afraid they would lose me. It affected the part of my brain where memories are stored. I don't remember anything from my childhood before eight. Since the accident my memory comes and goes."

It's funny how life works, I think. The father has total recall, the daughter can't remember her own father's rank in the US Navy. I wonder if she will forget him altogether.

"I remember he told me something about a loose ordnance he threw overboard," Corny says. "Daddy lived in the past. He had so many stories, I get them mixed up."

I pull a second folder.

"I'll make tea," she says and steps into the kitchen.

I find promotion papers including one that refers to him as a lieutenant. A third folder contains citations, commendations, good conduct reports, transfers, travel documents, training certificates and the papers from correspondence schools he attended. I know enough about the Navy to realize officers aren't promoted from the enlisted ranks without attending command school. I find no documents attesting to that. Maybe he lied. But maybe he didn't and just didn't keep all his records in this metal box.

"Corny, wouldn't your father have made a lot more money if he had retired as an officer?"

"I don't remember that money was a big issue with him," she says from the kitchen. "Daddy told us he traveled around the world three times and had enough of that. Mom said we were lucky to all be in one place together as a family. I had a stay-at-home mother and that's what Daddy wanted. He made enough money to take care of us all."

"It doesn't make sense," I call in to her. "He could have enjoyed a more affluent retirement."

"You don't get it, Dave." Steam screams from the kettle, and I hear metal scrape on metal. "Daddy loved Mom and wanted her to be happy. He believed in rules. He had strong principles. He would joke, but he would never break a law, or do anything that went against his standards or those of his country."

Never? I think, except for the time he threw my father to the sharks.

"He was my father," Corny says from the kitchen, "and in my mind he was perfect. I would love him even if he wasn't perfect."

I hear dishes clatter and steaming water being poured. "What about your brother?"

"What about Slick?" Corny says, and steps toward Leticia carrying two mugs.

"Didn't your father want him to join the Navy, follow his footsteps?"

"That's sexist, Dave." She hands Leticia a mug, sets one on the table and returns to the kitchen. "I'm the one who followed the family tradition. I joined the Navy. I'm a Vietnam vet." She reappears with a mug for herself.

"Where did you serve in Vietnam?" I ask.

"I never got to 'Nam. Had a desk job stateside."

"Did your father help you get that?"

"He told me I'd be safer here. I don't know for sure, but he may have pulled rank. He never told me he did. Daddy had Slick all set up to go to Annapolis when he graduated from high school." She sits, takes a long sip and places her mug on the side table. "My brother came home one day and announced he had joined the Air Force."

"Was your father upset?"

"My father wanted us to be strong, and to think for ourselves. He encouraged us to make our own decisions from an early age. He showed us how to use what he called deductive reasoning. Sure he was upset. He was a Navy man."

"But he wasn't angry at Slick?"

"He loved that little boy so much. We all did. Slick's a pilot now, flies civilian aircraft, corporate planes for executives. He's very busy. Daddy called him, but he rarely returned his calls. Something happened between those two. They haven't seen each other since my mother's funeral eight years ago."

"I want to see your father. Can I stop there now?"

"I'll call the funeral parlor."

I nod toward the bathroom as she dials the number, close the door behind me, and find the bug still stuck to the pipe under the sink. It has never been activated. I flush it down the toilet.

I'm cold before I slip my jacket on to go. It gives me little comfort, but I manage to tell the old man's daughter I am sorry her father has died. The words catch and crack in my throat. "You're not the only one who will miss him." I recall the teasing humor he used that wrapped his warmth around me, like a winter quilt. "I never had much of a relationship with my father. Your dad was special to me."

"I'm not surprised. I know he liked you," she says. "He laughed every time he told a story about you, and he told some whoppers. He said Murphy was particularly fond of you."

Leticia looks at me like I am a stranger. She walks me to the car, her arm holding me around the waist. The sun has disappeared. "Which way to the funeral parlor?" she asks, and slips behind the wheel.

The old man's daughter points, then backs inside the doorway with her arms wrapped over her chest. The temperature has dropped. The sun has settled. The sky has bleached gray.

A woman wearing a navy suit appears from a side office of the Borek Jennings Funeral Home on Main Street. "Mr. McLaughlin, Mrs. McLaughlin, your uncle is right this way."

Leticia winks at me as we enter the large room and walk to where the storm tossed sailor is laid out.

"Call me if you need anything," the woman says. "You may stay as long as you like."

I can make out a blurry horizontal figure along one wall. It takes several blinks before his features are clear. Yes. It's him. Absent is any trace of foam on this sailor's last wave. No flowers. No flags. No whispers in this room. No hushed silences or lies. No red Jell-O with bloated marshmallows. No weeping family. Not in this spare room. Not with this man. He lay there in his plaid shirt and red suspenders, wearing his reading glasses. He looks long laying there, still a big man in death.

"Leticia," I say. "Meet James H. McLaughlin. Admiral, this is my girl."

I stare at my mentor, resting there with a waffle weave blanket wound tightly around him, as if he were taking a snooze. His presence is huge, even in this large room. The flat calm of the carpet stretches out from him like a piece of gray ocean silk, a silent captain caught in the doldrums. I expect a playful wink or a snicker, but neither comes. He's quiet, has lost his biting humor. There is no sign of life in this man, just as there had been no hint of the gloom of death in the way he lived his life.

Did his rank matter? Was he a liar? I feel ashamed to question his dignity in death. I turn to hurry from the funeral parlor when a figure appears from a far corner of the room.

It's Pony. She must have been there all along. Tears stain her face, too. She gives Leticia a broad smile before she wraps one arm around my waist. We all walk toward the exit. No one says a word. She slips outside and disappears into the weather where drift upon drift of blown snow laps the landscape. I think it must look like his ocean looked slapping the cold shores of Kodiak Island.

Leticia drives me toward my apartment along drifts that blanket farmer's fields lending an austerity to the landscape. I'm shivering. We don't talk.

The sandwich she sets out at my apartment goes untouched. A vague fatigue takes hold as darkness swallows the sunset. I ingest my sobs. From time to time they erupt. It seems strange to be feeling so dreadful. I have known this man less than two weeks. I can't remember feelings, or crying at my own father's funeral.

"David." Leticia finally breaks the silence. "If he lied about his rank, can the rest of what he told you be true?"

"I don't know if he lied, honey," I say and gaze through the blinds at the streetlight.

I hear her check her home answering machine and watch her scribbling numbers. Looking up, she asks, "Have you listened to your messages?"

"My battery is dead."

She hands me her cell phone. I dial, punch the code, and listen.

"David, is that you?" The voice is familiar. "I hate talking to machines."

I swallow hard and whisper, "Leticia, it's him."

"I hope this damn thing works." His voice sputters from her cell phone. "Wondering how I got your number?" I can hear him snicker. "I thought you might. Let's just say I still have an old friend at the bureau." He clears his throat. "I forgot to tell you something important about your father." He pauses. "He was a sensitive man, a kind man. You should know that about him. I have a back-story if you want to hear it. Give me a call if you have time between arresting gangsters and loving your woman." I hear the disconnect click and the buzz of a dial tone. He didn't say goodbye.

CHAPTER 49

"Good detective work, Dugan," my case manager says from across his desk. "Sign your report and I'll recommend you be promoted to neophyte second class." He chuckles, leans back in his swivel chair and props his feet on an open desk drawer. "I read somewhere that one of these atomic sailors dies every four hours. How old was this guy?"

"Eighty-six."

"Well, he did one final service for his country before he kicked the bucket. He helped us nail Gibbons."

My boss was pleased the case was a wrap.

"Don't take it so hard, Dugan. You'll never last in this business if you get involved with informants."

"I liked the man."

"You're okay, Dugan. The target could have been recruited as an operative for a foreign nation, could have been trying to get inside the agency, or he could have been attempting to set up those two Navy grunts. Maybe his plan was to out them. Hell, they could have been spies, or worse: C.I.A. Or he could have been a screwball. Sometimes these retired guys don't get enough action or need money. Remember the MICE theory from boot camp?"

"Sure. An informant can be motivated to become a spy by any or all of the four factors: money, ideology, compromise or ego. McLaughlin did his share of drinking, and had some extramarital affairs, but the MICE theory didn't work on him.

Turns out he was just a straight arrow from Cheyenne country in Oklahoma."

My boss thumbs through my paperwork, and nods. "Too bad so many of these veterans died before they collected compensation for the poison the government fed them. I've read about the plutonium injections they gave platoons of soldiers just to see how they would react. This stuff gives me the creeps," he says. "It's too damn close to Nazi experiments. Too bad your first case puts our government in such a bad light. Trust me. We do a lot of good stuff."

I glance at him and grin.

"Okay," he says, "so don't trust me. That's probably smarter." He winks. "I listened to some of your first tapes from the restaurant in Swainsville."

I feel the kind of thud you get in your gut when something inevitable happens. "You did?" I say and remember the agent in the next booth who taped conversations with the admiral and Rudy. I start to sweat.

"Yes, I sure did. Have you learned anything since then?" he asks.

"Yes sir."

"Good," he smiles. "And that's the end of that."

I glance at the report he is holding and say, "McLaughlin's personnel records came up missing from St Louis, so I assumed they were burned in the warehouse fire. Turns out he had them all the time, or at least parts of them. His daughter pulled a fireproof box from his closet and let me look it over. It appears he retired as a master chief petty officer."

"Is that right? Why does his rank matter so much to you?"

I stand silent while my boss waits.

"I, I guess I don't like to make mistakes," I say, angry at the old man for lying to me, if he lied. Then I think about how many lives he touched, how many boys he cultivated into men capable of being fathers. I consider how much he has given me in a few short weeks. I think about what is right for the record. "The gentleman certainly acted like an admiral."

"Dugan, you missed something," he says, fumbling with a file.

"Sir?"

"These are his records from the Defense Finance and Accounting Service in Cleveland, the center for Navy pay operations and personnel data management." He pushes the manila folder across his desk. "Have you seen these?"

"Where did you ..."

"If you would have checked with the Retired Pay Department you would have found that McLaughlin retired the first time with a pay grade of rear admiral. A clerk informed me that men taking a tombstone promotion upon retirement were required to report for active duty whenever the Navy needed them. He was recalled to active duty during Vietnam. When he retired the second time he resigned his commission, reverting to his last earned enlisted position, master chief petty officer. Looks like the old sailor had had enough."

The End

AUTHOR'S NOTES

Jim McLaughlin leaned down to ask my breakfast companion Jenny Howard, if she had changed her mind about marrying him. That was in 2004 at the Big Boy in Brooklyn, Michigan, and the first time I met the man. He is real. And so is my neighbor Jenny, who blushed, then told him she had already buried three husbands and they were enough for her. At the time both Jim and Jenny were octogenarians.

I invited Jim to join us at our table, which he did every week for the next three years. During that time he shared sea stories, his humor and salty vocabulary with Jenny and me. When I asked if I could use his stories he gave me his written permission to turn them into a book or a movie.

I have never met a person with total recall before, so I checked his facts constantly. His information was the same each time I asked no matter the context, and accurate in my research. Each direct quote of his in this novel is darn close to what he told me across that breakfast table.

Admiral James H. McLaughlin died before the writing was finished. I will always be grateful to him for sharing his memories and the laughter surrounding our breakfast table.

Pony's character is drawn from a fusion of the real Jenny Howard, who died after Jim, and a retired WWII Navy WAVE octogenarian whom I met at my exercise class and is still pumping iron.

I created the FBI agent as the protagonist, and used his point of view to tell the story. His entire persona is fabricated as well as the people and events in his life. His character portrays that of an actual FBI agent according to a retired FBI agent who volunteered to be one of my unnamed editors.

My manuscript would still be stuffed inside a drawer if it were not for the constant encouragement of the Columbia Women's Writers group.

Retired Army Captain William Melms of a WWII ocean going supply ship, Navy submarine Commander Michael Riordan, retired, and Chief Warrant Officer Stephen Warro, also retired from a Cold War nuclear submarine all graciously checked my work for accuracy.

To all these colorful characters I thank and dedicate this book.

Laurice LaZebnik

Laurice LaZebnik has a BS in Education from Central Michigan University. LaZebnik taught secondary school Art and English, worked in international marketing and sales and in the local community as a volunteer. A licensed pilot and real estate salesperson, the author balances a social life with her husband with caring for elderly parents and her two dogs.

Also by Laurice LaZebnik:

STRONGHEART

A Dog Who Was A Coward is a story about Herbie before he was a show dog.

Buy it now on Amazon!
Available in paperback and Kindle.

“*A delightful first novel! Laurice LaZebnik gives us a story of redemption, the power of persistence, and the importance of learning from and passing on our heritage. She is skilled in the art of painting vivid images with her words.*”

— Patricia Tuttle

“*I absolutely loved being able to see the world through a dogs eyes. I have a dog and every time I look at her now, I try to think of what her life is like and what she thinks about. The whole concept of this book was really brilliant, the fact that the author was able to blend Herbie's learning of the Potawatomi legends with him gaining courage and facing change was really interesting to me. I have recommended this book to all of my friends and even my grandparents and teachers.*”

— Liberty Romanik, young reader